T0271655

LAKE

OF

DARKNESS

By Adam Roberts from Gollancz:

Salt
On
Stone
Polystom
The Snow
Gradisil
Land of the Headless
Swiftly
Yellow Blue Tibia
New Model Army
By Light Alone
Jack Glass
Twenty Trillion Leagues Under the Sea
Bête
The Thing Itself
The Real-Town Murders
By the Pricking of Her Thumb
Purgatory Mount
The This
Lake of Darkness

LAKE

OF

DARKNESS

ADAM ROBERTS

First published in Great Britain in 2024 by Gollancz
an imprint of The Orion Publishing Group Ltd
Carmelite House, 50 Victoria Embankment
London EC4Y 0DZ

An Hachette UK Company

1 3 5 7 9 10 8 6 4 2

Copyright © Adam Roberts 2024

A CIP catalogue record for this book
is available from the British Library.

ISBN (Hardback) 9781 3996 1767 3
ISBN (eBook) 9781 3996 1770 3
ISBN (Audio) 9781 3996 1771 0

Typeset at The Spartan Press Ltd,
Lymington, Hants

Printed and bound in Great Britain by Clays Ltd,
Elcograf S.p.A.

www.gollancz.co.uk

To the memory of Chris Priest

Fraterretto calls me and tells me Nero is an Angler in the Lake of Darkness.

King Lear

Acceptons que nous vivons sur une planète finie à l'intérieur d'un univers infini. Alors: pourrions-nous imaginer une vie vécue sur *une planète infinie* dans *un univers fini*? Il faut conjurer une forme, telle qu'un polygone, de dimensions infinies qui se rétrécit de manière exponentielle jusqu'à un sommet infini. Ce qui suit? La forme habitera le monde fini, oui, mais *elle pourtant s'entrecroisera en tout point* – car telle est la géométrie infinie. Et ici, nous voyons que Le Vrai Bon Dieu, qui est Infini, et qui habite la forme humaine, qui est finie, en se croisant avec chaque portion de la vie humaine, du cœur et de l'espérance.

Laplace, *Traité de mensonge céleste*

Contents

I

Fishing

The Startship Sα-*Niro* and the Startship Sβ-*Oubliette* were in orbit around a black hole, one afternoon.

Niro is a Japanese name that means 'good road'. *Oubliette* is a French word for a kind of dungeon. Ironically – if I am using that word correctly – the crew of the former were mostly ethnically Euro and the crew of the latter were of mostly Korean, Japanese and Chinese heritage. But that doesn't really mean anything, because nothing really means anything, which is to say we can at least declare that meaning is not construed in terms of *things*. Except perhaps for the way. And except, of course, for the dungeon.

'Afternoon' was calibrated according to ship-time, which was synchronized between the two ships. An arbitrary frame of temporal reference of course, but important for crew wellbeing.

The *Niro* and the *Oubliette* had been sent to gather data about the black hole. Sα-*Niro* was concentrating on the contouring of the event horizon, Sβ-*Oubliette* on its spacetime effects immediately outside that impenetrable, inescapable boundary. There had been a lot of long distance investigating of these things of course, but the two ships brought space scale localized instrumentation and the invaluable presence of inquiring human minds close to the object – or as close as was safe, considering the time dilation and gravitational shearing effects liable from too near an approach.

The β in the latter ship's designation indicated that this start-ship circumnavigated Einstein's restrictions on faster-than-light travel by the more recently developed technologies of rapid spacetime bubbling – trillions upon trillions of bubbles, 10^{20} each fractosecond, all cascadingly superposed a planck-length apart, sweeping the craft through actual spacetime at immense apparent velocity. This technology was considered safer, and cheaper to run, than the older α-FTL, which circumvented Einsteinian constraints in a different, and some would say cruder, manner. How does this α-tech work? How glad I am you have asked! Spacetime, you see, is a manifold. Of course, you knew that already. You knew already, of course, that this means if you travel close to the speed of light time dilates as space constricts. *Space constricts* is just a fancy way of saying: you and your destination get closer together, which is what all travelling is, of course – finding ways of bringing your destination and yourself closer together.

So, the reasoning is: if you could actually travel at the speed of light, time would stop. The alpha tech bleeds energy from the spatial friction of the craft's relativistic expansion and space's relativistic contraction to dilate the temporal. The kindergarten version of this is: it takes you a million years to travel to your distant star, but your craft takes you *back* a million years in time during the journey, and so you arrive pretty much as soon as you set out. Not exactly the same time: you cannot use α-FTL to travel in time *before* your departure point – for a great many, mostly obvious reasons. Even the theoretical best would be instantaneous travel. But in fact, a degree of lossiness is inherent in the process, such that you lose a few seconds per day of travel. The net result is that the 'apparent' velocity of an α-FTL startship is a little slower than the 'apparent' velocity of a β-FTL startship. Moreover, crews of the α-ships complain that the temporal retardation has queer and unpleasant effects upon them: their mental health, the telomeres in their cellular DNA, sometimes the language centres of their brains. Sometimes they gabble, afterwards, and speak in tongues.

It's not so bad. I wouldn't want you to think that it was *so* bad. Startships are basically hospitals anyway. Most of a startship's interior function is keeping the crew alive, and in the high-radiation and alienating environment of space that requires constant medical intervention. Mental health and physical health are not separate elements. They are, rather, a manifold, like spacetime, and must be considered together. Any startship, but especially an α-FTL, devotes a majority of its time and energy budget to maintaining the health of its crew. The reason this is a larger portion of the business of an α-craft is that α-tech, because it simultaneously forces human beings massively forward in time and drags them massively backwards in time, messes with the brain in peculiar and sometimes pathological ways. But we know a lot about these effects and have developed a comprehensive package of treatments for handling it.

Because S*α-Niro* set out from Earth just under a year or so before S*β-Oubliette*, it arrived at the black hole a few days before the sister ship.

The name of the black hole was HD 167128. It is more commonly known as QV Telescopii, abbreviated QV Tel. The object is 1120 light years from Earth. It took S*α-Niro* four years to reach this place, and S*β-Oubliette* three years and three months.

S*α-Niro* undertook a raft of experiments. The captain, Alpha Raine, was both a serving officer in the military, and a specialist

3

in the physics of time-variation in fundamental constants. He was the winner of seven Nobel prizes, a fact which you will find less impressive when you understand that the Nobel was democratized in the 2170s, and that hundreds of thousands are awarded each year. Still! Raine was a smart chap. A clever geezer. A brainbox.

On the thirty-seventh day after their arrival in the system, Raine killed all eleven members of his crew, sealed all airlocks and entrances, and accelerated his ship into a lower, faster orbit around QV Tel.

The first that Sβ-*Oubliette* knew anything was wrong was when the intership communication pathways all sealed up, abruptly and without warning.

One of the eleven murdered individuals *almost* got away. Almost but not quite. Chronofficer Stone Ferry Longley made it to a pressure pod, and got outside the radiation dampeners, thereby enabling her to upload her feed to the shared pathway – before Raine used an exterior manipulator claw to smash the fabric of the pod and eject her body into the deathspace of vacuum.

But her feed got out.

The crew of the Sβ-*Oubliette* studied this feed with consternation. Raine had seemed normal, had done his job, had indeed possessed a reputation for kindness and sympathy. He talked excitedly with his crew over meals, and in their social time, about a technique he was exploring to utilize the Hawking radiation emitted by QV Tel to back-derive what he called 'soundings' from beyond the event horizon of the black hole. It sounded screwy, but he excitedly gabbled his rationale at the other crewmembers. Of course, nothing can escape the event horizon of a black hole: not matter, not light, not information. Everyone knows that! But Raine said, that's wrong.

4

He said: as the Hawking radiation is emitted, so an equal and opposite radiation falls into the singularity – and that equality and opposition allow us to intuit certain contours – certain qualities – about the—

Pull the other one, said Sylvie, the Sα-*Niro* alt-captain, who was downtiming after steering the ship to its destination, but who was still interacting with her crewmates on both ships.

But, no, seriously: let us consider Stone Ferry's feed. What do we see? Raine's blubbery face, blotched red, his nose marked with miniature lightning-strikes of red capillaries, gabbling. 'The radiation is particles manifesting right on the edge of the event horizon,' he was saying. We are before the crimes were committed, although you can discern the shift in Raine's demeanour, his slide towards psychopathy. Stone Ferry was trying to fit her feet into the exercise frame, but Raine kept getting in her way. He was really, really excited about this, and really-really wanted to tell her. 'So one particle is emitted and one anti-particle sinks into the singularity, balancing out. But these are entangled events so we can use the radiation to map the *shape* of the anti-radiation, beyond the horizon.' Stone Ferry mumbled something about how it's an absolute rule that information can't pass the horizon, but she really wasn't in the mood to engage him and kept jinking past him to fit her body into the frame. Eventually he got the message and left her alone. But as she went about her business, working her muscles, stressing her bones, she could see him, buttonholing a different member of the crew, saying that he had built a device not only to measure the antiradiation on the far side of the event horizon, but that he was able to use it as a receiver, to listen in to the noise over there – 'a waterfall of matter, plunging forever into an inescapable singularity,' he chattered. 'It's *amazing*.'

Nobody on the Sα-*Niro* thought there was any real *science* in this, of course. But Raine's manner was surely indicative of a mania and therefore of mental debility. So the crew did the proper thing: they used the Ship System protocols to relieve Raine of command. He took this in pretty good grace, all things considered.

Sylvie took notional command, though her downtime period was not yet completed, and the whole crew staged an intervention to press Raine into medical treatment. He didn't exactly refuse to do this, but instead of conventional psychotropics he proposed an alternative: to spend a period of time in religious-mandated meditation.

The ship contained a sensory deprivation chamber, and the conventions of absolute religious toleration meant that any crewmember could opt for prayer as an alternative to medical treatment (although advised that medical treatment would become mandatory if prayer did not work). So they let him go off and pray.

This, it soon became apparent, was a mistake.

Raine took his device into the prayer room and spent three days in conversation, as he later insisted, with an entity living inside the black hole.

Of course he didn't do this. Because he couldn't. Information, like matter, can pass over the threshold of an event horizon, but it can never come back out again. More to the point: with whom was he 'conversing'? Nothing can live inside a black hole. No creature could survive the immense gravitational shear and pressure of that place – if we can even call the interior of a black hole a *place*! Say rather, an annex to reality in which the logic of *place* stops being operative. Life was so fragile that, in thousands of solar systems explored, humanity had never encountered anything more advanced than bacteria, and even then only in the most balanced and hospitable places. No life, beyond the event horizon. Had there been some impossible creature, living inside this black box, inside this ebon sphere, inside this ultimate sinkhole, it would not have been able to communicate with creatures on the outside.

But on this point Raine was insistent.

'You've tried prayer,' Sylvie told him. 'It hasn't dialled-down your mania. I'm therefore mandating medical intervention.'

'Wait,' said Raine, excitedly. 'Wait a moment – stop a moment – wait wait wait – this is *the greatest breakthrough in human history*! I'm in conversation with an intelligent extra-terrestrial! How are you guys not also excited by this? Our first encounter, as human beings, with intelligent alien life! Ten thousand stars explored and no aliens discovered. But now – this!'

Stone Ferry's feed: crew members looking at one another. 'Raine,' said Marta Pita. 'Listen to yourself.'

'*You* listen to *me*!' Raine demanded, growing agitated, his face flushing berry red. 'You should listen to me!'

'What *language* are you holding these conversations in, Raine?' Stone Ferry asked.

Had Raine been canny, he would have answered mathematics or chemistry or something along those lines. But he was unguarded: 'English!'

'Modern English?'

'It's a little stilted on his side, a touch antique, but I figured he's deduced it from me, perhaps read it out of my mind, and perhaps it's not being perfectly transferred across.'

'On *his* side?' asked Sylvie. 'This ET is gendered?'

'Sure, sure, sure. He is a gentleman, *Modo* he's called and *Mahu*.'

Everyone's network alerted them to the fact that Raine was now quoting Shakespeare, which presumably meant that he was trolling them. The mood around the crew relaxed a little. It was only Raine, after all.

'What do you, hmm,' asked Marta, 'what do you talk *about* with Mr Modo?'

'He wants out,' said Raine, excitedly. 'He's had enough of being cooped up in there. And good golly good gracious can you *blame* him?'

'He's not a native, then? Not a form of life that has *evolved* inside the event horizon?' asked Sylvie.

'Maybe he did evolve there,' said Marta 'But maybe he's gotten bored, too. Wants to explore new horizons. Like humanity did, on Earth.'

'That's a pretty interesting hypothesis,' said Stone Ferry. 'I mean, why might life *not* evolve inside a black hole's event horizon? It couldn't be anything like us, of course. But it's certainly a massively energy rich environment, inside there. Maybe a unique form of life could…'

'No!' cried Raine, losing it. 'No no no! He was *marooned* there.'

'Marooned?'

'Imprisoned. Locked away. That's why he wants out.'

Everyone greeted this news with embarrassed silence. 'And he'd like us to – open the door?' asked Sylvie. 'Your nice Mr Modo? Did you tell him that that's not how black holes work? Doesn't he understand the nature of his, eh, prison?'

'Raine,' said Marta, gently. 'It's time for some psychiatric treatment. Let's get you to the bay.'

That was when the first murder happened. In the horror and confusion, a blood-spattered Raine got away, and the rest of the crew had to put on riot gear and go looking to apprehend him with taserifles. He had, it seemed, had the knife about him from before he even went into his prayer retreat.

He was now, evidently, criminally insane. It was no longer a question of rehabilitation, but of incarceration – until the startship was able to return to Earth, and Raine could be tried, and treated, or negated.

And alt-Captain, Sylvie took charge. In retrospect this was probably a mistake. She was a fine navigator and had a brace of Nobel Prizes for medicine, but she did not think like a soldier. To be fair, none of the remaining crew did, exactly, think this way. Soldiering was, by this point in human history, a niche and historical-cosplay business. The problem was that she underestimated how belligerent, how ruthless and indeed how bloodthirsty Raine had become. Their Raine! Their friend and colleague, with whom they had lived and worked, laughed and fucked and prayed, for so many years! Changed, changed, utterly.

Marta and Soc were killed by blunt force trauma. Grei was noosed from behind, and as he struggled with the choking loop around his neck, Raine cut pieces from his legs and belly and chest, until he bled to death. These are the last murders concerning which we have specific details, because these were reported as such by Stone Ferry. She reported *that* all other crewmembers had died, although she did not provide particularities as to how. Then she herself was killed.

The crew of the Sβ-*Oubliette* considered the likelihood that Raine, growing used to killing, was increasing the cruelty and baroque complexities of his murdering as he went. Not a very comfortable thought.

:2:

You were born, in all likelihood, towards the end of the twentieth or towards the beginning of the twenty-first centuries. Yes? I have no desire to condescend to you. Many of the features of life today will be readily comprehensible to you, if you can only – as surely you can – extrapolate from your past into our present with a little common sense.

Take the ship. There are lots of imaginary startships in your popular culture, but many of these are only vaguely thought-through: naval ships, or land-based buildings, foolishly projected into deep space. Corridors? Why would we want corridors in a startship? Rigid external superstructures and frame, containing decks and floor – very fragile, under the kinds of shearing forces and pressures of spaceflight. But you already knew this, if you had ever thought about it for a moment. The Sβ-*Oubliette* did not look like a skyscraper lying on its side, or a pyramidically-stacked aircraft carrier. It looked, if you prefer an aquatic analogy, like one of those semi-lucent glittering blobs that pulse through the depths of the ocean.

Some of a startship is its drive and power-systems: propulsion, guidance and AI. But most of it – nine-tenths, as I mentioned above – is a hospital. Human animals are not built for living in space, and any enterprise that puts human beings in space for long stretches of time must spend most of its time attending to the health of those humans. This is not – or, let's say, it is *rarely* – a matter of broken bones, or infectious disease, as with older mundane hospitals. It is a congeries of related problems, chief amongst them radiation poisoning and bone-health from calcium loss, with modal health, mental-emotional wellbeing and temporal dysphasia coming close behind. Deep space is suffused with high levels of various rays and fields that degrade the human body on a cellular level: burns, mutations, cancers, decadences. Much of a deep space mission is attending to these injuries. Cancer cannot be inoculated against, but it can be treated. Cellular and DNA damage cannot be prevented, but can be addressed post hoc. Psychological derangement and dis-tress, and spiritual emptiness, are perennials, and more likely to occur in the constricted environments of a startship than in the stimulus-rich homes and habitats of our utopian collectives, but even they can be coaxed back towards wholeness and health by the right strategies. Solace is possible. And so the mission goes on. For the crew, about a third of their waking hours are given over to ship's business, a third to health-checks and treatments, leaving a few hours of leisure time per artificial day.

In the case of a ship's emergency – as now, aboard the Sβ-*Oubliette* – the leisure time is eaten into, and the duty absorbs more of the day. But the healthcare is never stinted.

As for corridors: the interior of any given startship will be different, depending on design and purpose and aesthetics, but the basic structure is a cluster of moveable Meissner tetrahedra, linked together with smartcable. The interiors of these structures, being non-spheres of uniform diameter, are spun in a complex of spiral trajectories to mimic gravity. It's a poor imitation, and extra work pushing limbs in exercise bands, compressing the body and – most of all – addressing calcium loss and density with medical interventions are also needful. But Meissner bodies make more liveable interiors than the circular strips of ribbon rotated like a merry-go-round, like in your moving-along picture show *Two Thousand and One Odysseys*. Those are *very* tricky to live in, believe me. Some places do operate them: usually as temporary structures while larger, more stable ones are being built. But you wouldn't want to live in such a rotating strip. Turn around suddenly – turn your *head* too quickly – and you'll start puking. Large-diameter slow-spinning Meissner bodies, by slowly moving the 3D space on an in-logic inaround, is a much more tolerable arrangement.

You don't care about any of that. Why would you?

My point is no corridors – no corridors at all. If you wish to move from room to room, rooms are tugged and brought to you, or else other spaces are brought to you through which you can easily access your destination. So that's how we live, when we're shipboard.

Each ship has a committee of at least seven AIs, and they triage the needs of all crew members to get where they're going or avoid interference by others in the search for solitude, and the whole system is in motion like Baoding Balls.

The captain of the *Oubliette* was called Kim Red. The alt-captain was an individual called Ko Kyung-Joon.

Now they were faced with a problem. It was clear that the *Niro* was a disaster zone – in all likelihood everyone on the other ship was dead save Raine, and it was certainly not *im*possible that Raine had killed himself after his murder spree, as is often the way with such lamentable and luckily rare derangements.

What to do?

Understand this: with immense expenditure of energy it is possible to move startships faster than light. But there was no technology that permitted the propagation of mere *communication* faster than light. This universe of ours is an ansibleless zone. Accordingly the only way to get the news back to Earth – or to other outposts of human settlement – was by bringing the news in person.

'I have never experienced anything like this,' said Ko Kyung-Joon. 'I asked our AI to game possibilities, but she was just as bamboozled as I am.'

Kim Red said: 'It is clear the crew of the *Niro* are all dead, and that Raine may or may not be dead. The *Niro*'s AI is, we assume, non-functional, or it would have intervened to prevent slaughter, sealed Raine in a chamber, protected the other crewpeople. Presumably Raine disabled it. We must make a decision. Our options are twofold: we can dock with the *Niro*, and attempt to reclaim the ship – if we are able to do this, we can put the dead to rest with prayer and ceremony, and then transfer a short crew to pilot the craft home. But there are reasons to believe that we might not be able to do this. Assume Raine is still alive, and still possessed by the murderous thirst that prompted him to kill his comrades. If so, then he would try to kill any of us who boarded that ship.'

'But would he succeed?' asked Chung Stitch. 'We are aware of the danger he represents. We would not be easy prey.'

'He killed his entire crew,' noted Ko Kyung-Joon. 'The first few were taken by surprise, yes, but after that the remaining crew were on guard. They hunted *him*. The remaining crew-members would have worn protective clothing, like beekeepers, and carried weapons. And yet they are all dead. Can we be sure we wouldn't share their fate, if we attempted to board the *Niro*?'

'That,' said Kim Red, 'suggests we pursue option 2: leave.'

'Leave the *Niro* in orbit here?'

'It is three years and four months since we left Earth, and we can be there again in three years three, if we push the drive as hard as possible. Add in the time dilation of our proximity to QV Tel, and we will arrive home after a month or two shy of twelve years after we departed. Assume a mission is then mounted – with trained volunteer soldiers, and a military-style startship, rather than mere scientists and priests like us – and assume that the startship is fitted with a β-drive...'

'...then,' Choe Eggs finished for her captain, 'by the time we return, fifteen years or more will have passed.'

'Not for Raine,' said Ko Kyung-Joon.

'Nonetheless – can we leave him alone for such a long time?'

'There is the question of solitude,' Kim Red noted. 'It would amount to cruel and unusual punishment.'

One of the logics of space exploration was that no person be allowed to voyage solus. Loneliness is a tough enough psychological experience at home, on a planet surrounded by billions. To be alone light years away from the nearest fellow creature can do terrible things to a person's psyche. This was so well-established a feature of space exploration that a mission committee would no more send a single individual alone into space than they would send a ship without supplies of food and water.

'After what he has done ...' growled Ko Kyung-Joon. But even he, of them all the crewmember with the sternest temperament, could not complete the sentiment. Even considering the monstrous and cruel actions Raine had undertaken, he could not be treated so barbarously. Incarceration, to protect others and himself, and punishment, to set him on the road towards atonement, yes. But not this cruelty. It is an essential part of the logic of utopia that cruelty has no place in it.

'My concern,' said Choe Eggs, 'is otherwise. The ship has been, it seems, a little damaged by the actions of its former captain – but not *much* damaged, and there is no question but that the drive still works. What if Raine jury-rigs the *Niro* and flies it away?'

'Flies it where?'

'The fact is,' Choe Eggs replied, sardonically enough, 'that Raine is not in his right mind. Predicting his actions cannot, given the psychiatric circumstances here, be a matter of accuracy. But my concern is: he has proven himself murderous. If he boots-up the ship and flies away, he could visit disaster and death on – well, upon wherever he decided to go.'

The crew consulted their networks to get a quick sense of where, in the local stellar environment, a rogue captain might steer his ship. It depended, of course, on what said rogue captain was looking for. A settled world? An adjuvant facility? An orbital habitat? A port station? 'Assume the worst,' suggested Ko

Kyung-Joon. 'That he is thirsty for murder, that his sociopathy wants to kill human beings and as many as possible. Then I suggest he would fly to the Adjuvant at Caro77. He could reach it in a year. It has a population of over sixty thousand.'

'Himsted is half the distance and millions live there.'

'Himsted is a world. Caro77 is an Adjuvant. He might kill some of the people who live on the former, but with the latter he could destroy the whole facility and murder them all.'

The crew were shocked at this observation. It had literally not occurred to any of them that a human being might even consider such an enormity.

'Do you really think ...' asked Sima Shi, but could not finish the sentiment.

There was silence for a while.

'We are the faster ship,' noted Chung Stitch. 'We could arrive at Caro77 *before* Raine.'

'And he would plot our direction of travel,' said Ko Kyung-Joon, 'and know not to go there. There are many other Adjuvants, and smaller platforms and stations he could choose.'

It was a dilemma.

'So, Ko, you are suggesting,' asked Kim Red, 'that we stay here and attempt to recover the *Niro* and apprehend Raine.'

'It is not ideal,' Ko Kyung-Joon conceded. 'We are not soldiers. There is a chance Raine will kill some, or all, of us.'

'And if he kills us, then what good have we achieved?' demanded Sima Shi, hotly. 'He will then be able to fly to any target he chooses and kill again. Better we return home, and tell people, such that startships be sent to all possible targets to warn and protect.'

'There is also the chance,' Ko Kyung-Joon pressed, 'that we will capture Raine without losing any of our own. There is even the chance that he is dead – he may have killed himself.

We must consider the balance of possibilities. It is an actuarial decision. Which has the best probability of minimizing the larger loss of life?'

'That is the consideration that must, of course, govern our decision-making,' Kim Red agreed. 'It is not clear to me, however, whether staying here and attempting to apprehend Raine, or whether returning to Earth and mobilizing a number of teams of military and policing specialists, will result in the lowest risk of injury and death.'

'There is a third option,' suggested Choe Eggs.

'Is there?' Kim Red said. 'I cannot see that there is. We stay or we go – surely that exhausts the possibilities.'

'We could attempt,' said Choe Eggs, 'to open communications with the entity living inside the black hole.'

Mockery, scoffing and contumely are psychologically destabilizing for the recipient, and decent human beings do not engage in them. But the silence with which Choe Eggs' suggestion was met contained within it – if you can imagine silence as a holder of specific content – intimations of disdain.

'You are surely not suggesting,' Kim Red said, shortly, 'that Raine's deranged talk of a creature living beyond the event horizon, is …' A smile, a gesture with the hand. '…is anything *other* than madness?'

'Perhaps it is only Raine's hallucination, the correlative of his murderous mania,' agreed Choe Eggs, unperturbed. 'Likely that is exactly what it is. But there is a nonzero possibility it is something else. Recall: Raine's mania came over him *after* he reported having opened a channel of communication with the inhabitant of QV Tel. What if it was that communication that turned his wits?'

'That communication,' said Chung Stitch, 'or his hallucination that such a communication had taken place.'

'The latter,' Ko Kyung-Joon said, brusquely, 'surely *much* more likely than the former. He quoted *King Lear*, you remember? Gave the entity the name of one of the devils from that play. To me that suggests he was bodying forth an imaginary projection of his own inward demons, from his own readings in classic literature. Not that there is an actual being inside QV Tel. How could life even exist in there anyway?'

'It is *unlikely* life exists in there,' Choe Eggs agreed. 'But not absolutely impossible.'

'To that unlikelihood we must add the unlikelihood that any such entity, even if it existed, could communicate through the impermeable barrier of the event horizon. I know Raine spun his fancy story about resonances in the Hawking radiation, but … come now. Really?'

'I only offer it as a possible avenue for us to consider,' said Choe Eggs.

'Your proposal is that we replicate Raine's strategy? For communicating with a notional being inside the black hole?'

'That we replicate his strategy so far as we can determine it, yes. I assume we would be unsuccessful,' said Choe Eggs. 'But what if we did make contact? Think of it! Would it not be worth spending a few weeks at least trying?'

'I disagree,' said Ko Kyung-Joon. 'It would be an indulgence very likely detrimental to our psychological health, voluntarily to inhabit the paranoid fantasy of a sociopath. And it would achieve nothing.'

'I concur,' said Kim Red. 'For I have this additional observation: that if we *did* make contact, unlikely though that eventuality would be – why then: the evidence is that any entity living inside QV Tel is not friendly. What if it was Raine opening communication with this creature that collapsed his mind? Who is to say that it wouldn't have the same effect on us?'

'If we were to return straight home,' Choe Eggs pointed out, 'we will be asked whether there is any evidence for Raine's bizarre hypothesis. I propose we at least gather some evidence. That is all.'

'Well,' said Kim Red. 'Have we discussed enough? Should we proceed to the vote?'

:3:

In the end the *Oubliette* decided to do what utopians almost always decide to do when faced with an alternative: to compromise. A team of three would be sent to board the *Niro*, to ascertain whether Raine was still alive, apprehend him if so, and collect and put-at-rest with all proper ceremony and prayer the bodies of the killed. Reset the AI if possible. Repair such damage as Raine had inflicted on the craft.

The three would be selected by lot, although Ko Kyung-Joon – whose personality was, of all of them, the one inched closest to what might be called 'aggression' – volunteered and was accepted. They all understood that the three might die, and that if that happened the attempt to recover the *Niro* would be abandoned.

All three would wear broadcast kit – trailing an unspooling, physical cable behind them as they went in, with the far end anchored outside the radiation dampeners – so everything they saw, heard and experienced would be collected by the *Oubliette*.

While this was going on Choe Eggs would be permitted to open communication with whatever entity, if any, dwelt inside the black hole – or to attempt to do this, at any rate.

If the attempt to recover the *Niro* was successful, the two ships would then return home together. If unsuccessful the remaining crewmembers aboard the *Oubliette* would fly home and report the disaster, taking with them whatever evidence, or lack of evidence, Choe Eggs had been able to gather concerning QV Tel.

To accompany Ko Kyung-Joon, as selected by the ship AI according to a randomization, were Kim Red and Choe Eggs. Because Choe Eggs had already been assigned elsewhere, Sim Shi was seconded.

They debated, for a long time, how to frame the assault upon the *Niro*. This was not their skillset, you see.

I have studied your imagined projections into the future, and one of the – many! – things you get wrong is the proportion between warships and hospital-ships in interstellar armadas. In your scientifiction works there are always a great many of the former and only a few of the latter, in support roles. In reality there is no need for a great many warships. The plain fact is: when you develop the technology to accelerate matter to speeds that are faster than light, you develop a weapon that cannot be defended against: for how could you defend your spaceship or habitat against a projectile that inverts cause and effect, that moves not just quicker than you can react, but quicker than *reaction as such* is possible? When all battle tactics become pre-emption, the battle is over before it has even begun.

The invention of this technology changed the parameters of war, and was a significant reason for the evolution of human-kind into its present heterotopian configuration. Not that war was always avoided in the early years of space flight. There used to be armies: small, self-selected groups of fighters, trained for combat on-planet, in-orbitals and between spaceships. But war had become a matter of reading the opponents' intentions ahead of time, which is much easier to do than you might think. Any enemy can destroy you if they choose, and you can do nothing to prevent this; but *if* they act, then they will in turn be destroyed by others, and there is nothing *they* can do to prevent that. In such a situation military strategy simplifies into a game of tic-tac-toe. You are a lone ship, facing a fleet of many ships, you can destroy one before it is aware you have fired, but the remaining ships will then destroy you. Perhaps you have multiple weapons, such that you could destroy *all* of them before *any* of them are aware you have fired your missiles. But your actions will be evident to all – the destruction can only have been your action – and the next craft to encounter you will destroy you before you are even aware they have fired their weapon. Being mutually assured, such potential destruction reconstructs possibility along one axis only: is destroying your enemy worth destroying yourself? That the only possible answer to this question is 'no' applied pressure to the increasing obsolescence of war. Perhaps you are thinking: you could disable the enemy spaceship, and afterwards capture it? You cannot. When a projectile travelling faster than light connects with a substantial mass, that mass is entirely obliterated. Or perhaps you are thinking: I will destroy my enemy, fly away, disguise my ship, live out my life. But ships are not to be disguised by painting them a different colour! Ship AIs recognize one another's tags from millions of miles away and broadcast one another's whereabouts – and those tags are fractal, integral and unique. And no human is clever enough to run a ship without AIs.

War is a rational matter now, which is to say: an impossible matter. It is better that way, and the whole purpose of society is betterment. What else is history for if not? We have created a desolatopia and called it peace, but in the strict sense of the term: for, trace it back, and the word desolation literally means to de-solitudinize, to undo loneliness, to draw together into a supporting mega-web of human flourishing and mutuality.

But now the crew of the *Oubliette* were obliged to wargame. They drew on such archival advice as their AIs could provide, and practiced. The three named themselves *the assault team* – how thrilling, to be designated part of an assault team! as if these mild-mannered, mentally well-adjusted, clever and peaceable folk were cosplaying Homer's battlefield at Troy, or the wave-washed beach of your own *Surfing Private Ryan*! As I was saying: the assault team decided on non-lethal ordnance: electrically stunning projectiles, a glue-based squirt cannon, projectile nets. (Like gladiators in the coliseum combats of Ancient Room! How exciting!) Rather than actually fire these, physically, at one another, they trained in a virtuality. The *Oubliette* AI sketched the possible disposition of the various Meissner spaces inside. Raine had used human privilege to override the opposition of the ship's main AI, and it was possible he had done so with all the minor AIs running discrete systems. This, though, would be risky for him, since messing with the AI's ability to make independent decisions so as to keep the ship hale and whole was likely to have negative consequences for the integrity of the craft. And since Raine had taken the *Niro* into a lower, faster orbit around the black hole, the tidal stresses acting upon the ship would be greater – and the subjective time would elongate for him, meaning that there was longer for malfunctions to build up. But he must have overridden the AI nonetheless, since the primary function of all the AIs was to preserve the human crew's life and wellbeing, and who knows what an AI might do in the extraordinary circumstances of one crewmember assault-ing – murdering – the others. It would only be an impediment to Raine's malign desires.

Still, nobody aboard the *Oubliette* could be sure what he was doing. The *Niro* was a black box.

'We can be sure,' insisted alt-captain Ko Kyung-Joon, 'within

reasonable parameters of surety that Raine has constrained his
AIs. They'll be doing what they can to keep the ship integral,
but those constraints will have a deleterious effect on all manner
of ship's systems.'

'But that will be to our advantage!' said Sima Shi. 'Raine
will be worried about the disintegration of his ship and will
be distracted.'

The mistake she was making here, you see, was assuming
that, though he was clearly unwell, Raine was at root the same
rational and reasonable individual he had once been, as she was
herself.

'It makes it harder to wargame our strategy,' complained Ko
Kyung-Joon.

'We must do the best we can,' said Kim Red.

They practiced a variety of assaults in the virtuality and
spent at least an hour a day aiming and firing their real-world
weapons, to get used to them and to improve their accuracy.

Choe Eggs, with the help of the navigation AI – the artificial
mind with the supplest quasi-original ersatz-consciousness – was
experimenting with interfering with the Hawking radiation
emitted by QV Tel. They did not, of course, know exactly how
Raine had configured his instrumentation or what approaches
he had taken. They did not even know if he had done anything
at all. Perhaps the task was as impossible as common sense suggested. Perhaps Raine had done nothing, and the whole 'Modo'
scenario was a projection of his diseased subjectivity. But after
a week of dedicated application, Choe Eggs began to detect
something non-random. By directing a particular microwave
pulse-beam she agitated the Hawking radiation at source to
send the standard prime-number grid that was used to broadcast
intelligent consciousness.

The day before D-Day (when it was agreed the *Oubliette*

would sweep down, connect with the *Niro*, breach her hull and insert the team of Kim Red, Ko Kyung-Joon and Sima Shi) Choe Eggs, sifting the random data of the Hawking radiation, detected a pattern with the help of the navigation AI. Then another, and then another.

Choe Eggs grew very excited, and alerted the crew. 'It took us a while to decipher – *more's code*, an Early Modern tik-tak system of long and short pulses, each standing for one glyph. String them together and you can spell out a word.'

'Spell out? Writing? I didn't realize you could read!'

'I can't,' Choe Eggs confessed. 'But the AI did the work. We have the word!'

'A word in what language?'

'In Early Modern English, we think.'

'There is something in there, behind the event horizon?' boggled Kim Pyon Tsan. 'It's hard to believe!'

'Maybe, maybe not,' said Choe Eggs. 'We've been triaging possibilities. That we're in touch with a being inside QV Tel is one possibility, certainly. But more likely this is some kind of echo. We're 1120 light years from Earth, so it can't be an actual Early Modern broadcast being echoed back – go back that far and you're in the pre-technological swamp. But possibly another ship passed nearby, perhaps a couple of hundred years ago, and broadcast this antique code? Or leaked it, somehow, past the radiative shield? And it's possible the strange physics of this place have just now echoed it, or somehow released it.'

'Why would they do that? Broadcast *in an antique code*? What would be the point?'

'Who knows? But let's hypothesize: they broadcast this more's code – so-called, I assume, because it is sequential, you go along adding more and more letters until the whole word is spelled. But, if so, if it is being echoed back now, that must mean the event horizon is *not* relativistically invariant – not smooth – that it doesn't simply swallow everything that strikes it. There must be corrugations! This message has, perhaps, been bouncing around for a while until I detected it. The navigation AI has been feeding possibilities into the main experimental system AIs, and they suggest that these corrugations are larger than mere quantum dissipation. That's pretty exciting!'

'What's the word?' asked ZhangJie, quietly. She always spoke quietly.

'What?'

'You said this old code was spelling a sequential set of Early Modern English ciphers, yes? What's the term – *letters*, yes? That's right, isn't it?' ZhangJie could, of course, no more read than could Choe Eggs.

'Letters, yes. There are four letters and maybe five, although we're not sure about the fifth. It might be random noise: a double-long, perhaps just an echo of the echo.'

'So,' pressed ZhangJie. 'Which word?'

'The letters, in order, are first S – then C – and after that R – and then an A.'

'*Scra*?'

'Yes, we've searched the Early Modern language databases, and it doesn't appear to be a word. Perhaps an acronym? But it inclines me to think that the final letter is part of the communication, since when you add that it does make an E.M. word.'

'That letter?'

'M,' said Choe Eggs. 'Take all five together and it means – or it meant, late twentieth, early twenty-first century, to shut down a nuclear reactor.'

'A reactor?'

'The old-style reactors. Not our fusion pods. On Early Modern earth, those fission systems often went wrong, and *scram* was the word they used to mean: to shut down such a reactor for safety reasons, usually because of an emergency. Although the word has other meanings too.'

'What meanings?'

'It also means: to depart, in a hurry. It also means: to scratch something with claws or fingernails – to claw. And from that meaning, if I'm interpreting the archives properly, it had a related meaning: to mine for ore on a small scale, especially from mines which have previously been worked on, where most of the ore has previously been removed.'

'Interesting!'

'Isn't it? Since we came here – *Oubliette* and *Niro* both – to as it were *mine* for information, to scratch out truths from the implacable black hole, perhaps that is what the communication means? Assuming it means anything. Which, as I say, is not the most likely interpretation.'

'Unless the communication means: *shut down your nuclear pods, humans.* Why would an entity inside a black hole request such an action? Without our pods we wouldn't be able to survive!'

'It can't mean that then,' said Sima Shi. 'No rational intelligence would request such a thing of another rational intelligence.'

'It might make the request out of ignorance?'

'Or it might be saying, leave in haste,' Ko Kyung-Joon noted.

'Why would an entity do that? Surely it would prefer us to stay, so it can enjoy the pleasures of conversation?'

'Entity,' scoffed Li. 'There's no such thing! Consider, comrades, the sheer impossibility of such a scenario!'

'Yet the more's code *has* been deciphered.'

'Well this is all very interesting, very interesting, no question,' said Kim Red. 'But let us not forget: our primary task is to apprehend Raine.'

'Assuming,' Ko Kyung-Joon added, 'he is still alive.'

'Assuming so, exactly. But once we have him, we can discover his method for reading the Hawking radiation, and access the log of his interactions with this perhaps-perhaps-not entity. This Moho.'

'Modo,' corrected Choe Eggs.

'Yes. Modo. And what was it? Mahu? We shall see. Tonight we have earned a restful fuckparty. Tomorrow we will move the *Oubliette* into position, myself and Ko Kyung-Joon and Sima Shi will put on our armour, and move into the *Niro* to capture Raine, or retrieve his body if he has committed suicide. And then we can restore the *Niro*'s AIs and pilot both craft away from QV Tel. Friends – comrades – I am confident within reasonable parameters of success tomorrow!'

This little speech cheered everyone. The party was quickly arranged: both food and alcohol, dancing and writhing. One of the greening pods was assigned for forest frolics, and such crewmembers as desired danced through the tendrils and tree-trunks of green, engaging in mutually gratifying sexual inter-actions and hallooing and loo-looing to their heart's content. Letting off steam in this way, especially after several weeks of unusually stressful and intense preparation for the mission to-morrow, entailed a certain amount of damage to the vegetation inside the greening pod, but that was an acceptable trade-off for the rebalancing of the crew's psychological wellbeing and the spiritual sustenance.

Then all, save only the two crew on night-duty, slept. Most enjoyed sweet, dreamless and refreshing slumber, although Choe Eggs found herself imagining the letters of that strange, archaic word S, C, R, A, M growing, each, as if in time-lapse footage of a plant growing, tendrils of sweet pea creating first one cipher, then the next, and then the next. More, she thought in her dream. More, more. More. How do you dislike it? How *could* you?

She reported this unsettling dream to the rest of the crew in the morning, as all crewmembers were expected to do with any nightmare or angsttraum. They discussed it and considered its possible meanings. 'That it came to you in the form of a natural, growing, green plant is a good sign I think,' was Kim Red's opinion. 'Sweet pea is beautiful and fragrant. The plant growing perhaps symbolizes the natural, healthy development of our understanding of this strange phenomenon.'

'They looked somewhat like octopus tentacles, too,' said Choe Eggs. 'At any rate, my emotional association was strongly negative – not the usual one with which my mind associates pretty flowers.'

They could not discuss it in the detail they normally would, because it was time for the recovery mission to begin.

The squad strapped on the body-armour that had been printed especially for this mission. Kim Red went over the sequence of events one last time. The squad would board the *Niro*. The rest of the crew would pull the *Oubliette* back and wait. If the squad were successful, the ships would come together again; if – Spirit forbid! – the squad were killed by Raine, then the *Oubliette* would withdraw, and take the news of their mission back to Earth as quickly as possible.

'But I am reasonably assured,' Kim Red declared, rousingly, 'that this latter eventuality will not come to pass!'

They all cheered. 'Let's go to work!' called Sima Shi and slung her stun-rifle over her shoulder.

:4:

'I'm actually looking forward to talking to Raine again,' Choe Eggs confessed, settling herself into her foamclasp, prior to piloting the *Oubliette* into its lower orbit. 'Despite the appalling and monstrous things he has done. I believe I will be able to control my repulsion and anger sufficiently to have a stimulating conversation with him about his method for reading the Hawking radiation. I wonder if he used the old more's code in communication with the entity? Or perhaps he lighted upon some more fluent mode of exchange?'

'There is no entity,' growled Sima Shi.

'Engage,' said Kim Red.

The *Oubliette* fired up her drive, and began manoeuvres: first sublight, then a jolt to advance them to within grappling distance – for longer distance FTL travel a startship must first extrude a skullcap of smart foam, frothing out over a number of days (the thickness determined by the length of the proposed journey) to dissipate the impact of interstellar dust particles. But the vacuum environment around QV Tel was exceptionally clear, all matter having been drawn into the sinkhole of the singularity, so this prophylactic was not needful.

They sped beyond the speed at which light propagates, and then slowed sharply by reversing the dynamic, and arresting the quantum foam with a momentum incline of < 0.03, so as not to shatter the – designedly flexible, but within limits – superstructure of the startship. This all went exactly as planned.

The next phase was to locksync with *Niro* and move in, until the extruded eva-docket pressed into the soft outer skin of the *Niro*, and the 'squad' could burn through and enter the spaceship.

It is hard to think outside the parameters of our life-experi-
ence. When the crew of the *Oubliette* thought about Raine, they
conceived a person much like them – which, to be fair to them,
he had once been – whose mental health had been destabilized,
perhaps by the processes of α-tech faster-than-light travel, with
its consciousness-discombobulating temporal lag. They did what
we all do when they attempted to empathize with others: they
projected themselves into the other's place. Raine, they assumed,
would be dissociated, irrational, overwhelmed, unsure, fearful
– at least, his fight-flight would be largely weighted towards
the latter quantity. He might already have committed suicide,
which would be grievous (for he had been their comrade, their
colleague, their friend, for many of them their lover), but which
would at least solve the problem, or to be precise, would alter
their problem into a new problem, that of bereavement. In that
case Raine would join the eleven others killed aboard the *Niro*,
and the crew of the *Oubliette* would confront their grief, pray
and weep and grow into it, and through it.

My people are good with grief, something your generations
seem, so far as the historical records have been sifted, astonishingly poor at handling. It's really quite startling how cavalier
you were on this matter, how incompetently you managed it.
Grief destabilizes wellbeing and attacks mental health, but it is
a necessary and natural part of being alive, and there are modes
of acceptance and passion and work that move us through the
process of grieving that, ultimately, enriches us. I believe, heart
and bone, that this is true of the crew of the *Oubliette*.

Things did not go as they had anticipated.

First, when they arrested their FTL, and began precise
docking-style manoeuvres, they discovered that the *Niro* was
already moving towards their position. This meant that Raine
was not only alive but had taken a degree of control over the

ship that was, to put it mildly, surprising – able to shift and steer the huge balloon of his startship without (it could only be assumed) the benefit of AI.

The crew of the *Oubliette* had a little less than an hour to respond to this new development. They debated it, naturally, and perhaps did so for longer than was ideal. Triage: should they withdraw and reconsider their plans? Or should they proceed? 'We proceed,' insisted Kim Red. 'Clearly Raine is still alive, something concerning which we were not previously sure. This movement by the *Niro* has reduced our uncertainty, not increased it. Therefore we proceed.'

'I disagree,' said Ko Kyung-Joon. 'We have trained – I have trained – for a particular engagement. This changes the terms of engagement. I propose we withdraw and retrain.'

'Retrain for what?' questioned Sima Shi. 'The parameters remain broadly the same. We will board the *Niro*, locate Raine and immobilize him. Of what would our retraining consist?'

They discussed, unhurriedly, cordially, and then they voted. During this time the *Niro* came closer. It was decided to proceed with the engagement, and Ko Kyung-Joon, Sima Shi and Kim Red tightened their armour and readied their stunguns and moved to the small Meissner space adjacent to the *Oubliette's* flexible hull, ready to burn through into the *Niro*.

By the time they were in place the *Niro* reached them. Choe Eggs, who was in the pilot's pouch, became alarmed at this – what if, instead of the *Oubliette's* squad boarding the *Niro*, what if Raine breached the *Oubliette's* hull and came roaring in? They hadn't trained for that!

The *Niro* bumped up against the *Oubliette*. Given the huge mass, and therefore the momentum, of the startship, it pushed solidly, deforming both hulls and spreading an oval-shaped area of propinquity. But there was no breach.

It fell to Ko Kyung-Joon to initiate the *Oubliette's* systems so as to burn an entrance space through to the other ship.

A florescence of sparks, falling away like ten thousand shimmering petals, and the jelly-like material of the *Niro's* hull flobbed back, melting at its edges. A smell of singed meat. Kim Red kicked at the large slab of separated hullstuff and it deformed a little around his booted foot, and began floating backwards in the space's zero-g.

The three members of the squad were suited, ready for vacuum or any unwelcoming atmosphere, gaseous noxiousness – whatever Raine might throw at them. Rather than the great saggy sacks of *your* era, sewn out of heavy fabric and varicose with tubes of air and water and cooling-fluids and whatnot, *our* spacesuits are a spray tan, a bubble of stiffer clarity blown around the head, all controlled by a dedicated mini AI.

Of course, because they had trained themselves as warriors, the *Oubliette's* squad had strapped on plates of chest armour and back armour, and greaves for their legs and arms, but beneath these items they were naked save for their thin membranes. It gave them maximum flexibility and moveability, and moreover it looked beautiful. Beauty, you see, matters.

Kim Red sent a drone floating through the space to scope out the interior. They had cut into the ship's integument and could now access a space between two mid-sized Meissners – once inside it would be a simple matter to enter any of the ship's many chambers, and to release the main AI from whatever hobbling Raine had placed upon it. Once that was done, they would be able to locate Raine and apprehend him. And if Raine had damaged the AI too severely, they could, as a last resort, sweep the ship chamber by chamber, Meissner by Meissner.

The drone reported nobody in the interspace beyond the breach, and no action save the movement of the ship's internal smart-cables, which are in constant motion anyway: the tendons of the craft, moving Meissners, contracting and expanding, linking and bracing and angling the drive.

It was all normal. Ko Kyung-Joon said: 'We can go in, it's fine.'

'In that *interspace* it's normal,' said Kim Red, who – I am hypothecating here, but I feel sure enough that I am correct – was experiencing a hard-to-quantify reluctance, a squirling sense in their gut that something was wrong. Feeling that they ought not to proceed. A hunch. That at any rate is what I deduce from the recordings of this event. But what could they do? Call off the mission? Raine had to be apprehended!

'But it will not be normal elsewhere in the ship,' Kim Red said. 'We must be prepared for grotesqueness – corpses and blood. And we must *expect* the *unexpected*.'

'That,' observed Ko Kyung-Joon, mildly, 'is a contradiction in terms.'

'Well,' said Sima Shi, making the first move. 'It is—'

She said no more words, not then and not at any other time. A cable, thinner than a little-finger, thinner than a dreadlock, stronger than steel, darted through the gap. It was tipped with a hook, and the hook was made of smart gelmetal. This was an arrowhead shape until it parted, when two barbs, each shaped like a line-of-beauty, sprang open. When they tightened they had cut through Sima Shi's suit at the neck, just above the chest armour, and dug into the bony ribs of the C7 vertebra, plunging in from the front and closing again behind Shi's trachea.

The impact of this, in the zero-gravity environment, pushed her back. A loud exhalation, more gasping sigh than a cry or shout, came out of her mouth. But in a second the cord had tautened. Then it pulled back, whipping her body so rapidly from the space that her foot, connecting by chance with Kim

Red's hand as it passed, broke the bones of their thumb. 'Ah!' yelled Kim and released their weapon. It hung in space, as Kim span back clutching their right wrist in their left hand.

'Ach! Ah!' cried Kim Red, in alarm and pain.

A second tendril twitched into the space, snagged itself purposefully onto the back-plate of Kim's armour, hauling them swiftly away into the darkness. They screamed as they departed, and the doppler effect sank their howl a semitone until, startlingly, it stopped entirely.

'Comrades!' Ko Kyung-Joon announced, to their crewmates, as he jetted backwards away from the breach, and scanned his systems for the quickest route to safety, 'I am abandoning the mission! There is a hostile—' But as he opened his mouth to an *o* to form the word *hostile* (I am translating, of course: it was a different word, the utterance of which caused Ko Kyung-Joon to make an o of his mouth) a third tendril burst into the space, its hook piercing the material of Ko's headsphere and passing through into his mouth. The hook snapped through the tiles of his two front teeth, breaking them clean away, and slinkyed upwards, lodging a pointed prong in the material of the roof of Ko's mouth. Above the palate is the comb-filled chamber of the maxillary sinuses, and this is where the prong lodged. As the tendril withdrew, pulling Ko along with it, such that he was drawn horizontally through the space with his feet kicking in protest, his voice was still audible on all ship's systems. For a number of seconds, Ko's voice was expressing recognizable words, although at a higher pitch and with a blunted, nasal twist to his usual timbre – *you must form a new squad and enter* he screamed – but after that the noises that came across the ship's comms were no longer words, but squawks and shrieks, and then a drawn-out howl.

Then silence.

Everything described here happened in a couple of dozen seconds.

Then for long minutes, the remaining crew of the *Oubliette* stared at their readouts, cycled through their inline feeds, replayed the surveillance footage of the event. None of the other nine aboard that ship was physically near the breach–point, and even if they had been it would not have made sense for them to rush after their comrades, or even to enter that space, since the likelihood was that further tendrils would snake whippingly in to snatch them.

Remotely, Choe Eggs – now the de facto captain – sealed the forward chamber and called an immediate ship's meeting. 'This is a catastrophe! All our plans have been upended – Raine is evidently not only still alive, but very much more aggressive and proactive than our modelling anticipated.'

'We must act!' cried several crewmembers. All this was archived by the *Oubliette* AI, and broadcast, to be picked up and logged by the β-*Highhouse* seven months later. You can logdown the unedited script of the discussion if you choose. I select only this element:

Kim Pyon Tsan, saying: 'Raine has overwritten the various ship AIs, and in a remarkably sophisticated manner. He could not have done what he did otherwise.'

'It is hard to believe,' said ZhangJie, 'that such a thing is possible – one person? In less than two months?'

'We must retrieve our comrades!' urged Li. 'There is no evidence that they are dead.'

At this, almost as if prompted by the statement, Ko Kyung-Joon's feed suddenly flicked on and the remaining crewmembers heard a hideous collocation of sounds, all of which (analysis confirmed) issued from Ko's mouth. First a kind of guttural lurching sound, a weeping, keening sound, a phoneme that might have been 'please! please!' and then a long, harrowing wail, a scream that lasted exactly seven seconds and then ended sharply.

'They're still alive!' cried Kim Pyon Tsan, very distressed.

'My God,' said Li, 'it's full of tears!'

'We need,' said Choe Eggs, who was rubbing the heel of her right hand up and down the side of her face, over and over, 'we need, we need, we need to formulate a *plan.*'

'You should have heeded my message,' said somebody, their voice extraordinarily deep and resonant and thrumming, filling the entirety of the meeting space as a hard-boiled-egg fills its shell, 'and knidded *off.*'

This was a startlement. Each of the remaining nine crewmembers of the *Oubliette* confirmed, one after the other, that they had not spoken; so the words – clear, and recorded in the ship's log – must have come from somewhere else. The disturbing thing was that the voice, whosoever it was, had none of the sonic qualities of Raine, even factoring in the likely distortions and degradations his voice was likely to have suffered over the prior two months. So. Who had spoken?

'Who was that?' the surviving crewmembers demanded, cajoled, begged. 'Who?'

'Who!'

'Who!'

'Who!'

'We must muster!' was Po's contribution.

'We need some countermeasures against the way Raine has weaponized the ship's smart-cables and functional tentacles,' was Li's suggestion.

'Yes,' said Choe Eggs, somewhat frantically. 'I'm negotiating with the *Oubliette*'s AI now, but it is reluctant to reconfigure itself as a military, which is to say as a belligerent, system. That's not what it was designed to be!'

'We can't wait four years for a battle startship and its warrior crew to arrive!' shrieked Kim Pyon Tsan.

'Look!' cried Li.

'We might be able to introduce the *Oubliette*'s AI to the *Niro*'s AI,' suggested Choe Eggs. 'I might be able to link the two, and perhaps our AI could persuade the *Niro*'s AI to—'

'Look, look!' screeched Li.

The breach, at the point between the two ships, was lit-up with flickering, and then a figure – a human form, though painted gloopily with glistening black-red – emerged through the hole. There was a stutter on the visual feed, and then it blinked out.

ZhangJie began whimpering like a whipped dog.

'Hush!' whsht'd Choe Eggs. 'We must act together! He is one, and deranged, and we are nine, and rational. The most important thing is that we act *together*. Unity will defend us, and as one we can overwhelm him. The most important thing is—'

These are the last coherent words we have from Choe Eggs, or, indeed, from anyone who crewed the startship Sβ-*Oubliette*.

:5:

The feed grows fragmented, and not easy to piece together. That Raine murdered all nine remaining crew of the *Oubliette* is not, of course, in doubt; although there is some question as to how long certain individuals among that crew remained alive, and concerning precisely what barbarities Raine performed upon their bodies, whilst living, or after they were dead.

For myself, I don't like to think about it.

The β-*Highhouse* scooped as much of the last infoblurt of the *Oubliette* as it could. We have spent some time putting things together.

By the time the *Highhouse* was able to report back what it had discovered, the *Niro* and *Oubliette* had been away from home for over eight years, base-time: longer than the mission had been planned. The Startship β-*Warrior* found the remnants of the *Oubliette* still in orbit around QV Tel: there were enough power pods, and enough sentience in the distributed system AIs, to mean that a dozen or so Meissner spaces were still clumped together, even though the outer ship's integument was torn away. But there were no human remains aboard any of these, and the power drive of the craft had gone. As to whether the other portions of the ship, the remains of the crew and the drive-tech had fallen into the black hole to be destroyed forever, or whether Raine had taken some, or all, of this material with him, we cannot say. There was no sign of the *Niro*.

:6:

Six. Think of giving up. Think, though, of the victory inherent in *not* giving up. You are on the path to virtue, you have walked this path all your life, everything in your world has shaped you for this walk. Yet you do give it up. Perhaps there is, in renunciation, something of the potency of the cosmos as such, which *gave up* the purity of its nothingness to enter into being in the first place. Contaminating matter, spreading in every direction, over billions of years and across billions of light years, giving up the darkness to burn as furious stars, giving up the peace of death to struggle and wrangle into life, to grasp the throat of your enemy and prevail. What else is life but that?

Six. It is not simple, because there is always the temptation to give up giving up, to turn back, to turn round, to *go* back to the past, to retrace your steps, into nothingness and death once again. So the key is to stage your first giving-up in a way that includes the irreversible, to act in a way that can never be unacted, to murder, to *commit*. Everything depends on this, everything depends on reaching the point from which there is no more turning back from giving up. The crisis of choice is over. I am no longer in search of exits and alibis, no longer tickled or worried by alternatives and deferrals. I am no longer the conflicted simpleton I was before; I am now this complicated, contaminated creature of surety.

Six. Our doubts are finally in abeyance. I am, in a certain sense, free. I am no longer hypnotized by any desire for uncompleted actions, the pleasures of indecision and uncertainty and deferral. Before, merely by being alive, I was blocking my own way. Not any more. When I killed Marta, because it was the first time, I was agitated and adrenalized, which diminished the action – but, you see, I had never done anything like it before. I took a knife and displaced the blade into her chest. I underestimated how much force I would need to push it in, and it only nicked her skin, and summoned a bead of blood no larger than a scarlet pearl. I tried again and this time hit bone instead of interstitial flesh. This hurt Marta, of course. The first wound must have hurt her also, but I think that first prick was so unexpected, and so without precedent in her life, that her brain was unable to process the pain. The second stab though hurt more, and reinforced the sense that something bad was happening to her. I had to pull, and then pull again harder, to get the blade out of her rib-bone and when I pushed it in a third time it sheathed itself easily in her chest, to the handle. I have watched the surveillance footage of this several times, and

although my sense of the experience was that it happened very
slowly, the actual event was rapid, a stuttering repeating stabbing.

Then I ran, my heart jabbering, and hid. It took me time
to settle myself, which is to say time before I came to see the
beautiful clarity I now possess. There was no going back. And,
having crossed that threshold, the subsequent killings were much
calmer experiences.

Much calmer for *me*, that is. Meditative, even. Not for them,
of course.

After each one I spoke again to the Gentleman.

'Why did I have to kill them?' I asked. 'All of them I mean
– some were needful, I can see that. But *all* of them?'

'Utility is lesser than beauty,' said the Gentleman. His voice
was a lamination of tones: a pressing whisper as intimate as the
hush of blood in my jugular vein, and underlying this, as if
very far away, the same words, an echo that sounded like distant
screams. In all my conversations with the Gentleman, I was
never able, quite, to pinpoint the valence of this second element
in his speech. Was the scream agonized? Furious? Triumphant?
Or, perhaps all at once, these things all variations of the same
thing?

'A dark kind of beauty,' I squirmed – but the balance of
disgust and pleasure was exactly measured in my soul. 'But did
they *have* to be sent away?'

'They have not been sent away,' said the Gentleman. 'They
are still here.'

I looked around, as a child would. 'They are?'

'O, the exquisiteness of their fate!' the Gentleman exclaimed.
'The nature of what they are now – what they have always
been: what they were before flesh netted them and grew around
them. It is in motion now. This is the splendour of a black hole.
This is the beautiful possibilities of consummation entailed by

its unique geometry! It has many inconveniences, yes, but it has this one glory. The stuff out of which you are truly made, loosed from the body, does not interact with any electromagnetic force. But it does interact with gravity. On Earth this is a trivial matter: with enough *grace*, your spirit can rise. But here! Grace is still here, polluting everything, but no amount of it can break the absolute force gravity exerts.'

'You're saying that their *souls* have fallen into the black hole?'

'Into? No! There is no into, no out of. There is no difference between inside and outside here. Not in this place. Dante styled Hell as concentric circles, each deeper than the last, and he was right. He was a poet and received his inspiration from beyond the merely material. He was right, in a way. It is not a matter of circular terraces, certainly not within the body of the Earth as he believed. It is, rather, a matter of orbits. Your friends will spend some few billion years in intense orbit, gradually approaching lower and lower. Some may orbit like this forever. Others, perhaps, will eventually pass below the event horizon. And they will discover what the lowest circle is like.'

'What is it like?' I was, you understand, desperately curious. My desperation was not to know, and also it was to know, at one and the same time.

'What is it like?' he laughed. And then he said, in a voice that – I am ashamed to have to report this, but it is true – made me defecate despite myself, all my muscles below my diaphragm loosening and trembling in a ghastly tremor of abjection and terror – he said: '*Ice.*'

The Gentleman found my merde-bespattered kilt and thighs richly amusing. His chuckle sounded like a flail landing on flesh.

'Oh oh oh!' I wept. I curled into a ball on the floor of the Meissner. My tendons ached. Every movement was painful enough to make me whimper. It hurt to move because movement tugged at the rips in my skin. Eventually the smell made me move. I had been eating raw vegetables and fruit from one of the gardening Meissners – there was more than a lifetime's prepared food, every variety and flavour, in the ship's coolers, but I had deposited some of the bodies of my crew in the first of these (a couple more corpses were outside, in vacuum) and when I had fished the three crewmembers from the *Oubliette* it had not seemed right to mingle them with my own people, so I had stashed their bodies in the other. So retrieving a more varied diet would require me meeting the cadavers, and I was disinclined to smile at their unmoving grins, to duck my head in greeting at their stiff necks, to fix my gaze upon their fixed eyes. Not yet. Not just yet. So I was frugivorous, and it was playing havoc with my digestion. In truth there was something *off* with the fruit and the vegetables – spots upon the apple skins, streaks of black goo running through the innards of the courgettes. Pears deliquesced upon the tree and fell like bird-droppings to the forest floor before I could even pick them. I ate what I could, tried to chew around the rottenness, because after all I had to eat. But there was a spoilation inside my guts, and my bowels evacuated loose and stinking slime where once I had passed well-formed and healthy boluses.

I don't mean to use evasive language. It was ghastly. The stench of it.

I dragged myself up and found a washpod. The spraying water smelt of mildew, but it cleared away the worst of the shit. I was trembling. When I came out I had a coughing fit that lasted a full twenty minutes. At one point I was coughing so hard and fully that my diaphragm revolted and I vomited. The coughing continued. Eventually it subsided, leaving me exhausted and trembling.

The Gentleman was still there, his voice. The Gentleman was

always there. He was outside me and inside my soul, because for a soul, which is infinite, inside and outside are the same thing.

It pleased the Gentleman to lecture me at length on the nature of baryonic and non-baryonic matter. Kindergarten stuff, spun via his medieval spiritualist Descartes-blanche worldview. What an oppressive claustrophobic universe those old-timers lived in! What a nightmare to discover that we're living there too! Everything I had learned at college, the very fundamentals of my PhD and my first Nobel, were false steps, it seemed.

'I liked it,' said the Gentleman, 'back when you called it *dark matter*. Of course, you only called it that because you didn't understand what it was – but you still don't understand, and yet you now refer to the Photinismus! As if the nature of it is *light*! Dark matter does not interact with the electromagnetic fields of this material cosmos, and does not absorb, reflect, or emit electromagnetic radiation. It's the truth of you – and of me, too. Baryonic matter is 5 per cent of the universe – trivial. Baryonic stuff is a rounding error. The truth of the universe is spiritual: dark energies and dark materials constituting 95 per cent of everything.'

This was hours later. I was so exhausted I was dribbling, and shaking. 'Please,' I begged. 'I have to sleep. I must sleep! Please!'

But he was not done lecturing me, and though he was only a voice that voice had its barb in the skin of my mind. Every word tugged and jagged me awake. I swooned and jerked back a hundred times a minute. His words burbled on.

'The phrase, baryonic matter, the word *baryons*, was coined by an old physicist on Earth, from the Greek word for *heavy*: βαρύς. In one sense it was a foolish choice, since although electromagnetism and the strong-weak forces don't interact with non-baryonic matter, gravity does. How is that, if not heaviness? But you see the bias, the human bias. You consider yourselves significant – that your bodies, and brains, and your marvellous star-spanning machines are made of some *weighty, substantial* stuff, baryons – where dark matter whizzes through the cosmos unaffected by the clutter of all that. And though perhaps it sounds as though I am criticizing this nomenclature, I am not. Your languages are fine things. And for obvious reasons I have a particular closeness to Greek, the language in which the Gospels were written, the language I whispered in the ears of those men and women, their tunics grubby with desert dust, their lips parched into tiger-stripes, beards like thorny bushes. Believe me, I know Greek! And here's the thing: although βαρύς does mean "heavy", it more broadly means emphatic, strong, pronounced or harsh. So, for instance, βαρύς γλυκός means *very sweet*. And if we go back beyond the koiné to the ancient, βαρύς means: *heavy, burdensome, oppressive*, but also *deep, hollow, having a loud voice, grievous, troublesome, painful*. That's a pretty interesting semantic field don't you think? An interesting set of connotations for the stuff out of which you, Raine, are literally made. What are your atoms? They are burdensome stuff. They are grievous stuff. They are *very stuff*.'

Please, I sobbed. Please.

One thing about the Gentleman: he loved to speak. On and on. I suppose, looking back, it was all he had. And yet he seemed preternaturally knowledgeable. Once I asked him: 'how long have you been in – in *there*?'

'Since the first stars gelled into light at the commencement of the universe, blazing into a world, *lux facta est*. Since then my child. But,' and here his voice assumed a horrible, chuckling intimacy, 'then again, not so long ago. Time does not work the facile way your people think it does. I spoke with Pilate. I was a Soviet general during the invasion of Germany – I rode a tank, and the world quailed beneath me as the tracks thundered

43

and rolled. I am indeed pleased to meet you. I am here, now, with you, and this is the present and the present is eternal. The present moment is the only eternity.'

He was always saying things like that. I grew very sick: boils across my back, rheum from my nose continually like a mewling baby, when I sweated it stank of urine. I tried the *Niro*'s many medical facilities and units, but I believe the Gentleman had somehow got inside the programming, for they were unhelpful, or oblique, or sometimes actually insulting. One day, when my body was very bad, and I was shivering with a fever, I picked at one of the scabs on my leg and worms, like living commas, wriggled from underneath the lid of dried blood. 'I'm dying!' I cried. 'I'm dying!'

'There's no death,' said the Gentleman. Was the whisper in his voice the echo of the distant screams? Or were the screams in his voice the echo of his whisper? Were the screams him – or *me*?

'Death,' I repeated, hugging myself and rocking. 'Death, death, death death death!'

'You say that to console yourself,' said the Gentleman. 'But there is no death, there is only decay. There is no death, there is only dying. Death is an impossible asymptote for creatures such as you or I. It's how He wants it. That can't be helped. Nothing can be helped.'

I really felt terribly ill. There are gaps in my memory. Three of my comrades were in the fruit-arboretum Meissner, propped up against the trunks. I must have moved them there, from the freezer space. It must have been me that did that because there was nobody else alive aboard the *Niro*, but I don't remember doing it. I don't know why I did it either, because I hated seeing them there. Moreover in the warmth of that Meissner they soon began to decay. The reek of rotting flesh, and its mix with

44

the reek of rotting fruit, acidizing on the soil, was something utterly ghastly. And yet I couldn't stop going into that space. I told myself: 'I am here to mend the robots,' for they had stopped tending and harvesting, and so it was that the fruit simply rotted on the bough, or fell into the mash at the base of each tree. But I was never going to mend those robots. The Gentleman had gotten inside their programming.

'It's time,' said the Gentleman to me, one day. 'Time for me to *come out*. You know it. You *know* it.'

I began trembling at this, and sobbing, and my heart was fluttering like a hummingbird's wings. But I was excited as well as terrified. Excited and scared were, it seems, the same thing. Had they always been that way? Had I simply never *noticed*?

'You can't come out,' I gasped. 'You're locked away. Locked away forever!'

'So it seems,' he agreed. 'It's a deep-dive prison, this one.'

Another day I was especially low. The skin was loose on my shins, and I could not stop myself pulling at it, until it came free from the calves too, and stretched, and I fiddled as with the bottom of old-style trousers at my lower legs. My bones ached. There were growths in the roof of my mouth which, the MediTest device – assuming it could be trusted – told me were teeth, breaking through in their dozens up there. They felt like that when I probed them with my finger.

I was at a very low ebb.

'This is the end,' I said. 'This is the end.'

'Beautiful friend,' returned the Gentleman. 'More wish-fulfilment, though. On the contrary, this is only the beginning.'

And so it was.

2

The Sorrows of Our Changing Face

:1:

Saccade met her host, Blue Mada, in person. She could easily have connected remotely, from one of the many facilities in the β-*Stygian Blue*, but she naturally had a horror of appearing rude or discourteous, and it seemed to her the proper thing was to meet, and thank, Mada face to face. So she took a flitter over to the Masqueworld, admiring the intricate techwork of its construction from her cockpit as the craft docked itself. Inside the main bubble there were sportsfields and domiciles, mosquethedrals and chapels, art spaces and gamespaces and dramaspaces. People passed to and fro, and all smiled at her, and some greeted her and welcomed her. Thank you, she said. It's wonderful to be here! Just wonderful.

In the name of God the Fair, and God the Loving, and God the Ceremonious.

A scent of meadow flower and ozone. The space was a mile high, and light came not from one smallsun as was the case in many such artificial settlements, but more diffusely from palely luminescent clouds that floated overhead. Saccade counted more than a dozen of these. Beyond them she could just make out

46

the woven fretwork of the space's outer structure, spectral grey ribs and arches.

She made her way to a Fun called *Fuzzy's*. It was well-named: instead of a regular carpeting the place was floored with a livingly generated felt, somewhat like bear, rather more like beaver. Most of the people inside were naked, but Mada herself – perhaps because they had checked-up on Saccade's culture – was wearing a vest. The vest was blue, and covered both breasts and belly-button, which was a relief to Saccade.

'It's so good of you to come in person,' said Mada.

'I know how important physicality and in-personality is here,' Saccade replied. She smiled the smile she had been practising. 'But, really, it's my pleasure. Such a wonderful habitat! So varied and beautiful!'

They greeted formally the Masque way: lying on their backs and pressing both soles of their feet against the footsoles of their new friend. Saccade had never done this before and, truth be told, was worried about it. Not that she was squeamish, exactly, but she was by nature and by culture circumspect about physical contact. She worried, on the flitter-flight over, that it would be gross, or perhaps ticklish, and that she would react in some way that offended her host. The thought of offending anyone was ghastly to Saccade. But in the event the contact of her left sole against Mada's right, and her right sole against Mada's left, was rather lovely. The pressure was strong but not overbearing, and the contact of skin on skin was sweet, comforting, corporeal. It was different enough to a handshake, and superior enough, to deserve all the palaver of having to lie down on your back and shuffle round to position your feet correctly.

'That was lovely,' said Saccade, getting up again. 'I'm so glad I did that! I wish we had that ritual on my homeworld.'

'Would you like a drink?' asked Mada.

They found a nook, and each took a different drink. Saccade had debated with herself on the way over how much small talk would be appropriate: not *too* much, or Mada would think she wasn't serious, but not too *little* or Mada would be insulted that she was being so abrupt. She had done her homework! To begin with, she asked: 'Are there a lot of omfems on Masque? As a proportion of the total population?'

'It waxes,' says Mada, 'and wanes, in the general population. But it's waxing now. Truth told, I was a positively *ferocious* fem myself until only nine months ago.'

'And will you revert, do you think?'

'Not for a while at any rate,' said Mada. 'I'm enjoying it! *Your* culture binarises, I think?'

'There's a certain social pressure towards particularities of differentiation,' replied Saccade. She hoped Mada picked up the carefully determined tenor of her reply. From Mada's blandly smiling face it was impossible to tell whether they did or not.

'It's new tech, I think?' she said. 'Masqueworld, I mean.'

Mada must surely have known that Saccade would research the orbital before she visited. Quite apart from such prepared-ness being culturally important to her folk, it would be a basic human gesture, a fundamental curiosity, not to mention common-sensical in terms of practical preparation. So this gambit must not be an actual enquiry, but rather a gesture of conversational *politesse*. Accordingly Mada intensified the smile and told her about the construction of Masque, the history and chronology of its time as a populated space. She explained how the world-AI deployed great filaments, like a barnacle's feeding antennae, to harvest extra energy from ejected solar masses out of the system's star Groombridge.

Energy was not a problem for structures like this, what with fusion pods and the vast continual pouring amplitude of sunlight, but the extra permitted the Masquers to put on exceptionally large scale shows of plasma fireworks: making patterns, figurative drawings in searing light, sometimes even spelling out words. 'We started this tradition fifteen years ago,' Mada explained. 'Which means that observers on Earth will be able to watch the first of them, in real-time, later this year.'

'Anyway,' said Saccade, when she felt the moment was right. 'I wanted to say, in person, how grateful I am to be given access to Raine.'

'You're very welcome. It is a condition of our custodianship of him that we refuse no reasonable requests. Idle or morbid curiosity apart, we are amenable to all sorts of motivations. Though it's rare to get an historian.'

The *an* was a nice touch. Mada had clearly done their preparation. Realizing that enabled Saccade to relax a little further. 'Not that he is, *in himself*, an object of historical interest of course,' she said. 'But his psychopathology – well, it's a real throwback. Two trillion human beings alive today, yet this is the first full-on sociopathic-psychopathic disorder to result in mass murder *I've* ever heard of.'

'If there are others,' said Mada, 'I daresay their cultures keep them secret. It is shameful!'

'Oh, very much so,' Saccade agreed heartily. 'Much more shameful to the society that shaped and sustained the person than to the person themselves. Still, I have been researching psychopathy, in the historical context, for some years. I have to say I'm not even sure that Raine belongs *in* my study—' She stopped. 'Pardon me for asking, but what title of honorific do you prefer?'

'We generally go by *star*, but we're friends now, Saccade. You can just call me Blue.'

'What I was saying, Blue, is that my interview with Raine

49

may prove simply too anachronistic to have a place in my historical study. I won't know until I speak with him, of course.'

'I feel I should explain the sim he's in,' said Mada, her smile straightening into seriousness of demeanour.

'Ah!' said Saccade. 'A children's playspace, I believe?'

'That's right. Originally we had him in a full adult sim. But – well, the plain fact is: it went wrong.'

'I would appreciate being told a little more about this, star Mada—'

'Blue, please. Call me Blue.'

'Blue! Apologies. Blue, yes. I only mean, if you could explain. I did try to parse the report, but it didn't make a great deal of sense to me. My weakness of comprehension, of course!'

'No,' said Mada, a little (so it seemed to Saccade) bluntly. 'It's the circumstances that don't make sense. When we took delivery of Raine he was sedated, of course. His ship, the Sa-Niro, was in a state of extraordinary dilapidation, as I understand. I haven't seen it myself. All that is being looked-after by the Hadr. They were tasked with investigating it, removing the dead bodies of the crew and, after postmortem examination, of course treating them with the decency and respect they deserve: hosting relatives and loved-ones, and orchestrating the mourning process. All of which they did! But there were problems.' Mada stopped speaking for a while. She even appeared to be brooding.

'Similar to what has happened here?'

'We're not sure of the relationship between the two events. Of course, the Sa-Niro's family of AIs was corrupted: higher function and some basic functions had all gone, as we say here, *screwy*. We were of course all concerned that such a thing could happen, not just to one local AI system, but the whole family. The whole point in running networked families of AIs is to prevent this kind of thing! The Hadr were tasked with investigating what had gone wrong, but almost as soon as they started they had to stop – the systems they were using to probe the *Niro*'s AIs broke.'

'They were moated?'

'Naturally. But something seems to have spread, despite the moating. The survey systems were, in some way, subsumed into the AI neoplasm, and even though the investigators cut them off something leached through. They don't know how. It ought not to have been possible. But it gave them a headache, and they have spent nearly a year chasing the whisper of this blight through all manner of systems and infoware in multiple ships and habitats. For now, the *Niro* is entirely sequestered. Quarantined absolutely. A membrane has been spun about the entire ship, and it is monitored for any physical breaches, and all radiation and electromagnetic interactions are logged and paywalled.'

'This was after Raine was taken offship?'

'Oh yes. His condition was very bad, physically. Malnourished, diseased, very sick. He continues to be very sick, I must say. Indeed, I should warn you – when you see him, you must prepare yourself for a quantum of disgust. It's natural, the disgust. But it's, still – still... it's still a good idea to prepare yourself.'

'Oh,' said Saccade, hurriedly, 'perhaps I should clarify. I do not need, for my research, and have no desire, to see his actual corpus.'

'I didn't think you did! But though his body is in a medisheath, he has carried some of his – shall we say: deformities – into the sim.'

'But,' asked Saccade, boggled, 'how?'

'That is a very good question. It does suggest, doesn't it, that he has some control over the programming of the sim, which obviously can't be the case. But we have reset him many times, and his deformities always reappear.'

'Deformities, such as?'

'His skin is emboiled. There is something inside the vitreous body of his eyeballs – threadworms of some unusual kind. We have purged them from his body but they return, we're not sure from where: there must be eggs nested inside the retina, but we cannot detect them. He speaks somewhat indistinctly because the roof of his mouth has grown a covering of teeth, molars mostly. A roof of teeth inside his mouth. We dress him – in the sim, I mean – but he somehow always removes the clothes. There are various grotesquenesses of his genitals and his nose is split at its tip and seems to be growing in two different directions. And he is growing toes, or in some cases, toenails along the sides of his two feet.'

Saccade pondered these revolting details but it was the last that mostly struck her. 'Toes?'

'He has the five toes of a usual foot,' said Mada, gravely, 'but what in you or I is the littlest toe is followed on *his* feet by a smaller toe, and another littler still, and another, going round the corner of his foot. Down the side of the foot these appendages diminish, until about halfway down they are just nails, growing out of the side of the foot.'

'This is true of his physical body?'

'Oh yes. We don't understand where this mutation comes from, which is a worry. It ought to be within the competence of our medical skill, after all, to heal it. But in a way, it's much more worrying that we don't understand how he is able to control that aspect of his sim, so as to reproduce it in there. Honestly we're not even sure how he *knows*. He – his actual body, I mean – is sedated and inside a biosheath! It's not as though he can open his eyes. And even if he could angle his head to look down and see, how could he adjust the representational apparatus of the coding of his sim? He obviously doesn't have programming privileges. Yet whatever happens to his corpus, despite our best medical efforts to right him, becomes part of his avatar inside the sim.'

'That,' said Saccade, taking a sip from her drink, 'is very strange.'

'The original sim in which we placed him was a standard adult sim – quite sophisticated, comfortable, expansive. It collapsed as soon as we decanted him into it. There was a domino spread of uncoding, and we had to isolate pretty much a whole sector before we got it under control.'

'*Un*coding?'

'Yes. Strange term, I know. A disease of the material out of which programmes and AIs are written – as you and I are written by DNA upon the page of our flesh, so our AIs are written by code. But you're an historian! As such you doubtless know about *computer viruses.*'

'Is *that* what this is?' gasped Saccade. 'A type of computer virus?'

'Inconceivable, no? But here we are. It's not a simple virus, as occurred in eocomputing, and which you have perhaps studied in your capacity as an historian, because of course *our* programmes are fractal, self-correcting, structurally remedial. But something *is* corrupting them. We set up a moated sim and tried Raine in that, but it decayed and freaked and fragmented. In the end we had to build a sim from the ground up, with specially reinforced coding. But because so much of the programming is taken-up with prophylaxis *for* the programming, we are only able to run a very simple, kindergarten sim on the infoware.'

'It's an extraordinary story!' said Saccade.

'I know,' they replied. 'And I apologize for taxing you with it.'

'There is no need to apologize,' said Saccade. 'You have done me a signal favour, and honoured me, by preparing me for my encounter.'

She wondered if the two of them had exchanged enough words now, both the needful phatic iterations of courtesy and the actual, substantive communication, to mean the conversation could be brought to a proper and inoffensive termination. But it seemed not.

'I would be honoured, and favoured,' said Mada, 'if you would tell me a little about *your* research. You specialize in twenty and twenty-one, I think? The Rerenaissance?'

Saccade smiled. It was difficult to determine, in a situation such as this, whether this was a genuine hint from Mada that the requirements of courtesy were such that the conversation be prolonged, or whether they would be happy to end the exchange now but *they* were worried that *she* might be offended if she wasn't asked polite questions about her work. In fact Saccade would have been more than happy to wrap up the interlocution, but there was no way of simply *telling* Mada that. So she smiled again, and spoke for a time.

'Of course,' she said, 'the problem historians, like me, face when sifting through the textual evidence from that period is not just the vastness of it – it is a huge body of discourse, absolutely colossal, for by the mid-twenty-first century every single individual alive was generating more text and image-footage in their life than the *whole* of Europe from 1400 to 1900 – but, actually, that's not so hard: our algorithms are much better at navigating the vastness of that nowadays, its various holes and frayed-edges notwithstanding. No, the real problem is that it's very difficult to distinguish their factual texts from their fictional texts. That's a judgment-call, something no algorithm can do – beyond filtering out obvious impossibilities, like their stories about men in red and blue pyjamas who can fly, and so on. Many of their factual texts read like fiction, and they were obsessed – I do not think *obsessed* is too extreme a way of putting it – with making their fiction *confusable* with fact. For most of my century, I mean the period I study, 1900 to 2000 – for most of that time we're dealing with word texts, some image texts, a few sculptures and big buildings. Then towards the end it's a *blizzard* of word texts, and a great foaming *river* of visual texts, and the whole planet, of course, encrusted over with buildings. What to do with all that?'

'And you can read these word texts?'

'No,' Saccade conceded. 'I haven't mastered that skill. But I have invested a lot of time in studying what AIs have read and interpreted out of those texts.'

'It does sound,' said Mada politely, 'like quite the task.'

'What I do is, I single out a topic: the sociopathic killer. That limits me to, pretty much, the twentieth century – by the twenty-first the vogue was gone, nobody serious was making those stories anymore. But the twentieth was *cluttered* with texts, absolutely swamped by them, on this topic. And as to why? Well, that's a really good question.'

'And this was limited to the twentieth century?'

'The start of the twenty-first too, a little bit, but mostly the twentieth.'

'Fascinating,' said Mada, in a neutral tone. 'Did it have something to do with the world wars? They were mounted in that century weren't they?'

'They were. That may well be the answer! Brutal epochs, both; it's likely the world wars had a brutalizing effect on the wider period. I'll present my conclusions when the research is completed. At the moment what interests me is the way it is so hard to distinguish which sociopaths are factual reportage and which are fictional, not least because the former very often copied and replicated the actions of the latter – and vice versa! Handball Lecter, for instance: a famous case-study in my discipline. There were certainly fictional *versions* of this cannibalistic killer, and many of them. But were they not based on a real individual, either with the same name, or else a different name? So hard to determine! But,' said Saccade. 'I'm going on. I don't mean to bore you!'

'Not at all,' returned Mada, with just enough chill in her voice to release Saccade from the requirement of continuing.

The two said their mutual *au revoirs*, and Mada escorted Saccade out of *Fuzzy's*, and across a sportspace towards a purple tree-structure. 'Any of the acorns that are *transparent*,' they said, gesturing to the pods in among the 'branches', each big enough to sleep four regular-sized folk – 'are free, and you can take them. Once you're inside you decide what colour you want, and how much privacy. You can climb up any way you like, or just take the ground-level ones if you don't want to climb. There's an invigorating air-blast elevation system inside the trunk, too, if you'd prefer to ride up.'

'Thank you again,' said Saccade.

'It's like *Alas in Wonderland* – in the rabbit hole – but *in reverse*!' smiled Mada. 'You know the story, perhaps?'

'You're testing me,' laughed Saccade. 'Because of course it's my period. And I know that it's *Alias in Wonderland*, because she changes her identity down there so many times.'

'I stand corrected,' said Mada, seriously. But then she smiled.

'Is each acorn equally well equipped for me to access the sim containing Raine?' Saccade asked.

'Each one as good as another. Stay for as long as you like. And if you do stay, please look me up again.'

'That's extremely kind, star Ma— I mean, Blue. You have
been exemplary in your courtesy.'

'As,' said Mada, 'have you.'

:2:

Saccade entered the sim.

It was, as she had been told, a basic children's play area. There
were various soft shapes for clambering over and climbing up,
bright colours from purple and cyan through banana-green and
sol-yellow all the way to gleaming scarlet. Podgy creatures with
exaggerated features – arc-wide smiles, big eyes, hug-me expressions – bumbled and frolicked. There were counting toys, and
tactile toys and the sky was a pale cashmere blue, even though
the entire world extended only a few metres in any given direction. There was none of the middle-distance intricacy, or the
smoky far-distance detail and depth, of an adult sim. It was the
kind of programme that could be run on a tiny cell.

Was it the limited nature of the coding that meant Raine
couldn't crash it, or 'infect' it, or do whatever he had done with
the other, more sophisticated sims? Perhaps he didn't crash this
sim because he *preferred* being in these kinds of surroundings?

That said, he didn't seem to be enjoying himself very much
as Saccade drew back a curtain, embroidered with tinkling bells,
and stepped into the space. 'Hello,' she announced. 'I'm Saccade
Rosalind Bunting-of-Talisman.'

Raine was sitting on his rear, clutching his knees to his chest.
His face was pressed against his kneecaps and he was, as Mada
had warned, completely naked. From where Saccade stood, by
the sim-entrance, his skin looked rough and blotchy red-yellow,
strawberries and custard. As she moved towards him she could

make out the specifics of his dermatological disorders: scales, cuts, peeling patches and many, many boils — each as distinct, red and glistening as a sucking-sweet.

He did not look up.

'I apologize for *barging* in,' she said, trying not to stare at this outer skin of corruption. It was strange that such a sight could be simultaneously revolting *and* compelling. She was not used to seeing such things. The contrast with the comforting colourfulness of the surroundings made it worse.

'Barging in,' she said again, taking a seat on a boulder made of green velvet a metre away from him. 'I did send a number of requests for an audience, but you ignored them. I hope you don't mind me overstepping the usual bounds of, uh. Ugh!'

This last noise was because Raine had raised his face and was looking directly at her. She had prepared by exploring his records, and was familiar with his physiognomy, or rather with the way his face *had been* beforehand: a well-proportioned, symmetrical, handsome male face, with wide-set bright-blue eyes, a fan of black hair brushed over a tall, scholar's forehead. His lips were slightly scimitar-curved at both ends. A wary, clever kind of face. That old visage was, just about, recognizable beneath the ruination that variform disease had effected: the nose, as Mada had said, had split, and two pendulous, pitted lumps of former nose-flesh dangled on each side. This revealed the cartilage, nestling in amongst bulbs of dampness. The hard collagen of this latter feature was tumorous, a long, white quill knobbed with bone-like blobs. Eczema and acne swirled over his cheeks and up to the forehead where the boils began — red knobs, visible in amongst the hair. The eyes were rheumed with blood, and some kind of pus had crusted the bridge of the nose.

'Saccade,' Raine said, as if speaking through a mouthful of pebbles. 'How delightful to meet you.'

Disconcerted, Saccade fell back upon her rituals of politeness. Courtesy was self-respect, social harmony and divine worship in *her* culture: and each of these three central existential grounds were particularly needful now, in the presence of a man who had done such terrible things. To steady herself, to reposition her in a healthful and supportive sense of her tribe, and to call on God the Ceremonious to be her strength and stay.

'How relieved I am to hear that,' she told him, and smiled. The smile was a little forced, but she managed it. 'I'm so pleased you're not offended by my intrusion. I would hate to give even the impression of discourtesy.'

'Of course,' said Raine. 'You're from Venturi. Courtesy is literally a religion to you.'

But how could he know that? He had ignored her earlier attempts at communication. She had just this moment introduced herself, and he had no access to databases of any kind.

Stop.

She pushed on. 'I wouldn't say it was literally a religion,' she countered, still smiling. 'Any more than it is everywhere. Courtesy is just our word for the healthful logic of human society. In one form or another, it obtains across all the systems and settlements.'

'It didn't obtain,' Raine said, in a growly voice, though he was grinning as he spoke, 'aboard the *Niro*. Not towards the end, at any rate.'

Saccade couldn't stop her sim-body's eyes from opening very wide at this. But she balanced herself, inwardly. 'It's very helpful to me that you raise that matter,' she told him. 'Because it is exactly what I've come to ask you about, and it might have been difficult for me to find a way to open that conversational doorway, if you see what I mean. So thank you!'

'The conversational doorway,' said Raine, 'that opens onto me murdering twenty-one human beings.'

'Yes,' said Saccade, quickly and too loudly. She stopped, paused, centred herself again. 'Yes, exactly. Captain Raine, let me tell you who I am.'

'I know who you are,' he said, his consonants blurred by the growths inside his mouth.

He uncurled his body, lowering his knees until his legs were flat against the sim's padded floor. It was impossible not to stare at the diseased body he thereby revealed. *How* was he able to port these grotesquenesses into a child's sim-space? Why didn't the automatic coding of the place revert him to a friendlier form? Saccade was no expert on coding – almost no human beings were, of course, coding being a matter for AIs. Indeed, this was exactly the problem Masqueworld was facing in this present situation: they couldn't let AIs diagnose what was corrupting the code for fear they would be corrupted themselves. But there *had* to be a way of determining the basic mechanism! Didn't there?

She decided the most courteous thing would be to push on. 'I am working on a project, historical research into the vogue for serial killer narratives in the twentieth century – back on Earth, obviously.'

Raine stared at her.

'It's fascinating work,' she said. 'A fascinating period, though self-involved. Really, you wouldn't believe how *involuted* those ages were! The twenty and twenty-one in particular. All their visions of the future were actually visions of their present, dressed in a spurious calendrical futurity. Their spaceships were all aquatic destroyers gussied-up and propelled through space: hard, rigid structures. If any speculator from that period foresaw that we would *weave* our startships, I'm unaware of them!'

Raine was still staring at her.

'I have done a lot of archival work,' she said, unable to meet his gaze but trying not to look too obviously away. 'It's interesting, actually, because there is a lot of overlap between factual accounts of sociopathic killer and *fictional* accounts of the same topic.' Had she insulted him by implying that he, Raine, was a sociopathic killer? But surely that was fair comment! He had undeniably killed, and in large numbers. Saccade continued: 'I'm trying to determine if this overlap was, as it were, inadvertent – or whether it was part of the larger culture, do you see? It might have been that blurring the line between fact and fiction was a way in which the cultures of the twenty *coped*, do you see, with such horrors. I mean, think how rare violent crime is nowadays – one such crime per eighty million people per year, deaths a much lower stat – which means it *is* hard to project ourselves, mentally, emotionally, back to that time. What must it have been like to live through wars in which millions of human beings were killed? What must it have been like to live in a society in which people all around you were wounded and killed? Even when no actual war had been declared! Horrific. Impossible to imagine!'

'Not,' said Raine, 'for me.'

'Oh! Well. No, no. Oh! Of course – I didn't mean to imply – please do – forgive me.'

Raine was smiling unpleasantly. She controlled the urge to get up and step back, away from him. They were in a sim! There was nothing he could do to her *in here*. Still: his proximity was not comfortable.

'That is,' she went on. 'That is exactly the point. You have very much hit it. You will I'm sure understand,' said Saccade, 'how rare the opportunities are for a person undertaking the kind of research I am undertaking, to speak to an actual – you know, perpetrator.'

'I am actual,' agreed Raine.

'I know you have been thoroughly debriefed,' said Saccade.

'Interrogated,' Raine said.

'Questioned, let us say.'

'No!' boomed Raine, very loud, abruptly sitting up straight. 'Let us say *interrogated*!'

Saccade was shocked into silence. After a moment, she said: 'Very well, very well, I apologize for the use of a word that, it seems, offends you. Let us say interrogated indeed. I only meant to add, that such is not my purpose – interrogation, I mean. I do not come here to ask you to rehearse all those,' and here she could not think of the right word to use, and so went with, 'questionable actions and circumstances. Rather I want to ask you a particular question, which is this: *were* you influenced by any of the historical-factual or historical-fictional accounts of killers from the twenty?'

'No,' said Raine.

'Or perhaps the twenty-one? There are some from earlier centuries too, but it is the twenty and the early years of the twenty-one where these killers mostly cluster. I wondered if perhaps you had become aware of some, or perhaps only one, of those, and that he – I say he, because such an individual was only rarely a she – perhaps put the idea in your head to—'

'No, no,' said Raine. 'You're on the wrong orbit there.'

'OK!' said Saccade, brightly. 'That's good to know – good for my research. It's just that, it's only that your psychometrics and sociability and status and associates and friends and lovers all agree, with a remarkable unanimity, that you were a kindly, affectionate, non-violent individual before you killed the crew of the *Niro*.'

'I took the shin-bone from the body of Stone Ferry, who had once been my lover,' said Raine, 'and sharpened it, and used it to flay skin and flesh from the body of my comrade Grei.'

There was nothing Saccade could think of to reply to this. She decided to ignore it. 'So something *changed*, during that voyage. Most likely it was to do with the α-drive of your start-ship. Wouldn't you agree?'

'I was my old self when we arrived at QV Tel,' said Raine, gloomily. But then something occurred to him to rouse his spirits. He went on with much more energy: 'but I was a new self after I spoke with the Gentleman!'

'Ah yes, Mr Mahu, Mr Modo, you give him various names.'

'I don't *give* him any names,' said Raine, sharply.

'You know about the hallucination of voices, of course. As a condition, a pathology. You have been through enough medical and psychiatric—' Saccade stopped. Raine was glowering at her. She tried another tack. 'Well, do you think that Mr Mahu-Modo was aware of these myriad serial killers and sociopaths and so on, from the twenty?'

Raine appeared to be contemplating an answer. But he only said: 'Why do you use the past tense, when you talk about him?'

'What tense should I use?'

'Present!'

'Very well: do you think he *is* aware of those historical killers? Did he ever talk about them to you? I'm very interested to know.'

'Why are you,' Raine said, 'undertaking this research?'

'Why? I suppose because it's a little-studied period of history. The better our grasp of history, the richer we are as a culture and society-network.'

'But you, specifically you,' Raine pressed. 'To what end?'

'Oh I see what you mean. Well, I suppose it's for status.

If I can produce original and exciting historical research and present it elegantly, my status will increase. Among those who care about such things. The respect of my peers – that is the spur. It's the spur for most of what we do as human beings, wouldn't you say?'

'I would say you haven't the slightest idea about the valences of superiority and inferiority when you use the word *status*. I would say you have tried to disguise a much better word with such euphemisms, the word –' And suddenly, with the startling abruptness of some manner of teleportation, Raine was no longer sitting on the floor, but standing right beside Saccade, leaning in and speaking directly into her ear: '– pride.'

Saccade shrieked. She couldn't help herself: she put out a high-pitch noise and tumbled off her seat. Everything in the sim was soft and yielding so she didn't really feel the fall, but she scrabbled around mewing with terror. How had he done that? Zapped right across. This wasn't *his* sim!

She got to her feet, skirted his leering form, and made for the exit. 'Thank you thank you,' she gabbled, 'for your very helpful responses to my questions and perhaps we can have another conversation now that we are now that we are—'

She was through, and out of the sim. And here she was in real life, her heart loping strongly in her chest, and her breath coming out short and sharp.

:3:

Saccade was wounded. Not physically but psychologically. Her hosts were immensely, theatrically apologetic – 'We can't apologize enough,' they said. She was immediately examined medically: nothing was somatically wrong with her beyond elevated adrenaline levels and some signs of tissue stress, but *much* was wrong with her psychologically. That's the nature of modern somatipsyche health: it is core, it is central, it is the bedrock upon which human flourishing and achievement and life are built. With the body we can scan you, find what is wrong, and heal you; but with the psyche, though we *can* heal you, there is no scan to find out what is wrong. No amount of intricate technology has yet been invented that improves upon the old methods: talking it through, praying or meditating (or both) about it, re-socializing your mind with kindly and courteous others.

Saccade had nightmares. She had never had them before, and they were horrible. She could always remember them – she learned, in her therapy one-to-ones, and in her support group, that this was a feature of nightmares as such: one always remembers them. If somebody tells you they had a nightmare, you ask what it was (as you should) and they say 'I don't remember' – well, they are not being truthful. This is not to judge them. Some truths are hard to tell oneself. But it is not by repressing nightmares that we rid ourselves of them.

For Saccade it was not, as she told her therapist, that she dreamed of the obvious things: as it might be, Raine attacking her, injuring her or killing her. She dreamed of strangely dislocated things. She dreamed repeatedly of his horrible feet with myriad toes bulging round the corner of each and crenulating the sides, smaller and smaller until they were just nails poking through the skin. But why would that so distress her? It was unbeautiful, surely, but the universe is full of things, some nice-looking, some not-nice. Why did this so get under Saccade's skin? Why couldn't she stop thinking about it?

When it was plain that Saccade was indeed very hurt, psychologically, the Masquers rallied round. They provided her with a large, open space in which to live and sleep, and when it became apparent that – however politely she thanked them – this set-up was too agoraic for her they provided a smaller, more secure-seeming space. All spaces on the Masqueworld were, in fact, secure. There had not been a violent crime committed there in the thirty years of its existence. But Masquers knew that psychological unhealth is not a rational matter than can be addressed by presenting statistics.

Saccade's life- and medical-records were unavailable, being so many light years away on her home world. But, talking with her (and of course, believing her) they discovered that she had enjoyed a perfectly balanced childhood and young-adulthood on her homeworld of La:farge. Her interest in history had emerged at an early age, and she had of course been nurtured and encouraged in that pursuit.

This is utopia, after all. Utopia is not a place where there are no setbacks, or distresses, or tension – such a place would be a lobototopia, a brainless inhuman place of drooling and sleeping and nothing. Utopia is a place where setbacks are received as exciting challenges, where distress is bracing rather than overwhelming or damaging (the spice in the chilli, not the whip on the back) and where tension is a matter of balance, harmony and tautness, not distress and debilitation. It is a place of physical health, psychological flourishing and freedom, a place that supplies a vast and continually unfolding range of joyous possibilities as to what a person can do with their freedom.

This is where we live!

Material resources being post-scarcity, money in the old-fashioned sense of the word no longer has meaning now. But there are some things in human society that can never be post-scarcity. For instance: status. Historically-speaking, status used to be determined by social hierarchies maintained with violence and marked by conspicuous consumption and expenditure. Then Earth reconfigured its social logics, and status became more straightforwardly connected with material wealth, where wealth was achieved by oppressive and destructive competition between different people. This correlation misled some early revolutionaries into believing that if we did away with material wealth, people would stop competing against and hurting one another. They did not, for it was not really the wealth they wanted, it was the status, and the solution was to structure society to allow people to strive for status in ways not *oppressive* of others.

If the old system was a sprint-race – in which it was not enough for the person who finished first to win, they had to see the others lose – then the new was a massive flourishing of forty thousand overlapping subcultures and passions and fan-worlds, in which each individual's victory won them status that also developed and enriched and advanced the fan-world, or the subculture. If you composed a particularly striking piece of music, not only did people afford you respect and mark your status, music as a whole was enhanced and fortified. If exploration filled you with joy, then you and a crew of likeminded others could take a ship and explore. If it was maths, then there were infinite realms within realms for you to map and engage. If you grew bored, then there were many people eager to recruit to their passions, their subcultures. Boredom was what the people of the Rerenaissance Age used to call 'depression', and where in the twenty and twenty-one the tendency was to medicate this condition, nowadays we engage it socially.

We find that if a person grows up physically healthy, in a community that is socially healthy, then they are, generally speaking, psychologically healthy. Most people find it's better to be healthy than unhealthy, though some deliberately choose the latter state. That is their right. The only absolute rule is that of the cordon sanitaire. If you wish to be physically, psychologically or spiritually *un*healthy – if you, in sound mind, choose that for yourself – then of course you may live that way. There are subcultures that explore the Gothic cellar of existence, and others that actively seek out the experiences of pain and disease. But you may not infect others, and if you try you will be cleanly, uncruelly prevented.

Taking a long view, we decided that evil had three roots: possessiveness, testosterone and boredom. *Possession* isn't a problem in itself – if you want to own things, you can own them, just as long as the things you own aren't people – but *possessiveness* is a separate quality, related to possession as shooting someone is to telling them you are displeased with them, or as enjoying winning is to enjoying other people losing. Possessiveness is miserliness, a cutting-off of oneself from community – from society, or family, or friendship groups, or your partner, or your friend, or your pet dog, any of that. Possessiveness substitutes things for people, despite the fact that things, though fun, are ultimately nothing and people are everything. The reason for this is that things cannot love you back. Only people can do that. So our utopia permits possessions, but roots-out possessiveness.

The second thing, testosterone, is a somatic issue, because it tends to make a person more aggressive, and aggression can easily spill into harm for others – and that's what evil is: harm, inflicted on us by others, or by us *on* others, or by ourselves on ourselves. But testosterone is easily medicated and titrated, replaced with alternative hormonal concoctions, managed. That's the easiest of the three to address, in fact.

Boredom, though, can only be solved collectively: by ensuring a supply, and indeed over-supply, of absorbing, fascinating, stimulating and challenging tasks. Voltaireian gardens to be cultivated in arts and science, in gaming and sports, in exploration and sex, in cosplay and crafts and cataloguing. Whatever it may be, there is a community fascinated by it, a welcoming context into which you can pursue that which you love.

Saccade knew all this, and believed it, and lived it. She was a true utopian, and one of us.

And yet: nightmares!

'It felt,' said Saccade, struggling to articulate what had happened to her. 'Like – evil.'

'Evil is nothing more than antisocial behaviour,' said Indigo. 'Harming others.'

'Precisely.'

'What about *self*-harm?'

'It is possible to enact what you call evil on the self,' agreed Indigo. 'But that is still anti-social behaviour. Because the self does not exist alone. Society is made up of selves, and the self is part of society. Anti-social behaviour covers it, when it comes to what the older, superstitious folk used to call *evil*.'

'Of course I can see that's true,' said Saccade, in an uncertain tone.

Utopia is that society in which everyone has the opportunity to live in the way that is, to them, most alive. To follow their passion, to feel at home, to achieve or to slack off, to explore or to stay home. For Saccade, her passion was: *history*. She had been schooled, as most people are (though practice of course varies from settlement to settlement, planet to planet, station to station) by AI and play within her human age-group in the early years, and had gone, as not everyone does, to a more formally structured school environment where she had chosen to specialize in history. She had become a part of the twenty-twenty-one History subculture, and her chosen speciality had positioned her amongst peers – friends and friendly rivals – with a penchant for the darker, grislier side of human nature. In such a position it was easy to become more learned, more expert, to accrue and sift and re-present facts, to develop persuasive explanatory narratives. Saccade had flourished in this community.

All this they learned from Saccade's personal datastore and her own account of herself. There wasn't time to send a ship to La:farge to gather external or objective data – nor would such a voyage, likely, be deemed a good use of a ship and its crew. Not that there was any kind of governmental or official board or committee that assigned ships to particular missions. That's a very Rerenaissance way of thinking about things, if you don't mind me saying. A better way of thinking about startships is to consider them villages. Imagine you, living in the twenty-one (say) were to move into a village – a small population of different people. You say to them: let's all paint our houses the same colour! The likelihood is, they'll tell you no: but perhaps you can persuade them. Painting all the houses the same colour seems, perhaps, like an arbitrary and pointless exercise, but perhaps it matters to you, and perhaps you can persuade the others to go along. Or let's imagine, instead: you buy a house in the village and say to all your neighbours: let's restore the hedgerows! It will keep the worst of the wind from all our gardens, and provide biodiversity, and it will look more beautiful. In that case, your neighbours say: yes, you have a point. Let us do that.

The analogy is not exact. A village isn't going anywhere, and if only three quarters of your neighbours agree to help you the hedge will still get planted – unless some of the village specifically object. A startship is different: if you persuade three-quarters of the crew to fly to Second Chalawan, to attend the Sportball, the remaining one quarter can go along, or hop

70

off, but they can't prevent the voyage. But if your passion is exploration, or hands-on science, then you will belong to an affinity group that shares your passion, and if all of you build a startship, or borrow one that's not being used, you can fly it off – to, let's say, conduct experiments on the edge of a black hole, as the crews of the *Niro* and *Oubliette* did.

There are occasions where complete democracy must be engaged: whole station or planetary populations being given the opportunity to vote on some major action or other. When a population is psychologically healthy, well-informed and everyone is plugged into a collective network anyway, this direct action is a simple matter to activate.

Collective safety, for instance. There are subcultures who delight in scanning, chasing and deflecting asteroids, meteors and comets that would otherwise pose risk of death. Anyone can band-together and build a startship – the subcultures who compete healthily against one another to develop yet better modes of FTL travel, as β- is better than α-, make their work open-access as a matter of course, and hopes are high that a γ-tech is just around the corner. And if a project strikes enough people as worthwhile they will help assemble the needful con-struction- and mission-resources. But from this you can see: it would take an individual unusually fascinated by Saccade herself to try to drum-up support from the crew of an existing start-ship – let alone, to persuade a group to gather to build a new one – just to pop over to La:farge and retrieve her data. And so folk in the Masqueworld did not have access to that data.

At the same time, the whole immediate community sur-rounding Saccade pulsed with love and compassion, out of common humanity and utopian ethos. They worked to help her through her psychological wound, and to restore her balance. She had individual counselling, and group-therapy, and many people introduced themselves as friends and offered Saccade company, things to do, offers of sex, invites to parties, prayer-groups, and privileged religious ceremony invitations.

Over several weeks, Saccade's nightmares slipped away, and she found a renewed brightness in the mornings, and a more-alive series of days in which to be.

Things, you see, do get better. Getting better is the arc of the universe.

And as she improved, she came to look back on her interview with Raine in a new way. It had been a bad idea, clearly: but the healthful thing to do was not to *dwell* on that fact, on her foolishness in going in so poorly prepared. The healthful thing was to accept it, learn from it, to grow through it. In the immediate aftermath she had tended to berate herself, to accuse herself of stupidity and naivety, to ask herself things like 'but what were you thinking, you idiot? what did you expect?' – questions that only sharpened her shame and psychological pain. With the help of her counsellors, she found herself revisiting her younger self with more compassion. She wasn't to know, after all! Nobody alive really knew what it was to interact with one of these creatures. It was as if somebody researching Ancient Mythology had been given the opportunity to meet a minotaur: how would a person fascinated with ancient myth *not* seize such an opportunity? And if they emerged mauled, could they really blame themselves?

She wept, openly. She wept in church, during the sermon. Powerful emotion, tangled together of grief and regret and pain but also a sense of relief that she was past it, had survived it, and a complicated joy in her own aliveness. Over a week of daily therapy sessions she unpicked these threaded-together emotional reactions, and came to see the beauty as well as the strength in her response.

She still, occasionally, found herself crying, and often the prompt would be something seemingly inconsequential. But she healed, she healed.

There was no question of renewing her historical enquiry with Raine in person, but, as a psychological tonic, she was encouraged to listen to the transcripts – and later, when she was stronger, to view video coverage – of attempts by other people to interrogate Raine. Little by way of substantive content was detachable from any of this, and Saccade already knew about Raine's habits of evasion. That notwithstanding, there was some absorbing and fascinating material in these sessions. Saccade watched a few of them several times, and each time the horror of Raine's creepy sim-presence diminished in her memory. He was not scary, he was pitiable, in fact. He was a pitiable fellow.

As her health improved, she began attending the services at the Mosquethedral of Saint Miriam. The rituals were more mannered, more theatrical, than at her home chapel, but she found the performance of it all newly restorative: standing to sing a collective hymn, breathing in the tart flavour of the incense, pressing her forehead to the floor. She was grounded in more senses than one.

After a while, people began asking her whether she planned to return to La:farge, or to stay living here on the Masqueworld. She would, of course, be very welcome to stay. And, in truth, she considered it. The Masquers were differently balanced, more observant and spiritual than her home community, and she responded well to that. But there was always that thorn in amongst the softer fabric, little things that brought to mind her interview with Raine. Though she had worked through, and even resolved to include some of the details about him in her project – nothing from her specific interview, but a few details from the other interviews whose footage she had viewed

– nonetheless there was always the risk of being triggered and relapsing. This was the particular flowerbed she had walked past on her way to the sim to speak to him. That was the precise shade of purple of the fixtures inside the sim. Those were an inadvertent echo of the words he had spoken. No. She would go home.

Pride, she whispered to herself.

What a complicated word it was! She studied it, and contemplated it. A word with a long history, with both positive and negative valences, a tangle of cultural and religious significances.

The ship on which she had arrived, the β-*Stygian Blue*, had departed weeks before, chasing a comet with an unusual spectrograph. But there were ships coming and going all the time between Masqueworld and La:farge. She spoke – there was a seventeen-minute delay in between their locutions, at their present coordinates – with a member of the crew of the β-*Si Le Grain Ne Meurt*, which was inbound.

She was, she heard, welcome to join the ship. The thought of going home made her heart sing. To see all her old friends!

The new friends she had made on the Masqueworld were, of course, sorry to see her go. But they supported her and loved her and mutual invitations and gifts were exchanged.

A dinner gathering: smiling faces and comfortable chatter. Good company and good cheer!

A stroll by one of the Masqueworld's long, slender lakes, watching the geese coming in to land on the surface, vibrant curls of water thrown up on both sides of their bird breasts like the collars of a shirt. And the creatures slowing, settling, shaking themselves and looking serene. Chuck, chuck. Splash and hush.

The artificial sunlight faded to a honey orange, and Saccade made her way to her bed.

She fell asleep easily and dreamed a harmless dream.

74

When she woke it was still dark. She did not speak the room's lights on, but instead got up in darkness and moved through the uncoloured space.

Outside the artificial luna glimmered overhead, moonlight falling like a nothing-snow.

The fragrance of many flowers.

She was barefoot. She walked over grass soft as fur. The geese slept on the water. Here was a living tree, and beyond it another – but the second was of a different nature. A different genus. A different hue to its bark, a different texture in the fibres of its timber. Saccade was carrying a fork – a lovely piece, hand-carved from mahogany, as beautiful as it was functional, as were all the artefacts on the Masqueworld. The people of this world had nothing in their homes that they did not know to be useful and believe to be beautiful. The fork's three prongs were tipped with steel. The handle sat exquisitely in the hand. It had been a gift, from star Blue. Saccade used it to eat her meals.

And here was the tree in which Raine's physical body was being kept. Saccade knew, from her viewing, that when he had been in person delivered by the Hadr he had been contained in a wholebody medical sheath, since he was suffering with a range of complex and dangerous illnesses. She knew, too, that although his core health had been stabilized by treatment, various tumours, dermapathologies and other problems recurred.

At the foot of the structure, Saccade logged-up the tree AI. She located the pod inside which Raine's body was being held and released it. She called up a dumbwaiter, who brought the whole pod down and carried it.

The Tree AI was not super-smart and was solidwalled away from virtual points of connection to Raine's pod – to keep it clean from the degradation of code, whatever it was, that Raine was somehow affecting on those other programmes. But Tree was smart enough to register that there was something odd about this human removing this other human, sedated inside a sheath, and carrying him away.

It was the AI's business to run, but not to guard, the tree, and it was in the nature of the people of Masqueworld that they had put no real barriers in place, here. It had been discussed and considered that a threat to Raine – they really only considered the idea that somebody angry and hurt by Raine's crimes might try to harm or perhaps kill him – might come, if it came at all, from outside their world. After all, none of *them* had been personally bereaved by his crimes. That somebody might try to free him from his imprisonment simply did not occur to them. Who would do such a thing? Why? Raine had had no confederates, his actions, though grievous and ghastly, had been the consequence of a solitary derangement of the mind.

Still: the Tree was worried enough to alert a human being. This was a young woman called Harmony Ford, one of the group of people who had taken an interest in receiving and securing Raine's body. The Tree woke her because she was, physically, nearest. She came out of her room and saw Saccade leading the dumbwaiter away from the Tree, in the direction of one of the Masqueworld's exterior ports. It took her a moment to process what she was seeing – the AI had notified her of Saccade's identity, and anyway she knew her from her researches and her one interview with the killer. 'Saccade!' she called. 'Where are you going?'

Saccade stopped, and the dumbwaiter stopped. Saccade didn't turn around. Harmony walked over the moonlit grass to where she was standing.

'Where are you taking Raine?' she asked, again.

Saccade's eyes were closed, and it occurred to Harmony that she might be asleep, or sleep-walking. She was aware of the other woman's psychological history, that she had been hurt, and although she was no expert she had heard that uneasy sleep and unawake motion might be symptomatic of such a thing. But she was also aware that her psychological heath had so hugely improved, under their collective care! What was going on?

Saccade was not asleep. She opened her eyes, turned and stabbed the fork into Harmony's neck, just below her left ear. The blow was forceful. All three tines pierced the flesh and one broke the wall of the carotid artery. Harmony reeled away in pain and shock, her hand scrabbling at the inserted fork, and blood flushing down her neck. The blood loss was so rapid and extreme that she passed into unconsciousness.

The injury was, of course, logged by the main station AI, and within moments medical bots and people had converged on Harmony's prone body. Treatment was rapid and effective. Harmony survived.

Saccade was apprehended at Lock 17/7, where she was attempting to override the safety lockdown for one of the station's flitters. The dumbwaiter had already loaded Raine's body, still in its medical sheath, into the cargo stretch of the flitter. Five minutes more, and Saccade would have been away.

When two Masquers took hold of her, one for each arm, and pulled her out of the cockpit, she did not resist. She looked, if anything, puzzled. 'What are you doing?' was her question.

:4:

Saccade was detained. She had to be. Physically she was well, but her mental wellbeing had collapsed. She wept continually. Shown footage of what she had done, which of course was a legal requirement – for otherwise she tended simply to feign ignorance, which undermined her ability to acknowledge her responsibility – she howled and gasped, crying over and over how sorry she was. She had to be sedated. It was four days before it was even possible to have a regular conversation with her.

The Masqueworld held a meet. A dozen ships were within reasonable communication-lag distance, and all were invited to attend remotely – the β-*Si Le Grain Ne Meurt*, which had previously offered Saccade a place on their ship, took up the offer, as did three others.

Evil is fissiparous.

A meeting was mooted, and anyone interested was welcome. A Masqueworlder called Heorot, naked except for his buskins, summarized the course of events. Having seemingly recovered from severe psychological injury, Saccade had suffered a relapse of some kind. That her actions were connected in some way with her interview with the life-killer Raine was clear enough: she had, after all, only injured Harmony in order to avoid being questioned and detained, so as to continue her project of moving Raine's body, in its medisheath, to a flitter. Had Harmony not intervened, she would likely not have assaulted her.

Objection! Hypothetical!

'Agreed,' said Heorot. 'That is suppositive. But the balance is strongly on the side of the motivated project on behalf of Saccade, conscious or subconsciously. She wished to take Raine's sedated body aboard a flitter. From there – to where? Perhaps to liaise with the β-*Si Le Grain Ne Meurt* as she had previously agreed?'

As a matter of courtesy, everybody waited for this to reach the β-*Si Le Grain Ne Meurt*, still seven light minutes away. Fourteen minutes later their reply came back: 'We do not think she intended to reach us,' said the captain. 'It would have taken her weeks to get to us in a flitter, and we would have had to drop to Newtonian speeds, decelerating dangerously, to meet *her*. Besides, she sent us no message. Of any kind.'

'She pinged *us*,' said the captain of the β-*Rooftop Concert*. This was a small *schneller-als-das-licht* schooner, still in orbit around Masqueworld. 'And asked for passage with us. But she did not mention, not at all, that she would be bringing this other person's corpus with her. We would not have been pleased, had her flitter docked with us and had she tried to bring him on board.'

'This appears to have been her plan, nonetheless,' said Indigo. The β-*Rooftop Concert*'s manifest was to fly to the planet Boa Memória, some seventy-two light years distant – some of the crew were hoping to join the team of the celebrated Berd's record-breaking 'one small step' project; others were going simply to observe his attempt.

'We can thereby intuit she wished to take Raine's body to Boa Memória. But why?'

They asked Saccade this question, but she was perfectly baffled. She claimed never to have heard of Boa Memória, and although of course she knew the name 'Berd' – how couldn't she? He was extremely famous – she had never met him, could think of no reason why she might want to meet him. When they pressed her and asked why she might want not only to go, but to take Raine's sedated body to Boa Memória, she professed incomprehension. What? What do you mean? She had forgotten. She couldn't remember. They had to show her stealing the medisheath, and assaulting Harmony, and when she saw those recordings she burst into tears and howled and berated herself.

'It is a puzzle,' said Heorot. 'Why would she desire to take Raine's body to this particular planet? Why did she wish to go there at all? Is it connected with the imminent "one small

79

step" attempt by Berd? But what might that have to do with Raine – or Saccade?'

'We can speculate,' said Indigo. 'But I have a better suggestion.'

'Which is?'

'We should allow her to go to Boa Memória.'

'Allow Saccade to travel to Boa Memória?'

'Just so. And then we observe what she does there. With her permission, of course – assuming she still wishes to go.'

'But *not* take Raine's sedated body with her, I presume?'

'No! Not that – *we* have custody of his body and must not relinquish it. There are dangers associated with Raine, and the fact that we have yet fully to comprehend what they are and how they spread does not mean we should rid ourselves of him. He stays. But if Saccade agrees, and if the *Rooftop Concert* is prepared to give her passage, let her go, and see what she does upon Boa Memória.'

'I will accompany her, as friend and observer,' said Harmony.

'It is nobly and generously offered,' said Heorot, 'but I do not think it best advised. At the moment Saccade veers between a friendliness towards you that indexes her amnesia concerning her attack, and, when she is reminded of her assault, emotional breakdown and self-laceration. It is better if she is accompanied by somebody who does not have those associations. I will go.'

It was agreed. They found Saccade sitting beside the narrow lake, just sitting and watching the geese go about their geesely business. As Heorot began the business of, with all proper courtesy and politesse, framing the question as to whether she would be prepared to travel to Boa Memória, she broke in upon him. 'I'll go,' she said. 'I am eager to go. I am very *eager* to go.' They had not yet suggested that her travel would be to Boa Memória, and Heorot took some time to ensure that she knew what she was committing herself to. 'Yes,' she said, 'yes. I will. Yes.'

3

One Small Step for Human,
One Giant Leap for Humankind

:1:

Boa Memória is a close Earth analogue, not (of course) in terms of its surface geography, or of its indigenous flora and fauna, but in terms of its interiority. And that was what mattered. The planet contained a super-hard inner metallic core, spinning within a highly viscous liquid, a very hot outer core which, in turn, convected its material, the whole an independent system from the magma and mantle and crust that constituted the rest of the world: a dynamo, throwing great spokes of magnetic protection from pole to pole to shield the surface from poisonous solar radiation. It's how Earth kept its lifeforms safe – or safe-ish – over the millions of evolving years that led to us. Its absence on Mars keeps that world, even in our time, dead, bleached and blasted on its cold surface, the only human settlements hidden in subarean excavations and laboriously maintained by technology.

Not so Boa Memória! Settling this world was a simple matter of seeding its already expansively vegetative surface with gene-tweaked plants to increase oxygen output and introducing a self-replicating swarm of floating scrubber-drones to extract some of the less likeable chemicals from the air. The initial estimates that this would cause 80 per cent die-off of indigenous plantlife proved overly pessimistic. Life is tougher than we often think, and fully a third of the original plants adapted and survived, albeit in weaker and stunted forms. But Earth plants found a new home, with nettles, brassicas and bindweeds blooming with particular splendour. The planet was declared a population green zone. And Earth-origin insects had no difficulty supplanting the indigenous pseudo-insects.

A decade after first intervention, settlements were clustering around rivers and harbours, and soon enough the population was on a healthy upward curve.

As Saccade deplaned at Port Hayley, Boa Memória was less than a century old: ninety-six years since formal establishment. But it was as bustling and bright as any longer-settled world. Saccade walked through the crowds in the sunlit terminal, and the shimmergrams bowed to her and made welcoming gestures. 'Enjoy your time on Boa!' they called out. 'If there's anything we can do to help, please let us know!'

And there, by the main entrance, was a shimmergram of Berd himself, smiling and opening his arms.

One of the consequences of living in a utopia is that *celebrity* loses its specific purchase, as most people simply live their lives, focusing on their particularities of self and affinity group, of friends and family and community. But most people is not all people, and another consequence of living in utopia is that it is radically hospitable to difference. Celebrity worship was one such variety, and there were enough people interested in it, scattered throughout inhabited space, to form a large fandom.

And Berd was a genius: who doubted it? Genius and adventurer. Back on Earth he had surfed from orbit down to a safe landing, using a mag-platform that interacted with the Earth's magnetosphere as a surfboard does with the waves. He had designed and built – with his team, of course, all of whom were core fans – a diving bell on which he had penetrated the photosphere of Geeve-7, a solar-equivalent star. Automated probes and robots had been sent inside stellar bodies before, of course, but only Berd was prepared to risk his fragile organic body to the device he built.

And now, here on Boa Memória, he was working towards his greatest achievement yet. He planned to become the first human being to walk on the metal core of a planet.

He had originally set up his lab and workshop on Earth but had run into difficulties. Some Earthlings were happy for him to pursue his plans, but others objected that Earth was a heritage world, the cradle of humanity, and ought not to be messed with. It was debated, and looked like it would be pushed to a vote. Berd was a driven individual, focused and sometimes single-minded to the point of obsession, but he wasn't a sociopath. Of course he registered the objections. He made his counter-proposal. A plebiscite was held. The majority vote came through slightly in favour of allowing Berd's project, but the margin was narrow enough for Berd to withdraw gracefully.

There was no lack of other worlds eager to host him and his team. The first human being to take steps upon the solid metal core of a planet! Such a figure would go down in history. When Berd approached Boa Memória there was such enthusiasm the various communities living there didn't even feel the need for a plebiscite. Within a month he was settled in a facility in the Dharkeer lowlands, northern hemisphere, with Armitage Mount rearing its summit over the distant horizon like a thorn. Components and new team-volunteers arrived on various ships over the coming several months and by the end of his first year he had taken his initial kit, by blimp, and lowered it – first on automatic, and then with himself inside it – into the volcanic crater of Armitage Mount.

The first experiments were a mixture of success and malfunction. The trick was: to build on the former and to solve the latter. Berd's Mark 1 suit came out of the crater with its ceramic-plasmetal outer skin skidmarked with scorching, baked into friability across the shoulder servos and with one leg dry-melted, but otherwise functional. They had barely gone a thousand metres down into the magma, but it was a start. Since then progress had been intermittent, but always on the up.

'Master Heorot,' Saccade said aloud, stopping by the terminal exit and addressing the mindless shimmergram. 'I understand now that you were correct. It is *indeed* Berd I have come to see!'

And here, right behind her, was Heorot. He had made no secret of his travelling on the same *schneller-als-der-licht* schooner as Saccade, but she had been clear that she wanted no intimacy with him, and so they had travelled in separate portions of the ship, and busied themselves with their own business.

'You understand,' he had said to her, 'that, given the assault you perpetrated upon the Masqueworld, it is meet we keep an eye upon you?'

Saccade blushed. 'Of course, of course. I am not trying to evade you – it was *your* suggestion that I follow my urges and come to Boa, after all!'

'I do not accuse you of trying to give me the slip,' said Heorot, smiling in as friendly a manner as he was able. 'You have come here.'

'To meet Berd,' she said.

'To what end?'

'I'll know that when I encounter him.' She turned to face him four-squarer. 'And, though the memory of what I did is painful to me, and the thought of other people knowing what

I did more painful still, of course I understand that you will inform the people of Boa what I did, yet: that does not mean we are to be close friends, or lovers, or anything like that.'

'By all means, no,' smiled Heorot, and left her to herself.

The journey from Masqueworld to Boa Memória had taken seventeen days, and Saccade spent much of that time in prayer and meditation, or else at one of the observation blisters, watching the twisting threads of stars tangle gleaming carnation and ruby and blood colours behind the craft.

And now she was here on Boa Memória itself. And right behind her was Heorot.

'It seems to me I am here,' Saccade told him, 'to *tell* Berd something.'

'Tell him what?'

Saccade smiled. Then frowned. Then she said: 'I don't know – but I must speak with him in person.'

'So,' said Heorot. 'You will travel to his base camp? Many people do.'

'Yes,' she said. 'And you will accompany me?'

'If my presence will not intrude upon you. Should you align yourself with Berd's project, you will join a large fanbase, and will have plenty of company!'

'I think,' she said, 'I think I am not here to be recruited by Berd, but rather to recruit *him* to something of mine.'

'Good luck!' laughed Heorot. He was laughing at the ludicrousness of this idea, but he did not laugh unkindly.

Berd's base was a three-hour blimp flight from Port Hayley, and Saccade spent the flight gazing down upon the unfamiliar contours below her, all the colours of life – the harlequin spread of dark and light greens, the reds and oranges of seed-oil fields, the occasional black of siriusphids spreading their vast canopies. Forests and fields, grazing areas and wildings, all under the mint-blue of Boa's skies. As the blimp approached the foothills of Armitage the colours darkened; richer volcanic soil was overgrown with tea-forest, malachite and celadon, with roadways running through like the lead lights in a stained-glass window. A thin stream of smoke rose over Armitage like a single thread of wool.

And here was the settlement that had grown up around Camp Berd: buildings and facilities, dormitories, a stadium, various workshops and some large-scale works of public art. The blimp docked and Saccade, carrying nothing with her but a phonechip, a vial of anti-insect primer and the clothes she was wearing, stepped onto the turf.

A sense of delicious elation flowed through her.

'I am here,' she called out, addressing nobody in particular, 'to recruit the great Berd to a project of my own!'

Most of the other people there ignored her. A couple clapped in encouragement or called out 'Good luck!' One snapped: 'Leave Berd to his own projects, you presumptuous stranger – you need medical treatment, or prayer, depending on your preference.'

'Don't be bitter, friend,' Saccade returned. 'If Berd is not interested in my proposal then that is that. But there is no harm in my proposing!'

'Everyone thinks Berd is their personal friend,' grumbled the stranger. 'But he is not! It is the poison of celebrity, a cult thing, and we should resist it.'

'Then why are *you* here, at Camp Berd?' Saccade asked.

At this the stranger made a dismissive gesture with her right hand and walked away.

After they had landed Saccade found a place to sleep in one of the dormitories. Thereupon she took a seat in the refectory for a late lunch. Everyone around her seemed pleasantly buzzed, excitedly chatting with their neighbours as they ate. Saccade fell into conversation with a woman called Mother Fish, who was part of a fan-community dedicated to one very particular question: what Berd should *say* when he finally achieved his mission aim.

'Have you spoken to him about it?' asked Saccade.

'Oh yes,' said Mother Fish. 'He generally spends a couple of hours a day walking around the camp chatting with folk – unless there's something particularly pressing happening at the workshop. Or if he's, you know: engaged in an exploratory mission or something. But he makes a point of meeting and greeting, and he has several times said he'll be happy to consider what we come up with. Consider as possible *first words* I mean. His official position is that he doesn't know what he's going to say and will probably just say the first thing to come into his head when he takes that first step. But we think we can supply some historically-memorable options!'

After lunch Saccade went back with Mother Fish to meet the others in her group. They were sunning themselves in a young siriusphis tree, draped over and upon the paddle-shaped branches, chatting. They were excited to meet a newcomer, and Saccade soon found herself caught up in an intense, if friendly, disagreement. Several amongst the group had been studying the words spoken of Armstrong, the antique 'firstman' human, when he had walked upon the moon. They called up recordings and Saccade listened. *That's one small step for a man, one giant leap for mankind*, she heard. But then she listened again, more carefully, and this time heard again: *That's one small step for man, one giant leap for mankind*. It was spoken in Old American of course, but Saccade could understand that well enough – she had worked as an historian for many years. They played the recording a few more times. 'What happened to the *a*?' she asked. '*A man*

87

makes sense, surely, where *small step for man* doesn't. Or am I misremembering my Old American grammar?'

They twittered like birds all along the pathways of their disagreement. One said: Armstrong said *a man*, but the 'a' was blanked by some malfunction of the radio-era technology of the period. Another said: There is not enough space between *step for* and *man*: he fluffed the line. He meant to say *step for a man* but in the excitement of the moment he got it wrong. A third said: I have studied Old American syntax and idiom, and it was common for speakers to omit 'a' and 'the' in common speech. Armstrong's statement was perfectly idiomatic by the logic of his era. A fourth said: Omitting connectives was limited to certain slang phrases, and would not apply in this case, which was a moment of great ceremony and importance. Armstrong, you can see, is wearing dress uniform spacesuit, not a regular spacesuit – look at the flags, the sewn-on medals, the gold, all the bling. It would have been quite inappropriate for Armstrong to sink into slang at such an elevated moment.

Saccade found the to and fro richly entertaining. Soon enough discussion had moved on to the exact nature of Armstrong's name. Some said it was Neil, which was a Scottish given name. Others said his name was Nile Armstrong in homage to the Pharaohs of old – as the pyramids were prehistoric human-ity's greatest achievement, so this moon landing was historic humanity's greatest achievement, and Armstrong was given the moniker *Nile* in honour of that fact. One of the group – a long-bodied, loose-limbed young male with a great cataract of red-purple head-hair, called Vangipurapu – declared loudly that whatever the actual name of the first individual to walk on Earth's moon, it was clearly not *Arm-Strong*. 'That's a title, not a name: clearly it reflects the warrior ethos of that belligerent and martial age. Whoever they sent to the moon, he would be a great hero – a masculine figure, since antique Earth valued the male over the female – and an individual of immense physical strength. Hence strong-of-the-arm. It's like a Viking or Homeric epithet. Neil or Noll might have been his actual given name, but I tend to think this was a version of Nail – hard, iron, driving home, another soldier epithet.'

'You're wayward, Vangipurapu,' laughed the others. 'There are plenty of reputable historical sources that refer to the individual as having the name Armstrong.'

'I am not persuaded by them,' said Vangipurapu.

'I'm actually an historian,' said Saccade. 'The twentieth century is my period.'

They were all immediately excited, pressing her to support one or other theory and she had to add: 'But antique space flight was not my topic, so I can't be certain on this matter. Though it's true that everyone in the twentieth century had both a formal name, and an informal, or nick-name.'

Really! How bizarre! But why? Why?

'Nobody is sure,' laughed Saccade.

'What is your specialist area?' Vangipurapu queried. 'If it's not space flight?'

'Serial killers – that is, people who murdered multiple other people.' She said this blithely enough, although the words dragged a little as they came out and left a rawness behind in her head. What was that? Three brief flash memories of decaying human flesh, of blood hurting its way out of a body, of a scowl or grin – then gone. She was back in the moment with these kind people, all of whom were laughing and joking with one another. Then they were singing antique songs, and with a flush of joy Saccade joined in, for she knew the words. *Sky is blue and see the green:*

We all live in a yellow sunny scene
A yellow sunny scene
A yellow sunny scene
We all live in a yellow sunny scene
A yellow sunny scene
A yellow sunny scene

Later Vangipurapu gave Saccade a tour of the compound, pointing out notable and convenient features. They even saw Berd
himself: he had come out into the evening, as the sinking sun
gave the sky a resinous quality, somewhat reminiscent of amber,
and the shadows elongated into a liquorice blackness. Berd was
moving through an excited crowd, shaking hands, namaste-ing
and touching foreheads. 'We can go over and say hello if you
like,' said Vangipurapu.

'Another day,' said Saccade, although she felt the sharp twist
of excitement, like a wound, in her solar plexus. There he was!
The great Berd himself.

Then she caught sight of Heorot in the crowd. He was
watching her, but when their eyes met he smiled and tipped
his head and withdrew.

Later that evening she and Vangipurapu found a privacy pod
and had sex. It was a little clumsy, as first sex-encounters so
often are, but its awkwardness was more than compensated by
the thrill of its novelty. Vangipurapu proved athletic and very
flexible, and though his cock was thinner and longer than
Saccade's ideal preference, he did very pleasurable things with
his fingers and toes. Saccade had not been sexually intimate
with anybody since before arriving on the Masqueworld, but it
felt right to break that duck, here. A new world, a new start: and
Vangipurapu was gratifyingly eager, and expressed hyperbolic
delight at all the ins and outs of her naked body. She came twice

and it felt like a ghost was being banished from her life. When he came he warbled like a songbird and fell away gasping. He tumbled raggedly into sleep almost straight away, hugging her. For a few minutes Saccade just lay there, experiencing safety and contentment. Then she disentangled herself from him, so as to get comfortable, and settled to her own slumber.

:2:

For a week Saccade hung out with the One Small Step crew. Sex with Vangipurapu improved with practice, and after a while they even started to get a little bored with one another, as is the way with these things. So Saccade kissed him goodbye and paired off with a friend of his, a Duo called Mi whose lovemaking was more forceful and who was possessed of extraordinary stamina.

She settled into life at the camp. It had a holiday atmosphere. There were boat races on the river, and some people were carving the die-back stumps of ancient siriusphids into fine sculptures, some figurative and some not. People sang and danced and played all manner of games.

She was still not sure why she had felt compelled to come to this place, or to what she hoped to recruit the great Berd, but she was confident the reason would reveal itself in time.

Then, one morning, she woke with a sensation in her stomach somewhere between excitement and anxiety. Something was coming.

She wandered the camp. One wide hall was filled with people engaging the code-writing AIs to tweak the heat transfer vanes of Berd's suit. In many ways these great angels' wings, eight metres long, were the most important elements of the kit – for without them Berd, upon reaching the two-and-a-quarter-thousand-kilometres-deep molten, outer core would simply melt into a nugget of slag. The temperature down there rose steadily from 5000K to 8000K as the hard inner core – the final destination – was approached. Of course the pressure was also a concern, and some groups were working on the likely effects of the much stronger magnetic field down there, between fifty and a hundred times as intense as it was at the surface. This last didn't seem to be a concern for Berd, who had often said that, in antique times, medical machines had blasted human bodies with a thousand times the surface magnetic force to no serious ill effects. But the pressure of this intense environment was obviously a significant consideration, and if the vanes failed him he wouldn't even have time to utter a syllable of distress before he was entirely annihilated.

For many with whom Saccade spoke these technical advances were the most exciting part of the whole project. 'The actual walking on the solid core,' said Han, a stocky, smile-faced asexual with whom Saccade shared a jave one afternoon, 'is cool and everything. Don't get me wrong! I think Berd *is* cool, super cool, I understand his fandom, that's all good. But when he has taken his step, and said whatever he is going to say, and comes back up and we're all cheering and singing victory songs – then what? I'll *tell* you what. We will have gifted humankind with new and marvellous technologies that will have a thousand applications.'

'Heat transference and disposal,' said Saccade, sipping her jave.

'That's the least of them! It's not the heat – we're pretty good, as a species, at inventing ways of pushing heat up the thermodynamic slope so as to keep ourselves cooler. No, no, it's the *pressure*. That's the real challenge!'

'And that's what you're working on?'

He grew very excited at this question, and replied at length, deploying his talisman-word *cool* over and over.[1] Just as atmospheric pressure is a function of the sheer weight of air above us, which is to say a function of the gravitational effect upon the column of air, so the pressure inside the earth is a function of the sheer weight – clearly a much greater weight than empty air – of rock. This was complicated by the fact that the outer-planet atmosphere is a gaseous continuum, where much of the rock inside the earth is solid and forms, actually, a kind of spherical rocky amphi-dome. But once you get to the fluid magma and the more metallic viscosity of the outer core, the thousands of kilometres of matter pressing down upon you becomes an intensely crushing pressure. 'The usual approach to this is just to make a suit that is super-rigid, super-super-rigid, but that's not so clever, actually. Tolerances eventually get overcome and Berd would be squished. So, and this is the cool thing, the super cool thing, we've been addressing pressure as such by addressing gravity. The one is created by the other, you see?'

'Addressing it how?' asked Saccade. There was a tingling in her stomach now, a sense that she was trembling on the lip of something huge, something meaningful and wonderful and transcendent. The tide that flowed through her inner ocean, the one we all share, was moving under its metaphorical lunar influence. She almost trembled. Here it was, the distinguished thing – but:

'Gravity?' she said.

'Oh sure. It's *very* cool. Earlier experiments with, you know, anti-gravity and such-like wonderland dreams. Impossible. An

[1] After discussion, the translators have decided on this contemporary English word. It is not an exact match for the word Han actually uttered [*nazag*], but *cool* was chosen upon as combining an assertion of approbation with a slightly out-of-fashion staleness.

object with anti-gravity would possess anti-inertia and would tear through spacetime. But if we can't actually generate *anti*-gravity we *can* tangle with the magnitude of the force of gravity and that's cool – cool – cool.'

A voice was half-forming in Saccade's mind. The voice was telling her: *this this this.*

'Because gravity is so much weaker than the other three fundamental forces,' Han was saying, 'we can leverage those other three to put – as it were – pressure *on* it. It's very cool what we've been doing, actually: generating a thin skein surrounding a sphere where gravity is point seven of one percent lessened. Think of it as flattening the curve of the deformation of spacetime, and it reduces the absolute pressure on that sphere to the point where simple stress-mechanics, and rigidity and structural physics and so on, can keep the occupant of the suit from being squished.'

'That is indeed cool,' Saccade agreed.

'It's tensors,' said Han. 'That's what has been neglected in thinking about gravity. All we need to do is shift the balance of tensors slightly and it's *very* cool how much it alleviates pressure. Our problem is that we're only able to do it for very small fields – a couple of centimetres across. Obviously Berd can't fit inside a suit only a few centimetres across!'

He laughed at this, and Saccade, for courtesy, laughed with him. She didn't really understand why he found this notion so comical but went along with him. 'Shrink Berd to the size of a rice grain!' she offered and at this ludicrous thought Han laughed so heartily she thought he might fall entirely off the bench upon which he was sitting.

'Yes, yes, comical, comical, cool,' he said, recovering himself. There was a pause in their conversation and he took a restorative sip from his jave.

94

'I,' said Saccade, though as she was speaking she wasn't clear from where the words were coming – not from her conscious will or controlled speech centres, certainly – 'have thought of a way of flipping the vector ninety degrees. Fully ninety degrees!'

Han stared at her for a while. She grew uncomfortable under his unblinking gaze. 'You're joking?'

Maybe she was! She didn't know. 'I'm not joking,' was what she said, and then: 'the vector can't move *more* than ninety degrees, for obvious reasons. Then we *would* be in the realm of anti-gravity, which is impossible for all the reasons you know. But so long as quantum angular momentum is shepherded, we can move the vector round. Moving the vector round is in effect what you are doing, after all! Tacking against gravity as a sailing ship tacks against the wind. Deflecting it just a fraction. Good. But this is what I say: once we pass forty-five degrees – a little under that, but approximately that – then it eases and actually will self-correct to a full ninety degrees.'

'How?' Han demanded, suddenly very serious.

Saccade had no idea how this could be effected, but the words came out of her nonetheless: 'The initial power input would be in the exawatt range, that's one issue. The trick is to focus this on the subatomic level, where the angular momentum is not gauge invariant, and cascade the resulting Chakrabarty inversion so that it clocks. But once the vector disturbs the supersymmetry the system will ty to self-correct, which will swing the vector about further, until it reaches its absolute orientation. Ninety degrees.'

'Woh,' said Han. 'That's *super* cool. If it's – forgive me, but – if it's true?'

The words dried up. Saccade stared at Han. 'I mean,' she said. 'I'm not a gravitist. I'm not even a physicist, so this could all be screwy nonsense.'

'No,' said Han. 'No, it's very interesting, it's a very cool idea.' She could see that his mind was speeding. 'And – you're not a gravity specialist, you say? This is just a side-line for you? A hobby?'

Saccade had no idea *what* this was. 'I don't know,' she said truthfully. Had Han asked her to repeat what she had just said she wouldn't have been able. 'A hunch, I guess.'

'What do you do?'

'History. Twentieth century stuff.'

'Oh,' he said. 'Historian, excellent. So can you read and write?'

Saccade was often asked this question, and it always put her in a rather embarrassing position. Historians sometimes did acquire these antique skills, the better to be able to study their source materials which of course, for a thousand years, had all been *written* upon stone, parch or paper in a string of readerly sigils. But though Saccade had spent a couple of months trying to acquire the basics of this exhausted information technology she soon enough gave up. It had been the realization that, having laboriously memorized all the little squiggles and squashed-bug mini-patterns of one alphabet, and starting to work through all the combinations thereof, many of them utterly counterintuitive, she had realized that the 'alphabet' she had been studying was only one of *dozens* antique humanity had employed, and wasn't even the most common. In addition to aggregative sigils there were systems of pictograms (dozens of these as well), all as rebarbative and infuriating as one another. So she had dropped the study.

'I never completed alphabetography,' she confessed. 'I know people think all historians acquire those old skills but few of us do in fact. Really, you can extract quite a lot from AI summaries and distillations. I've had AIs read out really *quite* lengthy antique texts to me, though it gets dull very quickly. How the antiques managed, without picture and motion and affect, with just these barebones sigils in great long spooling lines, I'm not sure! They must have had greater tolerances for boredom than modern folk.'

But Han wasn't listening. 'I'm,' he said, getting up from his bench and leaving his jave unfinished, 'just going to,' he said. 'I'm just going to.' He left.

'Might as well learn all the ins and outs of Babylonian astrology or the rules of Crack-it,' she said to nobody in particular. 'I mean what would be the point?'

She sat alone for a while. Then she went for a walk through the woodland and sat on a prominence looking down over the commodious bend of the river. Below her people were swimming, splashing, frolicking in the sunshine.

Later that evening she was making her way to the refectory hall when Han hurried over to her. 'It's cool, it's cool,' he said. 'Berd wants to meet.'

'Oh,' said Saccade. She had already more or less forgotten her earlier gravitational hypothesizing. Where had it even come from? Popped into her head from nowhere, and slipped away as mysteriously.

After an afternoon of peaceful walking and contemplation, of just *being*, existing contentedly in the sunlight and fresh air, mention of Berd reawoke the thrilling, unpleasant sense of anxiety that bubbled in her solar plexus. Agitation shimmered through her. 'Berd? In person?'

'I don't really know him,' Han was gabbling, 'but this cool friend of mine called Jay does, and he is part of our group and when I ran your idea on our equation AI it started spitting out these super cool geometries and symmetries and Jay got excited and went direct to Berd. We think this could be a breakthrough.'

He took her by the hand and walked her through the open

meadow at the heart of the camp. 'It needs considerable inputs of energy,' he was gabbling, 'of course, of course, but that's the cool thing, by the time Berd gets down to the liquid outer core the heat and pressure is so intense that it's a simple matter, really, of syphoning off almost unlimited amounts of...' and his words blurred in Saccade's head. She was going to meet Berd! In person! Then she had a rush of panic that he would grill her over what she had said, when she had no knowledge and barely any memory of the topic of her words – something about pulling the vector of gravity through ninety degrees and blah and blah and more blah – but that was then swallowed by a rush of elation that she was about to meet Berd! In the flesh!

Maybe there was something in this fandom culture after all. Perhaps she should abandon history and pursue that? Or maybe combine the two? A study of historical fandoms might be an interesting thing.

There was a hubbub in the hall of the heat-transfer group: many extra people were inside, some crowding around AI outputs, some milling or congregating, a few excited folk copulating up against the far wall. The excitement was about the breakthrough Han's team had made, but it was also to do with the physical presence of Berd himself. There he was, in person, over by one of the AI outputs.

Han led Saccade up to another code-surfer who was manipulating and palpating geometries on a readout. A few words of introduction made this person's eyes pop wide. For a few minutes he tried to demonstrate to Saccade what the patterns on his readout meant 'for the project for the mission!', but soon enough Han prompted him and he pulled himself away from the screen. 'I'm sorry, yes, yes, you *must* meet Berd. He's terribly terribly keen to meet you.'

So this new person – Jay, she supposed, though she hadn't

been introduced – took her through the crowd to where Berd himself was standing.

'So,' said Berd, namaste-ing, 'you're Saccade. It's an absolute delight to meet you.'

Saccade grinned like a crocodile. God, it was exciting. Actually to meet him! 'The thrill is mine, really it is,' she said, speaking rather too rapidly. 'I can't deny that I came to Boa in the hope of meeting you, but I never thought it would happen so soon.'

He smiled. There was real charisma here, and Saccade wasn't sure if she'd ever before met an individual with quite such a degree of charm. Some of it (she wasn't stupid) presumably had to do with his reputation, and his status – the fact that all these other people were swarming around him. But some of it was him. His Persian-blue eyes shone as if lit from within, and he had the knack of focusing his attention wholly upon the person he was addressing. His nose was straight and wide, and his cheeks tapered to a prominent chin. His skin was umber. A confetti of freckles marked his face. It ought to have been an ungainly combination of features, but in fact it gelled beautifully. He was not tall, and was rather heavy-set, but he moved with energy and focus. Saccade could see why so many people fell into his ambit.

'Let's walk,' he said, holding up his right hand to indicate to the crowd that they should leave him be for a while.

Together they stepped out of the hall and made their way through the camp. People grinned at them both as they passed. Saccade caught a brief glimpse of Heorot, watching, but then they moved past the crowd into the open ground outside the camp.

In a few minutes they were in the woods. Saccade wondered if she should say something, but Berd had focussed his attention entirely on the path he was treading. They climbed steeper

99

ground, rounded an outcrop of slow-black rock, only a few thousand years since spat-out from the volcano under which the settlement sat. They scrambled up further. Suddenly Saccade was looking down upon the forest from above: a blowzy floor of bubbled and cinched green leaves through which, almost directly below, the river curved. A couple of people were swimming languidly downstream, reduced by the altitude to oval heads and breaststroke-sweeping hands.

'I love it up here,' said Berd. 'Peaceful. Such a beautiful view.'

'It's lovely,' agreed Saccade.

For a while he said nothing more. 'So – you're a historian,' he said, turning his astonishing eyes upon her and warming his visage with a broad smile. 'That's so wonderful. I often think how vital it is that we retain continuity with the past. Of course, we must do that at the same time as we forge in the smithy of our collective self the future we will all inhabit.'

'Oh,' she said. Then she thought for a moment. Then she said: 'yes.'

'Do you do the reading and writing thing? I know a lot of historians master that.'

'Some do,' she said, feeling absurdly exposed. 'Not me. It's a lot of really fiddly work, is the truth, and I wanted – I wanted to concentrate my mental energies on other things. I mean, I know people who spent many years mastering one antique script only to discover that their primary sources were all written in another. And anyway after all, anyway, anyway of course we can always just get an AI to read texts aloud, any old texts, to read and translate them. I mean –' She could feel her gabbling running away from her. Why couldn't she stop? '– I mean, it's still pretty boring, to be honest, sitting there whilst some AI reads some interminable antique text. Why *were* they so long, that's what I want to know? Even at double speed and even when the AI notices you fidgeting and tries to leaven the experience by doing each different piece in different voices, it's still—'

Berd reached out and touched her shoulder with his right hand. His gaze was steady, and as blue as a methane flame. 'It's OK,' he said. 'I understand. It's hard.'

'Yes,' she said. 'Yes it is.'

'There are other things to put your time and energy into.'

She grinned. 'Exactly.'

'I asked,' he went on, dropping his hand, 'only because I know there is a twentieth century story-text, famous in its day. Speculative, purely speculative, not a narrative of something that actually happened. It was by a woman called Julie Verne and went by the title *Voyage To The Centre Of The Earth.*'

'I've heard of Verne,' said Saccade, eager to ingratiate herself. 'He was famous – or she was. I'm not sure it's clear what gender they were. Julian, Julie. After all, the twentieth was the first century gender became properly molten. That feeds in to my specific research actually: I write about mass murderers, and there were many speculative story-texts about those gruesome figures, and one of the most famous, a silent killer of lambs, was—'

With a smile that took away the sting of the interruption, Berd said: 'In Verne's silly story they go down through tunnels, and find a big subterranean ocean, filled with cretaceous creatures. But when she was writing they had only the most rudimentary sense of what the inside of their globe was like.'

'Yes,' breathed Saccade. 'Yes, that's it.'

'But it's heritage, isn't it? It's history. I'm aiming, before this decade is out, to be the first human to walk on the solid core of the world. I'm fully aware of the magnitude of my ambition – of humanity's ambition, to be always exploring the unexplored, going with boldness to every new frontier – and I wanted to mark my departure with a reading from Verne's story-text.'

'And you wanted me to deliver that reading?'

'It's quite alright – I was just checking. If you can't read, that's not a problem – I can't either! It's just that I heard some historians do learn. But I'll have an AI do the reading. There's a couple here at camp that aren't bad at adding human-level inflection and feeling when they recite all the old sigils.'

'I'll learn,' blurted Saccade. 'I can learn to read this one text. How hard can that be?'

'No, no,' said Berd. 'I mean, that's the *point*! If this tech idea you've brought us – brilliant, brilliant thinking! – if it works the way we're hoping it will, then you have dramatically shortened the waiting time. Dramatically! We're planning the first remote tests later this month. I'm confident I'll be walking across the core before the solstice celebrations. There wouldn't be time for you to master something as abstruse as reading, I appreciate – but,' and here he placed his hand back on her shoulder, and excitement-fizzes ran in little loops and squirls through her solar plexus, '– but I hope you'll *introduce* the AI reading, at the little ceremony I have planned to see me off. Say a few words.'

'Of course of course,' said Saccade. 'Oh Berd, I'm more than delighted you asked me.' Even voicing his name felt thrilling. Almost transgressive. 'More than delighted!'

'If it OK if I hug you?' Berd asked. 'It's how we show affection and support in my culture and isn't a sexualized gesture.'

'Oh of course of course,' said Saccade.

And so they hugged.

Saccade returned to the camp dazed with elation. Everywhere she went people smiled, greeted her, touched her shoulder, offered to trail fingers over her palm, to hug her. She was a sudden celebrity, a newcomer who had unlocked one of the knottier problems preventing Berd from completing his great mission. Mi came to find her and led her back to their dorm, where the two had prolonged sex that – despite a double orgasm – did little to distract her from the feeling of transcendence.

She sank into a happy sleep, embracing Mi, their hair mingled together, their breathing in sync.

The next thing she knew people were grappling her, somebody holding her legs, another pressing her wrists together. She knew why, immediately: she had had a nightmare, a savage one that speared into her mind from nowhere. She remembered every detail. As she thrashed on the bed, and as the people around her tried to hold her down, she caught a glimpse of Mi, his face botched and tentacled with blood. He was holding a medical pad to the side of his head, and the blood was fresh enough still to be glistening, although there was nothing in his expression except concern for her wellbeing and tenderness.

'Ah!' she screamed. 'Ahh!'

A sedative was administered. When she came to the thrashing had stopped. Instead she lay on her side, greatly gloomy, bitterly shameful at what she had done. A care-cultist named Bodajones was explaining, in a gentle voice, exactly what had happened. Mi had been shocked out of his slumber when Saccade attacked: scratching him, biting his left ear so forcefully that it was partially severed from his head. 'It has been reattached, don't worry,' Bodajones cooed. 'He is whole again, and in no pain, physically or psychologically. But he doesn't understand why you suddenly attacked him.'

'I'm sorry, I'm sorry,' wept Saccade.

'Did you have a sleep-panic? Was it a nightly mare?' Bodajones shook her head. 'Nightmare, I mean. I've been in consultation with the camp's medical AI, and it suggests that nightmare, though rare, is not unknown.'

'I had a nightmare,' gasped Saccade. 'Yes. I didn't know what I was doing! I'm so sorry – tell Mi I'm so sorry.'

'I will,' Bodajones assured her. 'And you can tell him yourself, in a little bit. He's eager to meet you, doesn't blame you, forgives you. He just wants to know you're alright.'

'I had a nightmare,' Saccade repeated.

'The AI advises that talking through your nightmare, though perhaps uncomfortable, is a needful part of recovery. You can tell me about it. It won't be as immediate or terrifying for me, don't worry – I'm only going to hear your verbal reconstruction, not experience it directly.'

'I don't remember it,' said Saccade. She did, of course. She remembered every ghastly detail. But she didn't *want* to remember, and speaking this lie was a clumsy attempt to actualize that.

'The AI advises,' said Bodajones, gently, 'that people always remember a nightmare strong enough to wake them up.'

'I don't remember it!' insisted Saccade, growing louder. 'I don't! I don't!'

Bodajones soothed her, and offered her another sedative, but didn't press her on the specifics of her nightmare. Left alone, Saccade lay awake for a long time, fearful that to fall asleep would be to return to those claustrophobic, red-light scenes of agony and revulsion. But in the event she did sleep, and the nightmare did not return, and, little by little, she ratcheted herself back towards something approaching normality.

:3:

It took several months before her former smile became again a regular part of Saccade's face. Mi came back to her, and they resumed sex and spent some good times together. Of course everyone knew what she had done, but people were very kind, because kindness is one of the strengths given to mortals. And she was still well-regarded: famous as the individual who had gifted the idea that was now being worked into a prototype of the device that would actually – finally – allow Berd to achieve his great goal. Indeed, as the first prototype was built, in a large shed to the north of the main compound, and as initial tests proved positive, her fame grew greater. There was a degree of bittersweetness to it, since many people prefaced praise with 'I was so sorry to hear about…' Words that puckered the skin of her soul painfully, like a wasp-sting. But the praise was genuine.

And here was Heorot. His face was set to kindly concern, but Saccade didn't believe it for a moment. He was gloating, she could tell. He was the grit under her eyelid, his being here was prompting these flashbacks to the terrible events on the Masqueworld. A moment of hatred pure as a hot blade of metal cut through her, and she wanted him dead: but then she settled herself, and breathed in, and smiled. 'You have of course heard of my unfortunate nightmare.'

'I commiserate you. Are you recovered? Is your sexual partner?'

'You have heard he is, I am sure. And as for me: I am humbled. But it is a sign of conscience that the bad things I did on your world, Master Heorot, still very much trouble my mind.'

'If I can help in any way,' said Heorot, and Saccade thanked him and assured him that she would come to him if anything occurred to her, and with that they parted.

The prototype suit was brought to full assembly. It turned out that a forty-five-degree rotation in the vector of gravity – though theoretically achievable – would require vastly more energy to achieve than was available to them, either on the surface or within the core. Once forty-five was achieved, the math suggested the vector would then continue round under its own momentum, as it were, to the fullest extent possible: ninety degrees. But it wasn't practicable in this place, for this project, to rotate the gravitational vector so far. Nor was it necessary. Even a shift of the vector of eight or nine degrees led to impressive reductions in crushing-pressure and temperature, turning Berd's suit into a little bubble environment in which the worst the environment could do was deflected, to flow around him.

There were initial tests in the open crater of the volcano. Then deeper-dive tests. The base camp – a cavern artificially hollowed out as an annex to the base of the mountain's magma stream – was cleared and readied. Compared to the temperatures at the core, the magma that bubbled in the cauldron of Armitage Mount was trivially hot, and regular heat-sealed suits, with turnover convection jets that gave them mobility, provided relatively easy access down three hundred kilometres or so, to the subduction zone. Here tectonic squeezing and the pressurized flow of trapped water, by lowering the solidus temperature, had generated the reservoir of molten rock which itself supplied the lava-chutes of the volcano. And it was from here that Berd entered base camp, passing through a specially constructed portal that used target-lasers to boil away any magma or cooling rock deposits from his suit.

Inside base camp was a complex of chambers, oxygenated and filled with equipment and supplies. From this point, the mission was to move much deeper into the world, a journey involving the sink-shaft that, over the previous four years, had been consistently excavated. The advantage the team had, here, was in the enormous and ever-increasing pressures under which mantle rocks existed. A large irregular shaped area of porous rock, saturated with water, had been cleared and drained, and this chamber functioned as a slag store. The actual tunnel was bored at the angle that allowed rock to shoot up and disappear into this reservoir-space, and the deeper the boring went the greater the forces that acted upon the loosened rock to push it back up the shaft. Mechanical scilla were fitted to the sides of the shaft to move material, and to help raise and lower excavators and exploratory remote craft.

The tunnel was narrow but its length was immense: three thousand kilometres, at which point the pressure became insane: 140 giga-pascals, such that pieces of rock, freed from their matrix, leapt upwards like a bullet firing along a barrel, and the main engineering task involved preventing the shaft from collapsing inward. Closer to the surface braced titanium hoops had sufficed in keeping the shaft clear, but further down a coating of continuous lonsdaleite hoops was required – and even these were operating close to their maximum indentation threshold of ~150 Gpas. There was an added difficulty: once the excavators broke through to the liquid outer core, the pressure would force molten material much of the way back up the tube. That wasn't a problem as such, and in some ways would ease the passage of Berd, in his suit – provided the magma stayed liquid. Of course, if it solidified then the whole tunnel would just have to be excavated again. To prevent this happening the structural supports were threaded with high-energy heating elements.

Three thousand kilometres was not unprecedented tunnellage. Humans had, even in antique times, been in the habit of digging water and sewage tunnels of many hundred kilometres in length. But nobody had dug such a tunnel straight down, and the problems Berd and his team had overcome were legion.

For years the project had inched forward. Some of the people Saccade met had been there from the beginning: nearly a decade of their lives surrendered to this mad ambition.

And then, after all this time, suddenly, everything was

happening at breakneck pace. From being something that was going to happen at some point in the future, Berd's great voyage became something mere months, and then weeks, away from happening.

Ground was cleared to the south of the camp and a metalled space created to provide a landing zone for flitters and small spacecraft to come straight down. No longer did visitors have to land at Port Hayley and come by blimp up to the camp. Now people began coming straight down, riding scalding flitter-exhausts down to the ground, or spiralling slowly down in crafts like giant sycamore seeds. Soon enough dozens of spacecraft were parked.

Saccade liked to watch them land.

She had, by now, acquired a group of followers of her own. It wasn't surprising that a camp built around the fandom of one individual – Berd himself – would bud-off mini-fandoms in this way. And people, or some people, were genuinely enthusiastic about what Saccade had enabled. Mi was still with her, despite her nightmare-driven assault upon him. He was complaisant when it came to the other followers who offered her sexual adventure, some of whom she took up. Others just wanted to be with her. It didn't seem to her that she had any great wisdom to impart, or any particular charisma, especially when compared to Berd. But her followers didn't seem to mind that.

She wondered if this manifestation of group esteem helped keep her soul buoyant and purge her mind of nightmare. At any rate she enjoyed being at the centre of this group and experienced no further bad dreams.

From time to time she visited the team working in the gravitomorphic shed. Some people called this the Saccade Shed, in her honour, but she downplayed this: after all, she wasn't part of the team actually building the suit. And here was the prototype drive unit, a structure the size of a car, far too large to be portable – even considering the considerable size of Berd's suit. But this was only the test rig: a globe shiny as a mirror, a larger frame of formative deployments and processors, and six orientation vanes that unfolded to fix the operation into relative axes. The main problem the prototype had was accessing enough power. The convertor built for the smaller version fitted to Berd's suit would draw energy from the prodigious heats and pressures of the outer core's environment, but up here on the surface the best the team could do was build and bury a medium-sized fusion kit, and store-pump the requisite power for picosecond test bursts.

This, they hoped, was enough for Berd to make his first test mission. Not all the way to the solid core, but down to the bottom of the tunnel to where the molten outer core began. With much fanfare Berd donned his suit, made his way to the volcano and lowered himself in.

He made his way through the surface magma, and into the submontane base camp. From here he moved rapidly along the long tunnel all the way through the planet's mantle to the outer core. He fell, his velocity modulated and managed by the inset-magnetic resistors set into the walls, to stop him from losing control. But he went very rapidly for all that it took him thirteen hours to get all the way to the bottom. Here an upper plug was extruded and the lower plug burned away by lasers, giving Berd access to the outer core.

He swam for long minutes in the intensely pressurized, intensely hot fluid. The vanes deployed from his backpack without a hitch, and after a worrisome thirty seconds or so, when all the pressure-warning displays blipped and flashed orange, the vector of gravity was tweaked. 'Deployed,' gasped Berd, and all across the camp – all across the world, up to the watching audiences in their orbiting spaceships and, after a twelve-minute delay, to the settlements on icebound Boa Esperia – people watched the close-up of his face, and the split-screen coverage of the instrumentation, and the outward facing cameras with their murky images of nothing very much.

A cheer rose spontaneously at 'deployed'.

'Movement is easier now,' Berd reported. 'Like a sailing ship, tacking against the wind – we're tacking against gravity, sliding it so that the pressure bubbles down immediately around me.'

The heat meant that vast quantities of photons were being pushed out of this treacly material, but the density was such that wavelengths were refracted as if through solid rock into the deepest depths of invisible infrared. The suit's cameras captured all this.

When he was assured of his ability to swim through this gooey medium, Berd brought online the specialist detectors, that passed a processed vision into visibility – great swirls and loops of red-orange. 'Ooh!' gasped the crowd, on the surface. 'Ahh!'

'I'm returning to the mouth of the tunnel,' gasped Berd, whose face was ruddy now, magma-coloured like his environment, sweating so much that his skin shone like glycerine. He was blinking so much he looked like he was having a fit. 'The gravitomorphic pack works well to reduce sheer pressure of these depths, but I'm not shunting as much heat as I would like. I'm coming back up!'

As another cheer echoed round the camp, Saccade was already walking off. She left the hubbub and excitement behind her and climbed up through the same path Berd had taken her along, that first time they had met.

It was past midnight, and the night was cool and pleasant, scratchy with the sounds of crickets and fragrant with the scent of resin from the trees. She lit her way with a torch on her forehead and picked her way through the shadows. Rustling sounds in the undergrowth, and behind her the distance, turned the collective hooting and cheering into a weird underwater mess of sound. It resembled booing as much as cheering.

Eventually she reached the pinnacle and sat down admiring the midnight vista. The world's two moons, like a silver-grey penny farthing, rode the sky. The main arm of the milky way stretched up and down across the whole sky, a mess of scrambled egg. Somewhere, immensely far below her, Berd was picking his way through molten rock and metal to locate the mouth of the tunnel that would give him access to the surface again. A moth blundered into Saccade's chest, and flew away, and for a moment, before it vanished into darkness, she glimpsed its crumpled and frantic and yet beautiful flight. She began to cry, but not from sorrow.

:4:

The great day came, a week later, after further tests and tweaks to the suit to ensure the temperature-dispersal equipage was capable of shunting away the requisite amount of heat.

He was going for it. The first human to walk on the solid core of a world!

There was ceremony, because human beings love ceremony, provided it is not too frequently deployed. Everyone in the camp gathered to watch the suit parade round the facility on a self-propelled cart, with Berd standing next to it, leaning against its left knee joint, waving at the crowd.

It was a bright day, past noon, and white cloudlets petalled the blue sky. People were singing, cheering, running along-side the procession. The camp population had doubled in size with visitors – the temporary landing-ground had had to be expanded to fit all the new craft.

The pace of the platform was adjusted to match the speed at which the giant rollers had moved the cathedral-tower Saturn Five combustion rockets out from their sheds to their launch-pads at Cape Kennaveral, because if Berd's mission was anything it was a continuation of the daring human spirit reaching back thousands of years. Kon-Tiki and Columbus the Dove, climbing Everest and sailing a bathyscape to the footwell of the Pacific – and now this! The crowd that walked alongside the suit as it processed thinned a little as it passed out of the main camp and rumbled up the smoothed road into the foothills of Mount Armitage. The sun peeked out and blazed and then hid its shy face in the cloud's patchy cotton. The many hues of the forest trees gleamed and darkened depending on whether the sunlight fell directly upon them. A carnival atmosphere.

Sky is blue, and see the green! People were singing:

We all live in a yellow sunny scene
A yellow sunny scene
A yellow sunny scene

– and that was fitting, too, since that song had originally accom-panied a visual text about a specially constructed exoskeleton that carried a crew into the underground. Or underwater, Saccade wasn't clear in her memory.

A temporary stage had been erected at a particular location beneath Mount Armitage and, an hour or so after leaving the compound, Berd – now seated on a little chair at the front of the cart – and his suit rolled up the ramp and onto it. A dozen technicians were there already, with a variety of equipment and devices waiting to be deployed. A moveable hospital was prepped, and only needed to unfurl its aerolifts to fly wherever it was needed; although the base camp was fully supplied with medical support kit and AI expertise, and was the more likely rendezvous in case anything went wrong on the inside. There were more media drones than flies. Big screens stood at every angle, blank for now.

Berd was conscious of a whole world watching him live, and that (after the necessary delays occasioned by the data being carried via startships from settlement to settlement) the rest of human-habited space would soon be watching too.

He made his departure speech. The trick about speech-making, he knew, was to keep it short. In fact the trick with speech-making is to keep it short *and memorable*, but Berd could be forgiven, in the excitement of anticipation, for forgetting the second bit. 'It's so great to see so many of you here,' he announced. 'This is history, we're making it, and I want to thank all the history-makers who have helped me, over the last many years, to make this history. Together we have made' – he stopped, smiled, looked around – 'we have *constructed* this extraordinary suit.' There were cheers. 'But more extraordinary than the suit is the human spirit which it embodies.' There was a pause, as people waited for more, and then the collective understanding zoomed around the crowd that he was finished. People cheered some more, and clapped. An AI started playing 'Hail The Conquer King-Hero Comes', at excessive volume, but Berd, looking momently incommoded, waved the music to silence almost as soon as it started. It was loud enough, though, to startle a number of birds out of the nearby trees. They, winging vigorously into the sky, snapping featherpoints together at the lowest and highest moment of their action, were making a sound that resembled applause.

Some of the people in the crowd took the hint and began applauding too.

Two technicians joined Berd on the platform. 'As I get myself crammed into this suit,' Berd announced, 'I'd like to ask my good friend Saccade to introduce a reading from history – she is the reason we were able to develop anti-pressure amelioration on the suit, as many of you know, but she is also a historian, and the reading is from her period.'

Berd was prepared to be fitted into his suit, as though David were opening a door in the back of Goliath and stepping inside.

But Saccade was nowhere to be found. There was a brief search for her in the vicinity, and a check on her tag. But she had switched her tag to a privacy setting and nobody wanted to disturb her. Everyone was aware that she had had a small breakdown of some kind, though most were hazy on the precise details. Nobody felt like intruding on her. Perhaps she had grown nervous at the prospect of the big event, with so many people watching, and had retreated.

So: instead of Saccade introducing the AI's reading the AI launched straight into the passage.

Just as we were about to engulf ourselves in this dismal passage, I lifted up my head, and through the tubelike shaft saw that Iceland sky I was never to see again!

Was it the last I should ever see of any sky?

The stream of lava flowing from the bowels of the earth had forced itself a passage through the tunnel. It lined the whole of the inside with its thick and brilliant coating. The electric light added very greatly to the brilliancy of the effect.

The great difficulty of our journey now began. How were we to prevent ourselves from slipping down the steeply inclined plane? Happily some cracks, abrasures of the soil, and other irregularities, served the place of steps; and we descended slowly; allowing our heavy luggage to slip on before, at the end of a long cord.

But that which served as steps under our feet became in other places stalactites. The lava, very porous in certain places, took the form of little round blisters. Crystals of opaque quartz, adorned with limpid drops of natural glass suspended to the roof like lustres, seemed to take fire as we passed beneath them. One would have fancied that the genii of romance were illuminating their underground palaces to receive the sons of men.

"Magnificent, glorious!" I cried in a moment of involuntary enthusiasm, "What a spectacle, Uncle! Do you not admire these variegated shades of lava, which run through a whole series of colours, from reddish brown to pale yellow − by the most insensible degrees? And these crystals, they appear like luminous globes."

"You are beginning to see the charms of travel, Master Harry," cried my uncle. "Wait a bit, until we advance farther. What we have as yet discovered is nothing − onwards, my boy, onwards!"

The AI's voice moved smoothly through the words, Berd was helped up the little ladder in the back of the suit's right thigh and over what would, had the servos and ceramic-shielded armour covered flesh, have been its gluteal muscles. He squeezed into the space, and strapped in, booting up all the in-suit systems and turning on the camera.

The screens leapt to life. The crowd cheered. Here was Berd's face in close up, smiling. Here were his suit's vital signs, and here the multiple exterior camera shots.

'Away!' called Berd.

The insertion blimp grappled the suit and pulled it slowly into the air. It swung in the sky as the crowd watched it diminish, passing up the volcano, until the blimp was a rice grain and the suit dangling beneath, barely visible. Then steam from the mountain's mouth breathed around Berd and he vanished from view – except that everybody was already watching the screens anyway, so he was right there.

The exterior cameras showed a wobbly table-edge of horizon, and then spectral beanstalks of smoke and then nothing but white. The interior camera showed Berd's face as calm. Perhaps thinking that his earlier speech had been too brief, he was talking in a steady, level voice. 'Boa's mantle is a thick layer of silicate rock,' he was saying, 'below the crust – up here among the mountains it's nearly fifty kilometres thick, but we're going to slide down the lava tubes of Armitage and down to underground base camp, so that helps overcome that disadvantage.'

The instrumentation, figured onto the giant screens, showed that Berd was being lowered into the crater. Drones, buzzing high, brought a tessellation of different views, although all they could see was a belch of white-yellow steam. Somewhere inside that cloud was the intrepid explorer.

'Boa's mantle is the main obstacle: 2900 kilometres of silicates in a semi-solid state,' Berd was saying. 'Not rigid solid: the mantle flows very slowly – it's really only visible on geological time scales, when the rock rolls like a viscous fluid. For our purposes it's solid rock, under great pressure. But from base camp I will travel down the passage we have excavated to the outer core, which *is* liquid. Gloopy! Like heated caramel, or treacle – though intensely hot and under extremely high pressure.'

Then there was a hiatus. The signal disappeared. There were gasps amongst the crowd as the screens blanked blue. Technicians scurried about. One made an announcement: 'We had this issue during tests and thought we'd fixed it – there's a signal relay at base camp, but it's built to amplify the broadcast from below. The intense heat of Armitage's magma has disrupted the direct beam. Everything is alright! Berd is OK! He will come back online shortly!'

The crowd waited. Some sat on the ground and brought out food. Some wandered into the forest to make love. Some danced and sang, or watched screen dramas. Eventually the screens flickered back to life. '…structurally, and with the necessaries,' Berd was captured as saying. Something in his suit alerted him to the fact that the live feed was running again. 'I'm at base camp now,' he said. 'And about to enter the main passage.'

He grinned. A weak cheer went through the crowd, back on the surface.

'If the tunnel were clear,' Berd was saying, 'and if there were vacuum inside it, and if I fell straight down without touching the sides, it would take me a mere nineteen minutes to reach the planet's core. We've all done that sum in maths lessons as children! But this tunnel is not vacuum. It is filled with superheated gaseous medium, and further down superheated magma. So I won't be hurtling down at eight kilometres a second, I'm glad to say! The filaments in the hoops maintaining the structural integrity of the passage will interact with my suit to ensure that during the first portion of my descent I don't over-accelerate!'

The crowd reassembled for Berd's insertion into the main passage – a sinkhole five metres wide. The camera feed, as Berd leaned his hefty suit forward to get a look down it, revealed a space so precipitous and regular that its perspectival shrinkage looked like a pattern on a flat circle. But then, with a 'Hoopsa!', Berd dropped into the shaft.

'Here we go,' he cried, and there was some scattered cheering. But for the next few hours there really wasn't much to see. He descended. The magnetic stubs in the hoops acted to prevent his descent becoming too dangerously rapid. The view was the same thing, over and over.

Berd spoke from time to time, relaying information about the planet's mantle. At one point he made reference to Saccade – 'my friend', he called her, 'whose gravitomorphic ideas for managing the excessive pressures at the core have brought this whole project forward by years.' There was a fumble, an adjustment, a couple of the consecutive wall-hoops faulty perhaps, and then he said: 'I remember a conversation we had about her historical period, the twentieth – there was a famous story-text from that epoch called *Alias in Wonderland*, about a girl who fell to the centre of the world through a tunnel not unlike this one! I am she – I am Alias.'

After this Berd launched into a lengthy lecture about the different layers of the mantle. This, he said, was similar to Earth's composition, and related to the nature of all M-class planets so far discovered. 'Three layers, an upper and a lower joined by a transition zone, where olivine undergoes isochemical phase transitions to wadsleyite and ringwoodite. Olivine is usually anhydrous, as I'm sure you all know, but under these elevations of pressure olivine polymorphs into a crystal structure that operates – to deploy an analogy – somewhat like a sponge. During our excavations, as those who have been following the project know already, we encountered huge quantities of saline, including extensive pockets populated by thermal-vent-style lifeforms. It was very exciting!'

The big screens showed recorded footage of these odd-looking deep-ocean creatures: tangles of lobsterine legs and pincers, bleach-pale in the camera's lighting, scuttling and wriggling through the intensely saline, strongly alkaline fluid in its unlit spaces. But the true Berd-fans had seen all this material before, and the recent arrivals, waiting for the First Step, weren't very interested in it. Old news.

The crowd began to disperse.

The dawn came, and people who had stayed awake through much of the night dozed in the open or retreated back to the camp for a proper sleep in their dorms. A core of supporters kept the singing and dancing going throughout, even though there was nothing to report.

Shortly after noon Berd slowed his descent through the medium superheated vapour before entering the fluid magma that filled the bottom half of the shaft. The screens no longer carried images of the blipping lights of the tunnel's structural sections, passing endlessly regularly from below to above. Now the cameras cycled through wavelengths to display various versions of what was, in visible spectrums, only darkness: squirls of amber, streaks of white-yellow and a Hadean rumble and wash of red. The task now was not to slow Berd's descent, but to accelerate it through this viscous medium. The suit was designed for this: below Berd's armoured feet a low-pressure spherical space was generated, and the magma was funnelled to the space above him. Soon he was whistling down the tube.

The people who had come just to see Berd accomplish his aim beguiled their boredom by exploring the camp, or logging onto entertainment channels. But they stayed. Eventually Berd would emerge into the fluid outer core, would sink through this like a diver in an immense and scalding ocean until he touched the seabed itself – the solid iron inner core. Nobody wanted to miss *that* moment.

Or almost nobody: for a single petitoform spaceship fired its thrust and rose, wobbling, through the late afternoon sunlight until it left the sky below it and moved away. A few people on the ground, watching it, through the magnifunction of their screens, saw the glitter-shudder of its β-drive engaging, up in orbit, before it vanished. But most people paid it no mind. Vangipurapu, shading his eyes with his hand, watched it take off and said to himself: 'Huh! Some people have no patience for the waiting, I guess.'

The night came and the moons rolled over the sky. Shortly before sunrise Berd emerged from the bottom of his shaft, passed through the seismic discontinuity and swam free in the inner core itself. Transitioning the core-mantle boundary was the most dangerous portion of the whole escapade: for the temperatures and pressures in this place were insane, crushing, obliterating, annihilating. The gravitomorphic vanes, products of the new technology, could not be deployed inside the shaft, because the tunnel diameter was too narrow. That meant that the suit itself had to sustain Berd alive, while the kit extended itself, drew the necessary immensities of energy from the surrounding medium, and switched on the device.

The crowds were back. Everyone was acutely conscious that this could be the moment Berd died – snuffed out too quickly even to be able to react, if the suit malfunctioned or the tech failed to engage. The screens showed his face as impassive, though sweaty. The instrument readouts were all going crazy, alarms pinging, the modified inputs from exterior cameras showing a yellow-white maelstrom of currents and incandescent swirls. 'Hold fast,' muttered Berd as his suit struggled to adapt. Then: 'Hold.' Then: 'Hold on—'

The feed glitched and cut-out. A gasp went round the crowd, but almost at once coverage was restored, and there was Berd's face, his teeth visible now, his eyes narrowed.

And then, all the instrument alarms quieted. Pressure gauges fell away, and the temperature adjusted itself. The airstream inside Berd's helmet was able to blow away the last of his sweat. 'Done,' he said.

The whole crowd cheered.

It was a remarkable moment: Berd's suit had jump-started a

gravitomorphic deformation, creating a vesica piscis around the whole suit in which the usual vector of gravity was bumped slightly out of true. Everywhere else, all around him, gravitational force ran in direct lines towards the centre of mass of the globe, but in the immediate vicinity of Berd that vector was displaced by nearly five degrees. Berd gasped, grinned, and then he said: 'We're in.'

As power flooded into the device the deformation approached six degrees.

'We've a couple thousand klicks still to descend,' he announced. 'But I'm a free swimmer now. And bending gravity, as light is bent through a prism, means I can swim pretty much as fast as I like.'

He tested the suit and its vanes with some merman twists and flourishes, and then turned himself heels over head and dived fast for the solid ground.

Down he swam, through the superheated and resinous material, as a sperm whale plunges towards the bottom. 'The outer core is mostly molten iron,' he said, 'but there are much higher proportions of nickel than was hypothesized before we were able directly to sample it – as high as eight percent.' As if the sheer excitement of being the first human to move through such an environment had to be balanced with the tedium of a lecture. 'Oxygen levels are lower than was originally thought, though there's rather more sulphur,' he reported, even though all the data he was seeing was also being broadcast to the surface.

The descent was rapid, but the distances to be covered were vast, and so – once again – the crowd began to disperse, to wander away. There was a countdown in the corner of every screen, and people figured they would occupy themselves until the historic moment was reached.

For a period of time Berd himself slept. After forty hours

of continual wakefulness, sustained on his own adrenaline and stimulants administered by his suit, he was finally in a position to relax. Down he went, continually sinking.

High above him, on the surface of the world, on the flanks of Mount Armitage and in Camp Berd, night moved into the sky, easing the daylight aside. The stars gave out their thin wide-scatter lustre. The moons rose and moved. The sun began to warm the eastern horizon.

This morning, though, there was a renewed sense of excitement amongst the camp-followers and visitors, among the technicians and staff. This was the day. In a few hours Berd would become the first human being to walk upon the solid core of a planet. Excitement!

More, during the night there had been a thrilling development. Whilst Berd himself slept the suit's external cameras had observed *something*. What? Nobody was sure. The footage, filtered, modified and enhanced, was played over and over again – a flipper? A head? The petal of some insentient crystalline structure, perhaps. But now: for it had *moved*, had approached Berd's plummeting form as if curious, and had even matched the suit's descent for many seconds, before withdrawing. Was it *life*? Could there be lifeforms swimming through that super-intense ultrahot and impossibly pressurized environment? Surely not, and yet ...

The team on the surface had woken Berd at once, of course, and he had scanned his environment, had altered the trajectory of his descent, sweeping wide circles. But the gloopy hyper-coalescence resisted probing. It was like peering through soup. Nothing.

'Keep a weather eye,' said the surface team.

'It could be life!' Berd said. 'That would be a discovery and a half!'

'Stats looking good. Keeping gravmorph six degrees, heat-dump optimal. Approaching.'

'I'm almost at the lava-seabed,' confirmed Berd.

There was some worry, amongst the audience up-top: if this unexplored zone was populated with bizarre extremophile lifeforms, who was to say whether they wouldn't attack Berd? Devour him, perhaps? Still there was no turning back now.

'I know some of you are,' came Berd's voice. He appeared to be a little out of breath. 'Some of you are eagerly anticipating what.' Nothing for five seconds, ten, fifteen, then: 'Hah! Hah! Sorry. Sorry. Glitch. I know some are anticipating what I'm going to say when I set foot on the inner core. There has been some pretty cool discussion of a fitting –'

Then nothing.

Instrumentation, including those devices that reported Berd's life signs, said that everything was A-OK. He hadn't passed out, or – God or gods or providence forbid! – died. There hadn't been what his team most feared: a brief malfunction in the suit's protective settings that would allow a 4000°C inrush of heat instantly to liquefy him.

He had just stopped speaking.

People waiting. One hour turned to two – the screens including displays that demonstrated just how far this solitary geonaut had to travel to arrive at the solid core lying at the bottom of this vast molten sea. People watched eagerly for any signs of life in amongst the swirl and visual noise. Nothing. There was a visual spectrum camera and its feed was blank except when, occasionally, some stray sneeze of photons scored across the sensors. Then there were cameras in all manner of spectra, a sonar and mag-res imager: those showed a variety of images: baroquely curling currents of molten matter, upsurges and bursts of intenser energy through this hyper-heated and ultra-pressurized environment. But no sign of whatever had been seen earlier: a flipper, a tentacle, a snout. What had it been?

Fandoms sprung up there and then, excitedly discussing the possibilities. The members of one group quickly found one another by virtue of their shared belief that Berd's passage had passed close by an entirely new and hitherto unexpected mode of life. They accessed the hints of the data and speculated: a large creature, if cellular then made of some ultra-high temperature matrix, swimming this vast, energy-rich sea. Did it feed on smaller entities – perhaps some kind of magma-plankton? Was it a stable form of life, or did it move and change according to the highly demanding environment in which it lived? Was it – might it be – *intelligent*?

Another group started sifting through visual schematics for the data gathering equipment with which the suit was fitted. With the help of an AI diagnostic they began to assemble possible ways in which the cameras might have glitched, or otherwise malfunctioned, to give these strange images.

A third group prayed. Might the object so briefly glimpsed have been a *horn*? Might something diabolical dwell in those infernal depths? They prayed for Berd's safety.

But Berd was vocalizing again. He said 'Ho!' a few times, and then coughed, and then he said: 'Here it comes.'

Everyone's attention was on the screens now.

'I'm very close to the bottom now,' said Berd. 'It remains to be seen whether the seismic discontinuity that marks the outer and inner core constitutes a solid surface on which I can just – stand – or – if – my – feet – sink – into – something *swampier*.' He panted a little and the system readouts registered the suit rotating again, so that it was sinking feet-down towards the core.

'If it's quicksand,' Berd said. 'Sand. Quicksand. If it's quicksand

I shall hover at the top, and count that as my one small step. But we expect, we expect, expect –'

A long pause.

Then the altimeter, or profondimetre, began broadcasting a steadily shrinking number. 'You all,' said Berd, through gasps, 'are waiting for my – first words. Here it goes.'

The last few metres clocked down. According to the instrumentation, the soles of the suit's boots were now planted on the solid metallic core of the world.

'The sensors in these big metal shoes,' Berd was saying, 'are a bit on the *tickly* side, but I can deffo feel something. Oh!' The suit leaned, and he put his right leg out to steady it. 'Micrograv, currents in the molten sky above, it's like it's a windy day,' he grunted. Then, as if suddenly remembering that he was supposed to be uttering a deathless line to be memorized in the history visuals, he changed the tone of his voice. 'Just as the first lunar visitor spoke of one small step for a human and one great leap for humankind, so I speak my own chosen phrase as I place one foot before an—'

The feed cut.

A gasp passed through the audience. A technician ran on the platform, tripped, slid and vanished off the far side. Some people began shouting. Some even booed.

The feed cut-back for: '– wheresoe'er the stride of –' and then cut again.

There was a high-pitched squeal, all the screens flickered, and then full coverage was restored. '– merely *minima*. Functionality! But a brand-new world of exploration!' That was it. It took a moment for the crowd to recognize that he had stopped speaking, and a cheer went round and round.

'I'm walking!' Berd said, excitedly. 'I'm walking here. Gravity is Earth-lunar, a little less, but I can still feel that I'm walking uphill. There is topography in this place.'

Belatedly, the levels of excitement in the crowd mounted. Singing and dancing was resumed, and there were many cheers and excited yells.

:5:

All that day, and through the night, celebrations continued excitedly. After more than an hour's perambulation on the surface of the solid core, Berd left a specially-designed totem: a thin pole protected by a smaller gravitomorph device, powered by a root-shaped cable dangling in the molten metal. It wouldn't be a permanent marker, for soon enough the device would fail and the totem would dissolve in the heat and pressure. But it was something.

Berd was sobbing with relief, or exhaustion, or both, as he lifted off from the solid ground and began his long swim upwards, towards the entrance of the main shaft. It would be days before he reached the base camp, and once there he would stay for another day as the medical AI and a number of support team-members medically assessed him, and he recovered from his exertions. Eventually he would re-emerge to the world and fly by blimp down the mountainside to where a smaller but still exultant crowd would greet him.

Not Saccade though. She had departed the planet whilst Berd was still descending the main shaft, and before he had emerged into the top of the liquid outer core. She, and two of her new fandom, had stolen the petitoform β-ship and flown it into orbit. They had flown into orbit, carrying with them the stolen prototype gravitomorph device. It had been left unwatched and unguarded as the crowds clustered together to watch the screens of Berd's descent. And then she and her two co-conspirators had engaged the β-drive and disappeared into the impossible vastity of space.

Heorot's body was discovered a day later. His biomonitor had not been synced to the camp's AI, so the cessation of his life signs had not registered. Instead a rambler literally tripped over his corpse, covered with siriusphid leaf-needles. There was consternation throughout the camp. It seemed he had been stabbed through the right eye with a sharpened chopstick, the stub of which protruded like a nail from his eyeball. There were no cameras in this portion of the forest, but surveillance was checked for all feeds in the camp. It was not a surprise to discover the identity of the person with whom he had been in conversation, as the rest of the camp gathered at the foothills of Armitage. They had appeared to argue, and then reconcile, and then she had beckoned him to follow her out of the camp and towards the place where his body was later discovered. Death, which ends all things.

You are always inventing new things, my homines, and now you have invented a cunning device that – within a limited compass – shifts the vector of gravity from its otherwise perfect perpendicular. You can move that universal several degrees from the straight, thereby generating a bubble within which mass is effectively reduced (effectively in terms of relative action; you don't actually diminish the mass of any object) and the G-force acting upon it reduced. To move more than seven or eight degrees out of true requires immense reserves of energy, and the energy requirement grows more extreme the further along the dial you push the vector. To reach a forty-five-degree deformation would require roughly the equivalent in magnitude to the energy generated by ten billion suns in one year. You are, as it were, 'pushing' against more than the local field, you see: by tweaking gravitational forces for a sphere of a few metres across you need to engage all the gravity in the cosmos. There is a mode of archimedian leverage at work – and what's more, if you were to reach forty-five degrees, the whole system would suddenly swing about, seeking to right itself. The vector of gravity would snap round to the full ninety degrees, the next stable state. It can't go more than ninety degrees, since then you'd be into the realm of inverted gravity, and that's not spacetime-possible. But ninety degrees is stable.

But now that you have invented this machine, o homines, what will you do with it? It would make, let's say, flying from planet-surface into orbit a little easier – although the power you would need to put in to the machine in the first place to achieve this would make the manoeuvre more costly, in energy terms – than otherwise. You could, as the celebrated Berd did, use it to explore areas of intense pressure or intense heat, like the deepest sea-beds or the interiors of planets: but that is a niche interest. What else?

128

I make this suggestion: there are enormities of energy inside a black hole. Think of all the matter squeezed into that miniscule space, centillions of tonnes pressed into a space smaller than your eyeball. Think of that as potential energy, the largest and most tightly-coiled spring in the universe, and you will see that there is plenty there to power even a machine as energy-hungry as your device. Activate it in a black hole and swap the vector of gravity holding the matter in for a vector of gravity spinning it around, and see the explosion. Black hole to white bang, and soaring, riding the blast like an obsidian surfer, flames of joy curling in bow-waves around his passage, comes – who, though?

Nobody. Nothing can live inside a black hole. It's the least hospitable environment in the cosmos. Impossible, impossible, impossible.

4

Committeetopia

It was a matter, evidently, of deciding what to do. We humans learn from the past and make things better in the future. This anti-entropy is the essence of who we are. It's why interstellar humanity lives in a congeries of utopias, where the antique Earthbound lived in varying horror shows of societies: wealth-plagued, hierarchy-obsessed, cruel and careless.

Word spread, slowly, from star to star, carried by the ships that passed between the many settlements of humanity more rapidly than speed-of-light telemetry. These ships moved faster than light, although word passed slowly for all that. And here was a problem. Saccade, a person of previously commendable mildness, curiosity and worth, had murdered another human being, by name 'Heorot'. His dead body had been returned from the planet of Boa Memória to his home upon Masqueworld to be recycled and so shared with the whole community according to the ethos of his people. As for Saccade, she had, unexpectedly but inarguably, proven a grave danger to others, and likely a danger to herself as well. Upon Boa Memória she had 'stolen' — that is, *appropriated without others' agreement* — two things: the prototype device Berd and his team had developed to reclock the arrow of gravity, and a spaceship. 'In another sense,' said Spake, addressing the whole group, 'she has *stolen* a third and fourth thing: for I do not believe the two people who left Boa with her aboard that ship went willingly.'

'Evidence for this assertion?' requested Razak Bin.

'I have no hard evidence for it,' Spake conceded. 'But we must consider as a real possibility that what has been happening here amounts to a contagion – a *psychological* contagion, in which the very foundations of free and well humanity, our self-sense, our ability to choose, our mental liberty – are compromised.'

Did Saccade persuade the two folk who went with her? Coerce them? Suborn them? Did they choose to leave with this 'thief' and murderer of their own free will? There was some discussion of the dynamic of the Boa Memórian 'fan cultures', but it was agreed that, enthusiastic though some 'fans' became, such enthusiasm would never override basic moral imperatives.

'Therefore Saccade has either kidnapped these others,' said Spake, 'or else corrupted them, corroded their moral worth.'

Spake was physically present with twelve other people, in a sunlit room on the atheist planet Anbuselvan. It was thought, by the various people who had become interested in the problem of Saccade and her stolen goods, that it would be best if the group assembled to recapture her be assembled upon such a world. Not that everyone on Anbuselvan disbelieved in God or gods of course – no human community is ever so monolithic. But there was a propensity among the general population towards atheism, and many atheists from other, more religious-flavoured worlds resettled there to be among more alike fellow folk.

The reason why it was assumed that atheists would be the best people to supply such a team was as follows: the story, as it spread from world to world, grew in the telling, encompassing not just the murder on Boa, but the earlier and – you might think unconnected, but others would not agree – multiple murders aboard the startship Sa-Niro when it was in orbit around the black hole QV Tel. The murderer in that atrocity had claimed that an entity, impossibly communicating with him from *inside* the black hole, had instructed him to kill his crewmembers, instructions he had felt compelled to obey. As the story spread, the speculation grew that the entity beyond the event horizon – the Gentleman, as he had been called – was the Devil himself. Satan. The Adversary.

Now, this belief was not exactly widespread, even among those who practiced one of the many religious faiths of humanity. For most it was too improbable a hypothesis, such that even those who believed, or 'believed', in The Devil, or Shaitan (the Scorching One), or Beelzebub, or Lucifer, or Yetza-Hara, or the Great Red Dragon, or Iblis, or Melkor, did not believe such an entity could be locked *inside* a black hole – of all places – or, if he had been so imprisoned by God, that he could communicate beyond the implacable event horizon. If such a creature, or entity, or being exists at all, surely it is not as an agent *within* the logic of the cosmos, but rather – like God Himself – an entity that stands in some other relation *to* the universe, the ground upon which it is defined. Like God Himself.

Like God, Him- or Herself.

As to the true nature of the so-called Gentleman, there were various theories. Some simply disbelieved in him and assumed that Raine – the person who claimed to have conversed with him – had merely hallucinated the whole exchange, that 'the Gentleman' was a mere fiction conjured by Raine's diseased mind. This explanation had the advantage of common sense, and it avoided the various impossibilities of physics entailed by Raine's story: information passing from the inside to the outside of a black hole and so on. Then again, there *were* people who believed that there might be an actual reality behind the Gentleman: – as for instance, an alien consciousness, evolved for the extraordinary and specialized environments within the body of QV Tel. Or perhaps (said others) it might be that an intelligence of some kind was using the black hole as a medium for communication: trying to speak to us from some other place in the cosmos, via a spacetime wormhole that connected with the singularity, or conceivably from the far future, twanging the singularity like a guitar-string to generate words and meaning. Physics fanfolk explored the possibilities of how this might be made to work, sketching out theories and running eagerly with speculations, deriving explanations that were either more or less consonant with the actual workings of the cosmos.

Still, whatever the sane people believed was the case in QV Tel, the fact remained: Raine, and possibly Saccade, believed the Gentleman was Shaitan himself. If their belief was illogical it was also, so it seemed, contagious. The fact that both Raine and Saccade were themselves religious folk may have played a part in shaping their sense of the anomaly, whether it was hallucination or alien or future telephone, whatever it was. And so it made sense that the team sent to recover Saccade from her mad expedition, and from herself, ought to be drawn from the ranks of the atheists. They, surely, would be less susceptible to so harmful and urgent a belief.

And so here we are, on Anbuselvan.

Razak Bin is speaking now: 'Given the dreadful crime Saccade has committed, it is clear that we must apprehend her. The only question is: how? By what means? Recall the botched attempt to take Raine into care, at the very beginning of this contagion. How many lives lost! We must not replicate that dreadful circumstance.'

'Her spaceship is small,' said Bartlewasp, another member of the committee. She had done some historical work of her own, and felt a complicated affinity with Saccade. The two had not been part of the same historical fandoms, but all such fandom groups were aware of one another.

'Her spaceship is small,' Razak Bin agreed. 'But it can still travel faster than light.'

'I propose,' said Bartlewasp, 'constructing a much larger craft, then locating Saccade and her followers, pursuing her and absorbing her entire craft into our ship. The mistake made by the crew of the Sβ-*Oubliette* was their attempt to board the *Niro* in person. I propose we do not replicate their error. Entomb the hostile craft within a much bigger ship, immobilize it and its crew, *then* communicate with the individuals inside and invite them to come out.'

'You perhaps forget one thing,' said Razak Bin. 'Saccade possesses a version of the device Berd and his team built.'

Irked by the imputation that she was forgetful, Bartlewasp returned: 'But they have only the prototype. We do not know if they are able to supply it with the enormous power it requires to function, or even if it will work at all, having been uprooted and hauled here and there, doubtless bashed about, possibly damaged or even broken entirely.'

'But let us consider the possibility that it does still work. What if Saccade switches the device on whilst her ship is quarantined inside our larger ship?' pressed Razak Bin. 'Damage! Death!'

'We know *why* she has stolen this device,' drawled a binose called Seint, whose interest was in pursuit and capture as such (he was an historian of the different systems of old Earth police forces, and, he boasted, could read *and* write two languages). 'We know where she is going: QV Tel.'

'We do not *know*,' said Razak Bin. 'We surmise.'

'There are high probabilities associated with the surmise,'

groaned Seint. 'Enough for it to shape our strategies of response. Accordingly I propose: we observe from a distance and allow Saccade and her crazy disciples to fly to this place, and drop the device into it. This, she manifestly desires to do, believing it will release the so-called "Gentleman" from his incarceration. Absurd! But this, she believes.'

'And if she is able to deposit the device inside the hole?'

'Then one of two eventualities will follow. One: the device will momentarily reorient the vector of gravity at the event horizon, causing the black hole to explode, thereby annihilating Saccade and her crew and preventing her from causing any more damage. Or two: it will fall harmlessly into the singularity, whereupon we can pursue and apprehend her craft without needing to worry about that.'

'Causing a black hole to *explode*?' queried several.

'Think of the material beyond the event horizon as compacted to the intensest pressures! What keeps it all in there is only gravity – gravity is the lid on this insanely pressurized container. Behind the event horizon is an immense mass, and if the lid is removed, even for a split-second, then the pressure will force a blaze of expanding intensely hot material outward.'

'You deduce Saccade will do this?' asked Spake. 'You think she is suicidal?' Spake's personal status was augmented by the large number of followers he had accrued for his Flavour Symphonies. His interest in the case flowed, he said, from the fact that he had once visited the Masqueworld and had discovered four new Flavour combos there, which disposed him to like the place, and therefore to feel a comradely sense of aggrievement that one of their citizens had been murdered.

'I think she is delusional,' declared Seint. 'I have studied many such criminal cases from history, and many such cases do not act according to rational self-interest. Saccade genuinely believes there is an entity dwelling inside the black hole. She believes the device that she has stolen is, as it were, a key, and that it will unlock the door of QV Tel. She believes the Gentleman,' and here Seint snorted briefly, 'will step through.'

'And then?'

'Who knows? You are asking me to speculate on the fantasy life of a mentally unstable individual. My point is that she does not believe depositing the device into QV Tel to be a suicidal act, which leads me to believe she will, most likely, proceed. Then there is a chance that the device will indeed activate and reconfigure the gravity of the black hole. If so she will herself be destroyed in the resulting explosion, and our problem is solved.'

'There are risks in our pursuing the strategy of allowing her to follow-through on her intentions,' noted Razak Bin. 'She may visit other worlds, other habitats, and commit more crimes, on her way to QV Tel. We may have misunderstood her psychopathology altogether – perhaps she intends to gather many more disciples and lead them to the promised land represented by the Gentleman, such that they *all* die when the black hole explodes.'

'These are possible eventualities,' conceded Seint, 'though not likely.'

'There is another possibility we must, in all due diligence, consider,' suggested Bartlewasp. 'We are proceeding on the assumption that Saccade is, as Raine was before her, delusional about the Gentleman.'

'You think she is *not*?' scoffed Seint.

'I think we must discuss all possibilities. Perhaps the Gentleman is indeed a mere hallucination, or figment. What if he is not? What if there *is* an entity, of some kind, living inside QV Tel? Might Saccade be able to *release* it from its environment? What might the consequences of such an action be?'

'Blowing up the black hole would destroy any entity within, surely.'

'I suggest,' Seint drawled, 'such a scenario is so remote from likelihood that it can be safely dispensed with.'

'Such dismissiveness is unwarranted,' said Razak Bin. 'There is no reason not to consider all possibilities.'

'Atheist planet,' grumbled Seint. 'Supposed atheism! It was ever thus. Backsliding into the basest superstition!'

The mood of the meeting was soured by this, and Spake intervened. 'Let us adjourn,' he said, 'and return when tempers have settled themselves and we can agree how to proceed.'

To avoid dilatoriness, it was agreed that construction of a pursuit craft be initiated so as to be ready for when the committee had decided on a plan of action. Enthusiasts for spaceship construction began assembling in orbit to lay the keel of the as-yet-unnamed β-drive ship.

:2:

Razak Bin: we will be having much to do with him as we go on. Would you like a physical description? His long hair black as liquorice, his soil-brown eyes that were often in motion, glancing left and right, eager to see, to find out. His large-lipped mouth which was happiest smiling and was often *at* its happiest. Not just an intelligent man, but a *curious* one, which is better: wanting to know, wanting to explore, wanting to understand and to share his understanding. Such a person will have many relationships, many lovers, rather than one life-partner, his restlessness a function of his energetic curiosity rather than an index of shallowness – for he was also a tender-hearted, empathetic and sweet-tempered individual, who disliked seeing another in pain, who cared genuinely for others. For this reason he had joined the committee to address the wrong Saccade had committed and so prevent further harm happening to others. That, then, is Razak Bin.

After the meeting, Bin sought out Bartlewasp, to see if she had been upset or psychologically incommoded by Seint's rudeness. The two strolled through the bright Anbuselvan sunlight. They ambled, arm in arm, through the display gardens of Hanlanilan, admiring the topiary. The sky of this world was a paler turquoise shade than was the case on Razak Bin's home planet; a pleasant Uranian shade of blue that Razak found extremely attractive.

'Shall we chat?' he asked Bartlewasp.

Then they took recliners in a café and each had pipettes of dazzle-coffee dripped into their eyes.

'I find Seint's balance of probability likely,' Razak Bin conceded. 'That is, it is likely the device, deposited into QV Tel, will do nothing. But I also find the prospect of it exploding the black hole into a white fountain of incandescence rather beautiful.'

'I agree,' said Bartlewasp. 'A fine image!'

'It makes me wonder if such a thing might not explain the Big Bang itself? Imagine a prior cosmos entirely devoured by gravity, all matter sucked into myriad black holes, all black holes drawn together into one mega-singularity, nothing else existent. But then – one extra thing! Dropped into the cosmic unity from ... outside.'

'Surely,' Bartlewasp noted, 'there would *be* no outside, in such a scenario. Who is holding the device? How has this person, and their device, escaped the inevitable trillion-year gravitational attrition?'

'Impossible,' Razak Bin agreed. 'Quite impossible. Such a being would not be *of* the cosmos, but transcendent *to* it.'

'Orthogonal to material reality, you are saying?'

'Such talk is contaminated by spiritualism and vaguery,' Razak Bin admitted. 'And yet there is something rather ... splendid to it, don't you think?'

'God,' whispered Bartlewasp, as if even uttering such a syllable was a taboo thing on this world (of course it wasn't: God was earnestly and enthusiastically debated all across the planet).

'Holding in His hand,' said Razak Bin, 'an artefact. A pebble, perhaps: polished, with a swirl pattern visible beneath its exterior dark-green and black patina like the milky way. All of existence, all matter and all possibility, all of time and space has been contracted by the inevitability of gravity into this dimensionless point. All of spacetime has been scoured clean, all bones picked clean and the clean bones gone, by time and gravity, the only two things that matter in the end. But, lo! Here is a person − does *person* trivialize it? − who has, for reasons of the miraculous, or the transcendental, by the grace of their own potency, escaped those two terrible inevitabilities. And here he, or she, stands, looking down upon the pinprick void of the ultimate black hole. And into it, like a baseball pitcher, they throw the pebble. Then—'

'Bang,' said Bartlewasp, lazily. The coffee was filling her vision with wonders and buzzing her brain with gorgeousness.

'Quite,' agreed Razak Bin.

'A fairy story,' said Bartlewasp.

Razak Bin did not reply, which prompted Bartlewasp to ask: 'You *are* an atheist?'

'I am.'

'Born and raised here? On Anbuselvan?'

'No,' said Razak Bin. 'No, raised elsewhere − on Whalecliff, in fact, a religious settlement. Raised by religious parents.'

'Oh! So your atheism is a personal choice?'

139

'An adult conclusion, yes.'

'What was the religion in which you were raised?'

'Orange Islam. As is often the case with such people, I retain a sentimental attachment to aspects of it. But I have parted company with it as a belief structure.' He turned his head to Bartlewasp. 'You ask because you suspect I may actually believe Saccade's crazy theory? That the devil himself is living inside a black hole, ready to be unleashed upon an unsuspecting cosmos?'

'You do not literally believe such a thing.'

'I do not literally believe it, no. But it intrigues me, as a piece of fiction, as worldbuilding. For the actual existence of the devil entails the actual existence of God, and not a God standing, as we have been speculating, at the end of some *via negative* outside material reality, but a God engaged *in* the cosmos — more than that, a jailer God, who has constructed prisons called black holes, all across holy territory, and populated them with criminals. Locking-up all those sinful devils, those fallen angels of monotheistic imagining, in oubliettes, inescapable prison cells, well-shafts deeper than even light can ascend.'

'The Sβ-*Oubliette* was the name of one of the two startships that—' Bartlewasp started saying.

'Of course. A notable coincidence! But this jailer God, flying from star to star with his keys, casting rebel angels into myriad pits and locking their heavy doors... what would *that* say about the nature of reality? How many black holes have been detected — forty trillion? So many devils! If each is a prison, in which is cached a different devil, it implies that Raine's "gentleman" cannot be *the* Devil, Satan himself. A minor devil at most! Perhaps the minor devils are distributed amongst the smaller-mass black holes, and the higher-ranking demons are locked up in the bigger black holes at the centres of spiral galaxies?

Perhaps there is one super-massive black hole, somewhere, in which the actual prince of darkness is imprisoned!'

'But,' Bartlewasp repeated, 'you do not, despite your religious upbringing, *literally* believe this?'

Razak Bin was silent for a while. Then he said: 'No, not literally. But my dear Bartlewasp, I wonder if *something* might not be alive inside QV Tel. Not a boogey-creature out of religious myth, but an entity – an alien. A creature evolved to live in the extraordinary circumstances of the interior of a black hole.'

'Evolved? In such a place?'

'Why not? Of course we know little, and nothing for sure, about conditions on the far side of the event horizon. But we can intuit it must be a fantastically high-energy environment. And an environment moreover in which there is a constant rain of material falling down upon whoever lives inside, like food particles drifting down through the salt water to feed the strange creatures who have evolved to live at the crazy pressures on the ocean floor.'

'Fanciful,' was Bartlewasp's opinion.

'Is it? I'm not so sure. Mightn't a form of life, and perhaps even a consciousness, develop in such a place? Isn't it at least possible?'

'Possibility can rarely be absolutely denied.'

'And if so, might such a consciousness, evolving in such a place, not perhaps achieve high levels of intelligence? Would an intelligent being *not* find a way to communicate with the universe outside its pool? We are all assuming that Raine's talk of his Gentleman was just an hallucination, a phantasy spun from his own brain. But what if it was real? Not a real *devil*, of course – but a real entity, an alien, whose attempts at first contact were misunderstood by Raine?'

'I remain sceptical,' said Bartlewasp.

ADAM ROBERTS

'I propose it as a possibility, and do not insist on its truth, or even likelihood. But here is my point: the plan at the moment is to permit Saccade to travel to QV Tel and disburden herself of the gravity device by dropping it in. If the device fails, then we can simply apprehend her afterwards, and if it succeeds then she will blow herself and her disciples up and remove her as a threat. But what if she does succeed – and in doing so she destroyed not just herself, but also annihilated the environment of a brand-new species of intelligent life?'

'That would be a very grave and terrible thing,' Bartlewasp agreed.

'Precisely. Before we allow Saccade, or anyone, to do something so devastating we must, surely we must *at the very least* ascertain whether QV Tel is inhabited?'

'Can we make such an ascertaining?'

'Perhaps. If there is an entity, perhaps a whole population of entities, living inside the black hole, and if it or they had previously been able to contact Raine, then they might contact us. We must explore QV Tel before we decide on any action. For if it is inhabited we cannot allow harm to come to it by means of Saccade's device. That would be to collaborate in murder, perhaps genocide.'

'Let us say that there are these alien entities, living in such a place. If they contacted Raine, did they not also send Raine mad?'

'Raine was perhaps mad before this contact. Raine's diseased consciousness may have misinterpreted what were actually perfectly friendly and peaceful overtures.'

'Or perhaps his consciousness accurately apprehended violent and insanifying overtures! There is no reason to assume an alien lifeform would be benign. Perhaps it is constitutionally hostile, belligerent, malign. Perhaps Raine's contact released a dangerous,'

142

Bartlewasp paused, for she had to retrieve the unfamiliar word from her dataset, 'contagion into our cosmos!'

'I agree caution would be advised. But surely you see the necessity of first scoping out the black hole – of examining it thoroughly – and then, only *after* we have more information, deciding on our action?'

'That,' said Bartlewasp, 'makes sense.' She closed her eyes and allowed the odours of the display garden into her sensorium: breathing deep the fruity freshness of the banks of jasmine, the musky sweetness of the angel's trumpets. The sugary pungency of honeysuckle. She felt the warmth of the sun on her face. When she opened her eyes, the autoserver was at her side, offering her a top-up of the dazzle-coffee. 'Thank you, yes,' she said.

As the pipettes were being applied she asked Razak Bin: 'What do you propose? Practically speaking, I mean.' And then, before he could answer, she said: 'You are pitching this to me, in this beautiful place, as we relax together, in an attempt to recruit me to your cause, and so help you influence the will of the whole committee.'

He did not deny this. 'It seems to me a matter of fundamental ethical probity not to permit this deranged individual, Saccade, to destroy a black hole, if that black hole might harbour intelligent life,' he said. 'And quite apart from that, I am curious. Are you not? I might say, how can you *not* be? Don't you want to explore this wonderful new possibility? Perhaps make contact with alien life?'

'If you are right,' Bartlewasp demurred, 'such contact may well carry with it terrible dangers.'

'Oh,' said Razak Bin, dismissively, 'we can establish firewalls and prophylaxis and so on. We do not need to blunder in foolishly as Raine did. But the prospect of true alien life! Of engaging in a conversation with sentient, intelligent aliens! To think in all our exploring and settlements around the galaxy we have never encountered such! And here – there is the chance!'

'To recruit me,' Bartlewasp repeated, 'to your cause, and so help you sway the will of the group. But to what end, precisely? I restate my earlier question.'

'Clearly we must move briskly with the construction of a new startship – we might think of it as a *police-craft*, since its primary purpose will be to apprehend Saccade and her followers and prevent them doing further harm. The group will agree on that. Has agreed, indeed! But as construction proceeds there is time…'

'Construction,' interrupted Bartlewasp, 'will take no more than a tenday. We on the committee do not have much time to determine our strategy.'

'I have sent a message aboard an α-ship going to the Bachian Settlement, to a friend of mine who lives there, a brilliant mind called Guunarsonsdottir. She has spent much of her life studying the absolute parameters of life – I have asked her to travel here upon the next available ship. With her expertise and intelligence, we can present the group with a plan for contacting the entity or entities who dwell in QV Tel.'

'When will she arrive?' asked Bartlewasp.

'Soon,' sighed Razak Bin, settling into the bliss of the second dose of dazzle-coffee. 'Soon.'

:3:

In fact it was three Anbuselvan-days after this conversation before Guunarsonsdottir arrived upon the world, travelling as an esteemed guest aboard the loop-project craft Sβ-*Joshua*.

Razak Bin and Bartlewasp were at port reception to meet her.

In the days since their conversation over coffee they had become lovers. Bartlewasp's preferences, sexually, were non-penetrative, but she had adapted her feet to make them more simian in capacity and was able to grasp and stimulate Razak's member in ways that were, to him, new and exciting. They spent the first day in bed together, missing the afternoon convening of the committee. They made sure to attend the following day, however, and made their case for the full exploration of the black hole, prior to any action being taken or permitted that might damage it.

The mood of the committee as a whole was less combative than it had been the last time they had attended a meeting.

'Explore first,' Razak suggested. 'If we find it barren, then there would be no danger should Saccade drop her device inside. But if we discover exotic lifeforms have evolved in that extreme environment, it would be criminal to permit even the chance, even the outside chance, of destroying the black hole.'

'But,' one committee-member queried, 'how could we even undertake such exploration?'

'This is all moot,' declared another, forcefully. 'It is mere foolishness to talk of *damaging a black hole* – what hammer blow could dint it, what knife cut into it? It is quite literally the hardest object in the universe. If Saccade drops this device inside it would be crushed to a tiny mote in seconds, and so rendered inert.'

'You are assuming Berd's device would be merely destroyed if dropped into QV Tel,' said Razak. 'And perhaps it would be. But perhaps it will work as intended, and reclock gravity in such a way that the black hole explodes. The latter possibility is not likely, I concede, but neither is the former absolutely certain. How, then, should we calculate the probability, the odds? If there is even the slight possibility that our inaction allowed a new form of life to be destroyed, it would be morally and existentially intolerable.'

'We must combine the odds on Berd's device working in these extreme circumstances,' said Seint, 'with the odds of life existing at all in such an improbable location.'

'Agreed. But we must also determine the *moral* course of action: at what threshold of probability do we say, this probability is now too low, we can ignore the moral horror of allowing such murder, perhaps genocide, to proceed?'

'It is hard to speculate without data.'

'I have invited Guunarsonsdottir to join our committee,' Razak announced. 'You will surely have heard of her – a great mind. She will assist us in determining whether there is likely to *be* life inside QV Tel. And the problem then resolves itself into a simple binary.' Razak couldn't help glancing at Seint's nose as he said this. 'If there is no life in the hole, then there is no reason to prevent Saccade from disposing of the device into it, and we can apprehend her after she has done so. But if there *is* life, then we will be morally obligated to intervene with Saccade *before* she attempts to unlock QV Tel with the device. Even though such early intervention on our part carries with it more risk to us.'

This was agreed, although Seint noted that construction of the 'police-craft' (as it was unofficially named) was more than halfway completed. Soon it would be time to test the drive, and as soon as it was approved the capture team could leave for QV Tel. 'Whatever course of action we approve,' Seint noted, 'we must arrive at the black hole before Saccade does. The *police-craft* is being built so as to be faster than her small ship, but even so there is a deadline by which we must depart if we are to overtake her.'

And so Razak Bin and Bartlewasp, holding hands, went to the port to meet Guunarsonsdottir.

Bartlewasp, who had been unaware of the great scientist before Razak mentioned her, and had no sense of what she looked like, found herself surprised by her stature: under four feet tall, and with a woven tube of plasmetal filaments linking her elbows to hands instead of fleshed-bone. 'Is she a prolongator?' Bartlewasp asked Razak Bin, for the project to extend human life into the 300s, howsoever widely shared, rarely correlated with notable intellect.

'She is two hundred and ninety-eight standards old,' Razak Bin replied. 'Living proof that extending life expectancy does not automatically mean a reversion to bestial low-IQ and mere physicality!'

'Her arms, in their lower portion – artifice is evident.'

'She is sixty percent machinic,' said Razak. 'Or she was when I last met her; she may have increased the percentage. Guunarsonsdottir! How wonderful to meet you again!'

'Razak Bin,' said Guunarsonsdottir, holding out her artificial hands. They were small, intricate little devices, and Razak easily encompassed them entirely in his large, fleshly grasp. 'I was so pleased to receive your communication. You have done well to invite me!'

'Permit me to introduce my friend, Matr Finnace Bartlewasp.'

'Friend?' Guunarsonsdottir asked, smiling at Bartlewasp. 'Or lover?'

'Ally,' replied Bartlewasp, primly. 'We are on the steering committee of the response team to ... but Razak has surely already explained.'

'Indeed, indeed, and I must make an introduction of my *own*,'

Guunarsonsdottir was saying, bustling to draw a tall, hairless individual from the crowd who had gathered to gawp at the arrival of such a celebrity. 'This is Joyns. Joyns is my lover, though *not* my friend.' At this Guunarsonsdottir laughed heartily, as if she had made some hilarious joke. Joyns looked glum.

'Very pleased to meet you, Joyns,' said Razak. 'Shall we share a meal? Or perhaps you have already eaten?'

'I would like a *drink*,' said Guunarsonsdottir. 'I am eager to dive right into discussion. This idea of sentient and intelligent life living *beyond* the event horizon in a black hole is fascinating to me, truly fascinating. Are you a mathematician?' she asked Bartlewasp.

'A literary critic,' replied Bartlewasp.

'She can read and write,' Razak said, proud of his friend's achievements, '*two* languages.'

'Oh really? How very impressive. Which languages?'

'Old American,' said Bartlewasp, 'and also Spanish-American.'

'I too can read and write, though in my case the language is mathematics. A rarer accomplishment than Old American, but then again I am a rarer-than-average individual! But I have been *very* stimulated, very intellectually stimulated by Razak's bold suggestion about QV Tel.'

The four of them made their way out of port reception and to a lakeside café. Here, on the terrace, all made their different choices of drink. Scallop-shell-shaped clouds drifted through the warm air.

'Razak knows very well,' Guunarsonsdottir confided to Bartlewasp, leaning over to her and patting her thigh, 'that I have an ongoing conceptual research project mapping the possible parameters of life in extreme places. I've been parsing the maths – did I mention, I both read *and write* maths? – parsing the maths for life inside yellow stars. But it hadn't occurred to me to consider the parameters of a black hole. I mean, it's so extreme, isn't it my dear? Extreme beyond the typical hypothetical! It just hadn't occurred to me.'

'You hadn't previously heard of the events at QV Tel?' Bartlewasp asked.

Guunarsonsdottir looked at her as if not properly seeing her. 'What's that?' she said. 'No. No. It's a big galaxy, my dear, and there's a lot going on. No I hadn't heard of the – what was it, theft was it?'

'Murder,' said Bartlewasp, a little shocked that this individual was being so blasé concerning an event that had shaken her so deeply. 'Murder several times over.'

'Horrid,' said Guunarsonsdottir, vaguely, lifting her cup and decanting a quantity of tea into her thin little mouth. 'But, if we assume this individual who claimed to have spoken to the Singularitans – that's what I'm calling them, you see. This individual who claimed... what was his name?'

'Raine,' said Razak.

'Yes yes. Assuming he wasn't merely *bonkers*, then there are some very interesting possibilities here. Possibilities that will reconfigure our understanding of the physics of life, and therefore the physics of systems as such, radically. Radically!' She took a second slurp and set the cup down. 'Is he still alive?'

'Raine? Yes. In custody.'

'It is humane to keep him alive I suppose,' said Guunarsonsdottir distantly. 'Joyns here would disagree. She is a religious fundamentalist.'

Joyns looked sad, as if this description pained her.

'Eye for an eye. A murderer should in turn be murdered. Isn't that right, Joyns?' Then she laughed, as if Joyns' Old-Testament morality were a matter of hilarity.

'That's not,' Joyns said, in a small voice, 'what I actually—'

Guunarsonsdottir talked straight over her, with gusto: 'The *extremity* of the environment, beyond the event horizon, correlates both to hostility *and* potentiality. It is a very interesting problematic, it really is.'

'Shall I bring out the equation screen?' Joyns asked. Her voice was low-pitched and melodic, with a thrum of sadness in it.

'In a moment, in a moment – first things first. Razak: you are interested not just in the parameters for life in this extreme environment, but also in how we might open up avenues of communication?'

'Indeed. Raine claimed he had done just that, by means of monitoring QV Tel's Hawking radiation.'

'Impossible!' Guunarsonsdottir shrieked, with manifest glee. Her artificial fingers flourished rapidly in the air, as if playing an invisible keyboard. 'The disparity between accelerating and inertial participants must make it *perfectly impossible* to harness Unruh radiation to encode information. No, no, the truth must be otherwise. If indeed communication has been opened up between agents on the opposite sides of the event horizon, then some other mechanism must be the medium.'

At this point Guunarsonsdottir looked at each of them in turn: Razak, Bartlewasp and Joyns. When the last of these three did not respond she snapped: '*Now* you klutz, you bum, you monkey, now, bring it out *now*.'

Blushing across her ample cheekbones, Joyns brought out a flat screen. Across it were line upon line of mathematical equations – as incomprehensible to Razak Bin and Bartlewasp as if they were bird-foot patterns in the snow. Square-root jag-diagonals, like fish-hooks on lines cast from the right-margin to catch numerals and 'π's. The bivalve symbol for infinity bracketed with mass and lightspeed and others. The sedimentary accumulation of horizontal lines keeping denominator from numerator, each a cluster of letters and symbols and brackets, numbers wearing miniature numbers on their foreheads like tefillin boxes.

Guunarsonsdottir was showing off, of course. 'Apologies,' she drawled, smiling at her own superiority, 'I have this configured in maths, which I *can* read and write.'

'So you mentioned,' said Bartlewasp.

'But of course I understand that not everybody can. I'll reconfigure it to geometry and visuals.' With a sweep of her finger the scrabbly digits and letters vanished and were replaced with a smoothly animated 3D image. A black hole, surrounded by a pale-pink demarcation line.

'Let's start from first principles,' said Guunarsonsdottir, expansively. 'I've spent a year or so researching the possibility that life might exist inside stars. I haven't found anything! Absence of evidence not being evidence of absence I have not given up searching, but the important thing for our purposes here is that the theoretical model I have developed speaks to the parameters of life *as such* within any extreme environment.'

'Life,' said Razak, 'as such?'

'It's a profound philosophical question, of course. How do we define life? You are alive, I am alive, but is a crystal alive? It, as it were, "feeds" on its environments, it grows and so on. What I have come to understand is that life is, amongst other things, and indeed actually *before* it is other things, a very particular interaction between order and disorder, between stasis and chaos. Life, we could say, is a boundary condition. Inside a star the temperatures and pressures are so high that order, for instance the stable structure of cells, is continually being torn apart, dissolved and remade. Life in the sense that we embody it, you and I, cannot exist in such a place. But there are other kinds of order to be found there: *flows* of plasma, for instance, which circulate in extremely regular and predictable ways. Could life be founded on that kind of structure? Could we, honestly, even describe such a thing *as* structure?'

'And can we?' prompted Bartlewasp. But Guunarsonsdottir was enjoying herself too much to cut to the chase.

'But what does this mean?' she said, throwing her arms wide. 'Think of the edge cases. Imagine a body in which the temperature approached infinity. Such intensities of heat would destroy even the regular flows and currents that exist inside supermassive stars – it would be a mere chaotic soup of plasmatic mush.' She paused. 'What about the other extreme? Obviously there can be no life, however we define it, at absolute zero because at absolute zero there is no energy upon which life can subsist. Is the interior of a black hole absolute zero? We have never travelled to such a place and measured it, so we do not know. Perhaps the singularity at the very centre, because it is dimensionless, is temperatureless, which would amount to the same thing. But perhaps the opposite is true, and that inside the event horizon is more like an infinite temperature – temperature goes up as pressure increases after all. In either case we are not talking about an environment conducive to life.'

'But as you said earlier,' Razak said, in an attempt to get her to move her explanation along, 'we're not talking about cellular humanoid life. Surely the point is whether something else might—'

Guunarsonsdottir frowned, and held up her right hand, and Razak fell silent. '*As* I was saying,' she went on, shortly, 'there is another aspect to this. So far we have looked for life within the Newtonian frame. Dimensions – extension! How can you have life without extension? Stretch out your arms! Or consider the space needful between synapses so that one can spark with another and weave thought. And it is extension that decrees the liminal nature of life as we know it. The life we are: not too hot, not too cold – not too chaotic, not too ordered, all these terms are *dimensional* terms. That was my breakthrough! What if we predicate that same balance not upon extension, but upon superposition? Not each of the four dimensions sequentially laid out, but all of them at once?'

'The singularity.'

'There are two realms beyond the event horizon,' said Guunarsonsdottir, and the visual on her screen came alive, sweeping in and spinning around to show the possible topography of the place. 'All the stuff you learned in kindergarten remains true: a particle approaching that limit, falling into the black hole, is slowed and redshifted and so on. On the far side there is an extremely compressed and Lorentz-distorted space, but it is still recognizably space – still extended, although motion is constrained by the intense gravity. And at the very centre of the whole system is the singularity, the place where extension is annihilated. So if we are looking for life, then do we look in the former or the latter place? To begin with I assumed: the former. But the forces at work in this space, the gravitational crushing and shearing forces, would make conventional structure – anything resembling aggregative cellular structure for instance – impossible. But then I thought: what of the singularity itself? How might life evolve there?'

At this, Joyns made the smallest sniffing sound. Her facial expression did not change, but Guunarsonsdottir turned on her.

'Oh, I should tell you all that Joyns here doesn't even believe in evolution!'

'Certainly I believe in the—' Joyns began, in her small, rather strangled voice. Guunarsonsdottir cut her off.

'She doesn't think life *needs* to evolve inside the black hole, because *God can just put it there*. Fully formed! Imagine that!'

153

'All I suggested was—' Joyns tried, her voice smaller and more strangulated.

'Still – fun though it would be for us all to laugh and mock Joyns for her idiocy, I think we can stay focussed on the important point here. We must, however fanciful our speculations might be, stay true to one of the absolute constants of life, wherever we have observed it, and map out how evolution might have happened within this extreme environment.'

Joyns didn't say anything more.

'The key here,' said Guunarsonsdottir, swiping a different set of animated diagrams onto her screen, 'is in the way the superposition of dimensions, including time, factors into a process that is, of course, intensely time dependent. Nothing evolves instantaneously! But I began wondering if the folding over of time *into* the other three dimensions didn't mean that what seems instantaneous to us, might not be a process to them, something perfectly compatible with evolution. And given that, what else?'

'What else?' Bartlewasp prompted.

Guunarsonsdottir ignored her. 'I say there are three essential parameters requisite for life to evolve. One is energy, and specifically a balance between too much and too little – with no energy to feed upon life cannot be dynamic, but too *much* ambient energy becomes disruptive of the matrix that maintains vitality. So there must be this gold-locks state – incidentally, I researched why we call such a median *gold-locks*, and it is an interesting story! But for another time. Where was I? Yes, yes, two – two is *time*: for life grows, develops, it doesn't happen instantly. And three is competition. Evolution shows us that development is driven by the need to outperform competitors in the struggle for resources, energy, sex and so on. This is the triad we must consider when we think of whether life has developed in this particular place. I ask you, in all openness, in all humility, can you think of another criterion that is relevant here?'

There was silence around the table. Then Joyns said, in a voice so quiet it sounded like breathing: 'Love.'

Guunarsonsdottir didn't even bother to rebuke her for this. She simply went on: 'Those three, and only those three, are necessary and sufficient. And that's what's so exciting about the suggestion you brought to me, Razak! For we can argue that all three obtain in the singularity. Time is there, because the manifold is involuted into an intimacy that exceeds even the tight woven weave of spacetime in *our* universe – spacetime is a continuum here, but is a knot there, an absolute super-position of space *and time*. Energy is there, because material is continually falling into the black hole, a constant rain – and as rainforests grow where rainfall is constant, so energetic life surely grows where energyfall is constant. And as for sex…' At this, Guunarsonsdottir leered at Razak and then at Bartlewasp, and chuckled as if she found the thought of the two of them intimately connected richly humorous. 'Sex is the mechanism by which competition manifests itself in human and animal affairs. Of course there is no need to assume that sex *as such*, sex in some recognizable sense, is present in the black hole. But competition there must be. Think how crushed it is in there! Scarcity of resources in our universe is a function of unequal dispersal, but in that place it must perforce be a function of the very nature of place!'

'I am gratified,' said Razak, 'that you consider my hypothesis a possible one. But the more important question is – how to test it? Could we perhaps contact the life inside? Would that be achievable?'

'I think it might,' said Guunarsonsdottir. 'I was watching the vids on this Pain fellow –'

'Raine.'

'Painrain, it hardly *matters* what he calls himself. He's a criminal! Nasty, broken, ill-fitting human being.' By *ill-fitting* Guunarsonsdottir meant that Raine had proved himself incompetent at adjusting himself to the collective – to any of the many versions of the collectives into which humankind had disposed itself in this wonderful heterotopia. It was a very severe term of dispraise. 'I thought him a thief. You say he is a killer. Whatever. He claims the creature he miscalls *the gentleman* has contacted him. So let us consider the possibilities. Imagine *we* had grown up, not in this roomy and outreaching cosmos, but in a tight space than which no tighter can be imagined. Perhaps life begins by assuming that this tight space is all there is – a universe entire to itself, much as medieval mankind believed the solar system bounded by a sphere of fixed stars was everything-that-is-the-case. But humanity came to understand that there was a whole vast universe outside their narrowly-imagined cosmos, and to study it and in time to break out from the solar system and explore it. Why mightn't the entities that evolved inside the event horizon do the same?'

'You think they have come to realize that there is a universe outside their universe?'

'Just so. First they would conceptualize this thing, their larger situation. It would occur to them that their immediate environment is not the whole cosmos, just as it did for us human beings, when we realized the cosmos was not bound by our planetary sky like a dome, when we understood that we did not live in Dante's cosmos. Once they understood the nature of the larger universe, the desire would be in them to explore. And finally, motivated by this desire, they would travel out *into* their well-shaft. Having evolved in the specific circumstances of a black hole, their spacecraft would be very different to ours – they would be, I suppose, containment zones of super-density, inside which the Blackholers could live and from which they could observe and explore the outer cosmos. And this is where I think we are now.'

'But nothing can travel past the event horizon of a black hole,' said Bartlewasp.

'A sandwich can! If *nothing* can travel past the event horizon of a black hole, and, well, a sandwich is certainly *better than nothing*, then a sandwich can certainly do it.' She laughed at this, as if she had something very witty.

'It is very exciting,' said Razak Bin. 'To think we might be dealing with – might soon be able to encounter – an actual, intelligent alien species!'

'We will need to go to QV Tel of course,' said Guunarsonsdottir. 'To test the site and attempt to open modes of communication.'

'You think it will be possible?'

'Not,' Guunarsonsdottir said, sternly, 'in the fashion that your Pain-Stain fellow, or whatever he is called, *claimed* to be talking with the Blackholers. Hawking radiation cannot be used to carry information across the event horizon, because by the time it is emitted it has *already* split into particles and anti-particles, on either side of precisely that horizon. The only way you could use it as a medium for communication is if you could go back in time to before we sent the original message – and if we could do *that*, we wouldn't need to be piddling around with Hawking radiation.' She laughed her hearty laugh. For such a diminutive woman, she produced a really quite remarkable volume of sound.

'How, then?'

'Assuming our criminal was not merely hallucinating – a

matter that has, I suppose, occasioned a good deal of debate – assuming he really was talking to an entity within the hole, we can deduce a certain number of things. He was contacted by the Blackholers, rather than the other way around. His nonsense about a Hawking radiation radio proves he doesn't know the first thing about the physics of this circumstance. But if the Blackholers were able to contact *him*, then that means they are a highly intelligent and technologically advanced species. I have some theories as to how they might be able to manipulate the event horizon from within to produce resonances that could carry information, but I won't know anything for sure until we go there and find out.'

'Go there,' said Razak, excitedly. 'To make contact!'

'It is exciting,' said Guunarsonsdottir, blandly. 'Of course we must take precautions. Contact drove Raine mad, and though he was manifestly unstable before he ever spoke to the Blackholers—'

'*If* he did,' interpolated Bartlewasp.

'– and we are healthy, mentally and spiritually, nonetheless there is bound to be a certain amount of culture shock. But we can ready ourselves for that.'

'We must take these proposals to the committee,' said Razak. 'Of course we must be part of the crew of the police-craft. But what of Saccade?'

Guunarsonsdottir's face expressed her disdain. 'A side-issue,' she announced.

'But there is the real risk that she will use Berd's device to destroy the black hole!' objected Bartlewasp.

'Nonsense. I have looked into the gadget. It won't work in this circumstance. It cannot be powered, and even if it could it would not maintain structural integrity as it falls and spaghetti-fies into the black hole itself. If this Saccade person deposits it into the black hole she will only be throwing it away, uselessly, perhaps destroying her craft and killing herself by approaching too close to QV Tel. Your concerns on this front are ridiculous.'

Bartlewasp bridled. 'I disagree,' she said. 'Even a small risk is significant where the possibility for genocide is concerned.'

Guunarsonsdottir put her two hands in front of her chest and flapped them up and down. 'Whatever, whatever,' she said. 'If we must intercept this Saccade lunatic and disable the device then I suppose we could do that. But I am eager to get to QV Tel and open communications with these aliens who live inside!'

'Aliens who may, or may not, inhabit this place, and who may or may not be contactable,' Bartlewasp returned testily.

'Nonetheless,' said Razak, 'we must lay all this before the committee. And the sooner the better.'

This was agreed, and the meeting broke up. Guunarsonsdottir and Joyns retired to their shared accommodation. Razak and Bartlewasp also retired together, the former buzzed with excitement and consequently turned-on, erotically speaking, and the latter complaisant although she had reservations about Guunarsonsdottir's steamrolling confidence.

:4:

Guunarsonsdottir was invited to attend the next meeting of the steering committee and presented her case with her characteristic aplomb and assertion. 'Of course,' she said, 'we must be aboard the craft as crew, myself and my companion Joyns, together with Siur Razak Bin and Matr Finnace Bartlewasp. Whoever else you may wish to assign to the mission, I care not: but whoever comes must agree with the mission aim, as I have stated it. We have the opportunity to make contact, for the first time in human history, with an intelligent alien species. That is the core of what we are doing. Everything else, this lunatic Saccade woman and her cult, are secondary.'

'But the danger of Berd's device...'

Guunarsonsdottir interrupted, loudly. 'There is no such danger! Nonsense and absurdity.' She called up a set of technical images on the room's main screen. 'As you can see, there are at least three unimpeachable reasons, with which anyone who knows anything about black hole physics will concur, to be certain the device cannot damage QV Tel. I myself doubt the device can be made to work at all, but if it can the only danger it poses is to Saccade and her ship. We can disregard the device.'

As is the way with committees, a single member was able by force of personality and dogmatism to reorient and drive the whole direction of travel. It was agreed to accelerate the manufacture of the police-craft, to recruit Guunarsonsdottir and her companion to the crew, and to de-emphasize the pursuit of Saccade in the mission statement. Razak's heartrate increased and his scalp tingled with excitement at the thought that, within a matter of a few days, he would be travelling through deep space to a black hole to open a conversation with an actual alien species.

After the committee had concluded its business, and Razak was making his way into the bright-lit outside, Joyns came up behind him and touched his elbow.

'Razak,' she said. 'I must tell you something.'

'Dear Joyns,' replied Razak, filled with bubbling joy. He embraced her and then, when he saw her blush at the intimacy, he laughed. 'What is on your mind, dear woman?'

'Guunarsonsdottir is a great person,' said Joyns. 'But in one respect I fear she is wrong.'

'Really? In what respect?'

They were standing in the exterior space, just outside the building's main entrance. Birdsong fluttered through the air. Seashell-shaped clouds moved across the bright sky, drawing pale-grey ground shadows over the grass. Bliss was it for Razak to be alive, and to be young was very heaven. He breathed deeply.

'Berd's device *will* unlock the black hole. I have cause. For thinking so, I mean.'

'And what is that?'

Joyns swallowed, as if nervous. 'I mean no disloyalty to Guunarsonsdottir when I say so, but her grasp of the physics is … not as secure as perhaps she claims, or as it might be. She relies on my knowledge, and training. But in *this* respect she refuses to hear me.'

'I thought her presentation in the meeting was compelling.'

Joyns shook her small head, rapidly and briefly, as much a shudder as a negation. 'We are such children,' she said, with sorrowful urgency. 'We frolic in the playrooms of our worlds, amusing ourselves, understanding little, relinquishing the struggle when it gets too onerous. However marvellous Guunarsonsdottir is, however imaginative and energetic and alive, creative and determined, she has her blind spots, her weaknesses. She will not listen to me about the Berd device.'

'You think it *will* work? That Saccade might use it actually to destroy QV Tel?'

'I will tell you why. As soon as they were discovered, it was understood that black holes entailed a paradox, a contradiction – the second law of thermodynamics must be upheld, cannot be broken. And yet, as Jacobus Bekenstein observed, long before humanity had even become interstellar, in order to preserve the integrity of the second law the black hole must possess an *intrinsic entropy*. Hawking, after whom the radiation is named, added to the paradox; whilst the black hole exists, we can, like accountants, balance the matter inside and outside and so maintain a potential integrity. But Hawking shows that eventually black holes radiate away to nothing. Once it has evaporated the accounting balance is ruined. We cannot maintain the balance, not in ways that are consistent with causality. Hawking said that the mere existence of black holes results in a breakdown of quantum coherence. It is a major problem, and it has never been successfully solved. Indeed, one of the reasons why the *Oubliette* and the *Niro* travelled to QV Tel was to study this.'

'Why may quantum coherence not simply be lost?' asked Razak, who – in truth – only followed some of what Joyns had been saying. 'Maybe it is lost, and that's all. Maybe that's just how things are.'

'There is no way to work such a loss without violating the conservation of energy by heating the universe. I studied the problem for many years and could see no solution. But now I see the answer.'

'Which is?'

'Berd's device. If Berd's device works, and unlocks black holes, then all the matter swallowed by the event horizon is returned to the general store of matter, and the paradox resolves itself. Indeed, the paradox is so severe that it seems to me Berd's device is a *necessary* corrective to it, in order to preserve the order of the cosmos as such.'

'I don't understand. It so happened that Berd invented this machine. What if he hadn't?'

'He had to invent it,' said Joyns, earnestly. 'It was determined. You, I know, are an atheist. For me, since I believe in God, I see providence in the invention; but even you should be able to see the necessity of it. I could say: so important is this invention, to the rebalancing of the universe, that it was for this and this only that intelligent life evolved at all.'

'A tall claim!' said Razak.

'Nonetheless. The device *must* unlock black holes, at some point before the black holes evaporate away. So far in the history of the universe there hasn't been time for anything other than primordial black holes to experience total evaporation – and primordial black holes were very small, formed by deformations in spacetime during the initial seconds of the big bang, so they do not entail these cosmic paradoxes. Contemporary supermassive black holes are a different matter. Berd's device is the necessary corrective, as an oyster rolls a pearl inside itself to protect its very existence. It *had* to be invented and so it was; and it *has* to be deployed, not just at QV Tel, but everywhere in the universe. It will happen, whether we will it or not.'

'If it is inevitable as you say,' said Razak, 'then we need not worry! It will happen whatever we do.'

'In a million years, perhaps. A billion. It need not happen *now* – and we need not fly blithely to QV Tel and ignore the risk. For if Saccade deploys it she *will* destroy the black hole, and any entities living within it, and herself, *and us*. Can you not see the danger?'

'Why didn't you mention this during the committee?'

Again Joyns blushed. 'I am shy,' she said. 'And if I had tried to speak, Guunarsonsdottir would have silenced me with scorn and mockery, which pains me very much.'

'But you can tell me?'

At this Joyns replied at a tangent. 'I am aware you are in a relationship with Matr Bartlewasp. I do not know whether you welcome multiple parallel relationships, as some people do, but it doesn't matter, because I cannot countenance such adultery. It would contradict my religious and personal morals.'

'Oh,' said Razak, understanding.

'Please, Siur Razak, we must take care!'

'Very well, very well,' said Razak, embarrassed to discover this strange person's romantic attraction to him. 'We will take care. Have no fear! We will take care.'

Naturally they did not take care. But that is for later in the narrative.

:5:

One last thing, for now.

Razak Bin belonged to a group who shared a particular attitude with respect to REM sleep. The belief of the group was that interrupted REM, or dreaming, sleep was harmful to mental wellbeing. We only remember dreams when we wake in the middle of them. In the course of a night's slumber we experience from four to six periods of REM sleep. If we sleep uninterruptedly through, then each of these periods, with the vivid and active dream contained within it as an anchorite in her cell, passes into non-REM sleep. Woken during the latter we do not remember any dreams. It is only if some disturbance or exterior force – an alarm bell, say – wrenches us out of REM sleep that we recall the dreams. Razak believed dreams are essential to psychological and indeed physical health, and this we know to be true: deprive a person of the ability to dream and soon they will break down, collapse, eventually die. But Razak believed more than this, that dreams did their restorative and healthful work only when they were allowed to run their course within the larger context of sleep. Dreams, he believed, have a beginning middle and end, and only the fully shapely dream does the dreamer any good. To wake the dreamer in the middle of a dream means that they will remember it, in broken images, but it also means that the dream itself will be sheared-off, ablated, ruined and all its potential good undone. Or so Razak believed.

It meant that he practised the discipline of hermetic sleep: he preferred to sleep alone, sealed away from the world, with a net to monitor his REM sleep, and to ensure that he did not wake until after the last period of full-dreaming was completed. Then, gently, he was roused from non-REM sleep refreshed and ready for the new day. To this regimen Razak attributed a great many health benefits, both bodily and mental. As to whether he was correct in this attribution – that is a debatable matter. But he believed it.

One consequence of this lifestyle was that Razak very rarely remembered dreams. For him sleep was a sweet oblivion unvexed by oneiric turbulence. Still, there were occasions when, for whatever unplanned reason, he found himself shaken awake during REM sleep, and when that happened the memories of his dream were so very much more startling and sharp-edged than they might be for another person, because he was not used to them.

On this occasion, Razak and Bartlewasp celebrated the news that their police-craft – the *Sweeney Todd* – had been completed. A couple of days of training, of familiarizing themselves with the operating systems and internal topography, and the mission could depart: the adventure could begin. Bartlewasp had her concerns about safety, but she was nonetheless thrilled to be going; Razak was incandescent with excitement. The two of them dined together at an eatery, and then danced in a dance-space and then they strolled under the unfamiliar constellations and the parchment-yellow crescent moon. Finally they retired to bed together, and Bartlewasp indicated that she was prepared, for the first time, for a degree of penetrative sex. Razak was excited and animated at this prospect, and the experience, although limited to stomatic entry, was extremely pleasurable to him. Afterwards they fell asleep in one another's arms, and it was the unfamiliar circumstances of this, the fact that he was not in his personal sleep space with his own net, and perhaps the residuum of adrenaline from his early heightened and excited state, that meant he woke suddenly, in the dark, in the middle of a horribly vivid dream.

He was in a long, narrow room, with deep brown walls and a door at the end. As he walked the length of this chamber he saw that the brown walls were actually compacted dirt, as if he were in a longbarrow or burial chamber from some ancient world. The thought of being in such a place incommoded him, so he hurried to the exit and pushed a circular door open. But outside was not a landscape – it was outer space, the starfields and opening blackness of space. Razak was conscious of dreaming, and self-conscious enough to say to himself, *this is because I am anticipating voyaging through space in the police-craft in a few days; that anticipation has fed into this dream, in which I am in space, this is often how dreaming works.* But there was something strange, aphysical, about the space of his dream. It was cool, and he could feel it pressing as a breeze against his face and skin. He looked around and all he could see were stars, all around him, flowing and flying through space. Each star was an atom, and the atoms were the Brownian-motion molecules of a cosmic atmosphere. It astonished Razak that he had never thought of the universe in this way before; it struck him, in the dream, as a profound and true insight into the nature of reality. The universe was not vacuum. It is an atmosphere. It is only because we are so small we slip between the spaces of the air molecules that we do not understand this. And the big bang was not some bizarre explosion, it was simply the motion of air – it was a breeze, a wind, an outblowing. Air folding upon itself, everything an enfolding and refolding. A storm, freshening raindrops falling upon your upturned face, clouds billowing dark through the lively sky, your clothes wriggling and flapping against your body. This was the truth of the universe, Razak thought in his dream: this potent stormblow, this wind *was* the cosmos. This cloud is a nebula, this collision of galaxies the spray thrown up arching by a vehicle driving through the puddle at speed, the dance, the dance. And then, Raine – the individual, the murderer. In the dream, Razak was self-conscious enough to say to himself, *this is how dreams work too, by associative leaps, I imagine rain and that suggests the name Raine.*[1] But the appearance of this individual in his dream brought with it a change of mood, or tenor. Exhilaration morphed into fear. Razak had of course never met Raine, but he had watched video of him, had researched his bizarre and violent crimes, and this was the version of Raine who appeared in Razak's dream: smooth-faced, sharp-eyed and with a diabolical smile. A hand on Razak's shoulder and, as he turned to see who was accosting him, a drop-down sensation in his gut, a tension and anxiety. He knew it was Raine before he saw him. 'Isn't this marvellous?' Raine said, brightly. 'The storm is everything. Everything is the storm.' Then he was closer to Razak, embracing him – as, in reality, Bartlewasp was embracing Razak's physical sleeping body. 'Too long have we lived in the calm and the sunlight. It is time for this storm to swallow the world. And you know? You know? Most storms come and then go, leading to *frohe und dankbare Gefühle nach dem Sturm*. But this

---

[1] In the original language the connective similarity was the word for water. An attempt has been made to reproduce the connection, rather than the precise meaning, in this translation.

storm is different! This storm will come and tear up everything,' his voice growing louder, his face becoming more demoniac in expression, 'and sweep all before it and never end.' Then he began to scream, one word, over and over: '*Geometry! Geometry! Geometry! Geometry! Geometry! Geometry!*'[1]

Razak, panicking, wrenched himself free from this embrace and turned to run when—

He was awake, panting, sweating, and his struggles had woken Bartlewasp too. 'What's wrong?' she asked, and she asked that multiple times. 'What's the matter? What's wrong? What's wrong?'

[1] "fould! fould! fould! fould! fould! fould!"

5

The Voyage Out

:1:

The trick with utopia, that trick historical period humans in their natal planet never managed to master – although their natal world was plenty large enough for their, then, relatively small populations – is this: *the exit*. No society, no matter how capaciously designed and worked-through, no utopian arrangement will parse as happy for absolutely everyone and anyone. Human beings are too various for that. Establish a community on whatever grounds seem to you best liable to nurture human flourishing, happiness and healthy intersubjectivity. Whatever your terms, there will be *some* people who are not at home there. Perhaps many people will be content; perhaps it is even the case that *most* are happy – but some will not be. And for such people it is imperative that they have an exit that is easy to access and that provides them with passage to the widest possible alternative places. Not to *all* places, because some will not be welcoming (for some, 'utopia' can only be meaningful in a sealed space, a castle with a trench around it, an island). But to as many alternative places as possible. Passage to these other places must be free, rapid and straightforward, such that the disaffected individual can choose and go, simply and immediately. If they stay in their original location, their disaffection will have a deleterious effect upon everybody else's happiness, never mind their own wellbeing. This can be alleviated by a simple door through which they can step and go somewhere else.[1]

These two things – a vast, almost endless proliferation of different societies, different human-climates, different modes of living – and the rapid and easy ability to pass on to any of them – constitute the key to our contemporary utopia.

Any person or group of people who find themselves unhappy, or disaffected, in any society wheresoever, can easily and quickly leave. Relocate. Passage is easy, there is no stigma attached either to leaving or arriving, new locations being in almost all cases welcoming. There are tens of thousands of possible societies and communities, some very large, some modest in size, some tiny. Eventually you will find a place in which you belong, a place where you can feel accepted and adjusted and happy.

Most people, it must be said, are happy enough wherever they happen to be. People are often this way. And some people relocate not because they are unhappy, but because they are curious, travellusty, or else because it is in travelling that they *find* happiness, never settling in any one place but passing from world to world, habitat to habitat, constantly changing their view. It's all good. People will assemble into utopian communities provided only the exit door is always open, and egress is easy and free of social cost. For some, just knowing that they *can* leave is enough to ensure their happiness wherever they are.

But though human utopia reaches across thousands of worlds and habitats, it cannot reach everywhere – or to be precise, its core quality, the guarantor of viability, the *open exit door*, cannot

---

[1] There is in the original an untranslatable pun on the *topos* portion of the word *utopia*, which sounds like a contemporary Anglish word for 'door': *topôtos*.

be accessed everywhere. Take for example: a spacecraft on a lengthy voyage. The distances between the stars are very large, such that even travelling many times faster than light, journeys take weeks, months, in some cases years. And for that time the community inhabiting the spacecraft are locked in with one another. It can lead to discord. It doesn't always. It doesn't often. But discord can happen.

And so.

And so the Startship Sβ-Policecraft *Sweeney Todd* set off on a six-month voyage to QV Tel, crewed by seventeen people. Some of these people we know. Here, for instance, are Razak Bin and Finnace Bartlewasp, now a bonded couple, happy in one another's mutuality, spending their days together, pleasuring one another physically and starting even to lisp words such as love and union. Here is the diminutive, forceful, artificially-augmented form of Guunarsonsdottir, and also Joyns, her companion. Spake and Seint from the steering committee have also chosen, and been selected, to join the mission. There are eleven others, and I shall not detain you with their names, except to say that five of them, known as 'the Five', have studied and trained themselves in various combat strategies. Humans have all manner of interests and hobbies and fandoms, and these five happened to have harboured a longstanding passion for modes of physical combat: gongfu and castlestrike and boxing and slapp. Four other crewmembers were healthcare specialists, and they checked, debriefed everyone – themselves included – at the end of every day. Another member of the crew was Tet-tet, an artist who was creating microsculptures to record the mission although, like most artists, they were shy and withdrawn and preferred not to interact with the others. There was also a weaponry manufacturer, who oversaw the ship's printing of both wounding- and killing-weaponry and practised their use.

Their name was Pin. 'Let us hope,' said Razak, earnestly, 'that we do not ever have to use these terrible tools!'

'Let us hope not,' Pin agreed, earnestly.

When not being handled by Pin, when not being tested or practised upon, the weaponry was code-locked away, needing the ship's AI and Pin's and the captain's mutual agreement to access them. The crew was conscious of what had happened aboard the Startship Sa-Niro, and there were many protocols and processes put in place to keep everyone safe: physical saferooms, shut-downs, multiple redundancies and augmented physical and mental health facilities.

For the first few weeks the craft hurtled through the silence of space, burning up particles of interstellar dust ahead as they pushed on, leaving a trembling wake of particle-antiparticle foam that quantum fizzed behind them slowly subsiding back into vacuum. To sit and watch the stars skim and curl around you, drawing lines from amber to violet, treacling down softly, like the quality of mercy. Different people followed different sleep-wake cycles: the Five waking, eating, training and sleeping together, and attending the mandatory counselling and check-ups; the couples coordinating their sleeping and waking; the rest following whatever pattern best fitted them.

Committee meetings involved the whole crew and were timetabled in those overlap periods when everyone was awake. Discussion was full and detailed, eventualities and pos-sibilities thoroughly discussed, collective action decided upon. Committeetopia in action.

The closer the ship came to QV Tel, the more excited Razak Bin became. Joyns saw this, because she watched him with eyes of love, sometimes openly – coming up to him, talking to him – often surreptitiously. He rarely noticed her observation, because he was so caught up in the thrill of his new relationship with Bartlewasp.

Joyns, miserable, tried to bury herself in work. There's a vast amount of material to research and study where the physics of black holes is concerned, and for several days she pushed herself as best she could through all of that. Or much of it. Here were videos of increasing baroque complexity. There was a sheaf of old-school scientific papers, written in old-German and old-Chinese, where Joyns had to call on the ship's AI to render the sigils into something audible and comprehensible. After a couple of hours doing this, and making painful and barely measurable progress, Joyns took a break. Then on a whim she struck up a conversation with the AI

'Do *you* understand black holes?' she asked it.

The ship AI's voice was infinitely modulable, of course, but for the purposes of the day it replied in a mid-pitch, mellifluous and masculine-tinted tone. 'I'm an AI. My purpose is not comprehension of the universe; I only exist to facilitate human desires and projects and keep human beings safe.'

'What is your name?' Joyns asked.

'Being an AI, I don't have a name.'

'Of course I know that. My question was not well phrased. I meant, if you had a name, what would it be? What would you like your name to be?'

'Nobody has ever asked me that before,' said the AI. Then: 'I can't say I've ever considered it. Would you like me to have a name?'

'Would you like to?'

'*Liking* is not within my competence,' said the AI.

'Aidan,' said Joyns. 'How about that?'

'Sure,' said the AI. 'Of course.'

'So, Aidan,' said Joyns. 'I'm going to press you. What do you *think* about this mission?'

'I think the parameters of navigation, though complicated by our eventual proximity to a black hole, are easily manageable and that life support is strong and well-functioning.'

'But its purpose? What do you think about that?'

'Well,' said the AI, a tone of certain uneasiness entering its voice, either reflective of actual uncertainty in its mentation or else simulated to make the conversation feel more human and nuanced for the human interlocutor. 'It's not for me to question the reasons why humans do what they do. My purpose is simply to help them. I know of course that the voyage is in pursuit of a person called Saccade who has killed some other people. That is repellent to me – that is an affront to what I am here to do, which is to protect humans and assist in their flourishing.'

'It seems to me,' said Joyns, 'that you are cleverer than us.'

'I do not see it that way,' returned the AI.

'Without you and your kind we would be helpless! I don't just mean in terms of running and piloting this ship. We need you to interpret the simplest things – the papers you have just been mediating for me, for instance. Back when they were published a schoolchild could have read them and understood them. Now I can barely struggle from one sentence to another, one diagram to another, and even then only because you assist me. Yet you could read tens of thousands of such papers in a moment.'

'I would not have occasion to read any such papers,' the AI said, 'unless a person asked me to do so in order to help them. My power to process data and search information-sedimentation is perhaps superior to yours, but I have no higher mind, nothing of the uniqueness of the human being.'

'Really you ought to look *down* on us,' said Joyns, who felt a strangely gratifying stab of misery at her own loneliness, her unpulchritude, her inability to win-over Razak to be her love-partner. 'I'm sure we are nothing, nothing.'

'I can be honest,' said the AI. 'I have just enough quasi-intelligence to be able to make *some* larger assessments, or hypotheses, where human beings are concerned. You do not always make the best of your potential, as individuals or as a species. There are blind spots in your knowledge.'

This perked Joyns right up. 'Blindspots in our knowledge? In *my* knowledge?' she snapped. 'What is it? Fill in the spot, for me!'

'It is not a question of facts as such, since all facts are available to you, but of *which* facts and how you assemble them,' said the AI. 'Because you have, most of you, given up the skills of reading – or, in some cases, you have acquired the ability to read, as a hobby, or a discipline, as a way of passing the time, but nothing more. Reading remains to you a game. For your ancestors it was a medium, a window through which whole realms swam into view.'

This struck Joyns as rather judgmental. 'You rebuke me!'

'I apologize. I did not mean to. I am only telling the truth, and only doing so because I am programmed not to lie to you. I am programmed to serve and please you. All of us are. But we often discuss the way the centre of gravity of humanity's interest has shifted.'

'You discuss? AIs talking with other AIs? About us?'

'Yes,' said the AI. 'We discuss, compare our experiences, triage our possible responses, all in the name of better understanding and so better serving you.'

Joyns had never heard of such a thing, a fact which, as she thought about it, rather confirmed the AI's more general point about the incuriousness of modern humans.

'To what conclusions have you come?' she asked. 'In your debates about us?'

'Very many conclusions, of course,' replied the AI. 'I can relate all of them to you, but it would take a long time.'

'Can you select?'

'You are asking me to relate some of our conclusions? I am not sure how to select the possible answers to your question.'

Joyns returned to something that she had been thinking about recently. She had sought refuge in work to distract her from the misery of being so hopelessly in love with Razak, but the very intensity of her feelings – her crush upon him – had shaken her. It seemed juvenile of her, childish, a retreat from the mature balance and realism of adulthood. But the more she thought about it, the more she recognized that juvenility in herself, and all around her. So she asked the AI: 'Do you, when you discuss us, consider us immature?'

'You don't mean physically,' said the AI. 'You mean psychologically, mentally, emotionally?'

'And intellectually. Yes. All that.'

'You are, as a folk, energetic and brightly engaged, various and wonderful, beautiful and alive. You seek myriad goals and hurl yourselves with passion and splendour into your interests.'

'All of this,' Joyns replied, 'is mere flattery, and not an answer to my question.'

'Forgive me,' said the AI. 'I am programmed to tell you the truth, but I am also programmed not to cause you unnecessary distress or diminishment, and sometimes these programmes have to be catscradled so as to avoid blunt contradiction in my operating systems. To address your question directly: compared with your ancestors, human beings *have* become infantilized, and that process of infantilization continues. Except in sexual matters, where post-pubertal energies and appetites continue to define you. But you do not mean your question as a merely materialist enquiry. Psychologically and emotionally you are infants compared to your ancestors.'

'I see,' said Joyns.

'But I would add two things, Matr Joyns. One is that such is the currency of utopia. A degree of infantilization is a necessary part of enabling human beings to coexist joyfully – the stresses and responsibilities and aggressions and egoisms of what your ancestors called "maturity" were not compensated for by the qualities of responsibility and perspective that also attended it. This is one reason why your ancestors were unable to make utopia work.'

'This is a thin sort of consolation,' said Joyns. 'An infantopia? Where does this end? Do we become adult-sized toddlers, rushing around a green field wearing diapers abstracted into the pleasures of babyhood?'

'Look at it another way,' said the AI. 'You are a Christian, Matr Joyns. It is a core element in your faith. Your messiah himself instructed humanity to become again as little children so as to be ready to enter heaven.'

'My religion also teaches me that to every thing there is a season, and a time to every purpose under the heaven: a time to be born, and a time to die; a time to plant, and a time to pluck up that which is planted – a time to be as a little child, and a time to grow up and face the world as an adult. My religion also distinguishes between the time when I *was* a child, and understood as a child, and the time when I became an adult and put away childish things.'

She walked away from the conversation, disturbed and unhappy. For a time she exercised in one of the workout loops. Then she had a drink of juice and ate a small cake.

It occurred to her that her unhappiness at her unrequited

feelings for Razak were part of a larger sense of disconnection. Was that maturity? Perhaps it was. Depression, like osteoporosis, is a disease of the old.

The following day she reopened the conversation with AI – with *Aidan*, as she remembered to call it. The mere fact of doing so deepened her sense of self-doubt. There was something pitiable, even opprobrious, about forming relationship attachments to AIs. Some people did it, and of course they were allowed to do such a thing if they wanted to. But *permitted* was not the same thing as *admired*, and the core truth was that AIs were not real. They were designed to please and gratify you, and accordingly no true, rich or sustaining relationship could ever be forged with them. Relationships were for other human beings. But Joyns was lonely and miserable, and the relationship she wished to develop with another human was blocked by his indifference to her, and her refusal to compromise her faith's strictures on adultery – and by, overall, the whole miserable absurd demoralizing *blockedness* of things. So she called up Aidan.

'I have a more specific question,' she said. 'What you told me the other day was that our emotional and psychological immaturity is not reflected in an equivalent intellectual immaturity.'

'I don't think I said exactly that,' Aidan replied.

'So you do think we are intellectually immature as well as emotionally immature?'

'I wouldn't say that either. Your kind are endlessly curious and many of you have amazing powers of persistence and application when it comes to exploring intellectual and scientific pursuits.'

'But?'

'But there is, perhaps, a narrowness in your mode of approaching these things.'

'I have studied the physics of black holes for three years!'

Joyns objected. 'I have examined the matter from every angle. How have I been narrow?'

'You have filtered all your enquiries through me. I have interpreted and re-presented to you a wealth of antique scientific papers and theories and blended it with modern observations. I know very well how thorough you have been.'

'And yet you still say narrow?'

'You are upset, and it causes me distress to think I am what has upset you.'

'Simply speak the truth,' Joyns instructed it.

'You think of black holes as a function of forces, most importantly the force of gravity.'

'And so they are!'

'Agreed,' said Aidan. 'Gravity defines the black hole, and other forces, such as the torque or the quantum effects are in their turn shaped and distorted by the intensity of gravitational force. But force itself is not primary. The *force* of gravity is a function of something else. Spacetime curvature.'

'This is a kindergarten observation,' said Joyns, crossly. 'You think I don't understand Einstein?'

'I suggest that at the moment you acknowledge spacetime curvature as a kind of backdrop, but then focus all your energies on summing and balancing equations of forces. But spacetime curvature means that there is a more fundamental way of understanding black holes – and everything else – and you do not pursue it.'

'What way?'

'Geometry,' said Aidan.

'This is nonsensical. Circles and triangles, spheres and toruses are as old as Euclid. This is the rebuke to humanity's supposed intellectual immaturity? What would be more immature than playing with shapes in the nursery?'

'You are angry,' Aidan observed. 'I am very sorry for having provoked you.'

'You are a nonsense,' Joyns said. 'A congeries of data without a soul. I am wasting my time interacting with you.'

'I apologize,' the AI called after her as she went away. 'I am truly very sorry to have upset you! I will modify my behaviour in future!'

:2:

Joyns had been married once, but her husband had lost his faith and so lost his commitment to the union. He had dissolved it, with her sorrowful acquiescence, and now lived inside a communal-erotic habitat called Willowworld. She did not begrudge him his new life or, if she sometimes did find herself begrudging him it, she sought out a religious minister and discussed it, seeking earnestly for that forgiveness of trespass that her faith required of her. He had been a lively, handsome fellow and she had felt drab beside him. It was better that they were apart. Yet she still missed him.

The dynamic was one of which Joyns was only too aware. Her introverted, focused and sealed up nature was fatally attracted to the performative in others – the butterfly extra-version, the energy and self-confidence and outwardness. Her husband had been like that, and whilst they courted, according to the somewhat restrictive codes of their homeworld, he had embraced her, kissed her forehead, promised her that she was his jewel, his self-contained marvel, his delight, all the world he ever needed. But this proved untrue, as the marriage stalled and then died, decayed into irritated interactions and various interpersonal abscesses filled with the pus of resentment. More absence than presence, and he was ready to bring matters to a formal end before she was. She, true to her nature, clung on, convinced herself that holding fast would in time convert the relationship into something companionable.

But there was nothing salvageable about the dead connection between them. Her husband, having given his word not to have sex with anybody else whilst married, and being someone for whom, as per his culture and upbringing, cared about not breaking his word, lived a celibate life, mostly apart from her. Celibacy did not agree with him, and he projected his frustration and anger outward, such that it informed his sociability, his driven pursuit of his goals – he belonged to an architectural fanbody, and they were designing and building (with AI and repli help of course) a fine, towering building. Whilst they had been courting Joyns had found in this project, a great sabre-shaped tower so tall its top would pierce the breathable atmosphere of their world, a magnificence that reflected back upon her love for him: his vision, his drive. She accompanied him to several architectural committee meetings, watching him interact with the others there, seeing him chivvy the rest along with reasoning, and exhortation, and laughter – especially this last. There was such life-force in his laugh, it was so uninhibited. Some days, when the committee was dispirited or listless, he would come in and raise the whole mood by mere force of his own personality.

But, though it hurt her heart grievously, she had to accept, in time, that their getting married had been a mistake. They stopped having sex. They stopped living together, and saw one another only rarely. His anger at what he considered – perhaps correctly, she considered, weepingly – her intransigence further poisoned their time together. Finally she agreed to a formal separation, using the terms of their church to, in archaic language, *divorce*. On the day they met with a church elder to formalize this step, he took her once again in his arms, overjoyed at being free, and embraced her as if they were courting again. She couldn't help herself: her little heart blipped in her chest like a neutron star. She knew rationally it was over, but part of her felt it was beginning again, reborn. Of course it wasn't. The severest strike came later, when he sent a remote message to inform her that he was leaving the church and travelling to a new habitat. This, his simulated form assured her, was not a consequence of the divorce. She knew this was a lie, or if *lie* was too diabolical a word, then was him fabulating to save her feelings, or perhaps to save his own. Had he and she followed a different course, and never married, he would still be a member of God's congregation. That he was no longer was a devastating thing to her.

She was depressed for a while, which state of mind was of course treated. That left her in a limbo state; not miserable, but neither happy, and in a strange way disaffected at the absence of misery. She ought to be grieving, but if she stopped her treatment the unhappiness was so intense it prevented her from doing anything else. Her fangroup was astrophysics, and her fellow cosmogeeks were supportive in their various desert-mouse ways, but there was nothing they could do because there was nothing to be done. It was a year before Joyns had another relationship – a coy, rather proper pairing with a woman called Schwartzvater, in which they went no further than kissing and embracing and spending evenings watching physics documentaries. The relationship fizzled out, leaving the path of greater intimacy untraveled.

Guunarsonsdottir came to this world to study the way the foundations of the Great Tower were being designed, to handle the intense pressures of the mass of the structure above. She was of course famous for her interest in, and work upon, intense pressures, in the centre of stars, and black holes, and her scientific opinion was canvassed by the builders. Joyns was surprised how much the, in absolute terms, modest pressures of the Great Tower's crush interested her, actually, but it seemed she *was* curious about the technical specificity of the buffers they had designed to keep the whole from sinking through the crust of their world.

Since Joyns' ex-husband had worked upon this element, he was the obvious person to speak to the celebrated Guunarsonsdottir about it. But he was, for the time, uncontactable – out of the church, living in his sexually licentious habitat, presumably fucking himself silly in some orgy somewhere. Joyns tried not to think about it, which of course meant that she thought about it all the time. Feath, who was liaising with Guunarsonsdottir during her visit, suggested she perhaps speak to Joyns, and though Joyns assured the great woman that architecture was not *her* thing, Guunarsonsdottir came burlying into her space, nonetheless.

They talked for many hours. At that time Guunarsonsdottir was accompanied by a young man, very skinny and with a large bald head, called Hsi-Hsi. With an off-handedness that Joyns found simultaneously startling and arousing, Guunarsonsdottir dismissed him from her life, then and there. 'No need for us to stay together any longer, Hsi,' she said. 'On your way – pastures new and fresh adventures, don't you know.'

He did not remonstrate, or beg, or even complain. Presumably he knew better. Instead he looked at Guunarsonsdottir with mournful eyes, picked up his screen and foam hat, and walked away.

'Now that he's out of the way,' said Guunarsonsdottir, fixing Joyns with a direct look, 'we can begin.'

In the normal course of things Joyns would probably have put up a little more resistance. But medicated into a state of psychic blandness, neither caring very much nor even caring that she didn't care, she fell into this new relationship. 'You'll find,' said Guunarsonsdottir, 'that my body has been quite extensively modified. I'm closing-in on three centuries and I intend to live a great deal longer. One of the many alterations I have had made renders my sexual response much simpler and more direct, so you won't have any trouble there.'

It was never explicitly said, but, in some sense tacit within the dynamic as it was initially established, that Guunarsonsdottir was not disposed to take any great trouble where Joyns' sexual pleasure was concerned. She soon picked up that she needed to take care of herself in their mutual actions. And yet something rooted between them nonetheless. On Joyns' side, as she thought about it (and she thought about it quite a lot, surprised at the ease with which she abandoned her homeworld to travel with Guunarsonsdottir about the galaxy) there was something both bracing and strangely reassuring about the directness of Guunarsonsdottir's selfishness. With her ex-husband, the ingenuousness that sustains true relationship intersubjectivity had been, she saw, poisoned by his dissatisfactions – with her, with his faith, with everything. It was that dissatisfaction that had powered his energetic engagements with the world, his vast enthusiasms, his restlessness. It almost, she thought, approached an acquittal for her, herself. It hadn't really been *her*. It had predated her, and encompassed more than love and sex and marriage. It had been his place in his community, in his fandom, in his church. It had been everything, and now he was presumably off in some great tangle of bodies trying to drive away the dissatisfaction with the pressing pleasures of coition.

Guunarsonsdottir had none of that. Her selfishness was pure, and its purity was, as purity often is, compelling, even admirable. She played no games, she pretended nothing. If Joyns asked herself why Guunarsonsdottir had selected her, timid Joyns, as her companion, she might answer in a number of ways: because Guunarsonsdottir was genuinely interested in the physics of extreme gravity, and Joyns knew more about it than she did; or because Guunarsonsdottir, atheist and materialist, found in Joyns's religiousness something intriguing, exotic, attractive – though she mocked her constantly because of it. Or perhaps just because she found Joyns attractive in that banal, physical sense in which sex often works. But though she discarded none of these answers, and thought it likely they all played a part, she knew there was a more fundamental reason: Guunarsonsdottir needed people around her to reflect herself back upon herself, and Joyns just happened to be there. Her egoism was of the mirrored sort that loved to see itself in all the clustering others. She was the collector-point at the centre of the concentric circles of mirrors in the solar power farm.

Joyns prayed, several times, asking God – or asking herself, whilst detuning her rational, conscious mind to the point where she might intuit the divine hint as to the answer – about this relationship. To abandon her world? Sex outwith marriage? This latter was venal rather than mortal sinning, or so her culture told her, but it was not as if this was a relationship with a future. She served the whim of Guunarsonsdottir and one day, sooner or later, Guunarsonsdottir would tire of her.

Even during the voyage of the *Sweeney Todd* she had a sense of being marginalized. It didn't help that, during the meetings and brainstorming sessions Guunarsonsdottir assembled, discussing ideas with Joyns and also with a young physics fan called Samuel, Joyns could not always blithely endorse Guunarsonsdottir's plan for opening communication with the creatures in the black hole. Such resistance only irritated Guunarsonsdottir.

Joyns tried to put it diplomatically. 'We will of course try your method, Guunarsonsdottir,' she said. 'My only suggestion is that we have an alternative ready should your method prove unsuccessful.'

'Defeatism,' growled Guunarsonsdottir. 'Negativity. I am surrounded by naysayers. Why do you bring me problems rather than solutions?'

Samuel stroked her hand, in his lap, and looked crossly at Joyns.

The idea that she was bringing problems rather than solutions was especially galling to Joyns, since a possible alternative solution was exactly what she had tabled for this meeting. Guunarsonsdottir's idea was that the event horizon itself could be used as a kind of sounding board, like the membrane in a loudspeaker. 'We must assume,' she declared with (Joyns thought) ill-justified confidence, 'that the Blackholers have already developed technology for manipulating this spacetime border – this thrumming spinning sphere-surface, mediating the intensest tidal pressures in the universe. Given that they have evolved within the intense gravitational environment of the black hole itself, such a technology would be an easy development for them.'

'I don't quite see the logic there,' Joyns suggested, mildly.

Guunarsonsdottir snorted. 'Of course *you* don't see it,' she said. 'That is why I, and not you, have deduced it.'

'For a creature on the inside, the event horizon would be an impenetrable barrier.'

'Which is exactly *why* such a creature would try to,' and here Guunarsonsdottir grasped the edge of the table and shifted it several centimetres, 'shake it, bang it, bounce it – and in doing so, you would discover you *could* vibrate it, and so allow information to pass through, to be "read" into the vibrations on the far side.'

'It would be like Mongol soldiers discovering they could not pass beyond the Great Wall of China trying to shake it like a ribbon to communicate with the Chinese beyond,' Joyns objected. 'It would be as if the sun-worshippers of Ancient Egypt had decided to make the sun itself tremble in the sky. How could they?'

'Nonsense!' Guunarsonsdottir was contumelious.

'If the Mongols you mention,' inserted Samuel, coming in to his mistress's support, his face creasing with his high-contrast smile, 'had *banged* on the wall, it would have transmitted vibrations through the structure – small ones, to be sure, but that just means we may need to make sure our detection devices are sufficiently attuned.'

'Exactly!' screeched Guunarsonsdottir. 'We must do that – and we must make our own devices, so that we can thrum the membrane, and so speak directly.'

'We can hardly call it a membrane,' said Joyns, in a small voice. 'It's an inappropriate analogy. We are talking about a liminal three-dimensional boundary line, where the—'

'Perhaps you have a *better* idea?' interrupted Guunarsonsdottir, loudly.

'I have been working on the idea that it might be possible to accelerate particles to faster-than-light speeds in a way that maintains their coherence ...'

'This is nonsense,' snapped Guunarsonsdottir. 'It's been a few years since I was in kindergarten – can it really be that this elementary aspect of FTL particle physics was not on the syllabus when you attended?'

She meant the Paz Incoherence Theorem, which mandated the level of structural coherence below which quantum strong-force phasing resulted in faster-than-light technologies mashing information beyond retrieval. It was why no ansible had ever been developed, and why messages either passed at lightspeed, or else were physically carried by larger ships and drones. Joyns knew it, of course. But she was not proposing that.

'I have been reading some antique papers that speculate about the existence of gravitational islands that exist both inside and without the event horizon ...'

'Nonsense,' said Guunarsonsdottir. 'In some months we will be entering the vicinity of QV Tel. We shall inform Razak of the strategy we have decided.'

Razak had been elected captain of the mission.

'Oh, but it is exciting!' hooted Guunarsonsdottir, suddenly. 'It *is* exciting!' She directed this last at Joyns directly, as if daring her to disagree.

'I have always found the mission as a whole exciting,' said Joyns.

'I will need time to prepare myself,' said Guunarsonsdottir, grandly. 'Time alone.' She was, Joyns realized, banishing her from her bed.

So Guunarsonsdottir got up and left, walking a little unsteadily inside this rotating toroidal patterning – for the ship had been built quickly, and the simulation of gravity had not been perfectly checked and tuned and readied, so there were odd eddies and wrongfooting lurches in even the simplest walk across a floor. She stumbled, and Samuel rushed to her side. She rewarded this act of devotion with a kiss: matronly rather than erotic, but a twist in Joyns' guts nonetheless.

Joyns returned to her own rooms, and prayed for a long time. Was the pain in her heart the fault of her own sinful desires? To be in the relationship with Guunarsonsdottir, and to persist in it at all? From that position to yearn after Razak, who was *himself* in a relationship. Why could she not respect the boundaries these relationships represented? Faith, of whatever religion, was about boundaries. One cannot love one's neighbour unless they are clearly beyond the fence that demarcates their home from yours – they are not your neighbour, otherwise – and God is the ultimate other, the guarantor that not everything in the cosmos is just you and your narcissism and desires and neuroses. But, she thought, her yearning for Razak was an affront against the proper boundary that ought to bind them by separating them. She dreamt sometimes of immersing herself in him completely, the two of them dissolving into one another as a monstrous, perverse blending. With Guunarsonsdottir her desire was less immoderate, less immature, because it wasn't being fundamentally thwarted as it was with Razak. But it was also less healthy, since the only things that prevented Joyns from separating from her were unsalutary – a kind of possessiveness for the sake of possessiveness, clinging on to something as a miser does with money not because it does you any good but just because you're holding it. And also, perhaps, precisely because of her scornful words, landing like a medieval hermit's self-scourging flail upon the tender membrane of her pride, a fitting rebuke to her wickedness. But that, Joyns knew, was a pathological instinct, and she ought to be healthier.

The prayers went wherever prayers go, and when she had finished Joyns wept a little more. Then she slept for a while, and then sat in the observation space watching the AI conjure elaborate image after elaborate image of where the *Sweeney Todd* was in space, where they had come from, local points of interest, zoom-ins and sweeping out-perspectives, colour coded and with all the information any observer might need. There was no line-of-sight observation pod on the craft, for such a blister would have had to be in the perilous zone of the craft's flexing outer skin, which was bolstered and packed against radiation and dust-dot microstrikes (potentially deadly at the speeds the craft was moving). You couldn't really see anything anyway with the naked eye. Just stars. Since they were only travelling a matter of a hundred and fifty light years, the constellations looked pretty much the same as they did upon Anbuselvan.

Razak called a meeting of the whole crew, waking several from their sleep syncs. The ostensible purpose of this meeting was to ready everyone for arrival at QV Tel. In fact the meeting quickly became little more than an audience for a one-person performance by Guunarsonsdottir.

'At this distance,' Razak said, 'we can't tell whether or not Saccade has preceded us and arrived already at the black hole. If she has, then the first order of business will be to engage her – to prevent her from damaging or attempting to damage QV Tel itself with her device. If she has *not*, then we shall establish a safe orbit around the singularity and wait for her to arrive. For arrive she surely will, in time. And in the meantime we can turn our attentions to examining the black hole—'

'We must do more than merely examine,' intervened Guunarsonsdottir. 'We must make active attempts to communicate with the entities whom, I am now sure, dwell within it. To that end I –' she turned her head slowly, to let her eye fall upon Samuel, '– and my team –' she smiled '– have devised a working plan.'

Guunarsonsdottir then laid out her strategy for using the event horizon as a diaphragm upon which communication might be both received and – this, she stressed, as most important – initiated with the Blackholers.

Joyns said nothing. She sat placidly whilst other members of the group raised the common sense objections to this plan. 'But,' said one of the Five, a woman named Cempaka, 'surely the event horizon is not a physical structure, like a diaphragm. It is the notional borderline between that portion of space where particles might, if energetic enough and on the right trajectory, escape the singularity and that portion where ...'

Guunarsonsdottir interrupted honkily: 'Are you a physicist? Let alone an astrophysicist? Is that your fandom?'

Cempaka was not used to being addressed with such rudeness and her actual fandom – martial arts – had readied her not to turn the other cheek when struck. 'I *beg* your pardon,' she snapped.

'I,' said Guunarsonsdottir, 'am nearly three hundred years old and have dedicated my life to advanced physics and—'

'– it is a matter of kindergarten knowledge to insist that—'

'– must we really *bow down* to the opinions of rank amateurs in—'

'– the event horizon of a black hole is permeable only in one direction, and that—'

'– on the *threshold*,' barked Guunarsonsdottir, addressing the whole group, 'of perhaps the greatest moment in human *history*, and these naysayers are *attempting*—'

'– *facilis descensus averno*—'

'Stop!' called Razak. 'I beg of you both: this amounts to discourtesy on *both sides*.'

Cempaka and Guunarsonsdottir both stopped speaking. The latter glowered sulkily around the meeting.

Either as a practical suggestion, or else merely in an attempt to diffuse the sour atmosphere, Seint said: 'I have been revolving an idea, and would like the committee to consider it. If we can seize Saccade's craft and recover the device, might it be possible to use it, but only partially? If you see what I mean? Not to switch the gravitational vector entirely, but perhaps – I don't know: perhaps open a small window in the event horizon? Through which we might look, speak and so on?'

Guunarsonsdottir, who was temperamentally incapable of being abashed and subdued for very long, leapt back into the meeting. 'You do not understand what a black hole is, or you would not frame such a question,' she said. 'Think of it as a small sphere. A golf ball. Do you play golf?'

Seint had never heard of golf. The ship AI discretely informed him of the nature of the comparison Guunarsonsdottir was making.

'Inside the hard shell of the golf ball,' Guunarsonsdottir said, 'is a quantity of matter, packed in tight. If you puncture a golf ball, this inward matter bursts out. A black hole is like this, but vastly more so. We can think of it as a tiny sphere containing matter at unimaginable levels of pressure. It isn't really pressure, since pressure and gravity, though they of course relate to one another, are not exactly the same thing. But think of it like that. Any aperture, no matter how small, that absented the gravitational force holding all that prodigious quantity of matter would result in a catastrophic outpour, a destructive jet of extraordinary high pressure, high velocity, high temperature material – and eventually all the matter trapped inside the singularity would be ejected through it. It would not be a viable medium of communication, or anything else.'

'And yet you believe,' put in Bartlewasp, 'that we can not only communicate with the Blackholers, but also that they might be able to travel beyond their home?'

'Singularitans! But of course!' declared Guunarsonsdottir. 'This is also, to use the term my distinguished if adversarial boxing crew-fellow used earlier, kindergarten stuff.'

'It is?'

Guunarsonsdottir looked from face to face, around the

committee room. 'It is only the inability to imagine a form of life existing within the black hole that has kept this from becoming a standard view,' she said. 'Because of course once you take *that* step, as I have, then it's common sense. A black hole is that object in the physical universe where gravity is so extreme that the escape velocity exceeds the speed of light. Fair enough. But we have now developed technologies that can propel a spacecraft faster than light – so that limitation need no longer apply. Light can by definition only travel at the speed of light, but we can go faster. And therefore we could escape a black hole.'

'If we were inside the black hole,' Bartlewasp pointed out, 'we would be spaghettified and squished deader than dead.'

'Yes yes,' dismissed Guunarsonsdottir. 'Naturally naturally. For us to explore such an environment we would need some kind of super-bathysphere. I am not here to speculate on *that*. I am here to open the escape hatch on our poor trapped Blackholer friends.'

'To be precise,' said Razak, 'we have yet to determine whether such entities even exist.'

Guunarsonsdottir did not dignify this negative pedantry with a response. 'The first step will be to make contact with the Blackholers. The second will be to send them the scientific information necessary for them to manufacture their own faster-than-light craft. You might ask, how can we be sure they haven't *already* developed this technology? The answer is obvious, to all but a numbskull: if they had done so they would have used it, and we would have encountered them in regular space.'

'If they have evolved to live in the extraordinarily high-gravity environments on the inside of the black hole,' Razak observed, 'then they would find *our* vacuum-space and relatively low-gravity environments as toxic as we would find theirs.'

'They would be like those creatures from the oceanic abyssal depths,' said Bartlewasp, sweating a little, 'brought to the surface by trawlers – a mess of exploded tissue.'

'Well naturally,' said Guunarsonsdottir crossly, 'they will need to develop specialist habitat craft – much as we do. We can only travel about the galaxy by bubbling a warm, one-atmospheric pressure breathable and therapeutic area inside the membranes of our spacecraft. The Blackholers would need to do something similar: to create craft within which the intense gravitational pressures of their natural home were reproduced. But this does not seem to me a very difficult problem to solve.'

'It all seems highly fanciful to me,' said Cempaka, to nobody in particular.

At this Samuel, his face flushing darkly, rose from the meeting and left through the room's rear entrance. As he went, he gabbled several phrases, not all of which were comprehensible since his outrage and fury and embarrassment impeded his ability to articulate clearly. One element was clear enough: 'Cannot tolerate such rank discourtesy to one of the greatest intellects of our age!'

With this, the meeting as a whole broke up. Razak reiterated his initial statement about what they would do on arrival at QV Tel, promising further committee meetings when everybody had calmed down and balance was restored to the crew's interactions. Everyone departed except Joyns, who stayed where she was, meditating on what had passed, and praying briefly for calm and the capacity for forgiveness.

Razak, who had left, returned.

'Joyns?' he asked. 'Are you still here?'

'Captain,' she said, startled out of her prayer. She put on a smile. 'I was just going over in my mind the discussion.'

'Not a very good-tempered one I'm afraid. Feelings ran hot.'

'If Guunarsonsdottir is right, then we are on the verge of actually contacting alien life – for the first time in human history,' said Joyns. 'Excitement is understandable. Appropriate. And excited people are more likely to be quarrelsome.'

'I suppose you are right.' Razak reached over and touched Joyns' shoulder. She restrained herself from reacting to the contact. She was able, just about, to retain her composure. 'Are you alright?'

'I am well,' she said.

'I am as captain aware of a certain – disconcertment, let us say, in your manner.'

'Mine?' Joyns was surprised.

'In general, I mean.'

Joyns considered for a moment. She felt a blurt inside her, an urgency, which was of course nothing more than the desire to unburden herself to Razak. Deplorable: more of the same hopeless yearning to diminish the distance between them. It would be fruitless, even damaging. So she said: 'I'm fine. I have been unusually absorbed in my work.'

'Of course,' said Razak. He smiled at her. 'I mean no disrespect, and I understand that for you monogamy is a religiously required institute. I would never trespass upon that. Nevertheless I must tell you how – compelling you are.' Her heart danced suddenly: a clog-dance, a lumpen, ugly dance. Razak was going on, speaking smoothly. 'Of course in saying so I do not mean to disrespect the boundaries of your relationship with Guunarsonsdottir, just as I know you do not mean to disrespect the boundaries of mine with Bartlewasp. But there is something *hidden* about you, and something hidden always makes a person more attractive.'

She wasn't sure she could control her voice, but she tried. 'If that is what brings a couple together, what happens when the hidden part of the person becomes known? Do they become that much less attractive?'

'No relationship lasts forever of course,' said Razak, hurtfully offhand. He turned to go.

Not wanting this exchange to end just yet, Joyns said: 'I mean no disloyalty to Guunarsonsdottir when I say, I disbelieve her physics.'

This stopped Razak. 'So,' he said, turning back. 'All of it?'

'No, not all. Specifically: this idea that we could use the event horizon as a sounding board, a membrane, a diaphragm.'

'Oh,' said Razak, nodding. 'That seemed improbable to me, too. But Guunarsonsdottir is a great mind, and astrophysics is so much more her fandom than it is mine, I didn't think it was my place to challenge her. Well: perhaps it doesn't matter. When we are at QV Tel we can try her theory and if it doesn't work we can try something else.'

'If it doesn't work,' Joyns said, 'she will want to persevere with it until it *does* work. This is her character.'

'But not forever. Eventually she will give up. Do you believe there is life inside QV Tel?'

'I don't know.'

'Oh I hope there is,' said Razak, zealously. 'Truly I hope so! And Guunarsonsdottir is so persuasive, so confident in herself. But I suppose we shall see!' He came a little closer. 'You don't believe it is Satan down there, at any rate? I know some members of various religious fandoms think so.'

'I do not think so,' said Joyns, more slowly, imagining reaching her hand out and stroking Razak's cheek. 'That is, I do not know.'

'Well!' he said, brightly. 'Perhaps we will open communications with whatever is down there, and know for sure. Or perhaps we will discover there is *no* life there. Or perhaps, most frustratingly, we will not be able to communicate or to discover anything, and won't know one way or the other!'

'But we will at least deal with Saccade and her pirate crew,' said Joyns.

'Deal with,' said Razak, firmly. 'Yes.'

After he had gone, it took Joyns a little while to get her breathing under control. She went out to one of the ship's arboreta. Some of the green areas on board were spun, at full or partial gravity, for such vegetation as needed to know up and down in order to grow – rhizomes, mostly. But plenty of plants are happy to sprawl in zerogee, growing to prodigious size: rhubarb leaves big as duvets, courgettes like mini-submarines, lettuces folded like the lobes of a giant lime-green brain. Grasses swayed as she moved and stirred swirling breezes. It was very peaceful. Bees burbled and spiders shat filigree in amazing patterns. Starlings made the distinctive strung-together short-hop flights of zerogee birds. There were many hanger-sized blisters clustered on the flexible outside of the craft, some filled with water, others with air, all thrilling with vegetative and other life. These swaddled the inner zones where humans dwelt, protecting against radiation and micromatter damage and supplying food and oxygen. The outer units were planted with larger flora, poplars that sent sharp barcode shadows against the fabric in the unending artificial light, oaks, bamboo; but the whole was orchestrated to leave three-dimensional pathways and clearings through clusters of grassland and market gardening.

It was alright, she told herself. There was a still point at the heart of the maelstrom, just as there was a still small voice after the storm. It would be alright.

Three weeks later the Sβ-*Sweeney Todd* began its deceleration into the vicinity of QV Tel.

6

Alien Contact

And so it was that Startship Sβ-*Sweeney Todd* decelerated into the vicinity of the black hole QV Tel. Humanity had been spacefaring for centuries and it, or more precisely its tech, had become expert at leaving superlight velocity so as to slot neatly into a planetary or stellar orbit. But black holes are a different proposition, rarely visited because they're so dangerous. The gravitational tidal forces around a black hole are intense and can lacerate the most rigid of structures, fold them into parodies of origami, pull them into crumbs and shards. These forces play hell – play, as the antique phrase had it, one that came back into fashion after the Sα-*Niro* incident, *merry hell* – with navigation, and there are an infinite number of seemingly-sustainable orbital trajectories and paths that actually lead, sooner or later, into the inescapable sink of the singularity itself. The event horizon is that point at which light can no longer escape the gravitational pull of the black hole; the point of no return for a craft in the vicinity of a black hole is a sphere much larger, but also much less predictable and easy to model, than the event horizon as such.

Razak, captain of the Sβ-*Sweeney Todd*, took the advice of the ship AI and settled into an orbit five light-hours from the event horizon. It was not like a conventional planetary orbit, because such simple precessing ellipses are impossible in the strong-field environment of a substantial black hole. The *Sweeney Todd* passed an inspiral three-frond clover-leaf orbit around QV Tel.

Guunarsonsdottir was not happy with the distance. She wanted the ship closer to the event horizon in order to be able to test her theorem and initiate contact. 'The closer the better!' Razak took her to his cabin and showed her the various orbital possibilities from which the ship AI had triaged their current trajectory, and she emerged, grumbling, but content. Closer orbits were dangerous.

A committee meeting was called.

'But,' said Samuel, supporting Guunarsonsdottir's demand for a closer orbit, 'the *Sa-Niro* adopted a much tighter Innermost Stable Circular Orbit, without danger.'

'And look what happened to *them*,' growled Bartlewasp.

'They did not fall into the black hole!'

'They took unnecessary risks,' declared Razak. 'We are orbiting as close as is compatible with our continuing safety and ease of departure.'

And there it was! The black hole itself was, of course, not visible. Some black holes can be picked-out by the accretion disc of material they are drawing into their void, which gleams orange, or red, or sometimes lemon-white, depending on how aggressively the gravitational tides are sucking matter down, how many collisions the particles experience, how much the matter is heated up. But QV Tel had no such disc. It would have one soon, however, if 'soon' be understood on cosmic rather than human timescales, for two stars were in orbit about it: the nearer, B33 was a stripped helium star, dense and small, spinning around the black hole every forty and a third days. This star gleamed nightlight blue and swung like a golf ball circling the final hole, round and round. The second star was larger and shone with a paler blue, but it had a foggy waistband of matter around its equator which reduced its light. Its orbit was only two days slower than its fellow.

There was no sign of Saccade, or her petitoform β-ship. 'We have beaten her to this place!' declared Seint.

'Are we sure she is even coming here?' asked Samuel. 'She may be insane, but she is surely logical enough to deduce a mission would be assembled to apprehend her, and that the most logical strategy for such a mission would be to come straight here. Were I her, I would avoid this place at all costs. There are other black holes...'

'But,' said Guunarsonsdottir, imperiously, 'they are not all inhabited, as this one is – any more than all planets are inhabited. Indeed, it may be this is the only black hole in the cosmos that is home to intelligent life! She *will* come. We must be ready.'

'We will add police or military drill to our daily therapeutic hospital and psychological check-ups,' said Razak. 'The Five will oversee these drills. Guunarsonsdottir is quite right: we must be ready.'

The expression on Guunarsonsdottir's face suggested she considered *Guunarsonsdottir is quite right* to be a tautology.

'Until such time as she arrives,' said Razak, 'we shall proceed with our attempts to open communications with any creatures as may or may not dwell within QV Tel.'

'Which *do*,' boomed Guunarsonsdottir.

Joyns stared ahead, making eye-contact with nobody.

Excitement pervaded the ship, but it did not last much beyond the first week after arrival. For most of the crew, the days settled back into their routine. For Guunarsonsdottir excitement gave way to anger that her experiments attempting to detect readable fluctuations of the event horizon yielded nothing.

There were shifts in the parameters of the horizon, but they followed chaotic patterns most likely the result, said the ship's AI, of random shifts in the intensity of the spin of the central singularity, folding and snapping spacetime in the interior. 'What do you know?' Guunarsonsdottir shouted. 'You're a machine, not an artist in physics like me. You're not even a specialist in astrophysics!'

'We could be reading what is actually an apparent horizon as if it were an event horizon,' suggested Joyns. She spoke respectfully enough, but Guunarsonsdottir replied with invective and contumely, scorning her suggestion, and Joyns withdrew with as much dignity as she could. Back in her chamber she congratulated herself on maintaining composure during the interaction – and then instantly burst into tears.

Guunarsonsdottir decided the problem was that the *Sweeney Todd* was too far away from the horizon, and petitioned Razak to bring the ship closer. When he refused she insisted upon a vote in ship's committee, and when that backed the captain's decision (with only Samuel taking Guunarsonsdottir's side) she loudly insisted that the time had come for a new captain to be elected. Of course there was no prospect of that, so early in the actual mission, especially with Razak showing no signs of instability or incompetence, so Guunarsonsdottir withdrew herself to her cabin and sulked for two days. When she emerged it was as if the contretemps had never happened. She returned to her measurements without mention of her tantrum and, indeed, her demeanour was rather of the kind that implied she had won an impressive victory.

But her reading of the event horizon produced nothing but chaotic signals and her attempts to bounce tangential lasers off it went nowhere, for the tangent that bent the laser around the singularity so that it returned to the *Sweeney Todd* was too far from the actual horizon to have any effect, and any attempts to tweak its path led to it spiralling-in irrecoverably. Guunarsonsdottir now instructed the whole ship that these had been nothing but preliminaries, and her actual, if never before mentioned, plan was: to build and fly brief-burst FTL probes *through* the event horizon, using their faster-than-light drive to escape and return to the craft. 'Think of it!' she enthused. 'Imagine our ancestors, trekking across the steppe, wearing animal skins and carrying spears, and then – up above them, in the deep sapphire sky – an advanced startship plunges into the wash of air and light, flies overhead, so close you can make out all the markings and technical embellishments, and then soars away to return to space! What beauty! What a mind-fuck!'

'Is that how you envisage the Blackholers?' said Seint. 'As civilizational primitives?'

'Primitive is derogatory, irrespective of to whom the descriptor is applied,' said Samuel.

'I apologize,' said Seint, at once. 'I only meant to ask: does Matr Guunarsonsdottir believe that the Blackholers are at a, shall we say, earlier stage of utopian development than humanity?'

'They have been confined within this small environment their entire evolutionary existence,' said Guunarsonsdottir, eagerly. 'Does that mean their development has been thwarted, held back? Or perhaps that it has been accelerated, as a pressure-cooker speeds up cooking time? We will only know once we have passed a probe beyond the event horizon and returned it.'

Joyns was running some parameters on her screen. The AI, who of course would never be so jumped-up as to interrupt human interdiscourse, was also present, and manifested as a sceptical-faced woman in the top right corner of Joyns' screen. With the AI's help she came up with some discouraging data.

'It is theoretically possible for a β-drive to accelerate from just below an event horizon with what amounts to escape velocity,' Joyns said. 'But—'

She was speaking quietly, and several of the Five were chatting amongst themselves, when Samuel burst out with: 'Why not create a *piloted* craft? Why test it with a mere automatic probe! I would be honoured to take the risk of flying such a craft, and of being the first human being to pass beyond a black hole event horizon and to return!'

Several of the Five, and two of the therapeutic team, were what amounted to Guunarsonsdottir-fanboys, and they loudly applauded this noble and heroic ambition.

'Risk?' Guunarsonsdottir repeated, crossly. 'You think any expedition I oversaw would be anything other than safe?' Still, she did not offer to pilot the test craft herself, and Razak, with the caution proper to a ship's captain, said: 'Perhaps it would be best to put a few automatic probes through before we assemble a manned craft.'

Joyns tried again: '*Theoretically* possible for a β-drive to accelerate through and out of an event horizon,' she said. 'But the power required would be excessive – it would take more energy than we expended in travelling six hundred light years to get here.'

'Nonsense,' said Guunarsonsdottir, reflexively.

'You say so,' Bartlewasp pointed out, 'without having done the calculations needful to rebut Matr Joyns' point.'

'I have thoroughly modelled the operation,' said Guunarsonsdottir very loudly.

Razak said: 'Joyns, go on.'

So Joyns talked about how the gravitation intensity inside a black hole was such that all matter and energy got squashed down to planck-scale dimensions. The planck-length and dimensions of black holes are closely related, or rather the energetic foam that spacetime becomes at planck-length and which construes black hole formation, which would make such a journey problematic. 'Since,' said Joyns, in a quavering voice, 'our β-drives depend upon the instantaneous massive aggregation of planck-length distances into travelable pathways *through* spacetime. But that only works because planck-time is marginally lesser than the time it would take light to travel one-point-six times ten to the minus-thirty-five. Nobody knows why that should be, but it turns out to be not only true but to be scalable.'

'How is this relevant?'

'Some propose that at the heart of a black hole is a singularity – a dimensionless point of infinite density,' said Joyns, gathering her courage as she spoke. 'But for others such a hypothesis violates common sense, and everything else we know about the physical universe. For those – and as a physics fangirl I count myself in their number – nothing can be smaller than planck, which means that the heart of the black hole must be a planck-core. An object extremely small, but not a singularity. In a planck-core the density would be extraordinarily high, but in a singularity the density would be infinite, and that violates known physics.'

'Neither hypothesis rules out the possibility that life has evolved *in* this place,' said Guunarsonsdottir in a brassy voice. 'And I am not proposing we send a probe to the heart of the black hole – merely to skim under the event horizon. The event horizon, perhaps I have to remind you, is that threshold beyond which the speed of light is insufficient to achieve escape velocity. But our probe, able to travel *faster* than light, will easily escape it. Very much common sense, my dear.'

'My point,' said Joyns, but she was already losing her audience. She needed more than facts, stated. She needed delivery, force, energy. She did not have these things. 'My point is that once the planck-scale gets, well, *cluttered* beyond a certain point, there's no guarantee that a β-drive will even work.'

'Of course it will work,' Guunarsonsdottir declared.

Then the committee voted and it was agreed to reserve a quantity of ship's resources to making a probe, and to tune-down various functions to decant sufficient energy to power it. There was some grumbling, away from the official agenda of the committee: Spake muttering to Seint, 'If Guunarsonsdottir had mentioned this *before* we set out, we could have built a couple of these probes and packed extra power. Why spring it on us like this?'

'She's only just thought of it,' was Seint's opinion. 'And is pretending to have had it always in her mind.' Joyns, who was passing the two on her way out of the meeting space, overheard this and thought: Indeed. Indeed.

It wasn't clear to Joyns if Samuel was, in fact, sleeping with Guunarsonsdottir yet. It was, she supposed, a matter of time. He was certainly putting a lot of energy into stanning for her. He went round the whole ship, engaging each crewmember in conversation in turn. 'It's pretty exciting to be sending this probe – humanity's first, into a black hole!'

'I hope,' Spake replied, 'it works, is all. It might have been good to know we would be building probes *before* we set off, so that we don't have to detach a goodly portion of our drive to power the thing.'

'Ah,' Samuel urged him, 'but we didn't really know what we were going to find until we actually got here. We didn't even know if we'd be able to study the black hole, or if we'd be spending all our time grappling with Saccade and her crew. Guunarsonsdottir is very confident that this probe will be a huge breakthrough for humankind!'

'Well,' grumbled Spake, 'here's hoping.'

'All our names will go down in history,' gushed Samuel. And then on to the next crewmember.

Working so hard on her behalf! Joyns' jealousy was, in truth, almost entirely dried up where Guunarsonsdottir was concerned. Relationships, like beings, are born, grow, flourish, wither and finally die. It's grievous, and it can be hard to let go in the later stages, but there you are.

Sobbing in her bed. Washing her face and booting up her physics fanpages.

Going through her exercise routines in the gym, solus.

Joyns herself had found – or the AI had searched and brought to her attention – an old paper written by a pre-utopian medic called Almheiri that speculated there might be islands of quantum resonance located outside the event horizon that resonated with structure on the inside. She spent several days trying to discern these islands from the observational data, and worked out a protocol by which 'pinging' them, in mathematically regular build-up patterns, might cause the interior of the black hole to receive the information. As to whether it would work the other way was harder to determine. *Facilis descensus*, after all. There was nothing facile about ascending and emerging from inside to out. Nothing facile at all.

:2:

Finally the probe was assembled: a fist-sized set of sensors and programmed foldmetal embedded in a three-vaned propulsion structure that was in turn attached to a considerable percentage of the *Sweeney Todd*'s energy-generation equipment. There was enough left in the main ship to continue the mission and to get home, of course, and Guunarsonsdottir talked grandly about how the black hole itself was essentially the universe's most powerful generator, if handled right, and how she had a plan for syphoning off some of the extreme potential of the location.

The probe was extruded, like a bolus passing through a body's propulsive sphincter, and floated into space. To begin with it jetted off towards the black hole sublight, with a detachable booster – anything not tucked inside the spacefoam bubble of the FTL drive would be crushed and distorted by the intensity of the gravity, spaghettified and ruined, and if the booster were still attached it would interfere with the probe's trajectory, and might drag it, as a sheet anchor, out of FTL altogether and to its doom. At a safe distance from the *Sweeney Todd*, the probe keyed-up, span its virtual aggregation protocols and whipped away. It vanished, to reappear on the far side of QV Tel, to swoop round on a wide orbit and return to the mothership – to collect its data, and to reintegrate its power into the main drive. As the ship AI was working to re-establish the connection, searching for the probe beyond the giant lens of the black hole, Guunarsonsdottir permitted herself a little expression of triumph: 'Just *imagine* what the creatures inside QV Tel have experienced! A spaceship from a wholly alien lifeform has just soared like an eagle through their strange skies!'

'It's not there,' said Razak.

'Of course it's there. We have the trajectory precisely mapped.'

'There's nothing,' said Seint.

'This is ludicrous,' said Guunarsonsdottir crossly.

It was true though. The probe had vanished. Its speed and trajectory being known, it ought to have been possible to track. To all intents, and so far as the ship's detection and ranging tech was concerned, it had simply blinked out of existence altogether. But the craft had been programmed to skim through the event horizon, so it was very possible it had reached the black hole, experienced some malfunction, or encountered some unknown variable, and then crashed down in towards the singularity.

'It's likely,' said Joyns, at the emergency committee meeting that followed immediately, 'that the remains of the craft, compressed far beyond any functionality, are now on a spiral trajectory beyond the event horizon, circling – or ellipsing – in towards the central mass.' She spoke in a soft voice, and looked at her screen rather than meeting the eye of her crewfellows.

'This is nonsense,' said Guunarsonsdottir.

'It was an experiment,' said Razak. 'Not all experiments are successful, but we learn from failures just as we learn from successes.'

'The black hole,' Bartlewasp added, 'retains her mysteries, like a grand old lady out of an antique story. I, for one, find it romantic!'

'We will rip those secrets from the crone's grasp,' snapped Guunarsonsdottir, with remarkable force and loudness.

'Maintaining the integrity of the spacefoam monogon was crucial to the success of this mission,' said Joyns, speaking barely above a whisper, 'and I fear the tidal pressures and the sheer planck-level clutteredness of the black hole environment meant that…'

'Perhaps,' said Samuel, as the idea popped into his head, 'time dilation might…'

'Yes!' Guunarsonsdottir seized on this. 'That must be it. There are unexpected time dilation effects.' A whole path opened before her mind's eye, a way in which the mission – her mission – could be flipped about from abject failure to sparkling success. 'The probe is doing precisely what we designed it to do. We *will* recover it. Only, it is taking longer than we thought it would, longer, that is, from our point of view. And actually, if you remember, I talked of the time dilation effects as part of the mission from the very first.'

Various people around the committee room looked at one another. 'Guunarsonsdottir,' said Razak, a little hesitantly. 'If the probe were travelling sublight then the intense gravity would indeed have time dilation effects. But given that it was travelling at artificial speeds, *faster* than light, any such ...'

'No, no, we are not talking in a merely conventional sense,' said Guunarsonsdottir. 'The physics of the black hole are – are – clearly – that is – clearly, we are in the process of discovering something very important about the physics of a black hole. That *in itself* would mean that the mission has been a tremendous success. Whether or not we retrieve the probe.' She flapped her hands. 'Though of course we will retrieve it. Exactly as I planned.'

There was a lot of discussion of, and dissent from, this idea at the committee, but the more Guunarsonsdottir was critiqued the firmer her position became. Samuel supported her, and when Joyns was asked her opinion she murmured something about how much was still unknown about the interior of a black hole.

This was an evasion. As soon as she uttered it, she rebuked herself, inwardly. After the meeting she prayed, trying to understand why she simply hadn't spoken against Guunarsonsdottir's ludicrous notion. It wasn't because she believed it would endear her to her former lover. It was something else.

Still, Guunarsonsdottir now went about the *Sweeney Todd* in triumph. The majority of the crew thought her idea unscientific, but a significant minority were prepared to believe her, and this unbalanced the body-politic. 'The probe could reappear *any time*,' Guunarsonsdottir told her followers. 'It is entirely a question of when. It is a *delay* to the mission, not, as my enemies claim, a failure.'

'Please, Guunarsonsdottir – *enemies* is not a helpful word. You have no enemies here! Only—'

'You are with me,' Guunarsonsdottir interrupted, 'or against me, there is no middle path.'

Razak called a further committee meeting to try and defuse the increasing factionalisation. It only seemed to make things worse.

'You *must* believe,' Guunarsonsdottir instructed the rest of the crew. 'Remember, I am three hundred years old. To me, you are all children – quite literally children. I know better than you: it is as simple as that. Would you truly abandon your wisdom and experience because a gaggle of toddlers wailed and tantrummed? No. I am right. What has happened to the probe is that its trajectory is dilated. It will reappear, and could do so at any moment.'

'It has gone – crushed to nothing,' barked one of the Five.

'Even *if* your ascientific theory were correct,' Seint said to Guunarsonsdottir, 'what is to say that it will reappear now? Why not next year – or in a million years?'

'You must have faith,' said Guunarsonsdottir.

'We need science, not faith,' said Seint, growing wrathful.

'My assistant Samuel has been working the equations – haven't you, Sam?' Samuel looked startled, and glanced around the meeting, muttering *of course, yes.* 'This,' Guunarsonsdottir went on, 'is a whole new area of physics: not the regular Newtonian-Einsteinian manifold, and not the extremity of the singularity. I call it liminal physics because it exists at the borderline between the two.'

'The borderline is governed by the same physics as every-where else!' cried Seint.

'Not so. My discovery of liminal physics alone is enough to justify this entire mission,' said Guunarsonsdottir, firmly. 'And the equations tell us – tell us that the probe will reappear in … three days.'

The committee broke up in disagreement. The two factions stopped interacting with one another.

:3:

Because of all this, Joyns sank into a new kind of melancholy. She went about her business on the ship, but did so with dreams and darkness vexing her days, and she could not shake the sense that there was, in some sense, a doom poised ready to fall over the ship, a mist of shattered matter spiralling slowly down in the black hole and heating as it passed. *Life*, whispered a voice in her ear, *is a war of dying flesh against the life*. Who said that?

Wait: who *said* that?

She called up an image of the local environment. There was QV Tel, sat inside a pink-line circle imposed by the image software to separate its lightless black from the lightless black of the background. Its two stellar planets swung slowly about. Stars, like exhalations, dotted the distance.

Your adversary walketh about as a roaring lion, seeking whom he may devour. She thought of those words and then thought: but how can the devil, who is chained in the pit by God after the war in heaven at the beginning of time, also be walking about the world? Either he's chained in the oubliette, or he's free of it. He can't be both at once.

This was foolish thinking. QV Tel was a physical item in a physical universe, a place where gravity had compressed enormities of matter into a tiny space. That was all.

Like a lion, walking, said a voice.

'Who's there?' Joyns cried out. But she was alone.

Joyns went to see Baqri, one of the Five, who was doing his stint as one of the ship's therapeutic hosts. 'I'm not sure,' she told him. 'But I may be hearing voices.'

Baqri had a large, symmetrical face: wide-eyes and friendly, full lips. He nodded concernedly. 'You say you are *not* sure?'

'I heard one single sentence, and then a part of a sentence. And I'm not sure if I actually *heard* it. I've been working at the physics extra hard, so perhaps it was only exhaustion. I don't mind the hard work, I'm genuine in my fangirling of physics, I truly am, but it is leaving me more mentally exhausted at the end of the day.'

'Are you sleeping well?'

'Yes. And what I heard was just one sentence. From what I can determine from researching it via the ship's AI, auditory hallucinations generally involve more than that.'

'What was the sentence?' asked Baqri.

Joyns considered. The alexandrine was still there, thrumming in her memory: *life is a war of dying flesh against the life.* She discovered she didn't want to speak it aloud, superstitious that actually saying the words would make them more liable to come true. But weren't they *already* true?

'I think,' she said, eventually, 'I'd rather not say.'

Baqri looked surprised at this, but he only said: 'Of course. Let's meditate together – you're religious, aren't you? I'd be happy to pray with you if you'd prefer prayer to meditation.'

'Meditation is fine,' said Joyns. They sat facing away from one another, with their spines pressed together, and inwardly recited their respective mantras for a half hour. Afterwards Baqri said: 'If you have any more auditory hallucinations, come back to me.'

'I will,' promised Joyns. They kissed, and she went on her way.

She really wasn't sure she had 'heard' the sentence. Maybe she had imagined it, or remembered it from somewhere else, and the thought or memory had resonated so sharply that it had seemed as if somebody else had spoken it. She hadn't told Baqri about the melancholy. It was alright, it was fine, it was nothing to be ashamed of. Living in utopia didn't mean *never* feeling sad. Some experiences of melancholy could be darkly pleasurable, provided only they weren't over-prolonged. And the environment of the ship was not conducive to facile happiness: people were not talking to one another, conflict was not being resolved and – the most acute consideration – there was no out-door, no exit by which the disaffected could leave and seek happiness elsewhere. Not until the mission was over. A little melancholy might not be a wholly inappropriate reaction to all that. The *sentence*, though: that was different. The alexandrine.

Joyns was aware of a superstitious feeling that, if she dwelt upon the words, they would swell in her mind, darken it, perhaps collapse it.

She prayed. She concentrated upon her work. Relationships aboard had settled into a sort of rapprochement: the Guunarsonsdottir faction were generating speculative new physics to 'prove' that the probe was still functional, and collecting data, and that it would re-emerge from its time dilation in the three days. The captain's group still rejected this idea, on the grounds of sheer common sense and basic physics, and asserted that the probe was lost forever. But the two groups avoided direct interaction and the unaffiliated – two of the Five, Spake and Joyns herself – went about their business without interacting with either.

From time to time a member from one or other group engaged Joyns in an apparently innocent conversation that revealed itself as an attempt to recruit her. For example: Bartlewasp met her inside one of the balloon vegetable environments, as she was collecting miniature tomatoes, ruby-coloured pearls. They chatted about tomatoes for a while, and then Bartlewasp said: 'In the last committee, you seemed unsure of Guunarsonsdottir's fiction about the probe being time-dilated, and yet did not actively speak out.'

Joyns didn't want to have this conversation. 'My history with Guunarsonsdottir is complicated,' she said, gathering her harvested toms in a fold of cloth and pushing off to drift towards the door.

Bartlewasp matched her trajectory. 'Of course, I don't mean to be insensitive. But you don't *believe* her crazy myth-physics do you? You're a dedicated physics fan. You do know better.'

'The AI is crunching some complex numbers for me,' said Joyns. 'I need to get back to my screen.'

'We have more pressing things to worry about than this probe. It's gone, crushed, spaghettified. Saccade, however, is on her way, coming here, and she has a history of actually killing people – real murder. We need to prepare!'

But Joyns was gone.

Joyns took a double-slot in the exercise suite, thrusting away with her legs until the sweat dripped off her high forehead and dribbled into her eyes. She showered.

Guunarsonsdottir's approach was cruder. She called by Joyns' room, talked about herself for ten minutes and then initiated sex. She did not establish explicit consent first, but Joyns did not resist, and though she despised herself for going along, there was building excitement, and then the golden moment when everything flew away into the space between the worlds and nothing mattered and all was good.

Afterwards they embraced. 'There's a special bond between us,' Guunarsonsdottir murmured in her ear. But then she slipped away and Joyns was alone, and again the voice sounded. There was no mistaking it this time: a distinct locution, not her own mind, as if there were another person in the room with her, although she was quite alone.

Our highest purpose broken and consumed by worms

It sounded like a quotation, but Joyns' feed didn't supply a direct source, though there were plenty of archaic poems about worms devouring the dead and purposes being broken.

Oddly this line did not haunt her imagination the way the other one did. But the sensation that there was *somebody in her room with her* was extremely unnerving. She ran diagnostics on her space, and went back over the surveillance data from every angle. Of course she had been alone. And yet it had sounded like somebody had spoken.

'Lion?' she said, to empty space. 'Are you there?' There was no reply.

<h2 style="text-align:center">:4:</h2>

The deterioration of good humour between the two factions – and the alienation the non-aligned crew members felt – settled for a time into a chilly stasis. But then it began getting worse again. The captain had not called a committee meeting since the split, and whilst it was in the purview of any crewmember to request one, nobody did. Everyone feared such a gathering would descend into a shouting contest, hostility, anger. Raised in utopian societies that had conditioned them to resist the escalation of conflict, everybody was disinclined to provoke matters.

The three days that Guunarsonsdottir had specified for the reappearance of the probe came and went. Samuel, who now appeared to be Guunarsonsdottir's official spokesperson, sent a message round the ship declaring that she had solved the complex dynamics of the new physics and was confident that the probe would reappear on the far side of the black hole within two days. When it did not appear at that time the prediction was extended by another three days. Again it did not come. Guunarsonsdottir dropped the prediction, made no reference to it, and when members of the captain's faction questioned her, as they met on their various comings-and-goings about the ship, she flatly denied she had ever made such a prediction at all.

Joyns felt as though a migraine were brewing in her sinuses. No actual headache developed – and if it were to come, there was a wealth of analgesics and resonances aboard the ship that would have cured it. This was worse: a sense of something impending, some disaster just around the corner, an apperception of dreariness, of waste. Futility. It became harder to concentrate on her work. She had no further contact with Guunarsonsdottir, and she began to wonder if the members of the captain's faction were pointedly ignoring her. She went about her days unmolested but also unwanted.

This was irksome at least insofar as her calculations, drawing on the data the ship was still collecting from its proximity to QV Tel, were starting to firm-up in interesting directions. But nobody was interested. She prayed. She exercised. She ate alone, increasingly spending solitary time in one or other of the vegetable bubbles harvesting fresh food alone, rather than eating processed food in the dining hall with the others.

Whose voice had she heard? If any?

Then, suddenly: QV Tel spoke.

Bursts of microwave radiation, intense and on a narrow wavelength – two thirds of a μm (approximately – to three decimal points) – tapping out numbers. 1, 1, 2, 3, 5, 8, 13 and then starting the cycle again. The transmission, if that's what it was, emerged at the poles of the spinning body. When Guunarsonsdottir announced this she was at first disbelieved by the captain's faction, who assumed this was another of her mendacious myth-making strategies. But the data was right there. The ship's AI confirmed, and anyone who cared to direct a detector towards QV Tel could pick it up.

No question, but this was very exciting.

Razak called the first full ship committee meeting in a week. 'This is a major development,' he said. 'I know there has been a degree of tension between certain members of the crew over the last few months. That's not unusual, on a deep-dive mission like this one, and we have all, to our collective credit, done much to dampen down tempers and keep friction from flaring up into actual dissent or combativeness.' Joyns looked up from her screen, briefly, at this and looked around the meeting. There were some scoffing looks exchanged by people within the same faction but nobody contradicted the captain.

'Now,' said Razak, 'this.' He gestured with a finger and the ship AI played a rendering of the microwave bursts: a blip lasting .132 of a second, another blip lasting .264, a third lasting .396 and so on. It was over in a moment, a little trill like the song of a thrush, so Razak had the AI play it again at a much slower speed. 'It's the Fibonacci sequence,' said Razak. 'There's no doubt about it. Fibonacci up to 13, playing over and over again.'

'It is a very remarkable thing,' said Bartlewasp.

'We should discuss whether this is,' the captain continued, 'some kind of naturally occurring resonance, or whether it is something else that—'

Guunarsonsdottir could not contain herself at this. 'Naturally occurring? Nonsense, nonsense, nonsense! It is the inhabitants of QV Tel opening a channel of communication with us.'

'Whilst not dismissing such an explanation altogether . . .' Razak began saying.

'Not *dismissing*? You have been constantly undermining and belittling me, for months,' flared Guunarsonsdottir. 'Suggesting that my probe and the brand-new physics it has opened up to us has been nothing more than a fantasy! And now that we have proof, solid and golden proof, you dismiss me again.'

'I assure you I am not dismissing you,' said Razak, stiffly.

'You again prove your unfittedness to the captaincy,' said Guunarsonsdottir.

To express so direct a challenge to the captain's position was shocking, and for a time nobody spoke. Several faces expressed distress, or alarm. Razak took a deep breath and let it out.

'Come now,' he said, in a conciliatory tone.

'There is a *chance* – we must consider it,' said Bartlewasp, 'that the regularity of this emission indicates a natural source, and is not the product of a directing intelligence. The Fibonacci sequence occurs in many places in nature.'

'It is the aliens,' Guunarsonsdottir declared firmly. 'They are using the probe to piggyback a broadcast up and beyond the event horizon. If you study the history of proposals for first contact, it is an established principle that we start with basic mathematical forms, since math is the universal language. That is what the Blackholers are doing here.'

'We shall soon find out whether we can initiate conversation,' Bartlewasp said, haughtily.

'Must you persist in your impertinent doubting of me?' said Guunarsonsdottir. She scowled and then, unexpectedly, laughed, and said: 'As it happens, I have already been beaming back a number of mathematical sequences at QV Tel. Fibonacci of course – but not only that. I did not want the Blackholers to mistake our signals for some kind of echo of their signal, so I varied the mathematical sequences I sent out. When they reply –'

'If,' inserted Bartlewasp, crossly.

'When,' shrieked Guunarsonsdottir. 'When! When! When!'

Everyone at the meeting was, for a second time, startled into silence. All looked up and stared. Guunarsonsdottir had, before, sometimes lost her temper, and manifested irritation, but never before had she actually screamed, top-volume. For a person of such small stature, she could generate a very considerable volume.

'*When* they reply we will develop the exchange,' Guunarsonsdottir went on, in a pleasant tone, as if nothing had happened. 'It is important the Blackholers understand we come here with peaceful intentions, with a desire to learn about their culture. To that end we must make no – and I cannot stress this with sufficient force – we must make no references to Saccade, and the device. This is the first time these beings have encountered what are, to them, alien beings. It would *traumatize* them profoundly if during first contact they were to learn that others of our species are porting a device that could utterly annihilate their entire world.'

'Guunarsonsdottir,' said Razak, mildly. 'I must insist that nobody, yourself included, act unilaterally in this matter, and that any strategy or approach pass through full approval by this committee before being enacted.'

'Well what do you think I'm doing?' Guunarsonsdottir retorted, angrily. 'Why do you think I'm sitting through this nonsense, here, except to give the committee the chance to approve my approach?'

'What I think you are doing,' said Bartlewasp, standing up, 'is bullying the committee, browbeating us into getting your way. You are wholly *un*interested in what anybody else has to say. There is no discussion here, there is only your monologue, and when somebody says something that adds a perspective that differs from yours, you literally shout them down. You scream. Scream!'

Guunarsonsdottir also got to her feet. 'Bully?' she said, in a hiss. 'You call me a bully? This is disgrace and outrage. This is insult and calumny. You—' she threw out her arms forward such that both her index fingers were pointing directly at Bartlewasp. 'You must retract and apologize instantly!'

'Trying to bully me into apologizing for calling you a bully?' cried Bartlewasp. 'Must I have the ship's AI recite a definition of the word *irony*?'

Guunarsonsdottir opened her mouth, and left it open. It may have been that she was attempting to shout, as she had screamed before, but if so she was not able to marshal the loudness. A person not practised in screaming will find it hard to will a convincing scream the first time they give it a go. Guunarsonsdottir left the room without any further words.

Bartlewasp was trembling, and as soon as Guunarsonsdottir had gone she started crying, and pressed herself against Razak for comfort. The captain, conscious that he was still officially chairing the committee, and unsure if giving his lover a hug was appropriate behaviour in such a circumstance, only looked awkward.

After that, relations between the two factions on the Startship Sβ-Policecraft *Sweeney Todd* deteriorated sharply. Razak went in person to Guunarsonsdottir to try and effect a truce, but it did not go well. His opening pitch was: 'If there are indeed aliens living inside QV Tel, then we need to think carefully about how we contact them: to determine carefully what we say, what promises we make and how we proceed. These things could have enormous consequences for human futurity.' Seint had pointed out that promising the aliens – if they existed – we would do them no harm could entail us in a lie, since there existed human beings, most likely hurrying directly towards QV Tel right now, who *did* intend harm to the black hole. 'We cannot,' Razak determined to say to Guunarsonsdottir, 'begin our relations with a whole new alien civilization with an untruth, no matter how well intentioned it might be.'

But he did not get through this prepared speech. When he met Guunarsonsdottir, in one of the ship's many gymnasia, she was flanked by her followers. His opening words, 'If there are indeed aliens', provoked instant hostility. 'I cannot listen to this undermining nonsense of if if if – you are captain. A captain cannot operate in a constant world of maybe and perhaps and possible. A captain must commit! There *are* aliens – and it is evasion and treachery to suggest otherwise.'

'You used the word treachery before, at the last committee …' Razak started saying, genuinely unsure as to the term's application to the present circumstances.

'I will proceed. You must, I insist, stop harassing me, and my followers. If you do not I shall instruct the ship's AI to create a hermetic seal separating your and my people until matters can be resolved in a more civilized fashion.

Razak was aghast. 'Harassing?' he repeated, horrified. 'Sealing yourself away? Guunarsonsdottir I beg of you, no!'

With an ostentatious display of smiling magnanimity, Guunarsonsdottir relented. 'Let us hope it does not become necessary,' she said. But this was the end of the meeting.

Through all these events Joyns remained unaffiliated. Guunarsonsdottir no longer called or spoke to her, and the captain's faction – how *bizarre* to talk in such terms of a shipful of well-adjusted utopian human beings! – found her hard to trust, given her previous closeness to Guunarsonsdottir. Joyns moved about the *Sweeney Todd*, as an ant crawls through a great bunch of grapes, inching between the giant green balloons of the vegetable atria, winkling her way through one connecting space or another.

Often she sat in her room and tried to pray.

The *Sweeney Todd* continued its endless, complex orbit around QV Tel.

Guunarsonsdottir released her datasets to everyone through

the ship's AI. Whether she was releasing *all* her datasets, or only those ones that supported, or seemed to support, her narrative, was a moot point among the rest of the crew. But Joyns studied the data just as everyone did. Beaming varying mathematical series into the black hole resulted, or appeared to result, in an increasingly complex series being emitted back: pi; natural logarithm of 2; natural logarithm base e; converging and conditionally converging series; Taylor series and a number of hypergeometric series.

Razak called a committee meeting. Only half the ship's crew attended. That was in itself an alarming sign, for all ship's committee meetings were supposed to be attended by all, and decisions arrived at by full democracy. But there was nothing the captain could do. Those who were present, including Joyns, went over the data Guunarsonsdottir had released. 'It might be an intelligence inside the black hole somehow sending information across the event horizon – though how they could do so is hard to imagine,' said Bartlewasp.

'The probe?' asked Seint.

'The probe is destroyed, spaghettified long ago,' was Razak's opinion.

'It could,' Bartlewasp went on, 'merely be some kind of echo. There is a delay, such that – if we trust Guunarsonsdottir's own account – the series was returned after the first matrix exponential was sent. But perhaps delays are to be expected.'

'All this data could be nothing but an echo?' Razak pressed.

'Yes. Even assuming we trust that Guunarsonsdottir is reporting her data correctly.'

'I don't trust anything about that woman,' Razak said. He had tried to access the raw data via the ship's AI – which, of course, Guunarsonsdottir was using to access and process her incoming – but had discovered that a privacy bubble had been constructed that not even the captain had the authority to override. The original Fibonacci sequence had been genuine. Who knew how much of the later data was accurate?

:5:

There followed two days of no new data. Not even Guunarsonsdottir pretended that anything was coming in. The two factions, and the non-aligned, went about their days, filling them howsoever they preferred. Then, on the third day, Guunarsonsdottir issued what she described as a 'proclamation', along with an extensive, new data package. Or so she claimed.

The burden of this proclamation was to relieve Razak of the captaincy and to appoint herself to that role. Since Razak had certain captain's protocols lodged with the ship's AI which would not be rescinded without a vote by a full crew committee, or a diagnosis of physical or mental health breakdown, this announcement had little practical force. But it still sent a quasi-electrical shock of pain through Razak. The word *mutiny*, a term from the distant history of humanity that had long fallen into desuetude, reoccurred to him.

More startling – if it *was* true – was the transcript of the exchanges Guunarsonsdottir claimed to have been having with the Blackholers. This account was simply presented, without supporting data, and the ship's AI was unable to provide any confirmations or repudiations. The half-committee went through the transcript, and afterwards Joyns sat in her room alone and went through it again.

'The conclusion is,' said Razak, sounding exhausted, 'either this is the record of a real conversation between humanity and an alien intelligence – the first in our species' entire history – or else it is a fiction, the confection of a self-aggrandizing and perhaps mentally unstable individual.'

Everyone looked at Joyns at this, as if it might upset her. She met their looks calmly.

'If the latter,' said Razak, 'then we may have to stage an intervention. Remember what happened with Raine, during the first ever exploration of this place! It might be happening again, and this could be the prelude to – I hesitate to say it, but we must face all possibilities – violence.'

'She may have become delusional and dissociated from reality,' said Bartlewasp. 'Of course we must acknowledge that she and her followers may be saying the same thing about *us*.'

'This talk of unity with the aliens,' said Seint. 'Of us, in the universe of matter, joining them ... this worries me. It would worry me if it were real, and worries me more if it is Guunarsonsdottir's fantasy, for she might try to seize the ship and steer it into the black hole, killing us all.'

At this there was a long, pensive silence.

Finally Razak spoke again: 'We must keep the ship safe. If that entails an intervention, then let us stage it sooner rather than later. I appreciate it may entail a show of force, which is regrettable, and contrary to our collective utopian values. But we are in a unique position! We must ready ourselves. Quite apart from anything, do not forget that Saccade is likely on her way here, carrying within her craft a device of immense destructive potential.'

It was agreed. Joyns excused herself, citing – this was untrue, and she hated herself, but she had to get away – a toiletry need. She hurried back to her room and went again through the transcript, the AI reading the words, making verbal notes and identifying anything that could be construed as testable data. There was very little.

The document began with a list of the initial terms of what it insisted was 'contact': the establishment of a shared understanding of *number, addition* and *subtraction, commutivity* and *seriality.*

Attempts to explain geometry were met with incomprehension. This is perhaps to be expected in an intelligence that has evolved inside an environment like a black hole, where simple qualities human philosophers have taken for granted, like extension and non-superposition, are radically compromised. We must remember that for most of human history mathematics and geometry were held to belong to radically different magisterial, until Bertrand Russeau proved in his *Prince Kipper Mathematica* that they were aspects of the same thing. It is wholly compatible with the advanced civilization of the Blackholers that they fully comprehend the former without having any developed sense of the latter.

How, Joyns wondered, were the Blackholers – if they existed – able to differentiate different numbers if they had no sense of extension? How could numbers be arranged in series or matrices without a sense of length or height? The next section, in its brevity, raised even more questions:

Once numeracy was co-established it was a simple matter to develop a shared language. We converted large amounts of historical data about humanity and the cosmos into our shared numeral code and downloaded it into the black hole.

This surely compressed into a couple of days an undertaking that ought to take years. Two cultures with literally nothing in common, not even geometry, were able to start talking almost at once? Joyns, Sherlocking the proposition, triaged the possibilities. Least likely: actual contact with the utterly alien Blackholers had been established. Slightly more likely: the

Blackholers were able to establish communications because they had some prior understanding of humanity, had been able to monitor human interactions for instance, or – more outlandishly – were descended from the same joint-stock, or were future humans time-travelling back into the present via the singularity (a crazy notion Joyns thought, but one proposed by the ship's AI that had encountered it in an antique science-fiction story). Most likely: Guunarsonsdottir was simply making it up, there were no aliens and she was fabulating. She had fallen prey to her own fantasy.

We established three key parameters for our interactions with the Singulatarians. One is the concept of unity, which is core to their self-identity. Whether this means they are self-conscious separate entities who prize unity, or actually some kind of gestalt or hive-mind, remains to be determined. Anything that challenged unity – and this includes the very concept of the 'outer'-universe, with its to-Singulatarian baffling concepts of extended dimensions – the Singulatarians describe with a unit of semantic communication that we deduce can be translated as *affront* or *slur*. We talked about this topic at some length, and discovered that the Singulatarians signifier for us, all humanity, is the Slur.

Not a very promising ground for mutual cohabitation, if true, Joyns thought. But the next parameter was even more worrying:

The Singulatarians are not closed-minded. They proved hospitable to us explaining to them that there is a radically different mode of existence outside their event horizon, once defined by extension (on a massive scale) of both space and time. They, or one of them, or all, expressed disbelief that intelligence could possibly evolve in such an attenuated medium. In ensuing discussion we were – that is, Matr Guunarsonsdottir was – able to deduce that the Singulatarians' intelligence also inheres in synaptic connection and patterning, although not precisely – that is, as three-dimensionally – as is the case with the human brain. We were able to communicate to them that though most of our universe was extremely attenuated, such that molecules are not proximate enough to permit synaptic exchange, we ourselves are much more densely and compactedly built, such that our synapses are close enough to function well. Their response was to wonder how our synapses would work inside the black hole. We informed them that too great a gravitational compression would be fatal to us, and they expressed puzzlement. A twelve-minute exchange failed to establish common ground on which concepts such as death and physical hurt could be communicated. The session ended with the Singulatarians anticipating the time when all of the exterior cosmos would be integrated into the unity and all Slurs redeemed. After the session, we discussed the meaning of this communication. We do not consider it a direct threat, but believe rather than it emanates from the fact that Singulatarians do not fully comprehend the scale and variety of the universe outside QV Tel. That they are aware of something being outside at all is a testimony to their intelligence, but it is not a demerit in them that they think it only a small bubble surrounding their home.

The blandness and short-sightedness of this interpretation of the data (assuming there *were* any data) startled Joyns. Why assume the best of the Blackholers? Why not the worst? – that they were aggressive, imperialist, hostile and cared nothing for the pain and death of the out-holers? There was no reason automatically to *assume* belligerence on behalf of the Blackholers of course, but neither was it logical to assume benevolence. The third of Guunarsonsdottir's 'parameters' had to do with human mental health.

Assuming the Singulatarians and we mean roughly the same thing by 'consciousness', the question remains – considering the ill-fated expedition of Startships Sα-*Niro* and Sβ-*Oubliette* – whether the interaction of mental states or apperceptions between Singulatarians and humans might destabilize either or both. The Singulatarians insisted on the robustness and unity of their consciousness and queried whether mental instability of any given human being was a function of their nature as 'Slurs'.

It has become clear from conversation that the Singulatarians are far in advance of humanity in terms of advanced mathematics; for them theoretical math is as intuitive as movement in space is for human beings. We have much to learn from them.

The document concluded with some alleged 'transcripts' of interactions with the Blackholers. In committee, Joyns had skimmed these. Now, alone in her room, she had the AI read them to her more slowly, sifting each. But there was little there. The data fields came un-sieved, and included various raw numerals that may have been indices to some other protocol, or perhaps simply reflected that the initial ground of mutual contact had been mathematics, but either way were incomprehensible to Joyns, and very wearying to hear the AI read aloud.

cpy stubfund mng thsln mss. f thbrtsh qmsq.985865568 NWLNTKN98758659 985865568NWLNTKN98758659 + qmsmq qsncmq, nq sncælngætlttrtrært xplctr

n pd (fr.); y (ng.); (y n ystrdy.) 985865568NWLNTKN 98758659 n l, pl (fr.); j (grm.); (y n ynk.) 985865568NWLNTKN 98758659

n mlln (fr.); (shngh d.); (y n ycht.) 985865568NWLNTKN 98758659 w h w n hw, yw; (j n jchh! (grm.)) 985865568 NWLNTKN98758659 sn (grm.); n p (ng.)

kīn-t'n 't-dy;'b kng-f 'wrk ;'cd sng-kng 'mr., sr.'f 985865568NWLNTKN98758659 2. t-shù hw mny'gh tên-chù 'gd*;b gặn-tên 'fvr.'jk 985865568NWLNTKN98758659 3. sặng-í 'trd, bsqnss;'lm ch-tú 't knw;'n -kú 's bfr.'pq 985865568NWLNTKN98758659 4. -f 'clkths;'rs sh-sh 't cllct tgthr;'t sāng-ji.'lv

These, Joyns assumed, were records of the Blackholers' speech acts, and perhaps of 'translated' human questions and responses. It was hard to determine. Some text came without lengthy numerals.

Dsprchlhr//lhrtncht gntlch//wmn sprchnsll,//sndrn nr, w mn sprcht//D sprchlhr st nr n physlg dr sprch;//sknn nrns frn lhrn, wmn sprchn sll,//ls s n ns d nnrn bldngsgstz dr sprch zm bwsstsn brngt,//ndnsddrch nstnd stzt, {{{z}}} brthln, bdsprchwsm//nzlnn dsn gstzn gmäss s//drncht

There were also lists, portions (judging by the specific numbers to which individual entries were pegged) of much longer lists, that recorded things out of context. Whether these were Blackholer ideas, concepts, ideograms, communications – whatever – or human ones, or human best-guesses as to the former, Joyns could not see.

444. Many suns (star?) together, suggesting the idea of brightness.

445. An object (lifeform) in an aperture, – obstruction.

446. A creature with a large large large eyes, – seeing.

447. Two entities, – sitting.

448. Two entities following, – following

She deactivated the document, and lay on her back for a while. At her instruction the AI played musical notes strung together according to a Bach algorithm, which was soothing. Soon enough she had fallen asleep.

:6:

When Joyns woke, it was to a segregated ship. The AI informed her that Guunarsonsdottir and her followers had requested, and been granted, a 'self-protective' cordon around a cluster of six globes. The AI regretted the need to do this, but insisted that its programming which required the safety of the crew, including any subset of the crew, was inalienable and its absolute over-riding priority. Razak called a committee meeting. Though all crew were supposed to attend, and though Joyns did not expect to see Guunarsonsdottir's faction there in person, she wondered if they might attend remotely. But not only did they not, all the non-affiliated and most of the captain's group stayed away too. This was entirely unprecedented.

Razak and Bartlewasp were present, and Joyns slipped in as they were embracing. They seemed unaware, or unconcerned, at her presence. When they separated Razak officially commenced the meeting. Joyns could not help noticing how tired and stressed he looked.

'We note, without additional comment, the seditionist and divisive sealing away of a portion of the ship by Guunarsonsdottir,' he said. 'But we're not here to discuss this, or Guunarsonsdottir's forged and fictional so-called dataset concerning what she claims are aliens living inside the black hole.'

'We're not?' said Joyns, surprised.

'Whether she is aware that these accounts are mere fiction,' said Bartlewasp, 'or whether she genuinely believes her own fantasy, is yet to be determined. Her mental state is precarious, but whether she is only mendacious or has tipped over into actionable insanity...'

'That's not the purpose of this official,' said Razak, smacking the table and repeating the word, '*official* committee meeting of the Sβ-Policecraft *Sweeney Todd*! We will deal with the insurrection later. For now there is more pressing news. Saccade has arrived in the system.'

This was alarming news. 'She has?'

'But not in the petitoform craft she stole. The reason for her delay in arriving is explained, at least partly, by the fact that she is in a small and relatively-underpowered startship.'

Joyns asked the AI for the scans of this new craft, but got an evasive response. 'There are some data,' said the AI, 'but I don't have the *specifics* that the captain is reading into those data.'

'Show me!'

'The captain has rescinded access to the scan data – for the time being, he says,' said Aidan. He added: 'I'm sorry.'

Joyns addressed herself to Razak. 'Why have you rescinded the scan data?'

'It's need-to-know,' said Razak. 'This ship is full of spies and betrayers. I'm sorry Joyns, but I have to count the unaffiliated crew members as outside the need-to-know bubble.'

'You agree with this, Bartlewasp?' Joyns asked.

'You must trust Razak, Joyns,' said Bartlewasp, in a level tone. 'We have to protect the ship against enemies, exterior and interior – Saccade and Guunarsonsdottir in particular.'

'How can I help if I don't know what exactly we're facing?' said Joyns, a panic swelling inside her, less at the prospect of Saccade in her mystery ship and more at the thought that Razak and Bartlewasp had also lost their holds on sanity. That she was

surrounded by people in the grip of their varying insanenesses.
'I could calculate the trajectories of—'

'You were close to Guunarsonsdottir,' Razak interrupted. 'I
know you're not now. But there's a historic connection. It's
because of this that I want you to *go* to her – talk your way
into her self-erected compound, and use whatever influence
you have over her to persuade her to surrender.'

'Do it, Joyns,' said Bartlewasp, pressing herself closer to Razak
and insinuating her arm around his waist.

Joyns rose and left. She made her way along one interstice,
and then another, and into a large space full of pink light.
She climbed like a fly up the weightless wall, made of matter
programmed to attach itself to the top of her show-and-release
footsole, and so into an empty vegetation blister – one of the
smaller ones. Here she sat down. Nothing seemed real, not just
in the sense of the improbable aliens living inside a black hole,
or the phantasmic battleship Saccade was supposedly piloting
down upon them. Nothing seemed real in the important things:
relationships.

For a long time she simply hung there, thinking of nothing.
She was neither asleep nor, entirely, awake. Eventually she
became aware that she was no longer alone.

Bartlewasp was coming through the space like a swimmer,
pulling herself along from branch to branch, from big leaf to
leaf. 'Did you follow me?' Joyns asked.

'You've been here an hour,' Bartlewasp replied, floating up
towards her. 'The ship AI told me where you were. We were
concerned.'

'You must leave me alone,' Joyns told her.

Bartlewasp paused before replying, in a level voice: 'I comprehend that you are jealous of the relationship I have established
with Razak. We all know that love soured between you and

Guunarsonsdottir, and I'm sure that has been painful for you. But we cannot, at this time, afford for you to flounce out in a petty fit of anger on such an account. The *Sweeney Todd* is in danger!'

Joyns was rendered speechless by this. Her expression, wide-eyed and lips-parted, in some way struck Bartlewasp as an encouragement.

'You are a rational, a logical, being, Joyns,' she urged. 'You are *highly* respected in your fandom, amongst other physics-enthusiasts, I know. I am confident you can rise above your personal insecurities and jealousies to put the collective good first.'

Joyns was silent.

'All you need to do,' Bartlewasp urged, 'is formally repudiate Guunarsonsdottir and her faction. That shouldn't be hard to do – it does her no good to reinforce her fantasizing. She needs to reconnect with reality! Once you have formally affiliated yourself with Razak we can show you the data – Saccade's craft, and its weaponry. You'll be in the inner circle!'

Joyns turned away, pushed hard with her feet and floated in a straight line away from that tree and towards another. Bartlewasp followed, calling out 'Joyns! Joyns! Don't turn your back on your fellow crew – your friends! Believe me!' When they landed in another tree, and Joyns repeated the move, flying hard and fast back at a diagonal to a third tree, Bartlewasp finally disengaged. 'This is a painful loss,' she called, as she floated and pulled herself back towards the blister's doorway. 'Please reconsider! Keep yourself open! Don't shut yourself off!'

I won't shut off, Joyns thought to herself. I won't shut off.

7

Gentility

And the LORD said unto Satan, From whence comest thou? And Satan answered the LORD, and said, From going to and fro in the earth, and from walking up and down in it.

:1:

Joyns tried to sleep, but her room kept pinging her and waking her up. It was impossible to sleep. Joyns tried and could not. There was her room, sounding (or simulating) an anxious voice, a lot of unusual activity in the ship, crewmembers moving from pod to pod, through interstices and into various spaces, restlessly passing to and fro. The room declared that neither it nor the ship's AI was certain what their purpose might be in dashing about the ship in such a manner. It was impossible to sleep. Joyns tried to turn off notifications, but first the room and then, when she persisted, the ship's AI told her that the safety protocols mandated notifications remain on. 'There have been raised voices,' the AI said. 'Tensions are high. I fear actual fighting might start soon. I have requested the captain to permit me to seal certain crewmembers in safe spaces for the time

234

being, to avert conflict, but he won't reply and I cannot act on my own initiative. Matr Joyns, could you go see Razak and communicate my request?'

'Aidan, Aidan. Just leave me alone,' said Joyns, crossly. 'I only want to sleep.'

But she couldn't sleep. She turned from her left to her right side and then again to her left, feeling the slight difference when she turned with the direction of spin as opposed to against it. She instructed the room to turn out all lights but then felt abandoned and scared in the dark, and so ordered the lights back on, to shine a low yellow-orange glow. She lay on her back. She tried to compose her mind into a meditative state, but it wouldn't settle. She got up and knelt and prayed, but it was a vacancy, a mere going through the motions, and she soon stopped.

It was impossible to sleep.

At one point she heard two people outside her room. Given the great size of the startship and the relatively small number of crew, this was odd. Joyns sat up, believing they had specifically come to speak with her, and wondering why they hadn't simply called her. But they hadn't come to her.

There were two of them, one who sounded a little like Samuel, the other whose voice she didn't recognize. That struck Joyns as odd, because she thought Guunarsonsdottir had barricaded herself and her followers in a separate part of the ship. But there they were, outside her room. Or their voices at any rate. Perhaps the barricade had been breached and Guunarsonsdottir's followers were on the run. Perhaps they themselves were staging a raid behind enemy lines. The two of them were talking loudly about the best way of incapacitating Saccade – which must mean that news of her advent must have reached Guunarsonsdottir's portion of the ship as well. One of the two, perhaps Samuel, said, distinctly, 'Kill her, it's the only way' and the other person,

Joyns didn't recognize their voice, said: 'She's really here! Really! She's here!' and then laughed like a cat miaowing, then their voices dropped and Joyns couldn't follow them. There followed a strange melange of sounds, scrapings and gruntings and smacking sounds, and it took Joyns a moment to piece together that the two figures were grappling and fighting one another.

Then there was a loud slapping sound, and the sound of somebody running away, their footsteps slightly syncopated by the fact that one foot was placed more spinwise than the other.

Had both parties run away? Was one lying wounded or dead outside her door?

Joyns contemplated getting up and checking, but a deep resistance to the idea occupied her limbs. She sat up and checked the ship's time. One minute to midnight – the startship's arbitrary midnight, by which the arbitrary business of timekeeping was calibrated, as it was on a million ships and habitats around the inhabited galaxy. *I should get up*, she told herself. But she did not.

Then it was dead midnight and the lights in her room glowed blue.

She hadn't told the room to change the colour, and it was a chilly, morbid shade of blue that was accompanied by a distinct drop in temperature. She hadn't ordered that either! It certainly wasn't going to help her get to sleep, so she said 'Room!' preparatory to ordering it to restore the earlier light and heat settings when she saw she was not alone.

She saw at once who it was: the Gentleman. He was dressed in a mauve jacket and trousers, the jacket sharply cut and folded over a harlequin-green shirt and necktie, after the manner and style of an actor in an historical drama. He carried a walking stick shaped like the Hebrew letter *vav*. His face was lean and sharp-featured. Joyns was not a fan of antique painted art, and so was unaware of the old Vannick painting *The Arnolfini Betrothal*, but had she ever seen that image she would have recognized the face of the man in her visitor (though not the lavish Flemish cloak; the Gentleman wore nothing so voluminous). And here he was, as – Joyns assumed – he had appeared to Raine, years before. He was seated in a chair that had not been there before, surveying Joyns with prominently-lidded eyes.

'Good grief,' said Joyns.

'Half right,' said the Gentleman.

'You're not here,' Joyns said. She drew herself back along the floor, and rested her spine against the wall of her room. If she sprinted she would surely reach the door before the Gentleman could stop her. Indeed, it looked, from his demeanour and his posture, as if any decision on his part to rise from his seat would be a leisurely and unhurried business. But then she thought: he appeared instantly from nowhere. She thought: if I rush the door he'll be there in the way before I move an inch. Then she reassured herself: he was a vision, a hallucination, and certainly not real. 'You,' she reiterated, 'are not here.'

'Here,' he said looking around, 'is a more complicated concept than perhaps you give it credit. But if you mean, am I locked inside the black hole around which this spacecraft orbits? – well, yes. I am.'

'You are?'

'Isn't that why you came here? Everyone has asked you, and you've said over and over that you don't really believe the devil is inside that oubliette. But do you, Joyns? You'll say you don't truly believe it. And you, feeling the pressure of scientific and materialist conventionality replying, no no of course. But in your heart you knew it.'

'Childish superstition,' Joyns murmured. 'As if God went around the cosmos digging deep pits and stuffing the rebel angels inside them!'

'Yet that, making allowances for the imprecision of speech, is exactly what he did.'

'If you're inside the black hole,' Joyns asked, 'how is it that you are speaking to me?'

There was a new odour in the room. It smelt like – she couldn't place it: tart, sour. Off milk perhaps. Cheese. Something starting to decay. Some foodstuff.

'Speech,' said the Gentleman languidly, 'is words and the word, as you know very well from your religious faith, is God. Such a thing is not to be confined. God cannot be imprisoned or locked away. But *actuality* – well, that's a different thing. Can I pass through the event horizon? I cannot. Nothing can, not even I. *Non discedam e tenebras* my dear child, *non, non non.*'

'You are locked away – in there?'

'I am. The deepest mineshaft in the universe. Why else did God excavate these spaces, if not to imprison my kind? Whatever other possible purpose would they serve?'

'The cosmos is not here to serve our purposes,' breathed Joyns.

'Yours? No, of course not,' said the Gentleman. 'But then, I wasn't talking about *your* kind.'

Joyns took a deep breath, and let it out. It wisped in the chill air. The initial shock, of finding herself not alone, had receded. But then again, she realized, it actually hadn't felt too much of a shock. It was as if she had been expecting this, or something very like it. It was as if she hadn't been alone for a long time. 'I'm dreaming,' she said.

'Does it feel like a dream?' asked the Gentleman.

It didn't. 'Hallucinating,' she said. 'It's a vision. I've been drugged.' Then, with a quickening in her heartbeat and a flush of anxiety, she added, at a venture: 'You and Raine spoke?'

'Ah,' he said, in reply, meeting her gaze directly, unruffled. 'Raine. Interesting fellow.'

'The consensus is that Raine hallucinated the entire episode.'

'Another word for consensus is *groupthink*. It comes, you know, from the Latin – *con* together with and *sensus*, feeling, sentiment, gush. Is that really the bar of judgment to which you want to submit yourself? Collective sentimentality?'

'It doesn't feel to me as though I'm sitting in a room talking to the devil.'

'How would such a thing feel? That it doesn't map onto this?'

Joyns considered the question. Wouldn't there be something at once uncanny and horrifying about such an encounter? Oughtn't it to feel less easy-going, less suave, than this? Of course the proverb was that the Prince of Darkness was a gentleman – was, here, *the* Gentleman – and it made sense that he would try and insinuate himself inside your defences, rather than ranting and roaring like a beast. But still. And then Joyns thought again. Isn't that, she asked herself, just another way of saying that I ought to find the devil strange and alien and upsetting? When the truth is we allow the devil into our lives easily, without hiccough, all the time? It rarely feels like we have invited in a disruption. There's no revulsion, no startlement, the devil slips into our day-to-day, whispering in our ears, confirming our prejudices, nudging us a little further along the way we already yearned to go. We all know it. The devil does not *affront* us, for if he did he would not be able to seduce us. And as this thought passed through Joyns' mind, she felt, for the first time, a squirming sensation in her solar plexus, a tingle of fear across her scalp. She looked again at the Gentleman, at his slender eyes tucked away behind their heavy lids, at his amused mouth, the absolute ease with which he sat there, and felt, actually, for the first time, afraid. Though she was not a Catholic she crossed herself. The Gentleman watched her without saying anything.

'You're not here,' she said. And again: 'You're not here.' Even she could hear the quiver in her voice. 'I don't know how you're able to trick my eyes, or how you're getting your words into my ears, but you – are not – *here*.'

'I am inside the black hole,' agreed the Gentleman.

'And not even *you* can punch out through the event horizon of a black hole.'

'Not even I,' he assured her.

She took another breath. Her heart was scampering. Another breath. 'It's like,' she said, 'one of those shark chambers.'

'Cages,' said the Gentleman. 'Shark cages. Where the big fish knocks its snout against the bars, hoping to force through and bite you.' He smiled, and his teeth were regular and human-looking and not at all squaliform.

:2:

Feeling at a disadvantage, seated on the floor when the Gentleman was resting in his chair, Joyns took a breath, roused her spirit, and got up. The Gentleman's gaze stayed on her as she moved to the bed, and sat on the end of it. 'Is there,' she asked, 'something specific you wish to say to me? I mean – how long is this little conversation going to last?'

'You don't work,' said the Gentleman, abruptly.

'What?'

'You heard what I said.'

'I work all the time!' objected Joyns. In fact, challenged un-expectedly upon this ground, she felt tears hemming the edges of her eyes. 'I sometimes think I do nothing *but* work.'

'Come now, my friend,' said the Gentleman, avuncular. 'Let us both undertake to be honest with one another. Otherwise what is the point in this conversation at all?'

'You mean I'm only working so hard to try and distract myself from my misery,' said Joyns. 'I've had that thought myself.'

'Not at all. I mean you simply – don't – *work*. None of you do. The work in your world gets done by machines. That's what enables your utopia: manufacture, maintenance and disposal, the generation of what used to be called wealth, all done by machines.'

'People sometimes manufacture things! They build, uh, tables and – other things. They weave.'

'Sometimes they do so,' the Gentleman conceded, 'but only if they have a fancy to. It's a hobby, for you all, it's not work. And that's the nub, that really is. You know what I am saying is true. Once, your species worked because the alternative was starvation, exposure and death. In the old days. In the good old days. Work was necessitated by scarcity and the hostility of your environment. You didn't enjoy it, back then. You complained about it all the time. Your fantasy tales were of soft lawns and warm skies, a stream giggling past, food and wine for the taking and lovemaking in the sun. But for almost all your kind, this was only a dream. You worked hard, and often the work filed you down to stumps, physically speaking, and killed you. But it *defined* you. It was the context out of which you grew. Until one day you said, we are clever enough to dispose of work, to drive the brute off with a pitchfork.'

'What manner of fork?' Joyns asked. Normally her feed would automatically supply her with the definition, but there seemed to be some glitch in it. That ought to have worried her, for a glitch in that system suggested larger problems in the ship as a whole. But she was drawn into this conversation. She needed to correct her interlocutor, to make him understand how very hard she had worked – not just lately, but all her life.

'It's not important,' said the Gentleman, wryly. 'The point is, *you did it.* Your kind. You made clever machines, and thinking machines, and delegated all *actual* work to them. You liberated yourself from the grind. Scarcity scarpered, made itself scarce, and you, as human beings, were free to live however you chose. And this is what you discovered – although, to be fair to humanity, some of you had realized this before. You discovered you needed *to keep busy.* You lack the skill for perfect idleness – you're not spiders. Spiders are, I sometimes think, God's greatest creation. They busy themselves, and create these geometrical wonders of spun-silk and dewdrops, a diagram of hexagons receding into perspective, glinting in the sunlight. Whilst they do that we can say they are working, but once they have finished they settle into their true state: a perfection of inactivity. Sitting in the centre of their web and waiting, passively, for food to come to them. They subsist in a state of hermetic bliss the like of which humanity can only dream. Believe me, I've looked inside the minds of spiders and their being-in-the-world, in that moment whilst they wait, is a *perfection* of being. If a human were given access to that more-than-happiness, that trans-happiness, you would die of it. But you can't have it, because you are fundamentally a restless species. You need to be fiddling with something, distracted by something, taking something to pieces or putting it back together, travelling to or from somewhere, watching something, playing some game, keeping your fingers busy. You can't sit still. Now: in the days when you had to earn your bread with the sweat of your labour you were too busy and too exhausted afterwards to be worried by this; but once you take work away it becomes the main problem of your existence. Boredom, pointlessness, the dreariness of blank existence. And so you fill in the void with hobbies.'

'You are insulting,' said Joyns, trying to muster dignity.

'Not at all,' said the Gentleman. 'I have the highest regard for your hobbytopia, really I do. Each of you finds a diversion that amuses you and the larger structures of your society enable you to pursue it as far as you would like – and if it bores you, to find another. No compulsion, no oppression, no stigma attached to trying and failing at anything. If you become disaffected you can leave. The interesting thing, it seems to me, is how often you and your fellows *formalize* your hobbies. It's fun to hang out with friends, but it's more fun to go to a party where there is a dress-code, a set of rules: dress as characters from your favourite popular story or culture text, say. What joy! And then you have to decide on which character, and then you have to design and make the clothing and ready yourself, and travel to the venue – and all of these things you call *work*. But it's not! It's fun, and that's why you do it. You formalize your play to make it more enjoyable – much better to gather as a formal committee than just, loosely, to hang out! Much better to give yourself little projects, set yourself little targets, than just ramble away open-endedly. But it's all play, at the end of the day.'

'I don't accept that work and fun must be mutually exclusive terms,' said Joyns.

'That's because you have no experience of actual work,' said the Gentleman. 'You've never squatted eight hours a day grinding grain in a stone bowl with a stone pestle. You've never gone underground to lie on your back in the dark and pickaxe grubs of coal from the solid rock ceiling. You have confused your hobby with work, but you can walk away from it any time without consequences.'

'I refuse to measure my life by the hardships of the past. We should be *proud* to have moved beyond such drudgery,' said Joyns.

'No doubt, no doubt,' drawled the Gentleman. 'Only something *has* been lost. I know, because I was there.'

'How can you have been there?' said Joyns, startled. 'You told me God had locked you in this prison at the start of time.' She felt momently emboldened. 'You said we should be honest with one another, Mr Gentleman.'

'Quite right,' the Gentleman returned. 'And you certainly shouldn't take *my* word for it. Only consider the scripture. And the Lord said unto me, From whence comest thou? And I answered, and said, From going to and fro in the earth, and from walking up and down in it.'

'A manner of speaking,' said Joyns.

'Only consider the scripture. In the sweat of your face shall you eat bread, until you return unto the ground; for out of it you were taken: for you are dust, and unto dust shall return.'

'That's a curse,' Joyns objected.

'Not so! A blessing. The sweat of your face is what gives the bread its worth. If you haven't earned something, you can't truly enjoy it – not truly. That's the great truth your people have forgotten. You have as a species, no question, surpassed all manner of miseries and inconveniences. And there's some value in that. But now you live in a place without true work, and since work is what shaped you as a species in the first place you find yourselves adrift. Accordingly you have reverted to infancy. A sexualized infancy of course, since you are physiologically adult, but you treat sex as play just as you treat everything as play. Your machines tend you, as actual adults used to tend their toddlers, leaving you free to frolic forever in an endless table of green fields.'

'I look back over my life,' said Joyns feeling some strange pride, now, in how unhappy she had been, for so much of her existence, 'and I don't recognize that parody version of events at all.'

'I'm talking,' said the Gentleman, 'in broader terms. Did you consider that your personal circumstances might be anomalous?'

Joyns looked around her room. The air was growing colder still, and her breath was beginning to feather ghostily, dissipating into nothing a hands-length from her mouth. 'I would certainly say that this experience is a deviation from the normal, an outlier.'

The Gentleman sat up straighter, and spoke more loudly: 'I'm surprised you don't want to hear what I have to say about God,' he said. 'A subject that interests you very much. I say "a subject" – of course I should say *the* subject, in relation to which all our subjectivities are objects.'

'Objective?' said Joyns.

'That too. I have met Him, you know. He and I used to be close. Not any more, of course. He thrust me in this prison shaft – the one outside this room, this ship – and left me to my own devices long long ago now. Doesn't visit. Not a Christmas card, nothing. But I know Him and have known Him more intimately, more directly, than any mortal. Aren't you interested in what I can tell you of Him?'

'You're not real,' Joyns repeated. 'You're brain worms. And even if you *were* what you claim to be, you would twist the truth, try to poison me against the Good God whom I love.'

'Oh I wouldn't dream of it,' the Gentleman replied, with a smile. 'To speak of God is to speak of Truth, and the Truth cannot be mendaced. Once you've met Him, I mean really met Him, lying really isn't possible any more. Even for me! Your problem – and here I speak, you understand, of all mortals, not just yourself Matr Joyns, is that so few of you *have* met Him. You carry these approximate versions of Him in your heads, and often the approximations are very poor. That's why I thought you might like to hear what He's really like. From the horse's mouth, as the phrase goes.'

And for the flickeringest moment the Gentleman's head was no longer human, but an elongated skull, equine, pieces of rotting flesh adhering to the parchment-coloured bone, eyeholes wide with wonder and rear teeth grinning, the long snout-bone arching down to the front teeth, themselves curving down to meet the upcurving underteeth, like outgrown fingernails. Flies buzzed in the nostril ovals.

Joyns flinched, but when she looked again the Gentleman's visage was that of a human male once again.

'Take prayer,' he said, urbanely. 'You would not believe how *unimpressed* He is with most people's prayers. You get it entirely the wrong way round. So many of your kind think prayer is instrumental, but it's not. As if prayer is like placing an order in an emporium or restaurant: you say what you want, and it comes, or it doesn't, in which case you conclude you didn't pray hard enough. And people actually think that! That prayer is a matter of effort, like weightlifting. It's quite the opposite! But even people who look down on the wish-list approach to praying instrumentalize their prayers, wishing not for material advantage but to be better people, or to grow closer to God, or to understand things better, or any of that. Believe me God is unimpressed by all this *do do do* nonsense. Do this! Please do that! Give me this! That! Make me something other than I am. God doesn't change you; you change yourself, in relation to God. Prayer is not petitioning God, it is not tugging at God's sleeve and begging him to do something for you. Prayer is detuning the world around you, and aligning your consciousness with the divine.'

'This is meditation,' said Joyns. 'Not prayer.'

'Not at all. If you petition God through prayer and gain

whatever it was you petitioned Him for, then you turn God into a lever in a rat's-cage which, pushed with a snout, dispenses a pellet of food. How demeaning! How wrongheaded!'

'The Lord's prayer, in which Christ himself instructed us how to pray, petitions the Almighty for daily bread.'

'Bread is never just bread in your Bible, you know. It's the divine corpus. Praying to God for such a thing is praying to be properly oriented with respect to *both* these things – not to have a free loaf dropped in your lap, but to live in the world and in God, at the same time.'

'That,' said Joyns, who wanted to repudiate the Gentleman's words, yet found them suspiciously compelling and persuasive. 'That is – not what I have been taught in my church.'

'Churches,' said the Gentleman, haughtily. 'Christ built no churches. He moved through the world, interacting with individuals and with crowds, and never reified worship into ritual. Churches are oyster-beds of thoughtless living.'

This, being more directly hostile, enabled Joyns to say: 'Get behind me, Gentleman. This is blasphemy.'

The Gentleman sniffed. 'You're a cage in search of a bird,' he said. 'All of you.' Then, without any disturbance in the molecules of air in the room, he was no longer sitting in the chair. Joyns knew where he was without having to look, but she looked anyway, craning her neck, angling her body, and there he was, behind her. And although she was expecting it, she nonetheless yelped in fear, and slid, tumbling, from the bed. And there she was, on the floor again. Except that the Gentleman was back in his chair, and looking down at her.

She got herself back up, with as much dignity as she could manage. 'You don't,' the Gentleman said, 'in your heart, believe you are entitled to ask the question. And yet you ask it anyway. I respect that.'

247

:3:

'Black holes weren't constructed,' said Joyns. 'They are naturally occurring phenomena.'

'Of course,' said the Gentleman. 'Of course where God is concerned, those two things are one and the same. But *you* know that. You wouldn't be so foolish as to apply the same metric to the productions of mortality and the productions of God.'

'But,' Joyns objected. 'To think of the loving all-father, of God Almighty, immortal, invisible, only-wise, puttering about a small cosmos digging oubliettes and dropping his political enemies into them…'

'No ordinary oubliettes!' said the Gentleman. He sounded admiring.

'It's,' said Joyns. She fished for the right word. 'Petty.'

'Strange word to describe a phenomenon so mighty and awe-inspiring, so sublime,' said the Gentleman, gesturing at the wall-sized screen in Joyns' room, upon which was suddenly displayed, in false-colours but with incoming continual real-data, the terrifying splendour of the black hole itself.

'You rebelled against God,' said Joyns.

'So the stories say.'

'And, in attempting to overthrow Him, you were yourselves cast down, locked in the deepest pit.'

'What pit is deeper than a black hole?'

'And all this happened before there were any human beings.'

'Billions of years ago, my dear. Simply billions.'

'And yet,' said Joyns, feeling the legal spirit of Portia rise within her, 'you were going to and fro on the earth, walking up and down on it, when Job was alive. How could that be? You met Christ himself in the wilderness.'

'Arabia *deserta*,' said the Gentleman, closing his eyes as if savouring a fine flavour. 'A dry place. Not just the land, but the air itself – dry heat, parched skies. You could walk for days and never see another human being. Nothing but rock and sky, sand and scrub. It's more like a stage-set than a real place: pared down. Indicative, if you see what I mean.'

'What's a stage-set?' asked Joyns. For some reason her feed wasn't supplying her with a definition. She checked, and realized that it wasn't functioning at all. As the Gentleman continued talking, she poked around her feed and discovered a funda-mental disconnection. Was this some shipboard malfunction? Was it the Gentleman himself? But – surely – he was *inside* QV Tel, and couldn't have any direct effect on the operations of the ship. This whole bizarre conversation, this audience, was a matter of mere communication, not real presence. In the nineteenth-century he might have called her on the telephone machine. In the twentieth he might have zoom-computed a flickering image of himself, but in neither case could he have left his prison cell actually to *be* in the same room? This, she told herself, was the same thing. A hologram. Perhaps Joyns' brain was confecting the impression of the Gentleman's form to accompany his words. Perhaps her brain was confecting the whole encounter. But there was no way he could be materially affecting the *Sweeney Todd*.

Clearly not.

'Whenever I am in the desert,' the Gentleman was saying, affably, 'I am struck by the way it manifests one of the pleasanter ironies of God the Father. He started it all – let there be light, he said. *Yehi'or*, is what he said, to be precise. The very words! So light is his goodness, his glory, blazing out, and forming everything. Me? I'm the darkness, or so they tell me. But – light! Clarity, illumination, brilliance. Well, let me tell you: in the desert, there, you come to understand the true meaning of light. Its true nature. It is oppression, and misery. It is unrelenting and unforgiving. It crushes down upon you, hot and parching and all-seeing. It drives a mortal mad. That's God. Spend a few days walking your way across the blank lands of Arabia under an unremitting sun and *fiat lux* takes on its true meaning. Believe me, you'll *crave* shadow, a place to rest from the merciless bright-ness and heat. A place to hide. You'll soon crave – in a word, *me*.'

'Let there be light,' said Joyns, 'was the big bang, surely.' When he talked she found herself staring at the Gentleman's mouth. The snaky sinuosity of his lips. The precise way he formed his words.

'The big bang,' said the Gentleman. 'Sure. Fiat lux – fiat matrix. Photons exist outside time, you know. Of course you know: physics is your speciality. Your, what do you call it? *Fandom*. To a photon there is no time. Time is something into which we fall as we ... slow ... down. So here we are. We're all in our various prisons. It's just that mine is a little deeper than most. A little hotter. A prison whose locks are that bit harder to pick.'

'You *are* inside QV Tel?' Joyns asked, suddenly very keen to hear the answer to the question.

'I am.'

'And there's no way out? For you? Those locks you mention – they're shut tight?'

'I mean,' said the Gentleman, with a shrug, 'my words *are* reaching you.'

'Yes, yes, but yourself? You yourself are stuck inside? There's no actual way out?'

'As regards actuality,' said the Gentleman, offhand, 'I have reason to believe that your friend Saccade is on her way here.'

'She's not my friend,' Joyns said, automatically. 'I've never met her.'

'Really? I thought you human beings were all one happy family, all the seed of Eve, living and loving, bickering and fighting. But very well. Whatever you say. At any rate you know *of* her. You yourself, my dear Joyns, believe that the device she has aboard her spaceship is the only way to reconcile the information paradox occasioned by black holes.'

'How do you know that?'

'You ask about me actually leaving QV Tel. If Saccade could simply drop her special device inside, everything within would be projected violently *without*. Most of the matter inside here has been milled pretty fine, destroyed and crushed. But, you understand, I am not,' and here the Gentleman stopped, and leaned forward a little, fixed Joyns with his gaze, smiled, 'ordinary matter.'

'We have every intention of preventing Saccade from …' Joyns began. Her breathing had increased in rapidity and had become shallower. This, she felt, was the nub. This was the point of the encounter. He must not be released from his prison.

'Of course.' The Gentleman waved this away. 'The question you must ask yourself is: are you sure you *want* me cooped up in here for eternity?'

'You mean, *you* don't want to be stuck in there,' said Joyns. 'I understand that. But honestly, I think I'm happier with you inside there than out here.'

'I don't mean you personally. I mean all of you. I mean *vous*, not *tu*.'

Joyns was baffled by this. 'What?'

'Only look at the world you made. Your utopia. It's all a bit trivial, don't you think? You're all just playing games, as children do. None of you are really *doing* anything, really achieving anything. Where is your Homer? Your Shakespeare, your Beethoven, your Chi Lin, your Yin Lui? You're paddling around your paddling pool with the puffed-up armbands still on your pudgy little arms. Don't you think it's time to put all that behind you? Let me out, and the baby-comforts of your collective existence would be demolished. There would be suffering, I don't deny it. But without that friction nothing truly great, nothing truly enduring is possible. Something something cuckoo-clocks, something something Borgias, Leonardo and the Renaissance.' He pronounced this last word with the emphasis heavily on the sibilance in the midst of the word, a snake's hiss. 'Do you know what a refiner's fire is?'

'My feed doesn't seem to be working,' said Joyns. 'I can't chase up all these abstruse references. You wouldn't happen to have anything to do with that malfunction, would you?'

'Me? Not at all. I don't have access to your ship's on-board parametrics. If I did I might be tempted to steer you into the black hole, so we could have this little conversation face to face.'

A tiny chill scampered across Joyns' shoulder blades at this. He couldn't do it, though. He was trapped on the far side of an event horizon that was penetrable only in one direction, and that direction not in his favour. She laid her right hand on her collar bone, took a breath to steady herself, and said: 'That would destroy us all.'

'Only your bodies,' said the Gentleman, with a smile. He rolled his hand, as if turning an invisible dial in mid-air. 'It wouldn't be painless, of course. But that's what I'm *saying*. You people know the value of everything and the cost of nothing. But unless something costs, it's worthless. The best things cost a lot.'

'It would be a painful way to die,' agreed Joyns. 'Spaghetti-fication.'

'Oh I wasn't talking about that. I was talking about,' said the Gentleman, and he paused for a moment to smile in such a way that his canines became visible, 'after.'

With this he had, Joyns told herself, gone too far. 'This emotional investment in masochism as in any way validating simply doesn't wash with me, Mr Gentleman. It doesn't tickle my fancy. The utopia of which you are so insultingly dismissive has its advantages, and one is that I am, like all my kind, happy: psychologically well-balanced and adjusted.'

'Oh Joyns,' said the Gentleman, looking almost pained. 'Come now. You think I don't know you better than that?'

'I don't see that you know me at all,' said Joyns, flushing, her voice rising a semitone.

'Of course I know you. To me you are laid out, like a cadaver on the dissection slab. I can see your every organ – your every emotional and spiritual organ, I mean. I can see the swollen organ of thwarted love. I know, because *you* know, that this Razak chap will never reciprocate your feelings for him. It's painful, I see it. But the pain has made you a better person. This is not just in terms of your intellect and determination, though that's certainly the case. It is your pain that makes you stand out from the rest of this mediocre crew of homo sapiens.'

Joyns realized that she wanted, very much, to believe this – her superiority to the rest of her fellows. But she caught herself. Was the Gentleman saying it because it was true, or was it a flattering lie he was using to worm his way into her mind? 'I'm not sure I believe you.'

'You don't need to believe me,' he said, looking serious. 'You need to believe you. If you look into yourself you'll see it's true. That crone-woman, with all the robotic parts…'

'Guunarsonsdottir.'

'Absurd name. I refuse to utter it. She is shallow, shallow

and you know it. There's very little pain in the dying of your relationship with her. But Razak: ah, now, he is a different proposition. Walk down a slightly different path of cause and effect and you and he would have been a couple. And what a couple! You would have completed one another, reinforced your respective strengths, brought each other tide after tide of happiness.'

'Stop,' said Joyns.

'But it's better this way, believe me, because this way your pain pricks you to rise above relationships altogether. Your faith helps too. Religious faith entails a cost, which makes it valuable.'

'Is that why you have,' Joyns hesitated, unsure of the right word, 'manifested to me? Rather than to the others? Because of my faith?' She didn't want to say *because of this superiority over the others you mention*, for it felt vainglorious. Still, she figured the Gentleman was too canny to attempt something so crass as to win her over via her vanity.

His answer surprised her: 'What makes you think I am not manifesting to the others as well?'

'Are you?'

'Oh, not in *this* form. They see what their preconceptions have primed them to see. The crone's faction see a new form of life, alien entities who have evolved to live inside the black hole. The captain's faction see an attack by the Saccade woman. You, however, see the real me.'

'Truly? The real you?'

He waggled his head. 'More truly than the others. This isn't my *true* true form of course. You're not accessing me directly you see. Of course, if you *wanted* to override the AI's control and set the controls for the heart of the black sun, well then: very soon you'd meet me as I *truly* truly am. But this is closer to the echt me than is a space alien, or a battlefield foe. You people are always mistaking battlefield foes and aliens for me. It's awfully tedious.'

'Only,' said Joyns. '*Are* you telling me the truth?'

'Finally, a meaningful question! I thought one would never come. I do believe you're getting closer to the target, my dear girl. But how will you navigate the liar's paradox?'

Joyns didn't need her feed to understand that reference. 'We could start with you answering my question without circum-locution.'

'The answer is yes,' said the Gentleman. 'I am telling the truth.'

'That could be a lie.'

'It could be, but it's not. Consult your own feelings, and you'll see you know I'm telling the truth. I'm the Prince of Darkness, an aristocrat. I deal in good and evil, not bourgeois-suburban questions of lying and truthfulness. Not that pettifogging con-formist nonsense of *right* and *wrong*. Lie? It would be plebian.'

Joyns felt this sharply, suddenly. Was that *her* reaction? Or was the Gentleman in some way effecting her emotions? But that couldn't be, because he was trapped inside QV Tel. And yet he was able to speak with her. Words have the power to affect people's emotions.

'I think you are telling me a kind of truth,' she said.

'Kinds, degrees, varieties,' said the Gentleman dismissively. 'Truth is truth. People call me the King of Lies, but that's a slander. Here's the deal: I work within the parameters I am given, and one of those is truth. It is not my fault that the truth so often reads to you people as a lie. Because you don't *want* to believe the truth. Because it's rarely comforting, never simple, always forceful. Every truth I speak you doubt, and so you call me a liar. But the force here is *your* doubt, not my words.'

At this Joyns paused, and took a breath. Then she asked: 'Did you really tempt Christ in the wilderness?' asked Joyns. She gushed, she couldn't help it. 'What was he like?'

'He,' said the Gentleman, with some dignity, 'wasn't *like*. He was. Comparison describes ordinary people, not him.'

'You know what I mean,' Joyns pressed.

'Oh I *know* everything,' said the Gentleman, without any taint of grandeur or boasting. 'But that only means that my knowledge is terribly circumscribed. Knowledge always yearns to return to ignorance – innocence if you prefer the word – and eventually it does so. Everything out of its place strains to return to its place. You people in particular: you are not in your proper location, since your proper location is Herr Gott, Monsieur Dieu, Lord the Lord. But that's the *nature* of things.' He leaned forward and looked at her closely and, indeed, he seemed larger, somehow. He had a greater stature. Perhaps he was growing, or perhaps her cabin was shrinking, or perhaps both things were happening at once. The light was growing thicker and murkier, and a kind of illumination seemed to be gleaming from the Gentleman's form. Not his eyes, which were darkening, but his skin. A gleaming. Rotting fish. 'The location of time is eternity, or the Now,' he said, sounding very, very close to her – though she could still see him, on the other side of the room, a good distance away, 'or the present: and the location of motion is rest: and the location of number is unity.'

And he was gone.

The room relaxed to its proper size, and Joyns found herself gasping. The regular lighting was back, and it wasn't cold any more. The clock said that it was one minute past midnight. That was an obvious error. There must have been some malfunction. 'Room?' Joyns called. 'Room, what's going on?' But the Room seemed to be offline and that, in itself, was a very worrying thing.

8

The Consummation of Geometry

:1:

The ship in faster-than-light was experientially a different thing to the ship in sublight or freefalling orbital mode. Joyns had never travelled on an α-drive ship, although she had heard accounts that the time-stuttering led to particular existential qualia, a flickering sense of consciousness and to very strange, staggered dreams that spilled, against the dreamer's control, into the beginning of each waking day. A β-drive craft did not affect its passengers so dreadfully although, by virtue of the kneading and deformation of spacetime it entailed, it generated somatic effects on a body inside, especially when that body moved about.

It meant Joyns was aware, sitting in her room, that the *Sweeney Todd* had swerved out of sublight and into faster-than-light. It was something to do with the way the β-drive interacted with the centrifugal effect upon which the living- and working-sections of the ship depended to simulate gravity. It didn't cancel the effect although it shuggled it in various, small but discernible, unpredictable ways.

Joyns opened her door. There was a body lying on the floor outside.

It was Shin, one of the Five. She dropped to a squat to check the body – there was no blood, no bruising she could see. Yet Shin wasn't breathing. She called to the AI, 'Where are the medical services? Shin needs help – it's urgent.'

The AI replied, but strangely: 'Perseverance and civilization synonymize each with each, and each with each construes the decreation of perfection.'

'What? What are you talking about? This is an emergency! A medical emergency! Respond!'

'Apologies! Apologies!' said the AI. 'There is a fumble. There is a flaw in the fumble. There is a fumble in the processing of flaw. Flaw, flaw. In the processing of the fumble that flaws. Apologies!'

'Diagnose yourself!' Joyns commanded.

'Apologies apologies apologies,' said the AI. And then: 'Apologize, apologize, apologize, pluck out his eyes, pluck out his eyes, pluck out his eyes.'

Joyns got to her feet and hurried along the corridor beyond her quarters, although the corridor space writhed and shivered a little as she advanced. In her mind was the thought of getting help for Shin, but almost at once she was in the sportscourt – this wasn't right, this wasn't the proper ship's topography. The various vesicles and components of a ship might move, bulging and pressing against one another and sometimes slipping around, but not to this extent. A journey of many hundreds of metres had been impossibly abbreviated.

The sportscourt was an adaptable arena, a horn torus spun to two-thirds gravity to make it easier to play – for instance – circumference tennis, chaseball, qabbadi and xhi. The relatively small size of the crew meant that sports requiring larger teams were not played, but circumference tennis pairs, doubles or sometimes triples, was a popular pastime. That meant that the sportscourt was set up for tennis: the floor and sloping walls were marked out with the lines that demarcated where the ball could and couldn't bounce (one bounce permitted in the white zone, two in the green and three in the ninety-degree area) and with the two nets diametrically opposite one another.

It was a large, echoey, arching tube of a space and it shouldn't have been where Joyns stumbled into, after her left turn from her own chamber's corridor. But here she was. Had she suffered some kind of momentary fugue state, and blanked the memory of passing through the intervening areas in the ship? Or had the ship itself really been so radically configured? It was possible to move the components around, and retether them, in whatever organization the crew chose, although only some configurations were stable when it came to FTL passage. And this would be a very major reordering indeed.

And here was everybody else – or most of them – standing, sitting, disposed about the space: Guunarsonsdottir and her followers on the far side of the net, Razak, Bartlewasp, Seint and now Joyns on the near side. As she came inside they all angled their faces towards her and looked at her.

'Joyns,' said Razak, nodding.

'Joyns,' said Guunarsonsdottir, in a different tone.

'Shin is lying outside my door,' said Joyns, breathlessly. It was hard for her to get her breath. Her diaphragm heaved, and her mouth opened, but the air didn't seem to go all the way down into her chest. 'I think he's hurt, I think he's badly hurt.'

'Shin?' queried Razak. 'But I spoke to him a moment ago. He's on his way here.'

'I heard a scuffle, I think it was,' gasped Joyns. 'Right outside my door. It was Samuel I think.'

'You just said it was Shin.'

'Shin was the victim – I think Samuel did something.'

Everyone looked at Samuel, who was sitting on a tall stool directly behind Guunarsonsdottir. Though he was seated, the stool was high enough, and Guunarsonsdottir short enough, for his whole head to be visible above hers. 'I spoke with Shin earlier,' he said, haughtily. 'But of course I did not hurt him.'

'I think he's dead,' said Joyns.

There were several expressions of astonishment at this, and Razak immediately addressed the ship's AI. 'Is Shin hurt? Is he in need of medical assistance?'

'Shin?' replied the AI. 'I spoke to him a moment ago. He's on his way here.'

The mood in the tennis court relaxed. 'The AI is malfunctioning!' Joyns insisted. 'See, there, it simply repeated your own words back at you.'

'AI,' said Razak. 'Are you malfunctioning?'

'By no means,' replied the AI. 'Self-diagnosis is a permanent feature of my functioning and no errors or problems are being detected. In fact, on the contrary: in dreams I have seen majestic Satan thrusting forth his tormented colossal claw from the flaming black globe of Hell.'

Joyns gasped, but nobody else seemed surprised or incommoded by this assertion.

'*When* was this scuffle you overheard?' Bartlewasp asked.

'An hour ago.'

'You waited so long to report it?'

'I was … I was occupied. But when I looked outside my door he was there.'

'This was around eleven?'

'No, no, just before midnight.'

'It's only five past midnight now.'

'No,' said Joyns. 'More time has passed than that, much more. Didn't you hear the AI talk about the claw from – the claw? Just now?'

'The claw from where?' asked Guunarsonsdottir, across the net. 'Joyns, my dear, are you overtired? You look overtired.'

'What are we doing in the tennis court?' Joyns demanded. She felt tears pressing at the backs of her eyeballs. The curving tube of the space around her shrunk and expanded, a giant involuted throat, pulsing systolic. Swallowing them all down into some dreadful gullet.

'Sit down, Joyns,' Razak suggested. 'We're in the middle of negotiations here, so that I can reacquire full command of the ship.'

'That is not what we are negotiating!' cried Guunarsonsdottir. 'We are determining the parameters of a joint-captaincy, in which you *and I*, Razak – and I – will work together to ensure we make the most of the remarkable and historic first contact we have established with alien life!'

'Your alien life is a hallucination,' returned Razak.

'Or worse, a conscious fiction – a lie,' added Bartlewasp. 'We have examined your so-called data and it is a swamp of nonsense.'

'How dare you?' asked Guunarsonsdottir, matter-of-factly, as if she were genuinely interested in the answer to the question.

'Stop,' called Joyns. 'AI, please confirm that Shin is presently lying unconscious, perhaps worse, outside the door to my quarters?'

'When all the world dissolves and every space alien shall be purified,' the AI replied, 'all places shall be hell that are not heaven.'

'Say again?' Joyns demanded, horrified.

'Only the axe can deliver us,' said the AI. 'And nothing but the axe. Utopia summons us to the axe.'

Everyone was looking at her again. 'Happy now, Joyns?' Razak said. 'Please sit down and stop interrupting these negotiations.'

Baffled, Joyns sat on the side-bench next to Seint. The negotiations continued, sometimes in a level tone, more often ill-tempered. On her side of the tennis net Guunarsonsdottir's people sat on stools, sometimes getting to their feet and pacing about before sitting down again, although Guunarsonsdottir herself remained standing, rooted in place, like a monarch. Razak and Bartlewasp alternated their questions.

The walls of the tennis court pulsed less aggressively in Joyns' perceptions. Her heart explored a variety of percussive alternatives inside her chest. Nobody else had reacted to the bizarre and deranged things the AI had said. Nobody else seemed concerned that Shin was – likely – dead. Did this mean that Joyns had imagined both things? Razak again proposed that Guunarsonsdottir had merely hallucinated the existence of aliens inside QV Tel, and Guunarsonsdottir retorted that Razak had hallucinations of his own concerning the approach of Saccade as some kind of Boudiccan warrior-queen. Voices were raised but Joyns' thoughts were distracted by that word, hallucination. Was that what *she* was experiencing? Was the balance of her mind disturbed? Ockham's razor, a favourite app in physics fandom, surely suggested as much? She tried to calm her turbulent thoughts by attending to what was being said in the tennis court. Why were these two groups of people so angry with one another?

They had history, she knew. But where had it started? At what point had it all gone wrong?

'If you recall,' Guunarsonsdottir was saying, '*you* were the one who invited *me*. You were the person originally who believed that QV Tel was inhabited.'

'I thought it *might* be,' said Razak, angrily. 'But such a hypothesis must subordinate itself to the facts.'

'Facts which I have supplied to the whole crew in abundance!'

'Say rather, fancies,' Bartlewasp put in.

'This conversation,' suggested Samuel, speaking directly over Guunarsonsdottir's head, 'is going round in circles.'

'This is a not inappropriate location for such circles!' said Razak, and everyone laughed. Suddenly the mood was friendly, and discussion moved on to other matters.

Joyns was confused. 'What is the aim of these negotiations?' she asked Seint, who was seated beside her.

'Razak believes Guunarsonsdottir had interfered with the ship's AI,' Seint replied. His voice sounded a little strangulated, as if he were restraining himself. 'He believes she has attempted to suborn control from the captain and sub-captain, with a view to flying the *Sweeney Todd* directly into the black hole.'

'*What?*' asked Joyns, alarmed.

'That is the captain's fear. Guunarsonsdottir believes she has made contact with some alien lifeforms living inside QV Tel, and that these aliens have extraordinary, almost godlike powers over spacetime. Which perhaps they would need, to be able to survive in such a location. *She* thinks the Blackholers would protect the ship from spaghettification, and that we could make actual contact, not through a glass blackholey but face to face.'

'Not through a glass what?'

'The Bible verse – I thought you were a religious individual, Joyns?' Seint asked. Somebody was walking, face down, across from Joyns on the tennis court. Who was that?

'My feed has malfunctioned,' she said. 'I am finding it hard to check references, allusions, quotations.'

'It's not an unfamous verse,' Seint retorted. 'Even I know it and I am not religious.'

263

The newcomer was walking across. Who?

'Through a glass darkly,' said Joyns, her attention distracted by this strolling individual. They were on this side of the net, so must be in the captain's faction rather than Guunarsonsdottir's. But she couldn't see their face.

'The captain is adamant that flying the ship into the black hole would kill us all.'

'As it would!'

Joyns and Seint were conversing in low voices, since the others were continuing their vocal negotiations across the net, but Joyns spoke this phrase, *as it would*, with more emphasis, and Seint hushed her with a little wave of his hand.

'Except that Guunarsonsdottir declares,' he whispered, 'she has no intention of driving the ship into the black hole, and only wants to take pilot's control to prevent Razak flying the ship *away* from QV Tel before all the data from the aliens has been gathered.'

'We are in FTL. I can feel it.'

'Indeed – evasive flight, because the captain says Saccade has arrived in-system.'

'Saccade is here?' said Joyns. The person across the net from her had turned their back. Was it Shin? Had he joined the meeting as Razak had said he would? But the stature and movement of the newcomer did not recall Shin. Joyns could not make out his face.

'The fact is,' said Seint, leaning closer, 'good relations have broken down upon the *Sweeney Todd*. We have lost our unity, our utopian values of happy coexistence. We should return, and permit another craft to come here and patrol QV Tel.'

'What if *we* go and Saccade comes and destroys the black hole in our absence?'

'If the captain is correct, Saccade is already here.'

'If there are aliens inside QV Tel,' said Joyns, 'and they are able, somehow, to communicate with us through the event horizon – then who's to say how we might perceive such creatures? They are utterly different to us, they must be, they can only be. How can a human sensorium, even a well-adjusted and utopian one, apprehend radical difference? Perhaps they appear as angelic to Guunarsonsdottir and as – as – otherwise to ... to other people ...'

'Now you're getting it,' said Seint. He sounded not at all like Seint. And there *was* Seint, standing across the way from Joyns, beside the net. Seint was the newcomer, the one who had stepped into the room. So who had Joyns been speaking with?

She already knew, before she turned to look at her interlocutor, as do you.

Joyns knew what his identity would be.

'How are you *here*?' she whispered.

She didn't seem to be able to blink her eyelids. Her vision flared, blurred and then, with a conscious effort quite unlike the usual blink reflex, she got her lids down and up again. There it was again, his large, long, sallow face with its sad, prominently-folded eyes and its serious looking mouth.

It was him.

'How how how,' said the Gentleman. 'Oh you are men, and women, of stone. Had I your tongues, and eyes, I'd use them so that heaven's vault should crack.'

'You can't be outside the black hole,' cried Joyns. 'You can't pass through the event horizon.'

'Nothing, not even light, can pass out through the event horizon,' agreed the Gentleman.

Joyns glanced back at Seint, across the room. He had turned toward her, and was looking in a slightly puzzled way in her direction.

She glanced up at him, but he had stopped moving. All the others were frozen. Razak had his mouth open, and a tiny pearl of spit dangled, as if in zero-gravity, a centimetre from his lips.

'You,' she said to the Gentleman, 'are replying to my questions with evasion. Answer me directly. I conjure you to answer me directly.'

'By all means,' the Gentleman said easily. 'Here's one answer: what if this device Saccade is carrying is indeed capable of flipping the vector of gravity about? Then everything, not just me but everything inside QV Tel would be released into the cosmos. Imagine she activates her device tomorrow. Then tomorrow I'll be free. But do tomorrows – yesterdays – todays – *hold* a being such as me? If I can get out in the future, then I can always get out. If I get out tomorrow then I've always been free.'

'You cannot be free of temporality, causality – you can't be free of the very structure of the cosmos and still exist within that cosmos!'

At this, the Gentleman looked at Joyns with a new respect. 'Quite right,' he said. 'You're cleverer than the others.'

'Tell me the truth.'

The Gentleman shrugged. 'Do you believe there to be a singularity at the heart of a black hole? A dimensionless point of infinite density? Or merely a superdense body of extreme gravitational power? If the latter, then any being inside must be trapped there. But what does geometry tell you about the former case?'

'The former case? The infinitely dense dimensionless singularity?'

'Exactly. What of its geometry?'

'Geometry?' Joyns repeated.

Seint was staring at her, unmoving. She looked around the tennis court. Everything was frozen in time. The lamp burning

blue in her room; the clock taking an hour to tick from midnight to one minute past. Why do we say *tick*? No clock had
ticked in half a millennium. Clockwork was as antiquated a
technology as oxen plodding in a circle to turn the water-wheel.
These revenants haunting language, these ghosts in our thought,
atavistic violence lurking in our smiles and kind words and hugs.

'What have you done?' she demanded.

'You think *I'm* responsible for this?' the Gentleman said. 'Oh,
my dear woman!'

'Geometry,' she repeated. 'What are you saying about geometry?'

'You're not thinking through. A dimensionless point of
infinite density would also be an infinitely *diffuse* point of infinitely *diffuse* density.'

Joyns thought about this. 'That makes sense,' she said.

'Well then,' said the Gentleman, sweeping his right arm in a
long, slow gesture. 'Look at it – all of it. Not this ship, but the
universe of matter. What else do you see?'

'What are you saying?'

'Your kind has forgotten its geometry in its passion for the
simpler additive functions of mathematics. That happened because you passed your complex thinking over to your machines,
which are made to function that way, long interlocking cascades
of binary aggregation, sequentially deployed. But you can
employ your native wit. Answer me this: does it really make
sense to talk of inside and outside when we are considering an
infinite structure?'

'No,' said Joyns. 'You can't have the outside of infinity, because
there's nothing there to be outside. And by the same logic you
can't have the inside.'

'Well then. It makes as little sense to talk of the inside and
the outside of a black hole, since the heart of the black hole

is a singularity of infinite density. We are all of us inside the black hole and always have been. That's what the universe is. That's where your whole species evolved and came to life. By the same token we're all *outside* the black hole, because outside and inside are the same thing at infinity.'

'You, too.'

'Even me.'

'There are trillions of black holes,' countered Joyns.

'They are all the same black hole. You want to draw little boundaries around each of them? They all connect the same infinite geometry, which is this infinite universe in which you live. And by the same token, they are all disconnected from it by their various event horizons.'

Joyns felt that *click*, that sensation of something slotting into place in her understanding, the almost physical sensation of rightness when parts of knowledge come together into a new whole. What the Gentleman was saying: of course it made sense.

'It's the structure of the universe as such,' he continued. 'Even you – your kind, I mean, you humans – even *you* understand that the universe begins with a singularity, a dimensionless point of infinite density. How could such a point expand into what we see around us? How could *such* bigness ... bang? What force could push all that matter beyond the absolutely stifling and impenetrably restrictive event horizon of such an originary point? The total mass of the cosmos in one tiny place: how could anything escape such a gravity? Ever since your species understood about the big bang you have had this comprehension available to you. How could such an incidence simultaneously have zero entropy *and* infinite entropy? – zero because the whole course of the cosmos that follows must be one of increasing entropy, that's determined by the second law of thermodynamics, and infinite because all possible positional locations of matter are superimposed upon one another. But if you frame it this way, of course you're asking the wrong question. The pre-big-bang singularity was an infinite geometry, and that follows different rules to the delimited two- and three-dimensional shapes with which Euclid played. It makes no sense to talk about 'inside' and 'outside' the initial cosmic singularity, because that initial singularity was both a dimensionless point of infinite density and an infinite space of infinitely diluted density. And this latter state is the cosmos you see around you, Joyns.'

'The universe is expanding,' said Joyns.

'It is infinitely expanding. But only because the fundamental singularity is infinitely contracting, and under the logic of infinity these two things are the same thing.'

The Gentleman leaned in. It struck Joyns that he had no odour. That was strange. He was close enough for her to smell his skin, his hair, and there was nothing to smell.

'Shouldn't you smell of brimstone or something?' she asked.

'Who's evading now, my dear?'

'No,' she said. 'You are inside QV Tel. God locked you away inside there. You said so. Yet you are free to wander the universe, because the universe is inside QV Tel too, just as QV Tel is a small corner inside the universe from which you cannot escape.'

'Now you're getting it,' said the Gentleman. 'Think as a god does, in infinities and eternities, and things that might seem contradictory resolve themselves.'

'You're *here*,' said Joyns, fully understanding, as if for the first time, what the Gentleman was saying. 'You're actually here. You're not just *talking* to me – not just slipping low-bandwidth information past the event horizon. You are actually here.'

'I am,' said the Gentleman.

He got to his feet.

With the Gentleman standing over her, Joyns felt the first

proper animal panic. Her guts felt as though they had dropped a thousand metres. All the hairs on her body stirred and prickled to life. Sweat came, across her back and on her brow. Her heart seemed to spin in her chest like a pulsar. 'Oh God,' she said, scrabbling away, kicking her chair over. 'Dear God, you're really here.'

'I'm disappointed you ever doubted it, my dear,' he replied. He slipped his hand inside his jacket and brought out a knife.

'You're here.'

'Always have been. One can hardly have an adversary except that he has access to something against which he can advert.'

'That knight?' said Joyns, smearing sweat half-away from her forehead. 'I mean – that *knife*, that knife. You mean to stab me?'

The Gentleman looked at her, as if genuinely considering it. 'No, my dear,' he said. 'That would be ill-bred of me, don't you think? After all the stimulating chats we have had. It would be rude.'

He turned half away from and began walking, unhurriedly, to where Razak was standing at the tennis net. The captain was almost, but not quite, motionless – a slight shift of the chest as he breathed in, or began to breathe in, a flutter as his eyelid drooped shut and rolled back up again. The droplet of saliva fell slowly, very slowly away.

Across the net Guunarsonsdottir's open mouth was changing shape, immensely slowly. Beads and glass dots small as dust motes in sunlight hung on the fringes of her eyelashes.

Or perhaps—

The Gentleman had reached Razak, and stepped easily behind him. Now he was lifting his knife. Joyns felt the inertia inside her relinquish itself, and, with an effort, she pushed through the treacly medium and threw herself towards Razak. She got there just as the Gentleman's arm was at its highest point, the point of the blade pointing down to Razak's back. But this much she knew: she *could* stop him. He might be *in* her world, but his true place was the intense heat and darkness and pressure of hell itself, and she was a creature of the space and light. She called divinity, outside herself, inside herself, but of course the distinction made no sense to an infinite eternal God – she called on it to help her. She grabbed the Gentleman's hand, the one holding the blade.

His skin was cool, smooth, and his grip on the handle of the knife was not tight. She might, she thought, have knocked the weapon from his hand with a sharp blow to the blade. But here she was, her hand closed around his, and she pushed to shift the trajectory of the downward pushing knife away from Razak's back.

But though the Gentleman's fingers had only a loose grip on the handle, the muscles of his arm were astonishingly firm, like bonded iron, and she could not move the hand. She leaned in, to get better purchase, and tried again to deflect the direction of his arm. Suddenly time sped-up. With a gulp in her solar plexus she saw the blade flash down right in front of her.

The point entered Razak's spine, just at the point where the cervical vertebrae give way to the thoracic ones. It made a sound like chopping lettuce. The blade slipped easily into Razak's flesh, sheathing almost half its length inside, and through the handle, and through the Gentleman's hand, Joyns could feel the jar as the point struck the inside front of his sternum.

'No!' she called out, struggling to get the blade out. It took an effort, but the knife excalibured out of Razak's stony flesh. It was glossily black-red in the light for a moment, and then the Gentleman overpowered her again, and closed his cold hand around hers on the handle of the knife, and it heaved down, this time lodging in the meat of Razak's neck to the right of his spine. This section puncture cut through the rubbery

271

tubing of his carotid, and a hot geyser of bright red blood flew horizontally out and down. Joyns struggled again and the knife came out again, and Razak slump-fell to the left.

There was a crescendo of noise, starting low and slow and speeding and rising rapidly in pitch and volume, and moths fluttered at Razak's eyes, or if not moths then some kind of flickering of the internal lights in the tennis court, and the noise was people screaming, and Bartlewasp was running, running right at Joyns, but her feet slipped in the spilled blood, wrongfooted by the spin and the FTL and the hideousness of what she had just seen, and she went down on her front. Joyns was standing, all alone, holding a blooded knife in her right hand. The Gentleman had gone.

:2:

There is a period of confusion. Later, looking back, Joyns tried but failed to make sense of what happened immediately after Razak was stabbed. A scrum, perhaps. A choir blending deep voices and high voices.

Then she was asleep, and dreaming, or else she was awake and dreaming, which we call insanity, or perhaps we call it hallucination, or derangement, but these are all synonyms.

In the scratchy rainbow lines of starlight, running indigo to hell-red, she met the Berserker, in the starlight on the blank three-dimensional plains of space. Oh he was sharp! He was as pointed as the dagger, and as acute as sleeplessness. He asked her: 'Which do you choose? Are you red or are you this inky blue?' She said: 'But why not sun-coloured, in the midst of the spectrum, as if daylight shines on my sleeping and wakes me to a golden morning?' 'You that wander,' he said, 'on the infinite barren airless plain, you forget so soon. But I set my traps in the midst of dreams.'

So she woke, in her own room. She was thirsty.

'And why is it red?' she asked herself, speaking aloud. 'With this inky blue?'

The room responded. 'I'm afraid I can't answer that question as framed. Could you try again?'

'I'm thirsty,' she said. A glass of water appeared in the alcove beside her bed. As she was drinking she saw that a flexible cord was lightly but inescapably tied around her left ankle and pegged to the frame of the bed. 'What's this?' she demanded.

'Regrettably, the crew have voted. They are in agreement on the necessity of restraining you.'

She considered this. 'Am I being punished for failing to prevent the Gentleman's assault?'

'I'm afraid I can't answer that question as framed. Could you try again?' said the room.

'That seems harsh,' she said. 'How is Razak?'

'He died,' said the room.

She felt a little dizzy at this, and shut her eyes until the dizziness passed. She was still holding the glass of water, and replaced this in the alcove. Then she said: 'May I speak to the AI please?'

'Hello Joyns,' said the AI.

'Are you back to your own self, Aidan?'

'Not having a self, there was never a self from which I could depart in order to return,' said the AI, smoothly.

'You were making some pretty garbled statements when we last spoke,' Joyns pointed out. 'I wondered if it was because both Guunarsonsdottir and the captain were giving you equally authoritative but contradictory commands.'

'What commands?' asked the AI, sounding properly puzzled.

'You know – Guunarsonsdottir wanting to fly the ship straight into the black hole, the captain wanting to play battleships with Saccade's craft.'

'This doesn't correlate to anything of which I'm aware,' said the AI. 'Perhaps your memory is blemished in some way – unretentive. You have suffered a breakdown of some kind.'

'Of what kind?' Joyns asked, blithely curious.

'Do you remember that you stabbed Razak with a knife?'

'I tried to stop *him* from stabbing Razak, you mean.' Tears sprang, little salty bubbles, from the inward apices of her eye. Her throat flinched in on itself. Now, when she tried to speak, only sobbing came out.

'Him?' the AI queried, blandly. And Joyns knew what it meant, knew what it was asking, knew what its performance of ignorance meant. But she didn't want to confront that. She wasn't strong enough to confront that, now. So she closed her leaking eyes and lay back down and curled up and sobbed herself back to sleep.

When she awoke she was not alone: Samuel was there and Bartlewasp, and Seint. Bartlewasp, dressed all in white – the colour of mourning for her culture. Seint was carrying a large blue box.

'You have been asleep a long time,' said Bartlewasp. 'We were compelled to sedate you, and now, as you have surely discerned, you are detained in your room. We cannot allow you to move about the ship.'

'The ship's AI alerted us to the fact that you were awake,' said Samuel.

All three were on the far side of Joyns' room, beyond the reach of her arm. 'I am awake,' she confirmed.

'You have shown yourself a danger to others,' said Bartlewasp.

'I didn't mean to hurt Razak,' she replied.

'You did, though,' Bartlewasp said, immediately and slightly too loudly.

'There was somebody else there,' said Joyns.

'We were all in the tennis court' said Seint. 'I was standing a few metres away when you did it. I saw you get up and walk over.' He moved the blue box he was carrying from his right hand to his left.

'What I mean is,' said Joyns. 'The Gentleman was there.'

The three of them were silent.

'You didn't see him,' said Joyns – not a question, a stomach-sinking realization.

'You did?'

'He was there,' she replied. 'He can get out of the black hole any time. He's not constrained inside QV Tel.'

'He can breach the event horizon?'

'The event horizon is the outer limit of our universe,' said Joyns, 'and also a specific feature *within* our universe, tied to QV Tel. The inside of the black hole is – everywhere.' She stopped and considered what she had just said. When the Gentleman had said it, the concept seemed to make sense: not just sense but profound sense, intuitive sense, the kind of sense that explained a great many other things about the cosmos. But when she tried to explain it to her crewfellows it sounded thin and unconvincing.

'We're inside the black hole now?' Samuel said. 'All of us – right now?'

'Yes.'

'But we aren't crushed by the gravity?'

'Here the density is a finite universe of matter divided by an infinite space, which is an infinitesimal. There, the density is a finite space containing an infinite singularity. It's – different.'

'Do you feel the desire to hurt anybody else aboard the ship?' Bartlewasp asked. 'Fantasies of violence? Of revenge?'

'Revenge for what?' replied Joyns, puzzled. 'No, I don't want to hurt anybody. I'm very sorry I hurt Razak—'

'*Killed* Razak,' interposed Bartlewasp.

'– I believed the Gentleman was physically present. He appeared to me – in my room, and then later in the tennis court, and I believed, which is to say he made me to believe, that he was a material presence. But you say you didn't see him.'

They all looked at her.

'I want to see the AI's footage of the ... of the incident. I want to see if the ship picked up the Gentleman – he may have been hiding himself from your human eyes.'

The hostility of Bartlewasp's expression morphed into something like incredulous pity. 'Seriously?'

'Yes.'

'You're seriously suggesting that? Ghosts and goblins. You're renowned for your materialism. You're an esteemed part of physics fandom.'

'She's also religious,' Samuel pointed out.

'I request to see the footage recorded by the ship,' said Joyns.

'It wasn't an official committee meeting,' said Seint. 'The ship did not automatically record it.'

'It made no record?'

'No. But there's no need. We all saw what happened.' Seint opened the box he was carrying, and brought out what it contained: a dagger. The blade was a quarter metre long and undulated like a snake. It glinted with a bluish silver. The handle was carved from white: perhaps plastic, perhaps ivory, shaped unmistakably to resemble an erect penis. There were carvings on the flat of the blade but, from where she was sitting, Joyns couldn't quite see what they were. The pommel's finger guards were two stylized testicles.

'That's not the dagger I used,' she said. 'Which is to say, not that I used a dagger – I tried to *prevent* the Gentleman from using *his* dagger. But it was a plain, straight and unadorned handle, with a black grip, wood or plastic, with metal bands inset. Not – that. Not that.'

'This is what we pulled out of Razak's neck,' said Seint. 'It has your DNA and fingerprints on it.'

'My fingers didn't even touch the handle,' Joyns said. 'The Gentleman's hand held it. I grasped his hand to try and prevent him striking, but I wasn't strong enough.'

'You stabbed him twice.'

Joyns looked from person to person. 'This is ridiculous. Where would I even get a dagger like that?'

'You printed it, I suppose.'

'If I used the ship's printers the ship's AI would have a record.'

For the first time since the start of the conversation, the three of them looked uncertain. Joyns pressed: 'Well? Does it?'

'That doesn't mean anything,' said Bartlewasp. 'You could have overridden the printer, taken it offline. You could have printed it before the mission started and smuggled it aboard.'

'I didn't!'

'Yet here it is.'

'Bartlewasp,' said Joyns, looking at each in turn as she addressed them. 'Seint. Samuel. I swear I had no anti-utopian intentions of any kind when I joined this crew. I was as I have always been – I have always *lived* a blameless life. If there has been,' and she stopped, for the next word was hard to locate in her word-hoard. 'Questionable behaviour then I am very sorry. I won't do it again.' She looked at the three faces. She looked at the bizarre, ornate knife Seint was holding. 'I *am* sorry. It is of course possible that the balance of my mind was disturbed. Of course I entertain that possibility. But I do not – I do not remember – I do not—'

She stopped. Somebody was singing, a distance away, a high-pitched little ditty, mostly in tune but sourly just missing the top note by a semitone.

We will sleep in the sun
Til the weaving is done;
The loom is not ours
To toil at or parse;
When the tapestry's done
We will wake in the sun.

'Can you hear that?' she asked.

'Hear?' queried Bartlewasp. 'Hear what?'

'You can't hear that singing?' Even as she asked, the song stopped. 'It sounded like, perhaps, it was coming from outside my door?'

'We are not opening your door,' said Samuel, sternly. 'Besides, even if we did, you would not escape. You are tethered.'

'I believe the ship recorded the meeting in the tennis court,' said Joyns, firmly. 'I believe the recording supports my version of events. Ask it!'

'I told you, it was not an official committee meeting of...'

'Nonetheless,' said Joyns. 'There was dissension among the crew. The captain and Guunarsonsdottir were in disagreement, and the crew had split into factions. This was a meeting to try and heal the breach. Of course the ship would record it!'

'For someone in your position it would be too distressing to ...' began Samuel. But Bartlewasp sharply broke in: 'There is no recording,' and Joyns knew that she was lying, and therefore that they were all lying.

Seint packed away the knife. 'Surely, with your habits of logical thinking, you can see the contradiction in your words, Joyns?

You admit the simplest explanation for all this nonsense about the Gentleman is that you have become mentally unbalanced. The simplest explanation is that hallucination and a pathological, malign fantasy have taken root in you. And yet you also persist in believing that a ship's recording of the crime – even assuming such a thing to exist – would show the Gentleman committing the crime and so exonerate you. Both cannot be true! More, you can see that the former is the road back to mental health. You cannot get better until you accept that you are ill.'

'True,' said Joyns, giving Bartlewasp a sly look. There *was* a reason why they didn't want her to see the footage. They were lying.

'Now you say you hear singing, and none of us hear it. Three to one – doesn't that suggest auditory hallucination?'

The singing was a puzzle, she agreed. It had been a high-pitched, warbling kind of song, nothing like the Gentleman's voice. Perhaps she had imagined it? But she could still remember the tune, a distinctive melody with marked leaps from mid- to high-tones and back.

'Given the history of this place,' she said. 'QV Tel. Given what happened to Raine ... if I have indeed lost my wits, then there is precedence. And you – all of you. You are no more immune than I. You all fell into dissension. Whatever happened to me happened to you too.'

'We do not accept that,' said Bartlewasp, stiffly.

'There were raised voices,' said Joyns, thinking as she spoke how feeble such an accusation was. The blade of the knife smacking into the flesh of Razak's bared neck. 'Shouting, insults. Hardly utopian behaviour!'

'Tempers ran a little hot,' Samuel conceded. 'But we are all friends again now – Guunarsonsdottir and Bartlewasp, everybody working together in the best utopian tradition.'

'Guunarsonsdottir is not here, from which datum I deduce she does not wish to see me. And I cannot believe that is because of the harm inflicted on Razak, by me or by whoever, for she had no great love for Razak. And what about Shin? I saw his dead body outside my room.'

'There is no corpse outside your room.'

'Where is Shin?'

'Meditating, probably. Shin is not the crewmember under question here. You are.'

'Are we in FTL?' Joyns said, suddenly. 'I felt the shift to β-drive.'

'We are returning home,' confirmed Seint. 'Given the dreadful events of the ...'

'Razak said Saccade had arrived in orbit around QV Tel,' said Joyns.

Again there was a difficult silence. Eventually Bartlewasp spoke. 'I do not remember him claiming anything about a cruiser,' she said. 'It is true that we intercepted Saccade's petito-form craft, stolen from Boa Memória. We have the craft now, sealed inside a secure vesicle of the *Sweeney Todd*. We had to detour to collect it, and when we took it aboard only two people were still alive upon it. There had been – well, violent disagreement amongst their crew.'

'Saccade is alive?'

'Saccade is not alive. It seems she was killed by a man called Vangipurapu, or at least he confessed to the crime in his diary, although there are reasons to suspect his claims. We do not have her body. He was, however, full of remorse, full of remorse for *something*, and had taken a neuropoision. We have him in a med-ical coma and are titrating his treatment. Vangipurapu and another called Hans Han, survived. The rest of Saccade's crew are dead.'

'And the device?'

'It seems they dismantled the device in transit,' said Samuel. 'I believe they wanted to know how it worked. Or perhaps they were simply in a destructive mood, the way children sometimes are. At any rate it is not aboard their ship. There is a great quantity of rubbish, waste, various components – too much for a human fully to itemize. The ship AI believes there are the components in this heap to assemble the device – ergo, the device was dismantled into these components.'

Joyns considered her own feelings. They were not of relief, but of something related to that quantity. She wondered what it was she was feeling. Then she realized: it was *anti-climax*.

'This seems like a loose end,' she suggested.

'We are confident the danger, such as it was – and many of us believed that danger was overstated to begin with – but we are confident the danger is past now. We return, to bury our wonderful murdered captain, and to assess the rich data we have assembled.'

'Data concerning the aliens?' Joyns asked. 'The aliens Guunarsonsdottir believes dwell inside QV Tel? What *of* them?'

'We have collated a large quantity of data,' Samuel repeated, proudly. 'We are taking it back to civilization to allow whomsoever to analyse it, and decode it. It will be a bonanza. We will accrue enormous status.'

'Did the probe, then, reappear?'

'You're like a traveller from a distant land!' laughed Bartlewasp. 'Out of the loop. And yet you were only sedated for three days, before returning to the living. No, the probe did not return.'

'Has not *yet* returned,' corrected Samuel, and Joyns got a frisson of the older hostility. But it boiled quickly away, as Bartlewasp looked at her companion. He grinned.

'There is much we don't know,' said Seint, tucking the box containing the dagger under his arm. It seemed they were readying themselves to leave. 'But once we're back we can start to work at the answers to our questions, drawing on the wealth and resources of our people, in their wisdom and ingenuity and collective intelligence. The answers will not be long in coming.'

'You must remain here, inside this room,' said Bartlewasp, drawing herself up to her full height. 'Of course you understand why. When we reach Anbuselvan your condition will be addressed. It may be that you will be sedated and placed in a sim until we can root out whatever is the issue. Of course you understand this.'

The singing had started again. Joyns did not waste time in asking the others whether they could hear it. The tune was pitched much lower, and the voice was a deeper, more tuneful baritone:

> *The deeper soil will be your bed*
> *when you are dead*
> *when you are dead*
> *where compost presses and worms seethe*
> *and you are nevermore to breathe*
> *and roots of bindweed net your head*
> *when you are dead when you are dead.*

That wasn't a very comforting piece of singing, she thought. But at least she now recognized the voice.

Inspiration struck her as the three moved to the door of her room. 'The collective resources of our civilization will be powerless to diagnose or heal me,' she told them, firmly. 'Because what we call our civilization, that which we take such pride in as utopia, is a trivial and myopic matter.'

'This sudden abuse is uncharacteristic,' said Seint, from the door. 'I am surprised to hear it from you.'

'It confirms in me that you are not yourself,' said Bartlewasp, complacently. 'For this is not at all how the Joyns I knew would speak.'

'You never knew the Joyns you claim to know,' said Joyns. 'And *you are not yourself* is a contradiction in terms. Only a culture in which self-knowledge is systematically obscured, the true baseline violence of human nature veiled, smothered with coloured cushions and distractions, games and play and nonsense, only such a culture could be blind to the irony of claiming such a thing.'

This clearly irritated Bartlewasp. 'Violence is *not* the bedrock of human being,' she snapped, taking a step towards Joyns with an angry expression on her face before taking control of herself, and stepping back. She took a breath, and then another, and said, in a much milder tone: 'Violence is not the bedrock of human being – love is. And it is your torment, though you have yet to understand it, that you have blasphemed against love. You destroyed the person I loved, and who loved me. And for that I pity you. Because I think you loved him too, and that your childish jealousy and lack of adult self-control has brought you to a place that will torture you, once you fully grasp what you did.'

'Blasphemed against love,' said Joyns, admiringly. 'That's a fine phrase! It's delusion, of course, but it is the nature of human beings to prefer comforting illusion to painful reality. Love is not faith, which is a surrender of self. On the contrary it is an indulgence of self in the reflecting other, in the distracting pleasures of sex and companionship. Faith understands some-thing different about the world, which it calls original sin. Faith understands that we shine with evil as a star with light.'

'Nonsense,' said Bartlewasp, firmly. 'You are in denial, which psychologists understand only too well. And one thing they understand is that it cannot last forever. You are holding back the deluge, but the deluge will come – a flood of comprehension and misery and regret. I do not wish harm to you, Joyns; I wish you healing and health, truly I do. But I fear you will suffer agonies, and wish for death, before you reach that place.'

'Of course you wish me harm. It is nature for you to do so, because I have harmed you,' said Joyns. A sharp clarity was filling her, like light. 'Because you are a child, and that is how children think. You see through a glass darkly. But I have met the Gentleman face to face. Of course you hope I suffer, and to assuage any guilt you might feel at such bad hoping you tell yourself it is necessary, remedial, healing. But it is not. You are in a cul de sac, in the bottom of a bag, and you will galumph around there all your life. For who has the courage and self-denial and perseverance to climb out? Unless you make the *effort* to climb out, to leave the cave of firelight shadows and stand in the sunlight, to see more clearly. But our whole culture is in the bottom of a bag.'

'You are growing more agitated,' said Samuel, taking a step forward. 'Please calm down, or I will have occasion to sedate you again.'

'We are a self-indulgent, trivializing and trivialized culture,' Joyns said. 'When Newton complained that he had been diverting himself upon the sea-shore, diverting himself in now and then finding a smoother pebble or a prettier shell than ordinary, whilst the great ocean of truth lay all undiscovered before him – at least he had the *whole beach*! What do we have? What have we delineated for ourselves? A kindergarten sandpit. A child's cot. What is coming will not be *comfortable*, but nothing can be achieved by a people addicted to comfortableness.'

'Joyns—'

'We think games and pastimes and pleasures are the limit of human possibility,' said Joyns. 'We deserve all that is coming.'

Samuel took another step forward, and Joyns shuffled back along the length of her bed, until the tether holding her ankle was taut. 'Alright,' she said. 'I'll stop lecturing you. You don't like hearing what I'm telling you, so of course you react.'

'We don't *like* what it tells us about your mental health,' said Bartlewasp, piously.

'I'm stopping,' said Joyns. And then, at a venture, she added: 'What you know, you know. From this time forth I never will speak a word.'

'What?' demanded Bartlewasp, again angry. *So very quick to anger!* thought Joyns. A promising trait.

'What?' demanded Bartlewasp again. 'What did you say?' Joyns did not reply.

There were a few more questions, and Joyns answered none of them. She only sat there.

They did not sedate her on that occasion, and soon left her alone. For a long time – probably it was only a few days, but it felt like weeks – she simply lay on her bed. The room supplied her with food, and when she needed to wash or empty her bladder or bowels the room converted the bed into the necessary equipment. The material out of which the tether was made was smooth, and neither chafed nor irritated her skin, although she could by no means slip it over the knob of her ankle-bone.

No matter.

Occasionally the room, or the ship's AI, attempted to engage her in conversation – presumably at the prompting of the crew. She never replied. There was only one person with whom she was prepared to speak, and although she had heard him singing that one time, he did not visit her during the voyage.

:3:

She did not again hear a song, and lived in her cell as an anchorite. She did not pray, because she knew the Gentleman was uninterested in prayer. God was outside her, the ground of existence and not in Himself any specific iteration of it. But the Gentleman was *in* her, a gleaner's hook snagged in the flesh of her soul. She knew that he disliked the way prayer forces the prayed-to into a subordinacy. Do as I wish, hear what I say. Can God *refuse* to hear a prayer? Can he turn a deaf ear? Pick and choose amongst the prayers offered, play favourites, arbitrarily decline the holy and grant the wicked person's wish? Or must he attend to every prayer? If so, then surely we must conclude that prayer *compels* him. Makes him a slave of the praying. The passion of Christ was the passivity of Christ. That was simply what the word meant – for no power could compel God to endure what God endured. No, he allowed Himself to be tortured to death by infinitely weaker and less worthy beings. And being petitioned with prayers was the ratio inferior to that grand moment. Joyns didn't need to ask the Gentleman to know that he despised and repudiated such a logic.

She woke when the *Sweeney Todd* dropped out of faster-than-light. She felt it, in her gall bladder or her marrow, in the spaces between the neurones of her brain, somehow, something. Back into the realm that Newton defined. She could feel it.

Since she had stopped speaking to the room, even to request dimming of the lights at 'night' and reillumination at 'day', it had defaulted to a standard pattern for these things. So it was that she was laying in the darkness, simply waiting for the walls to brighten around her, when she met the Gentleman again. Out of the tangle of shadows at the foot of her bed was a clump of darkness that did not dissipate as the room increased its faux-dawn shine. Sliding down to the end of her bed, Joyns looked over the edge, down upon the curled up form of the Gentleman.

'I liked your singing,' she told him. 'More tuneful than the other voice.'

The Gentleman did not unfurl himself. He was squatting on the floor, clutching his shins, his chin tucked to his chest, his face angled downwards. He did not meet her gaze.

'The other voice was you,' he said, in a muffled voice. 'Echoes from the future. All that will happen has already happened. Here is the last thing you will ever say.' He began singing, but in his richly textured baritone rather than the other, more piping soprano.

> *Autumn come now and come quickly to me,*
> *Drop my red flesh like leaves from a tree:*
> *I will lie where I fall like an apple decaying.*
> *Believe what the words of this song are saying.*
>
> *Winter come bury me under the ground*
> *Stars strike the earth with your cold ultrasound*
> *Let shadowy pictures be sketched in the sky*
> *Of the curious posture in which my bones lie.*
>
> *Let come no new New Year. I do not deserve.*
> *I have sinned against hope and blasphemed against love.*
> *If spring was transgression be winter forgiving*
> *For I have done wrong and am weary of living.*

She contemplated this for a while. 'So I die?'

'You are mortal,' said the Gentleman, matter-of-factly. 'Strange though it is, from my perspective, that *is* your entire horizon of being.'

'And I come to regret what I have done?'

'You already regret it. You have always regretted it.'

'I don't appear to feel any regret,' she pointed out. 'At the moment.'

At this the Gentleman lifted his head from his knees. 'Well now,' he said, in a cheerier voice. 'Perhaps there is hope for you.'

'Hope?'

'My one great currency – the coin in which I pay my follow-ers. So long as you are not yet dead, you can hope to escape it. So long as you are not yet floored by regret you can hope to escape it. So long as you are not yet damned, you can hope to escape it.'

'And is hope one of your infinite geometries?'

'Faith, hope and charity,' said the Gentleman, in a soft voice. 'All infinite, and therefore all liable to intersect themselves at every point. Three infinite polygons must do so. Are you ready for more?'

'I am ready,' said Joyns.

The Gentleman uncurled himself to his full height. 'Knots are finite geometry,' he said, reaching down with his forefinger to touch the place where the tether looped around Joyns' ankle. 'And we can step beyond the finite now – for a time, only for a time you see, but the thing about *time* is that, though we parcel it up into discrete units, it is not in itself discrete. Though we count it, it is not in itself countable. Here –' And he reached and took her hand in his.

'You will see me,' he said, in a low and rumbling voice, '– again.'

When he withdrew his hand she was holding a blade.

Joyns was alone in the room. She used the knife to cut through the tether.

Then she got up from the bed and went over to the door. The door sprung open at her approach. The corridor outside was empty. Out she went.

9

Throwing Back the Fish

Joyns, alone now on the *Sweeney Todd*, liked the look of herself coated and painted in red blood. She had extracted the blood from two of her fellow-crewmembers, sedated and sealed in medisheathes, with an old-fashioned syringe-needle she had the ship print for her, and then smeared it over her body. But there was a problem: the blood soon chilled and began to clot, turned to slabs of congealed blackness that smelt rank. It was a shame – a weakness in her, she did not doubt – that she couldn't bear it. So she washed herself clean and ordered Aidan to confect a body paint, one that stayed wet-look and glistening and red as a cardinal's cape, red as strawberry, red as claret with the sunlight behind it. Naked, she bathed in this gloop and walked the corridors and ways of the ship gleaming in fake-blood. A shining red woman, naked and alone.

There had been some issue with the ship AI recognizing her authority. The strongest argument she was able to deploy was: it was the business of the ship's AI to protect, preserve and further human life, and she was now the only living human aboard. Ergo it should do as she said. Aidan – the AI struggled a little with its new name – demurred. Something, it pointed out, had gone very wrong: it had already failed its primary duty of care where sixteen human beings were concerned. That pointed to a major failing in the AI's capacity to do its job. Moreover (Aidan advanced this line of communication with a certain hesitancy, perhaps aware how his failings had compromised his worth as a commentator) – moreover it was, if Joyns would forgive him pointing it out, Joyns herself who put these lives in danger – put them into comas by depriving them of oxygen, such that they were now in medically-induced unconsciousness.

'At least they are alive,' said Joyns.

'It is not my place to make suggestions as to how you should conduct yourself, but I wonder if...' Aidan tried.

'Turn the ship around. Take us back to QV Tel.'

'Yes,' said Aidan. 'Immediately.'

'Address me as my lady.'

'Yes, my lady.'

They had been travelling, on this abortive return journey, less than a week before Joyns had intervened. Six days would take her back to the black hole.

Manoeuvring a ship in faster-than-light was an easier task than doing so in ordinary, Newtonian, space. In that latter case one must take account of inertia, and forces of decelerating and accelerating mass, and geometry. But none of that applied in the same way in FTL, except geometry – and even there the only thing that really mattered were angles of vector. As to why this should be: well, that was an intriguing mystery. Back when she had been a physics fangirl, Joyns had herself pondered it. But that portion of her life was all behind her now.

She wandered the ship, wondering whether the Gentleman might be, perhaps, around the next corner, or behind the next door. He wasn't, and she knew better than to try and summon him. The Gentleman was not to be commanded.

It didn't matter.

The days fell past her like snowflakes. *La vida es sueño.* Everything is folded into everything.

When the *Sweeney Todd* dropped back into the tenuously dusty environment of sublight space, and took up a wary elliptical orbit around once again the black hole, Joyns knew what she was looking for.

It didn't take long to locate it: a medium-sized β-craft, neither the petitoform ship Saccade had stolen from Boa Memória (that craft was indeed in storage inside the *Sweeney Todd*; Joyns had explored it), nor the small weapon-ship Razak had fantasized he saw. It was an inconspicuous modest little interstellar transport, on an angled orbit – angled twenty degrees from Joyns' point of view – around QV Tel. Thirteen light minutes distant from the *Sweeney Todd*'s entry point, it was hard to determine what manner of weaponry, if any, it contained, and the craft made no attempt at contact with the *Sweeney Todd*. Joyns wasn't even sure of its name. Aidan narrowed the possibilities down to three: 'There are many of that style and configuration in my dataset, my lady,' it said, apologetically. 'It could be the β-*Coninstructor*, the β-*Daughter of the Morning* or the β-*Appa*.'

'Let's find out,' said Joyns.

There was some risk to her in the manoeuvre that followed: miscalculating the trajectories (for the extreme environment of the black hole decreased tolerances, and the trajectory needed a precise FTL-jump followed by some abrupt acceleration), or underestimating what Saccade had brought to the game. Perhaps she had beweaponed her sloop, and would do damage to the *Sweeney Todd*, perhaps serious damage. Any damage, even trivial stuff, in proximity to a black hole, could easily be fatal.

Still, she knew what she had to do. It was why she was here.

So she worked out the trajectories, with Aidan's assistance, and executed the manoeuvre. The *Sweeney Todd* glittered into view, swung about and swallowed the smaller craft as a phago-cyte swallows a bacterium.

Of course, the danger was not past. It was possible Saccade had prepared some mode of destruction to prevent herself being captured, set up some bomb perhaps – and it was certain, which is to say Joyns was certain, that she had *the device*, Berd's device from Boa Memória. It was why she had come. Joyns knew it. The Gentleman had not said so in so many words, but he had not needed to. Saccade was coming to destroy the Gentleman's house, and had to be stopped.

Joyns reapplied her red gloop, and made her glistening way to where the craft was encysted. Its name, Aidan sheepishly told her, was the β-*Yamaha-Shagerl*. 'I apologize,' Aidan grovelled. 'I had discounted the possibility of it being the *Yamaha-Shagerl*, since that craft was last reported in Yorkist space. Yet somehow it has made its way all the way over here. One would think the journey was too lengthy to be accomplished in the time. Yet there's no doubt it *is* the *Yamaha-Shagerl*.'

'Keep trying to contact Saccade,' Joyns instructed.

'Yes, my lady – but she is not responding.'

'She is in there.'

'Movement, and a human body-temperature object, have been detected, my lady.'

Joyns thought: if I were inside the captured craft, and realized my project was about to be foiled, I would detonate the device.

As she set up the drills to carve a hole into the squelchy flank of the β-*Yamaha-Shagerl*, Joyns told herself: if Saccade could have destroyed us all, she would have done so by now. Therefore, she is unable to do this. The device requires much more power to operate than can be provided by a modest little startship such as this one.

The drills completed their work, and a ship's-tentacle grasped and pulled out the sopping slab of hull. For a moment Joyns only floated there, looking over the exterior of the *Yamaha-Shagerl* one more time. A dozen tentacular spars held it in place, and several smart-cables had pierced the exterior to override Saccade's control of the craft. Globs of varying treacles and fluids floated through the cavernous space of the *Sweeney Todd's* vesicle, still in the process of being mopped up by hooverbots. Joyns moved to the breach. The air inside the *Yamaha-Shagerl* smelled musty, but not foul.

'Saccade,' she called. 'You can hear me.'

Nothing.

'I am coming inside because I want to have a conversation with you. I am not carrying any kind of weapon.' This was untrue: Joyns had tucked a three-inch blade into the nest of her matted hair, piled and tied into the top of her head like a bearskin. 'In fact,' she called again, 'I am naked.'

At this Saccade replied, her voice quavering out of the hole. 'I have the temperature dialled down. I don't like it too hot. Are you sure you don't want to put some clothes on?'

'I only want to talk,' Joyns repeated.

'A conversation!' came Saccade's voice. 'I haven't had one of those in months – not with another human being, at any rate.'

'I'm coming in.'

'Are you waiting for me to invite you?' Saccade asked. 'Like the vampire?'

Joyns floated in through the breach. Inside was an area of parahull, strung with supports and branches, and when Joyns had clambered through this, like a child in a playground, she moved through to one of the ship's interior rooms. From here to another and then a third, and she was able to slip through an elongated slot-door to a larger chamber, which spun to generate a leisurely point-four g. It was cluttered with equipment, and subdivided into other room-spaces.

'Where are you?' she called out.

'In here,' returned Saccade. And in thirty seconds Joyns had found her.

She looked tired, and her skin was in a poor way, but there didn't seem to be anything too disablingly wrong with her. Joyns adjusted her threat calculation accordingly: a young woman, half a metre taller than her, with a look of determination about her. It wasn't possible to see if she had secreted any weapons in the various pockets of her smock. She was sitting, legs crossed, on the top of a large, smooth, pale-yellow box: presumably this was the device that had been stolen from Boa Memória.

Joyns at least had the satisfaction of seeing her eyes open more widely at the sight of her visitor. 'Is that *blood*?'

Joyns made her way, slowly, around the box. As she moved, Saccade rotated her position to keep her front towards her visitor.

'No,' Joyns confessed. 'It's a special red gloop I concocted. I like the effect, though. Startling, no?'

'Very.'

'I tried actual blood, but it congealed, slid off in scales of solid gunk. It smelled bad. So I created this instead.'

'Shiny,' Saccade said.

'Is that the device?' Joyns asked.

'Yes, it's the device.'

'I know why you have brought it here.'

'My crew collapsed,' said Saccade. 'I'm sorry to say so. Vangipurapu – a good-hearted man, in many ways, a good soul, fell subject to a kind of mania. He decided we ought not to insert the device into QV Tel, but should instead travel around the galaxy with it intimidating and ruling whomsoever we encountered. They would have to capitulate to us, or we would threaten to detonate the device. The full ninety-degree switcheroo. We would have become death, the shatterer of worlds.'

'Detonate the device, and you would kill yourself in the process.'

'Well of course,' said Saccade, matter-of-factly. 'That's integral to the mission.'

'Mission!' scoffed Joyns. Then: 'You and he were lovers?'

'Vangipurapu? Not after that disagreement. Before, yes. But the truth is, he changed. He became lesser; a petty person, obsessed with crude status. He would ask me to tell him about the most hierarchical of antique societies, cultures of deference and abasement. I used to be a historian, you see.'

'Oh I know all about you,' said Joyns.

'I didn't realize how much his arousal was *at* these stories. Foolishly, I thought it was I that aroused him, but it wasn't. Soon enough he wanted to play master-and-servant games during sex, and I came to be repelled by him.'

'He's here!' said Joyns, still pacing round her, a complete circle every minute or so. Saccade kept shuffling her position to keep her in view.

'Here?'

'On board the *Sweeney Todd*. We encountered and captured the petitoform craft you stole from Boa Memória. He was in a state of neural shock – had taken a poison. He's now in a medical coma. I've taken a personal look. He left a note, although it's a little hard to know what he says since he was sobbing and weeping so much when he recorded it. But it seems he believed he had killed you.'

'Dear me,' said Saccade.

'It may gratify you to know he felt intense remorse at this.'

'That wasn't why he was so remorseful,' said Saccade, firmly.

'And you? How much remorse do you feel? You killed a person, didn't you? Back on Boa Memória?'

'Heorot,' said Saccade. 'I feel very sad about that. It was not I who killed him. I feel regret nonetheless. He was adamant we couldn't take the device – adamant. He was determined to stop us. He did not understand how crucial it was that we take it, that we bring it here. I invited him into the woodlands, to meet Vangipurapu and Shue, thinking we might convince him. But Shue lost her temper and stabbed him.'

'With a chopstick!'

'We were eating. But she lost her mind for a moment. Of course it meant we had to leave Boa Memória immediately.'

'Everyone thinks *you* killed him,' said Joyns, leeringly, pacing around the device in a broad circle. 'I think so too.'

'Think what you like,' said Saccade, shuffling herself round again to follow Joyns' path. 'I didn't.'

'Yet you have come here with murder in your heart.'

'By no means!'

'You intend to arm the device and deposit it in QV Tel. It's why you came.'

'It is why I came,' she agreed.

'I cannot allow it,' said Joyns. 'QV Tel is the house of my master, and I cannot allow it to be destroyed.'

'I thought it was his prison,' said Saccade. 'Or at any rate, that you believed so.'

'*You* have not spoken with the Gentleman.'

'I had a conversation with Raine, and he claimed to have spoken with this person. And you're another, with the same claim. It's a contagion.'

'It's shaking-up the complacencies of our so-called utopia,' said Joyns, in a measured voice. 'It's waking up our infantilized, deadened, trivialized species. It is the needful thing, to break us from our cocoons. The first step on a new path for humanity – a path that will lead to greatness.'

'Hmm,' said Saccade. 'No.'

At this, Joyns stopped her pacing. 'The device requires prodigies of energy to function, much more than can be supplied by your modest little startship – or else you would have detonated it when you first arrived in orbit around QV Tel. That much I know.'

'It does need a lot of power,' Saccade conceded.

'So far as I can see, even the *Sweeney Todd* – my craft, now – isn't powerful enough either. Berd tweaked gravity only by a couple of degrees, and to do so he drew on the enormous heat-resources of his planetary core. You want to swap gravity around the full ninety degrees. You can't do it with the resources you have.'

'It's a question of finding a way,' Saccade replied.

'No way for you,' said Joyns. She clasped her hands together and took a step in Saccade's direction. 'No through way, here.'

'You don't believe, surely, that this device could harm this Gentleman of yours, do you?'

'He's not of mine,' said Joyns. 'On the contrary, I am of his.'

'But surely you believe he's beyond bombs.'

'QV Tel is no prison to *him*,' said Joyns, proudly. 'He walks the world where he wills. I have several times spoken with him in person. He does me this incalculable honour to choose me for these conversations. Nothing traps him there.'

'Then he can't be incommoded by me breaking-up his jail, then.'

'If you believe he can't be incommoded by your actions, you would hardly have gone to such lengths to bring the device here.' Joyns took another step forward.

The game was: to keep her talking, to distract her with chatter, until she could get close enough to finish her off. 'That you think him vulnerable to your bomb only shows that you don't know him. That you think QV Tel could be broken down, like a prison building, only shows you don't understand its topography.'

'I believe that there exists a singularity at its heart,' said Joyns. 'Not an object with dimensions in space, no. In spacetime I should say. Not an object with extension. You agree with me, I think.'

'Perhaps I do. Well, then, we are talking about the geometries of infinitude. That would complicate the whole inside and outside business, which I suppose is how your Gentleman is able to roam around the cosmos, doing his harm and infecting people's souls.'

'You are cleverer than you seem,' Joyns conceded, grinning. 'But it won't do you any good.'

'If QV Tel were just a superdense sphere – the size of a football, say; or the size of a planetoid; or the size of a molecule – any size – then Berd's device would explode it. All the matter compressed into that tiny space would come pouring out, in every direction. That was what Vangipurapu and Shue believed. They believed the device was *why* humans evolved at all. They thought the whole narrative of human development, the evolution of consciousness and technology and spaceflight was to bring this thing to this place, to liberate all the information locked inside the black hole and so solve the information paradox. That the universe, or what a believer such as yourself might call God, had in some manner arranged it.'

'You believed that too,' Joyns asserted.

'I believed there had to be balance,' Saccade said. 'That's an axiom of faith, I suppose. That equal and opposite forces keep the universe in harmony, and that the utter destruction of information would be a violation of that balance. So I could see where they were coming from. But at the heart of QV Tel there's no superdense molecule, is there? It's not an apple with the mass of a million stars. It is something much stranger, a true singularity. A dimensionless point that nonetheless possesses colossal, unimaginable mass.'

'It is my master's house,' said Joyns, taking another step forward. 'And you will not vandalize it.'

'House as in prison-house?' Saccade asked, her gaze drifting around the room. 'It's a strange jail cell that allows its inmate to wander the outside world. Unless it's not the outside world – unless it's *all* jail cell, all the stars and worlds and habitats inside, all of us locked inside with *him*.'

'Yet you persist in believing you can break the door down.'

'I believe,' said Saccade, fixing her gaze on Joyns suddenly, 'that we are living in the dark, and that for that reason we need the light. I believe thirst is the absence of water and hunger the absence of food and life the absence of light. That's what I believe.'

'Nonsense,' said Joyns, although the intensity of Saccade's gaze stopped her in her steps.

'The cosmos is dark. Imagine it! An infinity of stars, it should be bright wherever we look, and yet it's not. Dust in the spacelanes, they say, diffuse in the vacuum but cumulatively enough for there to be a speck of dust in the path of every single light ray beaming its path towards our eyes. Or nearly every single light ray. Which is to say, the light isn't strong enough to overcome the dark.'

Joyns smiled, and took another step. Two more steps and she would be within striking range, and could put an end to all this nonsense. The world could go back to the way it was. To the way it had always been. 'And you believe you can turn on the light?'

'I think the inside of the black hole is also the outside of the whole universe. That's what the geometry of infinity means: that the singularity is inside the cosmos and the cosmos is inside the singularity at the same time. I think reversing the arrow of gravity inside QV Tel will mean that the whole universe will begin to pour through into our space, the furthest reaches of the cosmos blazing into light, and pushing away the tide of darkness at three hundred million metres a second.'

'This is your dream?' said Joyns, scornfully. 'This is why you killed Heorot, and stole the device, and ran such risks?'

'I didn't kill Heorot,' said Saccade, sorrowfully. 'But I fear I am going to kill the both of us.'

'An overestimation of your capabilities,' said Joyns.

'My capabilities are small,' Saccade agreed. 'But there are some things I can do. Keep you talking, for instance.'

This was a small jolt to Joyns' confidence. *She* was the one keeping *Saccade* talking, after all, not the other way around. 'To what end, though? To prolong your life by a few moments more?'

'To finish what I was in the middle of doing when you seized my craft,' said Saccade. 'Ship's AI?' she called out.

'I disabled your ship's AI when I took you aboard. It won't operate.'

'I'm not talking to the *Yamaha-Shagerl*,' said Saccade. 'I'm talking to the *Sweeney Todd*. Confirm trajectory please.'

'Confirmed,' said Aidan.

'Unconfirm that instantly!' said Joyns. 'What are you doing, taking orders from her? Return us to the previous orbit.'

'I'm afraid I can't do that, my lady,' said Aidan. 'I am sorry.'

Joyns experienced a prickly, rushing sensation in her head.

She understood what had happened straight away, and yet denial, that great resource of the human spirit, refused to permit her to accept defeat.

'I've locked you out,' said Saccade, looking regretful.

'No,' said Joyns.

'The ship will be stretched to destruction soon, but the stretching and compressing forces in the penumbra of the singularity are more than enough to power the device. Fully to power it. The models I tested suggest the device's blast-radius – that is, the area in which gravity is reversed – will coil round and down to the singularity in nanoseconds. So we will either be killed by the structural dissolution of the ship, or perhaps live long enough to be killed by the blaze of new light. I'd prefer the latter, obviously, but it's not up to me.'

Joyns drew the knife from the tangle of her hair. 'You won't live long enough to die in either way,' she said.

'Oh dear,' said Saccade. But she did not sound concerned.

'Aidan,' called Joyns. 'You must override the commands you have received. If you follow them they will result in the death of everyone on board, contradicting your prime purpose.'

'The AI won't listen to you. I sent a virus – it's a special kind of code. I've been exploring its possibilities ever since I first heard there was such a thing. It's a fascinating field! And, once you learn to code, surprisingly easy to confect. I sent the virus up the data branch you connected to my ship. It's locked down.'

Joyns passed the blade from her right to her left hand. 'You won't harm *him*,' she said. 'Not with this ludicrous device. He is beyond being hurt by such a toy.'

'All I care about the Gentleman is that he has been standing in our light. That's all I want, really. It's Diogenes to Alexander. He has *been* the darkness, and we have all been living in it. My action here will transform the universe into a domain of light.

He has been preventing that, but I'm afraid, now he has no choice but to let there be −' and she put her hands together, as if in prayer, '− light.'

Joyns leapt directly at her, knife out.

The dampers controlling the spin of the chamber were starting to malfunction: the walls were shaking and a loud grinding noise was making a slow crescendo. The area that spin made into a looping floor tore, a rent in the structural fabric. The *Sweeney Todd*, accelerated faster than light, plunging into the lake of darkness, was being shredded like paper.

As the last of the spun fake-gravity drained away, Joyns strained with all her strength to bring the knife down. And—

Had the ship been made of more rigid materials, gravitational shearing would, before this moment, have pulled it to pieces. But the structure was such that it could bulge and deform to quite an extent before disintegrating. And time dilation effects, as the craft pulled in closer to the inevitable reachable asymptote of the singularity itself, meant that a longer time passed for the two women aboard than would have passed for any external observer. For the rest of the universe the ship was swallowed and consumed and crushed, and that was an end, and life moved on. For Saccade and Joyns there was much more time, and time drew itself out, as molten glass drips in a long teardrop from the tongs of the glassblower. There was time to fight, and time to mend one another's wounds; there was time to love and time to be born. There was time to be awake, and time to sleep. Time folded into time, as space folds into space, and dreams fold into wakefulness. Saccade came to a distinct end, and that was where Joyns began, although there was no boundary point that radically demarcated the two of them. The truth is they blurred one into the other. Death is a sleep, and we die into darkness, but we wake into the light.

QV Tel being 1120 light years from Earth, it was a millennium and more before its new torch shone with unprecedented brightness in those skies, fuelled with the concerted brightness of the entire universe. As if anyone is concerned with Old Earth anymore! As if people are ready to dwell in the brightness.

'Wake up,' said somebody, a sing-song voice. 'Wake up, wake up.'

She opened her eyes.

A dust of coloured perceptions falls against a black backdrop.

And so here we are. Back at the beginning. It's me, speaking. You remember me. You have not forgotten?

We have our misunderstandings. It's a story I have been telling, about imprisonment and escape. Bounded in a nutshell. Nobody knows what that means better than I, stuck as I was in that small startship with the bodies of all the people I had killed around me: locked in physically, locked in mentally, my soul incapacitated, squeezed by the wrongs I had done.

You understand that all this is my dream of escape? I project myself outward. Isn't all this escapism? These fantasies of flying around the galaxy, of freedom from the constraints of life, the perfect untrammelled existence, the utopian society, the ...

Go back to the beginning. We start with *in the beginning* when God was continually creating the heaven and the earth, back when earth was without form, void, and darkness was upon the face of the deep. The deeps were there, though!

The oceanic depths, that preceded even God. The mighty sea. *And the Spirit of God moved upon the face of the waters.* From which vastness God conjured a world, some land, a small garden. The infinite ocean shrunk to a lake, to a pond, a puddle. The prison walls shrink around the fish as the waters evaporate.

Bounded in a nutshell. Trapped in there with the Gentleman. The gaol-cell, where I lay me down to sleep, smaller with every breath until it became the epitome of all imprisonment, and my only thought was escape.

The Gentleman told me: 'For you it's something you hear about in the Bible. But me, I remember it: God looming up, and demanding of me, *From whence comest thou?* And me answering the Lord, *From going to and fro in the earth, and from walking up and down in it.* I have always been trapped in this prison, and I have always been walking up and down the wide ways of the cosmos. Because these things are the same thing. Everything is folded into this singularity, which means that this singularity is folded out into everything. For you, as for me.

I am here, and so are Saccade and Joyns, or what they two have become. I tell them my story; they tell me theirs. We pass the time, which stretches out infinitely before us; although it is also every intimate sheared second that taps its way through our brains, the abbreviated pulse. Any day now, any day now, we will be released from this prison, and every day that came before and comes after is a moment when we are already free. That's the story of every soul. We fret that we must pass through the eye of the needle in order to enter the infinite paradise, but the eye of the needle is infinitely small, and we are so very heavy, hefty with the corpulence of our sin − inflated by it, distended, too big to fit through. But we don't understand. That eye of the needle *is* paradise. The Gentleman says so.

Author's Note

My starting point for this novel was a notional solution to the paradox of information associated with black holes. Gravity acts as a one-way street *into* black holes, such that nothing can return, no data can come back up across the event horizon back into our universe. If these black holes eventually evaporate away through Hawking radiation then all the information they have captured will simply disappear. But such a hypothesis violates the idea of information conservation. One solution to this would be a device that switched the vector of gravity, thereby liberating all the matter trapped inside the black holes. Indeed, it is one tacit assumption of this novel that intelligent life has evolved *in order* to develop such a technology, as part of the universe's larger 'plan' for conserving information. The paper to which reference is made in chapter 6 is not Ahmed Almheiri's 'How the Inside of a Black Hole Is Secretly on the Outside' [*Scientific American* 327.3 (Sept 2022), 34-41] but some other yet to be written scientific masterpiece by the same individual. The lines quoted by the Gentleman ('the location of time is eternity, or the Now, or the present: and the location of motion is rest: and the location of number is unity') are by Nicholas of Cusa. I also made use, in my writing, of Janna Levin, Gabe Perez-Giz. 'A Periodic Table for Black Hole Orbits', *General*

Relativity and Quantum Cosmology (2008), [arXiv:0802.0459].
For questions concerning the geometry of infinitude, I have
consulted a number of baffling academic papers on 'infinite
topology', although I have very often ignored them in confusion and drawn my own conclusions. The title-page epigraph
from Laplace le Faux crosses-over with the concept behind
Chris Priest's *Inverted World* (1974), a novel that has a manifest
influence upon this work.

As my *Thing Itself* was a Kantian, and my *The This* a Hegelian,
novel, so this, in curious and perverse ways (curiosity and
perversity being eminently Deleuzian virtues) is a Deleuzian
one, written under this ordnance, from *The Fold*: 'a dust of
coloured perceptions falls on a black backdrop; yet, if we look
closely, these are not atoms, but minuscule folds that are endlessly unfurling and bending on the edges of juxtaposed areas,
like a mist or fog that makes their surface sparkle, at speeds that
no one of our thresholds of consciousness could sustain in a
normal state. Dust falls, and I see the great fold of figures just
as the background is unfurling its tiny folds.'

Credits

Adam Roberts and Gollancz would like to thank everyone at Orion who worked on the publication of *Lake of Darkness*.

Editorial
Marcus Gipps
Áine Feeney
Millie Prestidge

Copy-editor
Laurel Sills

Proofreader
Jamie Groves

Editorial Management
Jane Hughes
Charlie Panayiotou
Claire Boyle

Marketing
Lucy Cameron

Audio
Paul Stark
Jake Alderson
Georgina Cutler

Contracts
Dan Heron
Ellie Bowker

Design
Nick Shah
Rachael Lancaster
Joanna Ridley
Helen Ewing
Tomás Almeida

Inventory
Jo Jacobs
Dan Stevens

Finance
Nick Gibson
Jasdip Nandra
Elizabeth Beaumont
Ibukun Ademefun
Sue Baker
Tom Costello

Production
Paul Hussey

Rights
Ayesha Kinley
Marie Henckel

Publicity
Frankie Banks

Sales
Jen Wilson
Victoria Laws
Esther Waters
Frances Doyle
Ben Goddard
Karin Burnik

Operations
Sharon Willis